THE JOINING TREE

BLACKTHORNE FOREST - BOOK 4

CLAIRE FOGEL

Copyright 2017 by Claire C. Fogel

All rights reserved except as permitted under the U.S. Copyright Act of 1976, no part of this publication may be reproduced, distributed or transmitted in any form or by any means, or stored in a data base or retrieval system without prior written permission from the owner/publisher of this book.

This book is a work of fiction. Names, characters, places and incidents are either products of the author's imagination or are used fictitiously and any resemblance to actual persons, living or dead, business establishments, events or locales is entirely coincidental.

Please do not participate in or encourage piracy of copyrighted materials in violation of the author's rights. Purchase only authorized editions.

September 2017 First Edition
Printed in the United States of America

Print ISBN: 978-0-9908923-7-3
Digital ISBN: 978-0-9908923-6-6

Editor: Neil Fogel
Cover Design: Alexandre Rito
Formatting by Elaine York, Allusion Graphics, LLC
www.allusiongraphics.com

The Blackthorne Forest Series

Blackthorne Forest, Book 1

Elvenwood, Book 2

The Dragon's Song, Book 3

The Joining Tree, Book 4

DEDICATION

ONCE AGAIN, TO NEIL,
FOR YOUR IDEAS, ENTHUSIASM,
AND ENCOURAGEMENT.
I COULDN'T DO IT WITHOUT YOU!

CHAPTER 1

My heart was broken. Irrevocably. And yet it was still beating. Stupid heart. It hadn't gotten the message yet.

When Conor brought me home after I'd spent hours in the forest in total misery, my parents were sitting at the kitchen table wearing worried looks.

Mom asked, "Cara, what's wrong?"

I couldn't talk to her. If she hadn't been so typically overprotective, maybe Adam wouldn't have left and my heart wouldn't be broken.

My father reached out for my hand, but I pulled away and ran upstairs to my room. I didn't want to speak to either one of them.

But as mad as I was at Mom, I was equally mad at Adam Wolfe. He left without even saying goodbye. How could he kiss me like that, totally rocking my world, and then leave the next day without a word to me? I might have been able to talk him out of leaving. But he never gave me the chance.

I could hear Conor's voice downstairs. I had no idea what he was saying to my parents, but I prayed he wouldn't tell them that he'd seen Adam kiss me yesterday. No, I was pretty sure he wouldn't do that. He'd always behaved like an understanding big brother.

I remembered something Conor had said to me a few months ago when I admitted I cared about Adam more than I probably should. Conor had chuckled, saying, "He won't always be too old for you, you know." That ten-year age difference wouldn't be such a big deal when I was twenty, would it?

Couldn't Adam have waited four years?

I went into my bathroom and ran a bath, throwing in my favorite bath salts. Maybe I could soak my heartache away. I sniffled. There weren't enough bath salts in the world to take away the pain I was feeling.

After I was in bed, I heard a soft tapping at my bedroom door. It sounded like Mom. I ignored it. My phone had rung a few times after I got out of the bath. Probably Sean, the ex-boyfriend who wanted me back. I ignored that too.

Thankfully, I had a dreamless night. I couldn't have handled any more pain.

When I went into the bathroom the next morning, I took one look in the mirror and went back to bed. Tinted glasses wouldn't cut it this time and I really didn't want to answer any questions about why I looked like crap.

THE JOINING TREE

I needed a mental health day, maybe more than one. I wasn't going back to school until I looked normal. What I'd seen in the mirror was definitely not normal; red, swollen eyes and nose. I looked pathetic. I felt pathetic. I'd been dumped by the only man, or Elf, I'd ever love. I hated him.

Sighing. *No, not really.*

More taps on my bedroom door. I continued to ignore them. Finally, I heard my father's deep voice. "Cara, we love you and we're worried about you. Don't shut us out."

I went to the door and opened it a crack. "I need time to myself, Dad. Please leave me alone right now."

He sighed. I heard his footsteps head downstairs.

I had a lot of thinking to do. The past six months had changed me in so many ways. I didn't even feel like the same girl, dressed in pink, who'd seen her parents get married two days ago.

Six months of threats, attacks, injuries and fear hadn't broken my spirit. But in less than twenty-four hours, Adam Wolfe had broken my heart.

I went back to school two days later. When I came downstairs Wednesday morning, Mom asked how I was feeling. She looked worried.

I said I was fine, not hungry, and left.

I didn't know whether Kevin needed a ride so I drove around the corner and beeped. After a few minutes, he came running out.

"Are you okay, babe?"

"I'm fine, Kev. Need a ride to school?"

"Sure, just give me a minute to gather my books." He went back inside the house, returning in under two minutes, backpack over his shoulder. Hopping into my front seat, he took one look at me. "I don't believe you've been sick. You're never sick. What happened?"

I shrugged, not looking at him. "I'm not really ready to talk about it."

His hand was on my shoulder. I turned and saw the concern in his eyes.

"Kev, just be my friend without asking questions right now, okay?"

After a few seconds, he said, "Okay. But when you're ready to talk, I'll be here."

I nodded and drove to school. I knew I'd be forced to have the same non-conversation with Amy. I wasn't looking forward to it. Amy never took "no" for an answer.

As for Sean, I wasn't sure what to say to him. He'd called five times and I hadn't answered once. There'd be no way to avoid him. He would be sitting next to me in four classes, five days a week.

I groaned inwardly. It might be easier to just drop out of school.

Since I'd skipped breakfast, we were early and I was able to park right in front of the main entrance.

Before I could get out of the car, Kevin said, "Cara, I know what you've gone through in the past six months. Maybe it's all hit you at once, and maybe you'll never be the girl you used to be. And that's okay. We're all shaped by our experiences, the good and the bad, but you and I are still best friends. If you're hurting, well, I'm hurting too. Don't shut me out." The same thing my mother had said.

I sat there for a few minutes, then I nodded. "I know. When I can talk about it, I will."

He was right about one thing. The past six months had been disastrous in many ways: Arson, shootings, kidnapping, and murder, masterminded by the psychopath who was now in prison. I thought I had been coping fairly well but Adam's desertion had finished me.

We got out of the car and walked inside. It was really early. We didn't find Amy and Sean waiting for us. I wasn't even sure if that would continue to be our daily routine. But for today, it made this morning easier for me.

"See you at lunch." I left Kevin and walked down the hall to my first class. I had seen the confused, concerned look on his face. I needed more time. My emotions were too raw. Right now it was too painful to talk about, even to friends who loved me.

I was sitting in Science class, reading the textbook, trying to care about what I'd missed since last week, when Sean walked in. He sat down next to me with a hurt expression on his face.

"You stopped answering your phone, Cara. Or maybe you just stopped taking *my* calls. What did I do?"

I sighed. This would be harder than I expected.

"You didn't do anything, Sean. I'm in a bad place right now. I haven't talked to anybody. I'm not ready to talk. Not even to you." I touched his arm briefly, to let him know I wasn't mad at him.

"If you're really my friend, you won't ask any questions." I looked up at him and found him looking confused, as Kevin had.

"All right. But I'm not going anywhere. You can't chase me away," he said softly.

I nodded. I really didn't deserve his devotion.

For my next three classes, he sat next to me silently.

Avoiding Amy's questions would be impossible, so I went home for lunch. No one was home, which was a relief.

I made a quick sandwich, which tasted like sawdust. Ralph sat at my feet, looking hopeful, so I broke up half the sandwich and put it in his dish. The happy way he attacked it made me smile. After scratching his back for a minute or two, I drank some bottled water and drove back to school.

THE JOINING TREE

In Art class, Kevin nodded to me but didn't say anything. In P.E. we were still doing calisthenics, so I didn't have to speak to anyone.

Waiting at the main entrance, Kevin walked to my car with me, not saying much.

I thought I was home free, but I should have known better. When we reached my car, Amy was perched on the hood, her blue eyes focused on me like lasers.

"You can't avoid me, Miss Connelly. Or is it Miss Blackthorne now? No matter, I'm here, I'm your best friend and you will not shut down on me!"

I just stared at her. Today had been a strain, and I was not in a good mood.

Kevin stood behind me with one hand on my shoulder. "Should I take the bus home today?"

I shook my head, still looking at Amy's irritated face. "I'll drive you home if someone will get her butt off my car."

Her eyes narrowed, she slid off the hood, then gave me an annoyed look and hopped into the back seat.

I sighed as Kevin climbed into the front seat. I was still standing next to the car. Apparently, there was no escape from Amy.

I got in the car and drove Kevin home. I knew if I tried to drop off Amy first, she'd refuse to get out of the car.

When I pulled up in front of Kevin's house, he squeezed my shoulder and said, "It's gonna be okay, babe, whatever it is." He nodded at Amy and went in the house.

From the back seat I heard, "We started this conversation on Sunday, Cara, and we will continue it now." More gently, she added, "Come home with me. We still have a few apple tarts left."

I didn't answer her as I drove to her house. When we got there, she leaned over the front seat and said, "I don't care how bad it is, I'm on your side and I always will be."

That did it. I leaned my head against the steering wheel and let the tears run down my face.

She climbed over the seat and wrapped her arms around me, leaning her head against mine. "Oh, sweetie, I'm so sorry. Come on into the house. I'll grab a few tarts and we'll go upstairs to my room where it's quiet and we can talk."

I nodded and climbed out of the car, meeting Amy on the other side. She took my hand and led me into her house, pointing me up to her room, while she dashed into the kitchen and grabbed a few tarts.

Once back in her bedroom, she handed me a box of tissues before she handed me a tart. "Blow your nose, you'll feel better."

After I had a few minutes to blow my nose, wipe my tears and compose myself, she said, "Okay, Cara. You were so happy when you were here Sunday morning. What in the world happened after that?"

After a few long seconds, I nodded. "Amy, I'll tell you, but this goes no further, okay?" I didn't want anyone else feeling sorry for me. And that included Kevin and Sean. Although I suspected Sean would probably be relieved when he learned that Adam was gone.

"When I got home from your house Sunday morning, my father said he wanted to speak to me privately.

"He said Adam had left, that he was already gone." My voice was shaking. "He tried to explain it away by saying that Adam had always been a rolling stone, and now that I no longer needed a bodyguard, he'd decided to move on."

I felt tears welling up again.

Amy gasped. "Did you think that was the truth?"

"As he saw it, maybe. But I know that wasn't really the reason. My mother had made such a point of telling Adam how young I am, he must have thought he'd be in real trouble if anyone knew he'd kissed me. His solution to that problem was to leave. And what hurts just as much is that he didn't even say goodbye to me."

Amy shook her head, obviously shocked.

"Oh, Cara, I'm so sorry. Your heart must be broken."

I sniffled. "I don't think I have a heart anymore. Adam took it with him."

"Sweetie, it'll take time, but you'll get over it eventually."

She obviously didn't understand.

"Amy, Elves mate for life. For Elves there are no break ups, no divorce. Look at my parents. All those years apart, and neither one of them ever looked at anyone else. They were mated for life, even though Mom is human and didn't know about the 'mated for life' thing.

"I won't get over it. I've never felt, never dreamed of feeling, what I felt with Adam. And I don't think I'll ever feel anything like that again."

"What? So you think that at sixteen, your love life is over forever?"

I simply nodded.

"Well, boys will still be in your life. I don't think Sean will ever walk away. When you go to college, or Art School, there will be boys and men everywhere. You don't think you'll ever find anyone attractive again?"

"Not like Adam. That was a once-in-a-lifetime feeling. If I tried to describe it to you, you'd never believe it." I shook my head. "No, I won't find that again."

"So are you swearing off the male sex completely?"

"They're fine as friends, but not for anything else."

She hesitated, then asked, "Cara, what have you been doing for the past two days?"

"I stayed in my room, refused to talk to my parents. I think I lost five pounds of water just from crying."

"You have to talk to your folks sometime. They're probably really worried about you. I sort of understand why you're holding your mom responsible, but why your dad?"

"My overprotective mother insisted that Dad speak to Adam about my age. I know he didn't want to. He knew he could trust Adam, but he didn't argue with her. He just did what she asked and spoke to Adam about how young I was, blah, blah, blah. I told you about that, remember? That conversation took place under my bedroom window. Adam knew I heard them.

"That's not the only reason I'm mad at him. My father told me he knew Adam had feelings for me, but that he had confidence that Adam would keep those feelings under control because of my age. But when Adam told my dad he was leaving, my father did nothing to talk him out of it. I don't understand why."

"Maybe you should ask him that question, Cara."

"Yeah. Maybe I will."

"Sweetie, I've been hoping we could start having fun during our last year of high school now that Gaynes is in jail. But it doesn't sound like you'll be enjoying it at all. What are you going to do all year?"

"I've given it a lot of thought over the last few days. I'm going to concentrate on my classes and my art. My mother can forget about sending me to a four-year college. All I've ever wanted is Art School. From now on, she won't be making any of my decisions. I will."

Amy knew I wasn't in any hurry to go home so she invited me to stay for dinner. Mrs. Strauss had made Wiener Schnitzel, a dish I hadn't had since the last time I'd had dinner with Amy. It would just be the three of us. Her dad was out at a Chamber of Commerce meeting.

Naturally, their phone rang while we were eating. Mrs. Strauss handed the phone to me.

"Hello? I'm having dinner with Amy and her mom. I'll be home later. 'Bye."

Amy asked, "Is she mad?"

"She didn't sound mad. Just wanted to know when I'd be home."

Amy's mom knew something was wrong. "Cara dear, is there anything I can do to help?"

"No, Mrs. Strauss. Just letting me spend time here is enough. Dinner is great. I really appreciate this."

"Anytime, dear. Our door is always open, you know."

Amy's mom was one of my favorite people. She always seemed to understand, without asking any questions. Unlike *my* mother.

After we'd finished the Schnitzel, there were more apple tarts. Amy and I cleaned up the kitchen and then we went into the den to do some homework.

When I couldn't put it off any longer, I gave Amy and her mom hugs and went home.

CHAPTER 2

I sat in my car for a while when I got home. I knew my parents would be waiting for me, and I still didn't want to talk to them. I just wanted to go up to my room, get into bed, and tune out my miserable life for a few hours.

I looked up when the front door opened and a tall figure came down the steps, heading for my car. Crap. My father wasn't going to leave me alone.

He opened the passenger door and got in. He didn't say anything right away and neither did I. Finally, he said in a very soft voice, "You shouldn't be hurting your mother this way. She's devoted her life to you. Your behavior has made her cry, Cara."

That was the last thing I needed to hear. I exploded.

"But I suppose *my* tears are unimportant, right? It's okay if I get hurt because of *her* behavior. Is that what you're saying?"

He looked shocked. "Of course not. We hated knowing you'd been crying. We never wanted you hurt. How is whatever you're feeling our fault?"

"Dad, Adam is gone. I blame Mom for that, for being so overprotective. And I blame you for not trying to talk him out of leaving."

He didn't say anything right away. He sounded confused. "This is all about Adam?"

I hadn't meant to yell at him. I nodded, fighting back tears again.

He put his arm around me. "Sweetheart, I asked you several times if you were in love with Adam. You always said you didn't know what falling in love felt like. Quote, unquote. You said he was a close friend. When did this change?"

"The day you and Mom got married."

I looked over at him. "Dad, you told me that Elves mate for life, that once an Elf gives his heart, it stays given." I felt tears forming again.

"Cara, you believe that Adam is your *mate*?" He sounded dumbfounded.

"I do. He is the only man I'll ever love. And you let him leave. Why didn't you try to talk him into staying?"

"It was his decision, Cara. I had no idea you and he felt so strongly about each other."

"Let me ask you this, Dad. If you'd been the one who raised me, and I'd fallen in love with Adam, even though I'm sixteen and he's ten years older, would you have sent him away?"

He didn't answer right away. Then he sighed. "No, dear, I wouldn't have sent him away. Many of our Elven couples fell in love when they were quite young. It's not unusual in our world."

THE JOINING TREE

I just nodded. My life would have been completely different if my father had been the one to raise me.

"Cara, you've given me some things to think about. The only thing I didn't mention was that Adam asked if he'd be welcome if he came back some day. I told him he would, that he'd always have a home with us. I sincerely hope that means he plans on returning eventually."

I shook my head. "Dad, we both know there's no guarantee he'll ever come back." I felt a tear running down my cheek and heard a deep sigh from my father.

"Sweetheart, all I can do is tell you how sorry I am. I wish I'd been aware of your feelings. Let's go inside now. You can go up to bed. I'll talk to your mother. I don't want either one of you crying. I love you both." He reached over and gently wiped away my tear.

He opened the door and got out of my car, holding out his hand to me. I slid across the seat and got out with him. He held my hand as we walked to the house.

When we got inside, I went straight upstairs while my father went into the kitchen where my mother was waiting.

That night my sleep was anything but dreamless. I kept dreaming of Adam kissing me, over and over, as though it was on a loop. Every time was like the first time, the roaring in my ears, and the ground moving beneath me. I don't remember how many times I woke up with a damp pillow against my face. It was endless. I'd probably need the glasses with the tinted lenses in the morning.

Life really wasn't fair.

After that, the atmosphere at home was quiet. Actually, it was more like an armed truce. Mom didn't question me about anything, and I didn't say much to her. At dinner, my father made conversation with both of us, but we only responded to him.

I was still angry with my mother for her overprotective meddling, and with Adam for leaving without a word to me. I did understand that if my father had been aware of my feelings for Adam, he would have made some effort to keep him with us.

The rest of that week went by in a kind of dull blur. School, homework, my various art projects, and dreams at night that left my pillow damp. I didn't talk to Kevin about what was bothering me, and I barely talked to Sean at all. When he asked me if I was going to Friday night's game, I said no and his face dropped.

He still wasn't able to play football. Until his surgeon felt that his broken nose was completely healed, Sean would be sitting on the bench. His former Elven bodyguard, Gabriel, would no longer be there to help the team. Gabe had played for Thornewood High a few times, but without Sean and Gabe, the rest of Thornewood's football season would be challenging, at best. Sean was obviously stressed out about this.

As his friend, I knew he needed my support, but I didn't have any to give.

It was unfortunate that Amy and I had no classes together. She understood, and I could talk to her. We had lunch together, and I began driving her home after school when it was my week to drive. Kevin and I still took turns. I was beginning to get hurt looks from Kevin, which I hated. I would have to confide in him soon. Knowing Kevin, he probably suspected why I was so unhappy.

Kevin's patience finally came to an end one Friday a few weeks later when he drove me home from school. He pressed the button to lock all the doors in his Jeep so that I couldn't get out.

"Short stuff, I have been your best friend, confidant, and protector since we were five. Shutting me out while you withdraw from life ends now!"

He turned the ignition off and faced me, wrapping one long arm around the back of his seat. I could see how pissed he was.

"Cara, when has there ever been *anything* you couldn't talk to me about?"

I just sat there, looking down at my hands.

"Look, I know you've unloaded to Amy, but she's being a real clam, strange as that seems. She won't say a word about you. I may have to resign as your other best friend if you refuse to tell me *what the hell is going on*."

Those last few words were shouted. Kevin had made his point.

I turned and looked into his intelligent hazel eyes. "Kev, it's really hard to talk about, and I didn't think you'd want me crying all over you. I haven't cried on you since kindergarten."

He nodded, a slight smile on his face. "Babe, I didn't mind then, and I wouldn't mind now." He hesitated for a long minute. His voice was soft as he added, "I have a feeling this is all about that one Elf I haven't seen around lately."

I nodded, feeling tears forming again. "Adam's gone. He didn't even say goodbye to me."

Looking surprised, he asked, "Are you in love with Adam?"

I looked him in the eye. "I am."

He leaned his head back against his headrest. "Wow. I had no idea it had gone that far. Did he feel the same way?"

I hesitated. "I don't know. I think so, but he never said those words."

Kevin snorted. "I heard him call you 'love' dozens of times, and I wondered about that. When did you suddenly decide you were in love with him?"

"At the wedding. He kissed me, really kissed me. It blew my mind."

"Babe, the guy is a lot older than you. He probably figured your parents would disapprove, even be angry with him. Maybe he thought he should leave before it got to that point."

"Then he should have left *before* he kissed me, not after!" I couldn't help yelling.

"Would that have made it easier for you?"

"To be honest, no, not much. I think I've been in love with Adam for months. I just didn't realize that's what I was feeling."

"So what are you going to do now? Drop out of life? Ignore your friends? Wallow in this obvious depression? Snap out of it! Your life is far from over. We have our senior year to enjoy. You have Art School to look forward to. I have no doubt that you'll be a successful artist some day. And, not that it's any of my business, you're breaking Sean's heart on a daily basis."

I groaned. "I'm not in love with Sean. He knows that. That's not something that will change, Kevin."

"I know. But completely shutting him out this way? That's really cold, babe."

"At least be his friend. He has feelings too, Cara, and you're ignoring them completely. This isn't like you."

He was right.

"I can be his friend, but I can't be more than that. He wants more."

"Just let him know you're still his friend. We should all be trying to enjoy this year, especially after the past six months that we've all lived through. You most of all."

"You're right. But I don't think I can just stick my broken heart in a drawer and forget about it. It really hurts, Kevin."

"I know, but you need to start enjoying life again. Our lives are really just beginning."

I sighed. "Is the lecture over now?"

He chuckled. "Yeah, lecture over. Now come to the game with me tonight. Amy will be there. The three musketeers, as we used to call ourselves. Okay?"

I was reluctant but I couldn't bring myself to say no to Kevin.

"Okay. Now I have to tell my parents I'm going out." I rolled my eyes. "They may faint from the shock."

He chuckled. "The celebrating will probably start as soon as you walk out the door!"

I grimaced and nodded. "See you around six."

When I walked into the house, my father was in the kitchen. Mom wasn't home from the bookstore yet.

He smiled, as he always did, no matter how gloomy I looked. "How was your day?"

"A little better now, Dad. Kevin just finished reading me the riot act. I'm going to tonight's football game with him and Amy."

"Excellent! You need to make an effort to get back to normal."

I shrugged. "I'm not sure what normal is anymore, but Kevin's determined to make me start enjoying our senior year. He's not giving me any choice."

"Good for Kevin. I'll have to give the boy a raise."

I couldn't hold back a weak smile. "I'll make myself a sandwich. You and Mom can have dinner at the usual time. I'll be leaving around six."

I started walking out of the kitchen as he said, "Cara, does this mean you'll start talking to your mother again? I really think it's time." His green eyes showed me how important it was to him.

"That's going to be harder, Dad. I don't think my relationship with Mom will ever be what it used to be. You both have to let me make my own decisions from now on."

He nodded. "All right. But if you happen to make a bad decision, just know we'll still be here for you."

"Sounds fair. I'll be down in a few minutes. I just want to change my clothes."

I ran up to my room. Tonight was the right time for my red Thornewood High sweatshirt. And, of course, boots with my knives tucked inside. The threat was over, but I never wanted to feel defenseless again.

Once I was dressed, I thought about Sean. Maybe I should call him, just to say I'd see him at the game. I owed him that.

When he picked up the phone, he sounded shocked. "Cara? Is it really you?"

"Yeah, really me. I think I owe you an apology. I've been depressed for weeks and I've been ignoring you, along with everyone else. I'm sorry. I know I shouldn't take my problems out on my friends. I'm going to the game with Kevin and Amy tonight. See you there?"

"Absolutely. I'll be on the bench with the team. Can we get together after the game?"

"Okay. Maybe the four of us can go out for burgers or pizza."

"We haven't been to the Pizza Palace in months. Cara, just hearing your voice is a treat. Don't change your mind about going out, okay? I'll see you at the game."

"Okay, Sean. See you later."

He sounded so happy. Kevin was right. I didn't want to hurt my friends, no matter what I was going through.

I ran downstairs and found a peanut butter and jelly sandwich on the table waiting for me along with a glass of milk. My mother must be home.

She came downstairs just as I was finishing my sandwich. "Thanks for the sandwich, Mom. I'm leaving for the game now. We'll probably go out for pizza afterward. See you later." It was the most I'd said to her in weeks.

I kissed my dad and left the house.

Feeling strangely energized, I decided not to wait for Kevin to pick me up. I walked around the corner to his house and caught him as he was getting into his Jeep.

"In a hurry, short stuff? You would have called me if you'd changed your mind, right?"

"I just didn't feel like sitting around. I'm not really ready to talk to my mom."

"You're blaming her for Adam leaving?"

"Yes.

"By the way, I called Sean and told him I'd be coming to the game with you and Amy. I also apologized for the way I've been acting. He suggested the four of us go out for pizza after the game."

He looked over at me with approval as he drove around the corner. "You did good. I hate seeing anyone as miserable as you and Sean have both been for the past few weeks. Tonight will be fun now that you're back in the land of the living."

He raised one eyebrow and grinned at me. I rolled my eyes.

When Kevin and I got to the football field, we spotted Amy up on the top row of the stands, waving like mad at us. We climbed up and joined her just as she decided to shout to Sean, who was sitting on the team bench. He turned around, saw me and grinned, waving to us. I smiled and waved back. Until the team ran on the field, he kept looking over his shoulder at me, as though he wanted to make sure I was still there.

Tonight's game was against Parkersburg, another small town about the size of Thornewood. With Sean at quarterback, it would have been an easy win, but the game almost went down as a defeat until the last quarter when Billy Herron passed for two touchdowns. The crowd went crazy and, once again, I wished I had ear plugs.

As we climbed down out of the stands, Kevin muttered, "That was too close. Sitting on the bench must be driving Sean nuts."

We waited for Sean until the rest of the team left for the locker room. When he came running over to us, the first thing he did was wrap his arms around me, hugging me with a big smile. Kevin and Amy watched us, looking satisfied.

When he finally let me go, Sean asked, "Who's ready for pizza?"

Kevin drove us to the Pizza Palace, and the smells in the dining room were making all of us hungry. We'd ordered two extra-large pizzas. When they were put on our table, Amy looked at me with one eyebrow raised. "Better grab a slice, Cara. These two look like starved vultures." I had to smile.

Both pizzas disappeared quickly and before we could ask, more Root Beer was brought to our table. Someone had already dropped some quarters in the old jukebox in the corner, and we could hear oldies playing in the background.

The music took me back to last spring when Sean brought me here for pizza. We'd danced to the oldies until we ran out of quarters. It had been very romantic.

I couldn't help sighing. Sean must have heard me. Softly he said, "Good memories, Cara. Dance with me?"

Before I could answer, Amy jumped up and pulled Kevin up with her. "Come on, Kev. I know you can dance." He looked a little sheepish as he glanced at me. Thanks to our mothers, Kevin and I had taken ballroom dancing classes a few years ago. Kevin was a really good dancer, which Amy had discovered at the last Spring Dance when his moves on the dance floor left her almost speechless.

I couldn't help smiling when I watched them dancing. Since Amy was almost as tall as Kevin, they looked great together.

I turned to Sean, surprised to see the longing in his warm brown eyes. He covered my hand with his own and said, "I know you love to dance." He grinned. "Come on." He stood up and held out his hand to me.

How could I say no? I got up and followed him to the middle of the room, his hand holding mine. "Why Do Fools Fall in Love" was playing on the jukebox, one of my favorites.

When it ended, a ballad began to play. Sean murmured, "Another dance, Cara?" I nodded and he wrapped his arms around me while I rested my head in that comfortable place between his neck and shoulder. But it wasn't the same. I'd changed too much.

When I looked over at Kevin and Amy, she had her forehead against his cheek and he was holding her close. I don't know why that surprised me, but it did. Were Amy and Kevin more than best friends? That gave me something new to think about.

Sean whispered in my ear, "You have no idea how good this feels, Cara. I've missed you." His arms tightened around me. I had to admit that being this close to Sean was nice, but it was a different pair of arms I longed for.

The four of us danced to one more oldie, then returned to our table and gulped down our Root Beer. We were talking about different eras of music when I looked up and saw a tall, curvy brunette walk in with a good looking guy with long black hair, dark eyes, and an impatient look on his face.

Her eyes met mine, surprised. "Cara, hey!" She started walking toward our table when her date pulled her back rather forcefully and pulled her to a table on the other side of the dining room.

Sean said, "That's Miranda Ross. She sure looks different than she did last year. I don't like the looks of that guy she's with. Do any of you know him?"

I'd had a few Emails from her over the summer. I'd used the verbal power of *Vox* to stop her from braining me with a baseball bat last spring when I'd started dating Sean. Miranda was obsessed with Sean and had been bullying every girl who'd even spoken to him. I found out later that she'd been going through a rough time at home, with an alcoholic mother and a dad who'd bailed.

Apparently, using *Vox* on a person could sometimes stop self-destructive behavior, kind of like re-wiring the brain. Miranda never knew exactly *what* I'd done, but she'd been a different person after that. I realized I hadn't seen her in school this semester.

Amy said, "I know she moved out of Thornewood in August. She lives with her aunt in Greenville now."

Sean said, "That guy must be from Greenville. Miranda looks a lot older than she did last year. I think she wanted to talk to you, Cara."

"Yeah. We emailed a few times over the summer, but I didn't know she'd moved. I haven't heard from her lately."

Impulsively, I got up and went over to her table. "Miranda, I didn't know you'd moved. Is your email address the same?" She nodded, looking at her date out of the corner of her eye. I said, "Good. I'll be in touch." I smiled. "Have a good night."

When I returned to the table, Amy said, "I didn't know you'd become friends. You never mentioned her."

I shrugged. "Just a few emails. She apologized for that stuff last spring and thanked me for whatever it was I'd done."

Looking thoughtful, Sean said, "Yeah, I remember. After the baseball bat incident, Miranda really turned her life around. Her attitude changed completely. She called me to apologize too. But it doesn't look to me like she's picking the best kind of friends over in Greenville."

It was getting late so we left and Kevin drove us all home. Sean whispered, "Wish I had my dad's car tonight. I'd like to talk some more. Can I call you later?"

"Sure." But I was afraid he'd want some kind of explanation for my depression over the past several weeks. I couldn't tell him the truth. I didn't want to hurt him.

No one was in the kitchen when I got home. My parents must be in their bedroom, maybe watching TV. Thinking about my dad watching TV made me smile. His village, Elvenwood, had no electricity, no modern appliances, not even hot showers. But I had taught him how to make coffee in our electric coffeemaker, and he admitted he was enjoying the hot showers. Now that he was spending so much time in the human world, his life was changing. He even said he'd like to learn how to drive a car. Picturing my father behind the wheel always made me smile.

I made myself a cup of herbal tea and took it upstairs with me. I stopped at my mother's bedroom and tapped on the door. "I'm home." Then I went into my room and shut the door. I set my tea down next to my bed and got out of my boots, making sure my knives were still firmly in the boot sheaths I'd had made. I went into my bathroom to get out of my clothes and into my pajamas.

When I walked out of the bathroom, my mother was sitting on my bed next to Ralph, who was already asleep and snoring softly.

She smiled. "Did you have a good time tonight?"

Climbing up on my bed, I said, "Yes. It was good to be out with my friends."

She stood. "I'm glad. You should have fun this year while you can. The work in college will be harder, although I hope you'll make friends there too. All work and no play, you know." Smiling, she went to the door. "Sleep well."

She left, closing my door softly. I wasn't ready for the heart-to-heart talks we used to have.

I was lying in bed, just thinking, when my phone rang. I sighed. It was probably Sean, and I still hadn't figured out how to explain the weeks of depression he'd suffered right along with me.

But it wasn't Sean. It was Miranda Ross.

"Hi, Cara. I'm so sorry I couldn't talk when I saw you tonight. My boyfriend doesn't like me to see old friends from Thornewood. He says it's not good to live in the past."

"Seeing a former classmate and saying hello doesn't sound much like 'living in the past' to me," I said. I really didn't like the sound of that guy.

"Miranda, I wish you'd let me know that you were moving. Maybe we could have gotten together before you left town."

"Well, I did call your house, but your mom said you were visiting your dad. I didn't leave a message or anything. By the way, Cara, my friends call me Randi."

"Oh, okay. The week before school started, I was away at my dad's place. I'm sorry I missed you. Amy said she thought you were living with your aunt?"

"Yeah, my mom's sister. We were never really close, but at least she doesn't drink like a fish. My mom's in a mental health facility, although my dad prefers to say she's in 'Rehab.' He travels so he's not home much. I wouldn't mind living with my dad, but he said no, that I'd be alone too much. I miss Thornewood. It's hard to make new friends in your senior year, which is why I didn't want to move to Greenville. I guess I was lucky to meet Joey. He's the guy I was with tonight. He lives in the same apartment building. He's gorgeous, isn't he?"

"He's very good looking, Randi. But he wasn't very friendly. Is he always so possessive?"

She didn't say anything right away. "Yeah, well, I think he's a little jealous of the friends I had in Thornewood. But I see you and Sean are still together. Or is it 'together again?'" She chuckled.

"Yeah, you probably heard that we broke up in June just before school ended. He went off to baseball camp, and I didn't speak to him for quite a while. Another friend convinced me to accept Sean's apology, so I did and we're friends again."

That sudden memory of Adam convincing me to forgive Sean made my heart feel like it was being squeezed. Time to change the subject.

"Randi, can you get over to Thornewood once in a while? I'm sure your friends here would like to see you again. They haven't forgotten you. Do you still have that red BMW?"

"Yeah, still have the Beamer. I'd like to, Cara, but Joey takes up most of my time when I'm not in school, and he's not interested in visiting Thornewood. The only reason we were there tonight was because he was complaining about the pizza in Greenville, and I told him about the Pizza Palace. He loved the pizza, but said he thinks it's too long a drive just for pizza. So I don't know when I'll have a chance to visit."

"Well, if you get homesick, please call me. Maybe talking about Thornewood will help."

She laughed. "Thanks, Cara. I'll do that. It was really great seeing all of you tonight. Please say hi to Sean and Amy for me. I don't know the other guy you were with, but he's a real cutie. How did I miss him the past three years?"

I chuckled. "That was Kevin Sinclair. He's one of my best friends. I think Kevin's just come into his own this year. And you're right; he is a cutie."

She laughed. "We'll talk soon, Cara."

"Thanks for calling, Randi. Take care."

That phone call had been a nice surprise, but Randi's choice of boyfriend worried me. I had a bad feeling about him.

The next time the phone rang it was Sean.

"Hey Sean. You'll never guess who I've been on the phone with for the past half hour."

"Oh? Who?" Why did he have to sound suspicious?

"Miranda Ross. But she asked me to call her Randi. She moved away the week I was in Elvenwood before school started. She's not too crazy about Greenville. I think she'd like to come back to Thornewood, but her father wants her to live with her aunt."

"Cara, I never knew you had gotten friendly with Randi. Especially after what she tried to do to you during spring break."

"Well, it seems that using *Vox* on her was what snapped her out of that self-destructive streak she was on. She's been her old self since then. She emailed me a couple times during the summer, first to apologize, and then to thank me for helping her. She doesn't actually know *what* I did, just that everything changed afterward."

"Yeah, I knew she had finally calmed down and started behaving a lot better. So Randi knows that you did *something*, but she has no idea what it was?"

"Right. I was glad I'd been able to help her. She was having a rough time at home."

"Frankly, Cara, that boyfriend of hers looked kind of shady to me. I didn't like the way he pushed her around. Guys like that are bad news."

"I think so too. I even mentioned that to Randi, but she said it's been really hard to make new friends in a new place in her senior year. And Joey, that's his name, lives in her apartment building. I invited her to come back to visit whenever she can, but I think Joey has discouraged that."

He groaned. "That guy sounds bad. But let's leave the subject of Randi for now. I wanted to talk to you about whatever it was you were going through the past few weeks. Cara, you were like one of the walking dead. Even with all the crap you've gone through since I met you, I've never seen you like that before. I was really worried."

I couldn't tell him the whole truth. I sighed. "Sean, I've had some problems with my mom. She's made some decisions that have ended up hurting me pretty badly. I don't want to go into detail, but things are not good at home right now."

"Oh, wow. I'm really sorry. I always thought you and your mom had a great relationship. Hard to believe it's changed that much, especially now that your parents are married. Does it have anything to do with the way she kept you and your dad apart for sixteen years?"

"Well, that's one example of a decision she made that hurt me. I already told my father that I'll be making my own decisions from now on, that it's my life, not my mom's."

"How does your dad feel about that?"

"He understands. It's not his fault. He doesn't see everything the same way Mom does." I snorted. "I might have been better off if he'd raised me."

"No, Cara, don't think that way. Everybody makes mistakes. Even parents. I hope you and your mom will be able to get past this. I can see how unhappy it's making you."

We didn't say anything for a few seconds.

He asked, "Hey, what are you doing this weekend? Can we get together?"

"Well, I was thinking about spending the weekend in Elvenwood."

"Want company?"

"Maybe. Mainly I want to be out of the house when my mom's home. She'll be working Saturday, but she's home on Sunday."

"Okay. How about this. Spend Saturday at my house. We can do homework, maybe catch a movie. Then on Sunday we could ride to Elvenwood. What do you think?"

The only reason Sean knew about Elvenwood, my father's secret village deep in the forest, was because he had Elven blood, something we only became aware of when he met Conor McKay, Sean's look-alike and distant cousin. Conor was one of my father's Elves, and my close friend.

Being with Sean would keep me from brooding about Adam, but I didn't like feeling I'd be using Sean. He deserved better.

"Sean, let me talk to my dad. If it's okay with him, we'll do it. I'll call you back as soon as I speak to him."

"Okay, but don't worry about it. We can always find something to do. Lots of things to do on the weekend, Cara."

We said good night and I wondered when I'd get a chance to talk to my dad without Mom around.

I felt like slapping myself. What was I thinking? My father and I were telepaths.

Dad, Sean and I want to make plans for the weekend. He's invited me to his house on Saturday, and we're thinking about riding to Elvenwood on Sunday. Would that be okay with you?

Cara, I'm planning on being in Elvenwood Saturday, but I'll be here Sunday because it's your mother's day off. Sounds to me like you're trying to avoid seeing her.

My father understood me too well.

Dad, right now having the two of us in the same place isn't good for either of us. If I stay home, I'll just be in my room all day. I think it's better if I'm out with Sean. I'm trying to get back to normal, or whatever normal is these days.

There was no immediate answer. I knew he was thinking over what I'd said.

All right, dear. I don't really think your mother would disapprove of your plans. She wants to see you enjoying yourself with your friends. But I do want you to sit down with your mother soon. You need to get everything out in the open, talk about what you've been so upset about. Otherwise, this situation will never get resolved and it's hurting her. You have to understand, sweetheart. I don't want you or your mother hurt.

I wasn't sure how to answer him.

It's going to take time, Dad.

Cara, your mother loves you very much. Her only crime was doing what she thought was necessary to keep you safe. She hadn't had time to get to know Adam very well. I think she knows she made a mistake. You need to talk to her.

All right, Dad. But not right now. I'm not sure you understand.

I heard him sigh. *I do understand. I spent sixteen years with the same kind of unhappiness. But it's going to be up to you to make peace with your mother. And I expect you to do it as soon as possible.*

Okay, Dad. Thanks for listening.

I love you, dear. Your mother loves you too.

There was nothing more I could say. I looked at the clock. It wasn't too late to call Sean back.

He was thrilled that his plans for our weekend had been approved. "How early do you want to get up in the morning? I won't have the car, so can you drive over here?"

"Sure, no problem. What time will you be up?"

He laughed. "I'll be up at the crack of dawn if you want to come over that early."

I had to smile. "That's a little too early. How about ten o'clock?"

"Great. I'll even make you breakfast."

"You can cook?"

"Yep. I'm pretty good at bacon and eggs. Or you could show me how to make your Sunrise Specials. Your choice."

I told him I'd pick up bagels and be over at ten, with my books and art supplies.

"Ah, you're going to do some drawing this weekend."

"I will if the weather's good. I haven't done any artwork in weeks, and I miss it. But homework has to come first. I'll need those notes of yours."

"Great. See you at ten. This is going to be a really good weekend, Cara. It's good to see you smiling again."

And that made me smile. "Thanks, Sean. Sleep well."

But it wasn't Sean's warm brown eyes that I saw in my dreams that night.

CHAPTER 3

My phone started ringing much too early Saturday morning. It had to be Amy.

"Hey, Amy. Why are you up so early?"

She laughed. "I think it's just long-term habit. I can't seem to sleep past six. I just wanted to check in and see how you enjoyed Friday night. I really had a good time, since I was with three of my favorite people."

"Yeah, the company was great. It cheered me up a little."

"Only a little? Cara, Sean was so attentive, he hardly took his eyes off you all night. Looked like you were enjoying the dancing." She chuckled.

"Well, when we dated last spring, Sean brought me to the Pizza Palace several times and we always fed the jukebox and danced until we ran out of quarters. It was nice last night, but it also made me aware how much I've changed since last spring."

"I think what you're saying is that getting close to Sean doesn't mean what it used to, right?"

"Yes. Don't get me wrong. Sean is still the sweetest guy I know. I just don't want him to get the wrong idea, you know? I'm not in love with him, and I'm not going to be."

"You're sure about that? These things can change in a heartbeat. Don't count Sean out yet."

"Amy, I'm in love with Adam. That won't change."

"Do you mean that if Adam never comes back, you'll never fall in love with anyone else? Like ever?"

"That's about it."

"Well, then we'd better hope he comes back, Cara."

I snorted. I couldn't count on that.

"So what are you doing over the weekend?"

"Sean and I made plans for the entire weekend. I'm going to his house today to do homework and maybe watch a movie, and tomorrow, if the weather holds, we'll ride to Elvenwood for the day."

"Wow! He's not wasting any time, is he?" She laughed. "Gotta respect the boy's determination. Have you talked to your mom yet?"

"As little as I could manage. I had a long conversation with my dad. Naturally, he wants me to sit down and talk it all out with her, but I'm not ready. He knows that, but he expects me to make the effort anyway." I sighed.

"Cara, your mom's always been great. I have faith in you. You'll work things out."

"I don't know. Right now, I'm afraid I'll just start yelling at her and end up crying over Adam. I believe if it hadn't been for her, he wouldn't have felt he had to leave. That's really hard for me to get past."

"I understand, but give it time. Hey, if you and Sean want to do something Saturday night, give me a call. Kevin was talking about seeing a movie. We could all go."

"Amy, are you and Kevin *dating*?" I was dying to hear her answer.

"Uh, well, I think it's more like hanging out than dating. I always have fun with Kevin and we know each other *so* well. Plus, have you noticed how good he's looking lately?"

I had to laugh. "Yes indeed. That curly-haired, long, lean look has finally come together for Kevin. I was talking to Miranda earlier and she wanted to know who the *cutie* was last night!"

"Miranda called you?"

"Yeah, we talked for a while. She's really homesick. Doesn't much like Greenville or starting her senior year with strangers."

"I feel for her, but that boyfriend of hers has got to go. She must be desperate."

"Well, she asked me to tell you hi. I invited her to drive over when she has time. She doesn't seem happy living with her aunt."

"That's too bad. Give her my best next time you talk to her. I'd better go. We're making a couple of apple pies this morning, and one might have your name on it."

I groaned. "Apple pie, my downfall. Just let me know when I can pick it up!"

She laughed. "Okay. Talk to you later."

I looked at the clock. It was only seven thirty, so I dove back under my comforter.

I got up around nine, showered and got dressed. It was kind of a date, so I took more care with my clothes and hair. I started out with black tights, added a long sweater, and, of course, the ever-present boots. I was tired of the ponytail, so I blew my hair dry and let it hang down my back.

On an impulse, I got out my nail scissors and cut wispy bangs at my forehead. Everything in my life had changed so much, I was ready for a new look. When I was done, I liked it. I wondered how Adam would like it, then immediately deleted that thought, irritated at myself.

No one was downstairs. Mom had already left for the bookstore and Dad had left for Elvenwood. Good. I wouldn't have to listen to any lectures this morning.

Throwing both my backpack and messenger bag in the car, I drove to the deli downtown and picked up a bag of bagels. When I pulled up in front of Sean's house, he ran out to help me out of the car, grabbing my backpack and the bag of bagels.

Standing back, he looked me over and whistled. "You look great. New look?"

"Well, yeah. I needed a change. What do you think?"

He grinned. "It's a sexy look. And you look older." Looking down at my legs, he chuckled. "If you're going to be dressing like that from now on, I'll be fighting off the other guys on a daily basis."

Naturally, I could feel my face getting hot. "Thanks, I think."

Laughing, he led me into the house, going straight into the kitchen. "We've got the house to ourselves for the day. Mom's spending the day at some spa, and Dad's seeing clients all day."

"Do they know I'll be here today?"

"Yep. They both wanted me to tell you hi." He smiled. "I think Mom's especially glad you're here." He looked down, his face slightly pink.

Opening the bag of bagels, he said, "Okay, breakfast first. Let's make the Sunrise Specials together. I'm really hungry."

We sliced the bagels, he made bacon, I sliced up the tomatoes, and he took the cream cheese out of the fridge. I put it all together and we sat down at the table and ate.

Over our breakfast of Sunrise Specials—Sean ate two—we talked about school, his scholarship hopes, and all the catching up I felt I needed to do.

After breakfast, he cleared the kitchen table and we spread our books out along with all of Sean's painstaking notes. "I'll make copies of these while you're here. It'll make studying easier for you."

We went through several chapters in Environmental Science, and then moved on to History. Working from Sean's notes was a lot easier than reading every chapter. He was a great note-taker. We worked until he announced he was hungry again and offered to make grilled sandwiches for us.

The boy could cook, I'll give him that. His grilled cheese was every bit as good as my mother's, and he added ham to the cheese.

"Thanks for cooking, Sean. This was delicious. You can cook for me any time."

He grinned. "My pleasure."

After lunch we went on to English, *Macbeth* specifically. Neither one of us was really enjoying it. "It's too bloody," he said, "depressing too." I totally agreed, but we went over his notes anyway. We'd heard the mid-term exam would be tough.

Our Economics class was fairly easy. When we'd reviewed Sean's notes, we were actually done.

"I feel like I'm totally caught up. I really fell behind, so today has been a life saver. I owe you."

"Nah, you don't owe me anything. It's really the other way around. Studying with you is a hundred times better than studying alone. When we get close to exam time, let's study together and we'll both do better with our exams."

"Deal." I winked at him. "Especially if you cook." He grinned.

Before we put our books and papers away, Sean ran up to his dad's office and made copies of his notes for me. With everything school-related tucked

THE JOINING TREE

away, he asked, "What would you like to do now? There's still enough sun if you want to do some drawing. Our backyard is looking great this year."

When we walked out the back door to his back porch, I was amazed. The yard was full of mature trees, all kinds, along with large flower beds on both sides of the yard.

"Who's the gardener? Your mom or your dad?"

"That would be Mom. She says it's better than a tranquilizer."

"Sean, I never did finish a picture of you to give to your parents last spring. Other people kept showing up unexpectedly in those drawings, remember?" He nodded, smiling.

"I'll get one started today. The scenery in your yard is perfect and we still have a few more hours of sun."

We dragged a chair into the backyard. I sat down with my drawing pad, and Sean began doing some weeding in one of the flower beds. I would draw him in profile as he worked. His blond hair and blue sweatshirt contrasted nicely with the red geraniums that filled up one row in the bed. I drew in a few trees, the wood fence at one side of the yard, and many of the flowers that were still blooming, dozens of asters, one white rose bush, and a few hardy yellow daylilies. When I was able to add all the colors, it would be an extremely colorful picture. I drew in all the detail, but used my phone to take a picture so I wouldn't forget the colors of all the flowers.

"You can get up now, Sean. I've sketched the whole scene. I'll finish adding the colors at home."

He picked up the pile of weeds he'd pulled and deposited them in a can at the side of the yard. When he reached me, I handed him my drawing pad.

Sitting down in the grass next to me, he said, "If I'm not mistaken, this is even better than the drawings you were doing last spring. They were great, but there's more, I don't know, emotion in this drawing." He shook his head. "I don't know if that's the right word."

Adam had said he was seeing more drama, more passion, in my latest drawings. Sean was calling it "emotion."

"Thanks, Sean. I guess my technique is evolving." I smiled. "But I'm glad you like it. This one is definitely for your parents as soon as I finish it."

"Cara, their anniversary is coming up. I think I'll take this downtown and get it framed. It will make a great anniversary gift." He grinned. "Of course, knowing the artist personally will be a plus."

"I do hope they like it. I'll take my time finishing it."

"They'll love it. Now, what do you think about a movie tonight?"

"Amy said she and Kevin are going to the movies tonight. I have no idea what's playing. Want to join them?"

He laughed. "It's probably some zombie movie. Our local theater seems to specialize in horror. Hey, are Amy and Kevin *dating*?"

"That was my very question when I spoke to her this morning." I smiled. "She says it's more like 'hanging out' than dating, but I'm not so sure."

"You're not going home before the movie, are you?" he asked.

"Uh, no. Is it okay if I clean up here?"

"Sure."

We heard "Hi, guys," from the back door and looked up to see Sean's dad waving at us. We waved back. Sean picked up my chair and we walked back to the house.

After I washed up, we sat with Mr. McKay and chatted until Mrs. McKay came home.

"Cara, how are you? It's so nice to see you again. I'm still talking about your parents' wedding. It was so lovely, and they looked perfect together. I really enjoyed myself. I also loved your pink and white dress. You looked beautiful. How are your mom and dad?"

"They're fine, thanks." And that was when my phone rang. I knew it would be my mother."Hi, Mom. I'm at Sean's. We studied most of the day, and we're going to the movies tonight. We'll probably eat there. . . Well, nachos and hot dogs. I don't think it will kill us." Sean's mom was laughing at my end of the conversation. "Yes, that was Mrs. McKay. Would you like to say hello?" I handed the phone to Sean's mom.

Sean was trying not to laugh. I simply rolled my eyes.

When I got my phone back, I called Amy to see when and where we should meet.

Half an hour later, we left. When we reached the movie theater, I took one look at the sign in front and groaned. "Night of the Living Dead," the original film.

"That movie always gave me nightmares. Seeing it again is really asking for it."

Sean laughed. "I see Kevin and Amy by the box office."

I parked my car half a block away and we joined them. Amy was shaking her head. "I won't sleep tonight; I just know it. This has got to be the creepiest movie I've ever seen."

We gorged on nachos and hot dogs, and I watched the movie with my eyes closed most of the time. Amy, of course, shrieked a lot while Kevin laughed at her. But I noticed he held her hand.

Sean had his arm around me and my face was pushed into his chest a lot. He wasn't laughing, just an occasional chuckle. When it was finally over, Amy and I were both relieved. Horror films would never be my favorites.

As we walked out of the movie, Kevin said, "That's an all-time great flick, but there was one thing missing." When I asked what, he answered with a grin. "Dragons."

Which reminded me that I hadn't had a real talk with Rowenna in quite a while. I knew she was aware of how unhappy I was.

We planned to ride to Elvenwood Sunday morning so I picked up Sean before seven a.m., hoping we wouldn't be too late for breakfast at the dining hall. I was out of the house before my parents came downstairs but I left a note.

THE JOINING TREE

Sean and I walked to my father's camp and got our horses after saying hello to Conor, Gavin, and Kevin's dad, Kelly O'Rourke. It was an overcast day but rain hadn't been in the forecast. I thought we'd be fine on horseback.

Our greys obviously felt like running, so we made it to the gateway in less than fifteen minutes. When we stopped at the realistic looking barrier, Sean grinned at me as I said the Gaelic words and the illusion of trees and boulders disappeared.

"Can you feel the magic, Sean?"

He nodded. "I can almost hear the words, 'Welcome back!'"

I smiled. "It always feels that way to me too. Let's ride straight to the dining hall. I hope breakfast is still being served."

We dismounted, thanked the greys and sent them to the stable. Inside the dining hall, I was glad to see there were still a few people enjoying breakfast. We served ourselves ham and scrambled eggs, along with a pitcher of apple juice, and sat down. Two minutes later Arlynn dashed out of the kitchen with a basket of muffins and joined us.

"Good morning, Cara, Sean. I was surprised to see you two ride up. Are you spending the day with us?"

"We are. You just made those muffins, didn't you?"

She smiled. "Yes, and I'm going to help you eat them. I'm off duty now. I see you brought your bag of artwork. Will you be drawing today?"

"I will if these clouds clear up. I thought I'd at least visit Francis Sullivan and show him what I've been working on. It's always good to get an objective opinion from another artist."

I pulled out the picture I'd begun the day before and showed it to her. "I'm working on this as a gift for Sean's parents. You met them at the wedding, didn't you?"

She smiled. "Yes, it was a real pleasure to meet more of Conor's family. They'll love this drawing of Sean."

Grinning, Sean added, "My mother said she'd never met anyone as beautiful as you, and she told Conor that he should consider himself extremely lucky."

Naturally, Arlynn turned red. "Thank you, Sean, your mother is very kind. Please give her my regards. What are the two of you planning on doing here today?"

"Is Jason around? I thought he might like to join us."

She nodded. "My cousin Garrett is teaching Jason woodworking, and Jason is turning out to be quite an artist with wood. With Adam gone, Garrett really needs help. You'll probably find Jason in the wood shop."

The mention of Adam wiped the smile off my face. Arlynn noticed immediately but didn't say anything in front of Sean.

"Well, what are you doing today?" I asked her.

She blushed again. "Conor and I are getting together when he gets back from camp. Why don't you plan to meet us back here for lunch?"

"Sounds like a plan. I guess we'll go visit friends now, maybe pay our special friend a visit out in the old orchard."

She laughed. "Everyone looks forward to a visit from you, especially a certain seven-year-old."

"Yes, we'll definitely pay Ian a visit."

"See you two at lunch."

She left the dining hall and we took our time finishing our breakfast. When we realized we were the only ones left in the dining hall, we got up to leave. I stuck my head in the kitchen and thanked the ladies who were still cleaning up. They all smiled, asking if there was anything else we needed. We assured them breakfast had been great.

"They sure go out of their way for you, Cara. I'll bet they don't do that for everybody, do they?"

When I thought about it, I realized he was right. "I guess I get special treatment because of my father. Everyone here has always been so kind. The first time I spent a week here, their seamstresses actually made me green tunics and pants like they all wear. And everything fit perfectly."

He grinned. "I'll bet you looked like a perfect little Elf."

I smiled. "Probably. I want to get some apples for the greys. Let's stop by Kathleen's on our way to the orchard."

We found Kathleen sitting in front of her cottage writing in a journal. When she looked up and spotted us, she got up and greeted both of us with hugs.

"Just here for the day, Cara?"

"Sean loved his first visit here, so he's back for more of Elvenwood's special magic."

She chuckled. "Well, it's good to see you both. Cara, I haven't seen you since your parents' wedding. Where have you been keeping yourself?"

"At home with homework and artwork, but Sean has been coaxing me out so I've hardly been home this weekend."

She looked at Sean with a curious smile. "What's that bandage on your nose for, Sean? Don't tell me you broke it again."

"Actually, I got hit in the face with a baseball bat. My nose was badly broken and I had surgery to fix it. My doctor tells me it will look perfect, but I still have no idea what it's going to look like."

Kathleen looked fascinated. "Sean, do you think I could take a peek? I'll put your bandage right back on. Would you mind?"

He chuckled. "Be my guest. I'm curious myself. Maybe you can tell me how you think it looks."

"Come inside, lad. Cara, if Sean doesn't mind, you can come in too."

He chuckled. "I don't mind. After all, Cara has to look at it every day."

Kathleen sat Sean down on one of the cots and sat down on a stool next to him. Very slowly she peeled the bandages off his nose. I gasped when I saw it; then I grinned.

He looked alarmed at first, until I said, "Sean, you now have Matt Damon's nose! It's perfect. I didn't think it was possible, but you're even better looking now!"

Kathleen smiled. "It is a beautiful nose, Sean. Cara's right. It's perfect." She placed the bandages back over it. "I think your doctor will take these bandages off permanently the next time you see him. Your nose healed beautifully."

He looked excited. "This means I can play football again."

Kathleen cringed. "Football? From what the boys have told me, it's a particularly brutal sport. I know Gabriel loves it, but I certainly wouldn't want to risk that nose if I were you."

Sean grinned. "I'll be wearing a rigid plastic nose protector under my helmet. There's no way I want to break it again."

We left Kathleen's cottage as she wished Sean luck with his nose, and told me she'd be visiting my mother again soon. I could tell she noticed my lack of enthusiasm, but I couldn't really explain the reason for it in front of Sean.

As we walked to the orchard, Sean asked "What's this about Matt Damon's nose? What's so special about it?"

I had to smile. "He's got a great looking nose that turns up very slightly at the tip. Your nose used to be perfectly straight, even after you broke it the first time. But now, your surgeon gave you that slightly turned up tip and it really looks fantastic.

"Sean, I didn't think it was possible for you to look any better, but when that bandage comes off, girls will be throwing themselves at your feet." I giggled.

He turned red and rolled his eyes. "Come on, Cara." Then he grinned. "It won't matter. They all know I'm yours."

Now I blushed. "Knock it off, Sean." But the mood between us had suddenly become warmer. He took my hand as we walked into the orchard.

Grinning, he said, "I came prepared. He pulled off his sweatshirt, then pulled off a t-shirt he was wearing underneath, and I was staring at shoulders, arms and a chest so toned, he took my breath away. He had obviously been working out while his nose healed. He had a six-pack any guy would envy and his chest had a light dusting of blond hair.

He smiled when he noticed me staring and nonchalantly pulled his sweatshirt back on. "I brought the t-shirt for the apples."

When I recovered from the sight of that gorgeous chest, we started picking up apples that had fallen on the ground until the shirt wouldn't hold any more. He tied the sleeves together and we kept walking until we reached the old orchard where I'd met Rowenna almost two months ago.

"Oh, shoot."

"What's wrong?"

"I meant to stop and get Jason. I'm sure he would have wanted to come out here with us. He might have brought his flute and played for Rowenna. He plays beautifully.

"Since we don't have Jason's flute today, I'll just sing without it."

I began singing Rowenna's song and it wasn't long before we saw her leave her mountain home and fly toward us. I was feeling guilty. I'd been so depressed for the past few weeks, I hadn't sung for her very often, and we'd barely spoken. I'd have to apologize.

From behind me I heard a flute playing the dragon's song. Jason had known where I'd be. When he reached us, he began playing the melody again and I sang the words from the beginning. Rowenna flew to us and descended to the orchard in her usual spot, surrounding us with her magic. She closed her eyes until we finished her song.

That was beautiful. I've missed your flute, Jason. Cara, please tell your friend I am glad to see him.

I told Sean what she'd said, and he said, "It's always a thrill to see you, Rowenna."

We heard her rough chuckle.

Cara, why have you been unhappy? Your handsome young friend loves you, I know.

"Well, I've been having some problems at home that have been upsetting. Sean is doing his best to cheer me up. All my friends have been."

We will talk about these problems another time, Cara. For now, perhaps singing my song will bring you the same kind of comfort it brings me.

Jason nodded to me and began to play the melody as I began singing the words of the dragon's song again. Rowenna closed her golden eyes and we could hear that weird humming sound she would make that my father described as purring. When we finished her song, she opened her eyes.

Thank you, Cara. Thank you, Jason. Cara, I will speak to you soon.

Spreading her huge wings, she rose out of the orchard into the sky, her magic swirling around us. We watched as she flew to her purple mountain and disappeared from view.

Jason looked at me and I heard his voice in my head. *I know why you've been unhappy, cousin. I'm very sorry. We can talk when you're ready.*

I nodded as I stood up. The three of us left the orchard and walked back to the village. We had a t-shirt full of apples for the greys so the stable was our next stop.

Jason squeezed my shoulder. "Cara, I'm going back to the woodshop. Garrett is teaching me so much about designing and building furniture. I'm really enjoying it. We'll see each other soon, I hope. Good to see you too, Sean." Jason hugged me and left us.

I wondered how much he was aware of.

When Sean and I reached the stable, we saw people heading for the dining hall, so I knew it must be close to lunchtime. We each took half the apples and walked through the stable, giving the greys their treats. The sound of the greys' enjoyment as they whinnied and nuzzled our heads made us both laugh. Will accused me of spoiling them, but I knew he didn't mind.

Arlynn and Conor were waiting for us in the dining hall. Both seemed pleased to see Sean holding my hand, although I hoped they didn't think it meant anything serious.

I always loved spending time with Conor. He'd been a good friend from the day I first met him, before I knew he was an Elf. Before I knew Elves existed.

Lunch was great, as usual. Lots of fresh veggies just picked that morning and sliced turkey along with freshly baked bread. I was sure Arlynn had made the bread. I'd never tasted bread as good as hers.

Conor wanted to know how things were going in school, how Sean's nose was feeling, and what I was doing with my artwork. We filled him in over lunch and I knew he was glad to see me smiling again and doing normal things. Now that I was no longer crying myself to sleep every night, I thought I should probably make time to visit with Conor. His silvery eyes told me that he was reading between the lines. He knew I was doing my best, despite the sadness that was always with me now.

After we said goodbye to Conor and Arlynn, I wanted to stop and see Francis Sullivan before we left.

I knocked on the partially open door to his studio and heard him call out, "Come in, Cara." He always knew when it was me, and I had no idea how. Magic, probably.

"Hi, Francis. I brought a friend you haven't met, as well as some new drawings."

He was smiling as he wiped his hands on a paint-filled rag and walked over to us.

"This has to be a McKay," he said. "I'm guessing you're a relation of Conor's, young man."

Sean smiled and put his hand out. "I'm Sean McKay, Mr. Sullivan. It's an honor to meet you. My mother is a big fan of yours."

Francis took his hand. "Please thank your mother for me, Sean. It's always good to meet a friend of Cara's."

Turning to me, there was a twinkle in his eye as he asked, "What have you brought to show me?"

Opening my messenger bag, I took out all the drawings I'd done since the last time I'd seen Francis and spread them out on his table.

He looked at each one carefully, not saying anything until he'd examined all of them.

Smiling, he said, "Cara, your style is developing beautifully. There's a great deal of emotion in your artwork now that wasn't there before. Your love for the trees and everything that grows in the forest is obvious. How are you doing with watercolors?"

"I'm still getting used to them. It's a completely new skill. I love the vibrant colors I'm able to put on paper now. I didn't bring any with me because they're not good enough yet."

He nodded. "I'm anxious to see your watercolors. Don't wait too long. I have a few art shows coming up and I'd very much like to include some of your work along with my own."

I realized my mouth was hanging open. "You really think my work is good enough to be shown with yours?"

He smiled. "Yes, I do. If you continue to improve this way, you'll be having your own shows before long. Your pen and ink drawings should definitely be shown. Please put more time into your watercolors. As soon as you feel they're good enough—and I know you're your own harshest critic—bring them back to show me. I want my agent to see your work."

My head was spinning. "Thank you. I'm very grateful. I'll work harder with the watercolors."

"Good. Come back and see me soon."

He shook my hand and Sean's and returned to his easel.

As we walked out of the studio, Sean's eyes were as big as mine. "You couldn't have a better mentor, that's for sure. What a compliment that he wants to show your work with his!"

I shook my head, amazed. "I know. This is the biggest thing that's happened to me. I expected to be a 'starving artist' for years."

We talked about Francis Sullivan's upcoming art shows as we walked to my father's cottage. By the time we were in sight of the cottage, Ian came running over from his home.

"Cara, Cara, you're here! Hi, Sean, what happened to your nose?"

The little boy hugged me, clearly excited to see us. "How long are you staying?"

"Just this afternoon, I'm afraid. Sean and I both have school tomorrow."

He looked disappointed but then looked at Sean again. "Did you break your nose, Sean?"

Sean chuckled. "Well, my nose got too close to a baseball bat, but my doctor fixed it and it will look much better soon."

Ian looked confused.

"Ian, an angry boy hit Sean and Gabriel with the bat, but he won't be hurting anyone else again," I told him.

"Is Gabe okay?"

"He's fine, he just got a few bruises," Sean said.

"We were just going inside to have tea. Would you like to join us?" I asked him.

"I'd like that." His smile couldn't have been much bigger.

We walked into my father's cottage and I lit the fire under the kettle of water. While we waited for the water to boil, Ian talked about how much he enjoyed being at my parents' wedding.

"Your mother is really pretty. And I got to see your house and your garden, and I even met your friend Amy who made that beautiful cake. I had a really good time. My father is still talking about those little sandwiches. He ate a lot of them."

I couldn't help laughing. "I'm so glad you and your parents were there. I think everybody ate a lot of those little sandwiches."

Then, of course, he asked the one question I couldn't answer.

"I haven't seen Adam since the wedding. Where is he?"

Sean looked at me, obviously wondering the same thing.

My heart was pounding, but I had to remain calm, at least on the outside.

"Ian, you know I don't need bodyguards anymore, don't you?"

He nodded. "Yes, my father told me the bad man is in jail."

"Adam decided that since I didn't need a bodyguard any longer, it was time for him to move on. I think he's lived in a lot of places since he left home when he was young. My father hated to see him go, but it was Adam's decision to leave." I was doing my best to ignore the big lump in my throat.

Ian looked surprised. "Why would anyone want to leave Elvenwood? I wish Adam had stayed. I liked him."

What could I say? "Yes, I liked him too." I felt like I'd been kicked in the stomach.

We had our tea, and then I walked to the door to say goodbye to Ian. When I looked at the sky, it was no longer merely overcast. There were dark clouds moving quickly across the sky.

"Sean, we'd better leave now. There's a storm coming."

We jogged to the stable and led Pigeon and Cloud outside. As we mounted the greys, Will said, "You'd better hurry if you want to get back before this storm hits. Cloud will be fine, but Pigeon hasn't had much experience being ridden in bad weather. Be careful."

We asked the greys to run and we were at the gateway quickly. I said the magic words and the pathway into the forest appeared. We hadn't gone far before we heard the first ear-piercing clap of thunder.

Sean turned to me with a worried look. "Since Cloud has more bad weather experience, why don't you follow us?"

I nodded and let Sean pass me on the path. When we were about halfway to my father's camp, the clouds opened up and rain began pounding on us. We were both soaked in seconds. I could feel my muscles tense up. I was breathing too fast and was having a hard time concentrating on the path ahead of us. I felt the familiar panic rising in my chest and my stomach was tied in tight knots. The continual thunder didn't help.

Suddenly I saw Cloud leap over a downed branch on the trail, but Pigeon stopped short, almost unseating me. She turned around and began running back the way we'd come. She was obviously in a panic and wasn't listening to me. There were more claps of thunder. I pulled on her reins and she reared up, tossing me off her back.

I hit the sodden ground hard and saw Pigeon running away from me, back to Elvenwood. When I tried to stand, I slipped on the muddy ground and went down again. Memories of running away in the same kind of storm, slipping in the mud, and being chased by strange men overwhelmed me. I was in a panic. I'd even forgotten that Sean was with me. I believed I was in pain, alone in a raging storm.

In my mind, I was reliving that whole miserable experience. I didn't hear Sean calling my name. I was still on the ground, lost in memories, tears running down my face, trying not to vomit from the remembered pain in my head.

He must have tried to lift me off the ground, but I hit out at him, punching whatever I could reach.

I heard hoof beats but they didn't make any sense to me. It was just more noise added to the pounding of the rain and the frequent claps of thunder.

I no longer knew where I was.

CHAPTER 4

Suddenly, familiar arms lifted me off the ground and pulled me against a chest that smelled of the forest. I stopped struggling and was lifted up on the back of an enormous grey horse, who stood very still as the owner of the arms leaped up behind me and clasped one arm around my waist.

It felt familiar. It felt safe. A blanket was tucked around me. I began to hear familiar voices. My breathing slowed. My tense muscles began to relax. I heard Sean's voice, and gradually I remembered where I was.

I was on Smoke and it was my father's strong arm that was wrapped around me, holding me against his broad chest. We rode through his camp without stopping. We kept going until we reached my mother's back porch, and I knew I was safe.

My father lifted me off Smoke's back, and with one arm firmly around my waist, he led me into the house. I think Sean was right behind us. My mother immediately led me upstairs into my bathroom. She turned on my shower and then stripped my wet clothes off me. I was shivering so hard, I couldn't speak.

She led me into the shower and said, "Stay in the shower until you stop shivering and feel warm. I'll wait in your room." She left and closed the bathroom door.

I sat on the floor of the shower under the hot water, my arms wrapped around my knees, until I felt warm and my tight muscles relaxed.

My insane reaction to the storm was beginning to come back to me. For the first time, I had completely lost it. If my parents were looking for a reason to have me committed, I had just given them a good one.

My mother had left one of our new Brian-sized towels outside the shower and I wrapped myself up completely. The new towel covered me from neck to toes.

I didn't bother drying my hair. I just combed it and let it hang down my back. When that was done, I sat down on the toilet seat and wondered how soon it would be before they'd be fitting me for a straight jacket.

Unfortunately, I couldn't hide in my bathroom forever. Finally, I opened the door. My mother was sitting on the bed waiting for me.

"I got out your warmest sweats, Cara. Please put them on and then maybe you can tell me what happened."

"Is Sean still here?"

"Yes, he's been telling your father about the storm hitting on your way back from Elvenwood. From what I've overheard, it sounds as though the problem was more with your grey than with the storm itself."

I nodded. "It was a combination of both. The storm made me nervous, but I think I would have made it back here if Pigeon hadn't thrown me. The storm terrified her more than me. When I hit the wet ground, the rain was pounding on everything around me, I was in pain—I'm not sure why—and suddenly I was back in that tent where the kidnappers were keeping me. It was my nightmare, all over again."

"Cara, your wrist looks swollen. May I see it?"

I held out my right wrist and was surprised to see it was red and very swollen. "Oh, no, I hope it's not broken. I need that hand for drawing."

I moved it around a little and it was a relief to learn that I could move it, even though it was painful.

"It's probably sprained, Cara, but to be on the safe side, we'll get it x-rayed tomorrow. In the meantime, I'll wrap it up with an elastic bandage to keep the swelling down. How painful is it?"

"It throbs. That must be what I felt when I fell. I wasn't aware of what I was doing. Sean must have thought I'd lost my mind." I could hear my voice shaking slightly.

After she'd wrapped up my wrist, she said, "We should go downstairs if you're up to it. I'm sure your father and Sean both need to know you're all right."

"Okay. Poor Sean," I muttered.

We went downstairs and when I walked into the kitchen, Sean sprang out of his chair and rushed over to me. "Are you okay?"

"Sean, I'm so sorry. I totally lost it. I must have scared you to death."

"It's okay, Cara. I knew what was happening. You were having a flashback, right?"

I nodded. "I didn't completely lose it until I hit the ground. If Pigeon hadn't panicked, I think we would have made it home okay."

I turned to my father. "How did you get to me so fast?"

He frowned. "When the storm began before you got home, I felt your panic, then it felt like terror. By that time, I was out the door and on my way to camp. We weren't expecting that kind of storm today, and I knew you had to be out in it."

He shook his head. "I'm sorry Pigeon behaved so poorly. She hasn't had much experience being ridden in bad weather." He sighed. "I think I'm going to have to find you another grey."

"Dad, they're all too big. I can't mount or dismount without help. Pigeon is the perfect size."

He smiled sympathetically. "Don't worry, sweetheart. I'll find another horse for you."

Taking my hand, he asked, "Why is your wrist taped up? Did you fall on it?"

"Yeah, I think I used my right hand to break my fall. Mom thinks it's just sprained, but it's swollen."

"We'll get it x-rayed tomorrow just to be sure," Mom added.

I finally noticed that Sean was no longer in his soaked clothes either. He was wearing jeans and a shirt that was at least two sizes too big, obviously my father's.

"Is there any coffee?" I asked.

Mom nodded. "Sean, would you like some too?"

He smiled. "Yes, please. I should also call my dad and ask him to pick me up." Turning to me, "Cara, are you sure you're all right now?"

"Yeah, I'm fine. I think I just need a good night's sleep so I can function in school tomorrow." I forced a smile. "Good thing you take such great notes." I looked down at my wrist. "I don't think I'll be taking any for a while."

Dad asked, "Did you at least have a good time in Elvenwood today?"

Sean grinned. "It's such an awesome place. I love going there." Turning to me he winked. "And I think Cara has some news to share with you."

For a moment, I was at a loss. Then I remembered.

I told them about Francis Sullivan's offer. My parents were both impressed.

"Of course, now it may take a while before I have some watercolors to show him." I waved my taped wrist at them. "I won't be doing any painting for a while. Great timing, huh."

"Cara, I think your wrist will be fine in a few weeks. And I'm sure Mr. Sullivan won't withdraw his offer because you've sprained your wrist. Brian, please let Mr. Sullivan know about Cara's wrist injury."

"I will. I know Francis has several shows every year, in different cities. If you don't make the next one, there will be others."

After he'd finished his coffee, Sean phoned his dad. "He'll be over in about ten minutes. Mr. Blackthorne, thanks for the loan of the clothes. I'll get them back to you this week. Mrs. Blackthorne, thanks for the coffee and sandwich."

I looked at the clock and realized we'd missed dinner. "No leftovers, Mom?"

Looking slightly red in the face, my father said, "We had meatloaf, Cara. I'm afraid there are no leftovers."

I had to laugh. "You pigged out again on Mom's meatloaf, didn't you?"

Looking guilty, he nodded. "Sorry, sweetheart."

The doorbell rang and Mom got up to answer the door. She led Sean's dad into the kitchen. He looked surprised to see Sean dressed in clothes that were obviously not his own.

"What happened? Did you two get caught in that storm this afternoon?"

Sean nodded. "Yeah, we were both soaked when we got here. Cara's parents got us dried off and into dry clothes."

Mr. McKay chatted with my parents for a few minutes and then he and Sean got up to leave. At the door, Sean gave me a warm hug and whispered, "I'll call you later."

I whispered back, "I'm really sorry about my melt down."

He kissed my cheek. "Don't worry about it."

When I walked back into the kitchen, Mom asked, "Are you hungry, dear?"

I had to think about it. Food was the last thing on my mind. "Well, we had a big lunch in Elvenwood. I could probably eat a sandwich. I can make one myself, Mom. You don't have to make anything for me."

She gave me a questioning look. "Is this part of your new independence, Cara?"

I hesitated. There were a few things that needed to be said.

"I think it's time I began to be more independent, don't you?"

"You're still only sixteen, dear. I'm not really ready to cut you loose just yet," she said with a smile.

I knew it was unreasonable, but I could feel myself getting irritated.

"Mom, I may be sixteen on the outside, but think about all the crap I've been through during the past six months. I'm not a little girl anymore, not on the inside. I think you need to understand that."

She didn't say anything right away. I looked over at my father. He was watching us quietly. He knew this was between my mother and me.

"Cara, do you want to discuss everything that's on your mind now? I've tried to be patient until you were ready to talk. It sounds to me like you're ready."

"Okay. I guess now's as good a time as any. First of all, you need to stop being over-protective. I still have a problem with storms, but in every other way, I'm able to take care of myself. Second, I don't want you trying to make my decisions for me. For example, I don't want to spend four years in college to get a Liberal Arts degree. I want Art school, just art school. I want to study art, art history, and anything art-related, that's all. That's where I know my future lies. And I want to choose the school myself. I want to be close enough that I can come home on weekends. Blackthorne Forest is here. This is where I belong.

"Third, I can choose my own friends, and I can decide for myself who I care about, regardless of his age. You took that choice away from me once, and I may never feel the same way about anyone again." My throat was feeling tight.

I could feel tears welling up in my eyes and tried to force them down.

My mother's face had paled and was looking tight, but I wasn't through yet.

"Elves mate for life, Mom. I'm enough of an Elf that it's true for me. My heart belongs to Adam Wolfe, but because of you, he's gone. I may never see him again. Now you know exactly why I've been upset. I'm heartbroken."

My father still hadn't said anything. I went to the fridge, pulled out some cheese, made myself a sandwich, grabbed a soda, and went upstairs. There was dead silence in the kitchen until I closed my bedroom door.

Had I said too much? Had I gone too far? I really didn't know, but at least I got it all off my chest, and that felt better.

My cheese sandwich gave me indigestion anyway.

A little later my phone rang. It was probably Sean. I picked it up.

"Hey, beautiful. Have you recovered completely?"

"Hi, Sean. Well, I'm sure I'll find the bruises tomorrow, but yeah, physically I'm okay."

"You don't sound like yourself. What's wrong?"

"I just told my mother what I've been feeling and why I've been upset with her. I don't think it went down too well."

"Ooh. That couldn't have been easy. Do you want to talk about it?"

"Not really. My mother just has to realize I'm not a little girl anymore. The past six months have changed me a lot. I feel a lot older than sixteen, but I don't think she realizes that."

"Your mom can only see what's on the outside. And she still sees that innocent little girl she's had to protect since you were born. You may have changed, but she hasn't."

Sean's insight occasionally amazed me. "I wasn't looking at it that way. You're probably right, but I still think she has to start respecting my rights. I'm not as young or as defenseless as I look. I think you know that."

He chuckled. "Yeah, I do. You can definitely defend yourself. You're a lot stronger than you look. You're not the same girl I met last spring either."

I heard a deep sigh. "You wouldn't have survived if you were. Maybe you could give your mom time to get used to that fact. You probably made that point clear tonight, didn't you?"

"I think so. She'll have to deal with it now. I've been completely honest about how I feel. I know it sounds selfish, but at least I feel better now that I got it off my chest."

"That's good but there was one other thing I wanted to ask you about."

"Okay. Shoot."

"When you told Ian about Adam, your face changed completely. I think his leaving really hurt you."

I had to take a deep breath before I could answer. My heart was being squeezed again.

"Yeah, it did. He didn't tell me he planned on leaving. He didn't even say goodbye."

"Oh? I thought you and he were really close. I mean, outside of being your bodyguard."

"I thought so too. That's why it hurt."

I couldn't tell him any more. I didn't want to hurt Sean.

"I was just trying to understand why you were so depressed. So it was more than one thing, wasn't it?"

"Yep. And I'm still working through it. You've been really patient with me. I appreciate that."

"Whatever you need, I'm here. But I'd better get off the phone. I need to get some laundry done tonight."

"Okay. See you in the morning. And thanks for understanding today. I don't usually behave like a lunatic."

He chuckled. "I know that. Don't worry about it."

"'Night, Sean."

There were no taps on my door that night. I wasn't sure if that was a good thing or a bad thing. It took a while, but I finally fell asleep.

All I remember about my dreams that night was seeing Adam's cobalt blue eyes, watching me sadly.

Mom took me to Urgent Care after school the next day to get my wrist x-rayed. She was right; it was only sprained. It would be sore for a week or two and the doctor gave me anti-inflammatory pills for the pain, but I knew how lucky I was. He said a broken wrist would have been much more serious and would have handicapped me for months.

When we left the medical office, I thanked Mom for bringing me in and she asked if I'd like to go to The Grille for burgers.

"Your father will be staying in Elvenwood tonight. He won't be back until tomorrow night, so why don't we have a girls night out?"

"Okay. Burgers and a milkshake sound good." I was guessing she wanted to talk to me and figured The Grille would be a more neutral place than home.

The restaurant was fairly empty on a Monday afternoon so Mom chose a booth in the back where we'd have some privacy.

After we placed our orders, she said, "I've given a lot of thought to everything you said last night. I do understand why you've been so upset. I think heartbroken is the word you used. All the other points you made are minor by comparison. Of course, you should be making your own decisions about school, college, your friends, and so on. And you will be, your father and I both agree you have that right."

I was relieved to see the understanding in her eyes. She spoke more softly. "And I think I understand why Adam's departure has affected you so painfully.

"Honey, please think back to June when Adam first came here and your father assigned him to act as your bodyguard."

I nodded. "I remember. And I remember your reaction to him when you met him, Mom. You overreacted."

"Perhaps I did. But I didn't know him. Your father trusted Adam intuitively, but he didn't really know him either. You probably didn't notice the way Adam watched you that night. He barely took his eyes off you, and it was obvious to me that he was not indifferent to my beautiful, but very young, daughter. You can ask Kevin. I think he noticed it too."

I could see that she hoped I'd understand her point of view. "Some day you may have a daughter, and you may also overreact when you see a handsome man who can't take his eyes off her. You know, it's not so many years ago that I was sixteen, naïve and inexperienced. When I was seventeen, I met an incredibly handsome older man. I fell madly in love. There was no one worrying about the possibility that I'd get hurt."

She took a deep breath. "By the time I was nineteen, I had a child to take care of. I know your father was, and is, a good man, but he and I might have both been better off if there had been someone to rein us in until I was more mature. He knows that too. That's not to say that we've ever regretted having a daughter we both adore, but if I'd been a few years older, we probably wouldn't have lost sixteen years together. Does any of this make sense to you?"

"Of course it does. I agree your life would have been a lot easier if you hadn't fallen in love when you did. But how would you have felt if someone forced the man you loved to leave you, to go who knows where, because he wasn't trusted? I think we all know that Adam is a good man, not someone who would hurt me. If he'd felt he was welcome to stay, maybe he would have waited a few years for me to grow up." I was feeling emotional again, blinking away the tears.

"Cara, once I got to know him, I welcomed him into our home. He stayed with us while he recovered from that gunshot. By that time, I did trust him. I knew he wouldn't let anything, or anyone, hurt you. Perhaps I should have told him that I trusted him."

"I wish you had."

"Sweetheart, what happened that made him feel he had to leave? There must be something you haven't told us."

"Yes, I guess there is." I hesitated for a minute or so.

"Adam stayed out of the crowd at your wedding. He's like me; he doesn't really like crowds. I finally spotted him standing at the edge of the woods. I went over to him to ask if he'd gotten anything to eat. We talked for a little while. Then he kissed me. The one and only time he's done more than hold my hand. It wasn't a kiss on the cheek. It was a real kiss." I closed my eyes and took a deep breath, fighting tears again.

"Kissing Adam was like nothing I've ever felt before. I had always wondered what falling in love felt like. Now I know." I felt tears welling up again.

"One kiss and you fell in love? Are you sure, Cara?"

I nodded. "To be honest, I think I'd been falling in love with Adam for months. I just didn't know what it was that I was feeling. But when he kissed me, my whole world exploded. I've been kissed before, Mom, but it never affected me like that."

Our burgers arrived and we ate quietly.

After we'd finished, Mom said, "So that's why you reacted the way you did when your father told you Adam was gone." She looked into my eyes and I knew she understood.

"I felt like my heart had been torn out of my chest. I've never felt that kind of hurt before." I was blinking back tears again. "My life without Adam seems . . . empty."

"I see."

She paid the check and we left for home.

When we got home, Mom suggested we have some of Kathleen's herbal tea.

We sat down in the kitchen with our tea and Mom asked, "What about Sean? He's certainly been devoted since you two became friends again."

"What about Sean? Well, Sean and I are good friends. He's a good guy, but I'm not in love with him. I knew that even before I met Adam. To be honest, I hope Sean meets and falls for someone else when he's away at college. He thinks he's in love with me but I hope he'll outgrow it."

We drank our tea quietly for a while.

Finally she said, "I hope you know that you can talk to me about anything, and I do mean *any*thing. My memories of my teen years are vivid! I made some mistakes that I hope you won't make. But if you do, your father and I will still be here for you, loving you and supporting you."

"What if I never see Adam again? What if he never comes back?" My voice was shaking. "When he left, I think he took my heart with him." Tears were now running down my cheeks.

"That's a question I can't answer, honey. I'm sorry. Maybe you'll get over him."

Getting over him was simply not a possibility. Adam was, and always would be, my mate.

After Mom and I had talked it out, the atmosphere at home was no longer like an armed camp, but it wasn't the same as it used to be either. It was weeks before I figured it out.

That light, happy vibe that had existed whenever I was with both my parents was missing. Things were peaceful; no one was mad at anyone. Mom and Dad were fine, obviously in love and happy with each other.

I was the one who had changed.

Chapter 5

A few days later, Sean's bandages came off. As I had predicted, he was better looking than ever, and was the subject of even more longing glances from girls at school.

I did my best to focus on my studies, thanking Sean daily for his efficient note taking. He was actually a far better student than I'd ever been. When I asked him one day what his GPA was, I was surprised when he said, "Last time I checked, it was 3.9. Why?"

"Holy cow, Sean! Kevin's the only other guy I know with a GPA that high. You're definitely not going to need an athletic scholarship."

He just shrugged. I couldn't believe he didn't think his excellent grades were that big a deal. Gorgeous *and* modest, that was Sean McKay.

I wasn't really surprised to learn that Sean and Kevin were both taking SAT Prep classes twice a week. They both wanted to be well prepared for the SAT's in January. Kevin wanted to make sure he'd be accepted at the school of his choice. Sean was hoping for a scholarship offer from one of his chosen schools.

He was able to play in Thornewood's last two football games, both of which we won. His teammates made sure none of the players from the other team got anywhere near him and his "new" nose. Sean was an outstanding quarterback. Naturally. He seemed to do everything well.

Over dinner one night in November, Mom asked when I wanted to start visiting colleges.

"In less than a year, you'll be leaving home and starting college, dear. How many would you like to visit?"

She looked surprised when I said, "Just one."

"Mom, I got brochures for half a dozen schools from the Guidance Department. There's only one I'm interested in. Some of the colleges have decent Art Departments, but I've already decided I want to attend an Art School rather than college. There's one within driving distance, the Barrett Art Institute. They offer a three-year program that sounds perfect, and they're located in Syracuse. It's about a two-hour drive."

My parents looked at each other, obviously surprised that I'd already chosen a school. Mom asked, "How soon do you have to send in your application?"

"Well, Miss Burrows, my Art teacher, sent one of my drawings to Barrett's Admissions Director. They emailed her that they'd love to have me study there. I just have to let them know when I'm visiting. One of their people will give us a tour.

"I'd like to have both of you go with me to visit Barrett, check out the campus and the dorms. The brochure made it look like a lovely place, but pictures can be deceiving."

"Do you want to go before or after Thanksgiving?" Mom asked.

"Before the holiday, I think. Syracuse is north of us and they get even more snow than we do, so I'd like to go before winter sets in."

Mom chuckled. "The way you feel about winter, I'm surprised you didn't investigate Art schools in Florida."

"Nope. I want to be able to come home on weekends. Florida's too long a drive."

"Cara, I was joking."

"I know, Mom." I finally smiled, winking at my father who wore a big grin.

We made a date with the Barrett Institute for the following week. I think Mom and Dad were more excited about the trip to Syracuse than I was. Not that I wasn't looking forward to it, but I didn't get excited about much anymore.

It was a cool, sunny day when we left to visit the Institute, perfect driving conditions which I knew wouldn't always be the case during the winter months.

When I mentioned this to Mom, she said, "I'm sure even an Art Institute has opportunities for socializing on weekends. You should really plan on taking part, at least some of the time. You don't have to come home every weekend, you know."

I nodded, but I wasn't planning on pursuing a social life while I was in school. Art was my only interest.

Traffic moved well so we reached Syracuse in just under two hours. Barrett was located outside the busy downtown section of the city. The campus covered about six city blocks, full of trees and brick walkways that meandered between the buildings that housed the Institute. There was a little fall color remaining, but not much. Most of the trees were already bare. Winter was on its way.

I parked in a visitors lot behind the main building. We were expected so we went straight to the Admissions office on the main floor where Mrs. Gardner was waiting for us.

When we walked into the Admissions office, we got the usual reaction. Women simply stared at my tall, handsome father, their mouths slightly open. I heard Mom sigh.

I walked to the reception desk and introduced myself. Within seconds a door opened and Mrs. Gardner came out to greet us, smiling until she spotted my father. It was almost as if she was wondering if he was real, or simply a figment of her imagination.

Mom and I looked at each other and rolled our eyes.

Once Mrs. Gardner recovered, she welcomed us to Barrett and led us outside for the promised tour. We saw groups of students walking from one building to another, many dressed rather strangely I thought.

Mom commented, "I take it there is no dress code on campus, Mrs. Gardner."

Our guide, who looked younger than Mom, laughed. "They're artists, Mrs. Blackthorne. We're just happy they cover themselves." I stifled a giggle.

As we walked between buildings, she explained that there were two buildings where classes were held, three buildings holding the various art, sculpture, and photography studios, and two buildings for student dorms. She led us into one of the buildings so we could see some of the studios where students were working.

My father seemed interested in the sculpture studio where half a dozen students were working with various materials. "Fascinating," he muttered.

I was more interested in the art studios where students were working at large easels and the air was full of the smells of paint and turpentine. Francis Sullivan's studio smelled the same way. I breathed it in, suddenly feeling at home.

When I heard my mother gasp, I looked up at the front of the room. This was obviously the Life Drawing class, and there was a model posed on a table. He looked at me and smiled. He was a good-looking young man with long blonde hair and dark eyes. He was also nude. Very nude, completely exposed, with not even a fig leaf. He looked perfectly comfortable up there, a lot more comfortable than we were.

There was a young instructor walking around the room, commenting on his students' work. When he spotted us standing at the rear of the room with Mrs. Gardner, he walked over to us. "Is this your first tour of Barrett?" he asked.

When I nodded, he chuckled. "Mrs. Gardner seems to enjoy the shock value of my class." He shook his head at her, but she was smiling, obviously enjoying our reactions.

He looked at me. "Will you be studying at Barrett in a few years?"

I nodded. "Next year actually. I graduate in June."

"How old are you?" he asked me.

"Sixteen. I'll be seventeen when I graduate."

He smiled. "You're very young. What do you usually draw or paint?"

"Landscapes mostly."

"Any people in your landscapes?"

"Yes, in some of them."

Grinning, he said, "But I'm sure they're all clothed, aren't they?"

I could feel my face getting warm. "Yes, they're all clothed. I suppose I'll have to get used to the absence of clothes, won't I?"

"Well, yes, but not until your second year here. These students are all at least a few years older than you. I'd better get back to my students. What's your name?"

"Cara Connelly Blackthorne. And you?"

He bowed slightly. "Daniel Goldman, at your service, Cara." He also bowed to my parents and left us to check on the progress his students were making.

Mrs. Gardner led us through the building where we could peek into several more large rooms where art students were working. I was glad to see that none of the rooms seemed crowded. There was even music playing in most of them, creating whatever atmosphere that particular group desired.

We left that building and walked to another one where regular classes were held. "Here is where you'll learn all about Art History, going all the way back to the cave drawings in France. It's fascinating stuff, Cara. I think you'll enjoy it."

We walked all around the campus, and I was pleased that none of the buildings were very far from the others. The last building she took us to was one of the dorms.

Looking at Mom, she said, "The dorms are co-ed, and I don't know how you'll feel about that. Some of our first year students choose to live off campus."

We walked into what looked like a two-story barracks. There were rooms along a central hallway, and they seemed to be very close to each other. When she opened the door to one, I could see why. The room was tiny, and it held two beds, so dorm rooms were obviously shared.

Mom muttered, "It's the size of a closet. Two students are supposed to live here?"

Mrs. Gardner nodded. "I'm afraid so. They used to be single rooms for one student, but as we grew, students living on campus had to double up."

I had a feeling we were being watched, and I turned abruptly, facing the hallway where a young man clad only in a towel was standing in the doorway across the hall. He grinned at me and winked before closing the door.

Mom had seen him too. She and my dad exchanged glances. "I think we should investigate off-campus housing, Mrs. Gardner."

She smiled. "I thought you might. Most of the homes that surround the campus have been turned into apartments for students. Some are very nice, although a little pricey. You should drive around this part of Syracuse when you leave. You'll see the homes I mentioned that are rented to students. The best time to rent one is in June, when many students are leaving. I'll give you a few phone numbers before you leave.

"I haven't taken you there, but there's also a Café on campus where many of our students eat. It's not expensive and the food's actually quite good. It's run and staffed by students working part time, and many of them are extremely inventive cooks."

The expression on her face told me she was remembering a particularly memorable meal. I had to smile, wondering whether "inventive" was another word for inedible.

"We also have a small bookstore that carries a little of everything. Now, is there anything I haven't mentioned?"

Mom and Dad looked at me. "Just one thing. What's the deadline for applications?"

She asked, "Are you sure that Barrett is the right fit for you?"

I couldn't help smiling. "Absolutely sure, Mrs. Gardner. I can't wait to start."

"Good. You'll just need to schedule a meeting with our Dean of Students, but that can wait until January, and be sure to being your portfolio when you come."

We thanked her for the tour and walked back to the parking lot. Mom and Dad talked about everything we'd seen on our tour, but I was quiet, my mind full of how my life would change in the next year.

That night I dreamed of being at Barrett Art Institute instead of my missing bodyguard. It was a welcome change.

Thanksgiving was a week later. It had always been just three of us, Mom, Kevin, and myself. Kevin's mom always had listings to take, houses to show, and other real estate business to attend to, even on Thanksgiving. I wasn't sure the woman ever took a day off.

This year, however, we would have a larger crowd at our table. My father would be with us for the first time at Thanksgiving, along with Kevin and his dad. The Elves didn't celebrate Thanksgiving. They celebrated Harvest in October. However, we'd learned that our Elves were always ready for a big meal, especially if my mother was cooking it.

Sean and his parents were in Boston with his mom's family for the holiday. He wouldn't be back until Saturday. Amy's family always shared Thanksgiving with their next door neighbors. This was the first year our kitchen would be full on Thanksgiving.

Mom was getting the turkey ready to put in the oven and I was busy chopping celery and onions for stuffing when the phone rang.

I was surprised to hear Randi's voice, sounding a little depressed. "I just wanted to wish you and your family a Happy Thanksgiving, Cara. I'm really missing Thornewood today."

"Randi, it's always good to hear from you. What are you doing today? Is your aunt cooking?"

"Uh, no. My aunt doesn't really like to cook. She's going to one of her friends' houses for Thanksgiving. She told me I could go with her, but I don't really want to. Some of her friends are a little too friendly, if you know what I mean."

"So you're alone on Thanksgiving?" I was shocked.

"Well, yeah, but there are a lot of good old movies on TV today, so I can entertain myself. And the Chinese restaurant down the street is open; they deliver."

"Randi, do you have gas in your car?" Mom looked over at me and nodded. She knew I wanted to invite Randi to share Thanksgiving with us.

"Sure. My gas tank is full. I was considering driving to Thornewood today, but my dad's away so I really have nowhere to go."

"Yes you do. My mom just invited you to have dinner with us. How soon can you get here?"

"Cara, do you mean it? It wouldn't be an imposition? I mean, Thanksgiving is for families."

"Consider us family, at least for today. We really want you to join us."

She sounded a lot happier than she had when she called. "I can get there in under an hour. What can I bring?"

Mom said, "Tell Randi to bring an appetite. We don't need a thing."

"I think you heard her." I laughed. "Mom's making enough food for an army."

"Cara, please thank your mom for me. This is so nice of you. I'll see you in an hour."

I couldn't help smiling when I got off the phone. "Thanks, Mom. I think we just made one lonely teenager happy."

Mom said, "I feel sorry for that girl. Her family should be doing a lot more for her."

I agreed. I was reminded how lucky I'd always been. My mother had always been there for me, and my friends had always been welcome at our house. I had taken a lot of it for granted.

With Mom's recipe in front of me, I continued chopping and then mixed the stuffing ingredients together and got it ready to put in the oven later. I might not know how to cook, but I could measure and mix as well as anyone. I had just started peeling the sweet potatoes when the doorbell rang.

Kevin always came early, and always brought something we could nosh on before dinner. This year he'd brought caramel popcorn for us to munch on while the mouthwatering smell of roasting turkey filled the house.

While Kevin poured the popcorn into a large bowl, my father came in the back door with Kelly O'Rourke, Kevin's dad. They were both wearing big smiles.

My father was carrying a wooden crate. "This is my contribution to your Thanksgiving dinner, Alicia. A limited amount of wine is made in Elvenwood every year from our own grapes. I talked our winemaker into donating a few bottles for my first Thanksgiving with family and friends."

My father set the crate on the breakfast bar where I was working and unwrapped one bottle of wine. "It's a white wine, Alicia, similar to the Sauterne you're familiar with."

Mom took the bottle out of his hands with a smile. "It sounds perfect. I hope you don't mind; I like white wine chilled. I'll put it in the fridge until dinner's ready."

Glancing around at all the activity in the kitchen, Dad said, "I think Kelly and I will get out of your way and go out on the porch. Just call me if I can help with anything, Alicia." He poured two cups of coffee and they went outside.

Mom had Kevin getting down the special serving dishes she only used during the holidays, and I started grating orange peel for the sweet potatoes.

When Kevin sat down next to me, I gave him some veggies to chop for the salad I'd make later. "We'll have one more for dinner, Kev. Miranda Ross will be joining us."

I explained her situation in Greenville, and he asked, "So where's that boyfriend of hers? Sounds like everyone deserted her today."

Mom said, "We always have room for one more at our table."

When Randi arrived, I gave her a hug and introduced her to my parents. Mom welcomed her with a smile. "Glad you could join us, Randi." I took her out on the porch to meet my father and she reacted the way everyone did when they saw my dad for the first time. Once she regained the power of speech, she said hi to Kevin and his dad.

Dinner was as wonderful as always. Actually, it was more wonderful this year with my parents together and friends joining us. We all ate too much, of course, sitting at the table talking over coffee and tea long after we'd finished eating. I don't think anyone wanted to leave, which was fine with me.

As I looked around the table at the smiling faces, I was reminded that there was one face missing. I would have given anything if those cobalt blue eyes had been looking back at me. I did my best to push that thought out of my mind.

By the time we'd cleared the table and put away the leftovers, the sun had gone down. I thought it was too late for Randi to drive back to Greenville, so I invited her to spend the night. She called her aunt, but had to leave a message when there was no answer.

"I'm sure she won't mind, Cara. Most of the time, she's barely aware I'm there."

Mom smiled. "You two can enjoy a girl's night, staying up late and talking. I'm sure I'll hear you down here later for a midnight snack. Just have fun tonight."

And that's what we did. Randi did most of the talking. Her life had really been difficult for the past two years since her parents had separated. It sounded as though she hadn't had anyone she trusted enough to unload on. We talked until our eyes began to close around two a.m., and we never did get that midnight snack.

Randi stayed with us until Saturday when she had to leave because she had a date with—ugh—Joey. We'd actually talked about him, and Randi knew I thought she could do better. *A lot better.* But she hadn't been able to make any new friends at her new school, so Joey was better than nothing as far as she was concerned.

Before she left, I told her our door would always be open whenever she got homesick for Thornewood. Mom and Dad both let her know she'd always be welcome, and she left a lot happier than she'd been when she arrived.

The weather was warm for late November. I planned to spend some time in the woods in the afternoon, maybe even do some sketching. It had been over a month since I'd spent time at my favorite spot by the stream.

I wouldn't allow myself to think about the hours I'd spent there crying the day Adam left. But I thought maybe if I had a drawing pad in my hand, I might be able to think about my artwork instead of my broken heart.

When I reached the stream, I got comfortable on a bed of fallen leaves and focused on the autumn sunlight shining through the tall pines at the south side of the forest. I had drawn these trees so many times, it wasn't a new scene, but the play of the sunlight as it touched the ground captured my imagination. In one spot a hardy purple violet had clung to life as if to say, *I'm tough and I'll still be here in the spring.* That violet made me smile.

Like the violet, I'd survive and I'd still be here in the spring.

I drew the trees and the tiny violet, paying special attention to the way the light changed from one spot to another. Capturing the changes in the sunlight had me completely absorbed and it was quite a while before I realized someone was standing behind me.

When I looked up, Conor was smiling down at me. "I've missed seeing you drawing out here, Cara. We won't have many more days like this one, I'm afraid."

He sat down next to me in the leaves. "May I see what you're working on?"

I handed him my drawing pad and watched as he examined it closely, nodding in a satisfied way. "You've gone deeper into the small things that make the forest so alive."

He smiled at me as he handed the drawing back to me, his silvery eyes sparkling. "Well done, Cara."

"I'm glad you like it. I think I'm seeing more than I used to see." I shook my head. "I really can't explain it. It's like my eyes have been opened a little wider."

"You're right. I almost expected to see the tiny beetles that live just under the surface of the soil." He laughed. "So when are you going to start painting? Your father told me you're in the process of moving from pen and pencil to watercolors."

I groaned. "Yes, and it's a real challenge. But I can get more vivid colors with paint, which will bring a lot more life to my landscapes. Francis Sullivan

THE JOINING TREE

is patiently waiting for me to master watercolors. He's offered to show some of my work at his art shows next year."

"I'm not surprised. Your artwork is beautiful."

We both heard someone coming closer, kicking at the fallen leaves. We looked up as Sean came into view. He stopped, clearly surprised to find Conor sitting on the ground with me.

Smiling and looking slightly embarrassed, he said, "Cara, your mom told me where I could probably find you. I have Dad's car this afternoon so I took a chance and drove over. Hi, Conor. I haven't seen you since Cara's parents' wedding."

Conor stood up to greet Sean. The similarity in their looks was becoming more obvious the older Sean became. Two extremely handsome, tall blond men, keeping me company out here in the forest. It would make any girl green with envy. I couldn't help smiling.

Sean walked over and sat down in Conor's place. "What are you working on today?"

I showed him my drawing and he started to smile. "Cara, this is beautiful."

Conor added, "I've been telling her how much more she's able to see in the landscape now. This one will look great in color." He smiled at us. "Well, I'll be off now. Glad to see you both today. Enjoy yourselves!"

He waved to us, heading west toward my father's camp.

Sean said, "I'll be glad to keep you company if you want to stay and work on that drawing." He chuckled. "I'm so full of turkey, I thought I'd enjoy a burger later. Want to join me?"

Actually, a burger did sound good. "I think Mom was planning on hot turkey sandwiches for dinner, so a burger at The Grille would definitely hit the spot. Don't get me wrong, our Thanksgiving turkey was great, but I don't think I can face any more turkey until maybe next week."

He laughed. "Yeah. Even though we had turkey at my aunt's house, she sent Mom home with some leftovers, so turkey's on the menu at my house tonight too."

"Well, try to make yourself comfortable while I do a little more work on this picture. By the way, that picture I was drawing for your parents is finished. You can take it home with you."

"Oh, that's great. Thanks, Cara. I'll get it framed next week."

Sean sat watching me draw until the sun had sunk too low to add anything more to my drawing. I placed it in my folder and stood.

"Okay, I'm getting hungry. How about you?"

He laughed. "You didn't hear my stomach growling?" He stood up and took my hand as we walked through the woods back to my house.

I was reminded of last spring when our relationship was new. I sighed.

Sean looked over at me and said softly, "Memories, right?"

I nodded. "Yeah."

He squeezed my hand as we walked out of the woods.

After stopping at my house to leave a note for Mom, Sean drove us to The Grill. I could smell the burgers before we even walked through the door. Apparently, a lot of people were unwilling to face more turkey this weekend because the place was full, and we had to wait for a booth.

Sean wanted to hear more about the Barrett Art Institute while we waited. I had already given him the Readers Digest version of my visit there, but I hadn't mentioned the co-ed dorms or the Life Drawing class.

"Completely nude?" he asked, his eyebrows up around his hairline.

I laughed. "Yep. Not even a fig leaf. The instructor told me I wouldn't be in his Life Drawing class until my second year there, so I think I have time to become more accustomed to the adult world. The guy who was modeling wasn't at all embarrassed, but I thought my mom was going to have a stroke!"

"I'll bet. What about the co-ed dorms? Will you be living in one? Is there any possibility you might have a male roommate?"

"No, thankfully. I don't think I could handle that."

He smiled. "Well, if I were going to Barrett, I'd definitely volunteer for the roommate job."

I elbowed him gently, laughing.

"My parents are both in favor of renting an apartment for me off campus. Those dorm rooms were so tiny, I don't see how two people could possibly coexist in one. Mom described them as closets."

A booth had finally opened up so we took our seats and placed our order for burgers, fries, and chocolate milkshakes.

"You know, when I'm away at school, I'm really going to miss this place," I said.

"Yeah, me too. But you're planning on coming home most weekends, right?"

"Absolutely. At least I will when it's not snowing. Any idea where you'll be going to school?"

"No, I'm still waiting to hear about scholarships. I'd like to stay close to home too, but I may not have that choice."

When our food was brought to our booth, conversation stopped. I had to laugh as Sean bit into his first burger, rolling his eyes in obvious pleasure. I started remembering all the occasions when Adam and I had been here together, but quickly pushed those memories away.

Adam was gone. I knew I'd be better off enjoying the company of my devoted friend, smiling at me across the table.

On our way out, we stopped at several other booths to say hello to Sean's buddies, mostly other football players, a few of them with dates. I didn't know any of the girls, but I recognized a few of the faces that habitually gave me dirty looks. All of them would have loved being in my place.

I could understand why everyone thought I was Sean's girlfriend. We were together so much, both in and out of school.

The Grille was situated on the corner of Main and South Streets. South Street was a narrow side street that continued into Thornewood's industrial park on the south side of town. As we crossed the street to reach Sean's car, I looked down South Street and was surprised to see Randi's red BMW parked a block away. I stopped short.

Sean asked, "What's wrong?"

"That's Randi's car. She was staying at my house until this morning. She only left because she had a date with Joey this afternoon. I see Joey down there with those other kids, but I don't see Randi. What's he doing here without her?"

"Let's go ask him."

We walked to the end of the block where Joey was standing with a group of younger boys. I walked up to him and said, "Where's Randi?"

He looked over at me, obviously annoyed. "How the hell would I know?"

He couldn't be any ruder. "That's her car. What are you doing here in Thornewood with Randi's car without Randi? She was at my house until this morning. She drove back to Greenville because she said she had a date with you."

His eyes narrowed, he said, "I borrowed her car to take care of some business, not that it's any business of yours. Now get lost." He actually sneered at me.

Was he blind? How did he miss Sean standing behind me? Of course, Sean was no longer behind me. He'd walked up to Joey and got right in his face. "I think it is our business. Randi's a friend of ours." Joey was tall but very thin. Sean made him look like a toothpick.

Looking around at the group of kids standing there, Sean said, "Time for you guys to go home. There's nothing here for you."

They all knew Sean, of course. They scattered.

I don't think either one of us had seen the man slouched down inside Randi's car. He emerged from the back seat of the Beamer with a mean look on his face and a knife in his hand, pointed at Sean.

The moment he raised his arm, my knife buried itself in his hand. There was a look of total shock on his face as he dropped his own knife. He let out a pained scream, his eyes bugging out of his head.

Giving me a hate-filled look, he clutched his injured hand with his shirt. Joey pushed him back in the Beamer and pulled away from the curb in a hurry.

Sean put his arm around me. "Let's get out of here. That was some bad business that was about to happen." He shook his head. "We walked right into the middle of it."

I reached down and picked up the other man's knife and shoved it in my pocket.

When we got into Sean's car, I said, "What kind of business was going on? What did we walk into?"

Sean pulled out on Main Street and headed back to my house. "I've heard a rumor that a drug dealer from Greenville was hanging around, selling drugs to kids. I recognized some of those boys. One is only in Junior High, the rest are in Tenth Grade. I wonder if Randi has any idea she's been dating a drug dealer."

"Sean, I'm sure she had no idea. And she thought she had a date with that creep this afternoon." I snorted. "All he wanted was a date with her car."

He pulled up in front of my house, turned off the ignition, and turned to look at me. "I'm still wondering when you pulled your knife. It was so fast, I never even saw it in your hand. But thanks."

"When that older guy got out of the car, I saw something shiny in his hand so I slid a knife out of my boot, just in case. To be honest, I don't even remember throwing it. It happened the same way when one of Gaynes' men aimed a gun at Amy outside school. One of the cops called it an automatic response." I shrugged.

He slid over and wrapped both arms around me.

"Cara, I'm really glad you're my friend and not my enemy."

His arms felt so good around me, without thinking I snuggled up to him, resting my head against his chest, enjoying that sandalwood and clean laundry smell. His arms tightened as he kissed my forehead, then leaned down to kiss my lips.

I'd always liked kissing Sean, but it was a different pair of lips I wanted. I hated feeling I was taking advantage of Sean.

Sighing, I pulled away slightly and said, "We should talk to the Chief and let him know what happened . . . before I get arrested for assaulting that jerk."

"Yeah, we should. Should we mention Randi's car? The police might think she's involved with this drug business."

He was right. The last thing I wanted to do was get Randi in trouble.

CHAPTER 6

Sean came into the kitchen with me where my parents were just finishing their dinner. They both greeted us as Mom said, "This happens every year, Brian. It'll be a few days before Cara can look at turkey again." She laughed. "That's what you get for stuffing yourself on Thanksgiving, dear."

"I know, I know. I might be able to handle a turkey sandwich in a few days. But today Sean and I both craved burgers."

Mom smiled. "Well, sit down and help yourselves to coffee. What have you been up to today?"

Sean and I looked at each other. He whispered, "You'd better tell them."

Once I'd explained what had happened outside The Grille, Mom said, "Cara, please call the Chief. Now." She and Dad both looked worried. My father looked especially grim.

I nodded. Since I still had the Chief on speed dial, I dialed his one-digit number, muttering to myself, "Yeah, the fun never stops around here."

When Chief O'Donnell answered, I told him what we'd seen outside The Grille. He asked if we'd gotten their license plate. I didn't answer that question but told him I could describe the two men. "Actually, I can do better than that. I'll sketch them for you."

He chuckled. "I'd forgotten what a good artist you are. Would it be okay with your parents if I came over tonight to collect those sketches?"

I told Mom what he'd asked and she took the phone out of my hand. "Come on over, Tommy. The coffee's hot."

The Chief was at the front door ten minutes later.

Over coffee, he listened patiently to both of us as we described what we'd seen and heard on South Street. Sean was able to give him the names of the kids we'd seen with Joey. But Randi's car wasn't mentioned.

While Sean spoke, I quickly sketched both men and handed the sketches to the Chief.

He recognized the older man in my sketch and told us that the man was currently on a "Watch" list. He was known as "Nick Romanov," although that probably wasn't his real name. However, Joey wasn't someone the police were familiar with. At least, not yet.

I hadn't yet admitted throwing my knife at the older man. I think I was saving the best for last.

"Uh, Chief, the older man was angry that we'd chased those young kids away. He pulled a knife on Sean, and I, um, reacted."

The Chief closed his eyes for a second. "Tell me what you did, Cara."

52

"Well, when I saw him point a knife at Sean's chest, I threw my knife. It pierced his hand and he dropped his knife. They got into their car and drove away in a hurry." I handed the Chief the knife I'd picked up off the ground.

The Chief nodded, one eyebrow raised. "You're saying he left with your knife stuck in his hand, right?"

"Yes. Am I in trouble?"

Sean reached over to hold my hand. My mother's eyes were shut, but my father looked as though he fully approved of what I'd done.

Mom asked, "Will Cara be in legal trouble for this, Tommy?"

Chief O'Donnell shook his head. "I don't think so, Alicia. Cara has had a Concealed Carry Permit ever since Gaynes was on the loose so that she could carry her knives legally. I'll be speaking to the police chief in Greenville tonight. I'll fill him in." He sighed. "I'll also have to explain why Cara carries a knife and how expert she is with it. I don't think he'll want to charge Cara with assault. She was defending herself and Sean. Cara, did he say anything else to you?"

"No. He was screaming in pain when they left."

The Chief nodded. "He's a nasty piece of work, from what I've heard." He sighed and looked at my father.

Dad looked at me. "Cara, you may need a bodyguard again."

I shook my head. "No thanks, Dad."

The Chief said, "That's up to you. I'll alert my men so they'll keep an eye on her. And we'll all be watching for Nick Romanov. We don't want him or his people running around Thornewood. Greenville has had a serious drug problem for the past few years. We don't want one here."

He stood. "Thanks for calling me. I have to go call Chief Russo in Greenville."

Turning to me, he said, "Keep me on speed dial, Cara. Let me know right away if you see either of those men again." I was relieved he hadn't asked about the car again.

I said I would and my dad walked the Chief to the front door.

Mom still sat at the table looking at me and shaking her head.

"Well, Cara, here we go again," she said, looking resigned. I think she had finally accepted the fact that her daughter was a disaster magnet.

Sean was still holding my hand. "I'm afraid I have to get my dad's car home so I'd better take off."

We stood as my dad returned to the kitchen. My father said, "Sean, you'll have to be careful too. Keep your eyes open for Romanov and Joey, and let the Chief know right away if you see them again. I'm afraid you and Cara made a new enemy tonight."

I walked Sean to the door and he wrapped his arms around me. He whispered, "You have to tell Randi what happened."

"Yeah. Definitely. I just wish we could convince her father to let her move back to Thornewood. It's not safe for her in Greenville."

He nodded, then leaned down and kissed me. Having his arms wrapped around me felt so good, so comforting, I kissed him back. He deepened the kiss until I pulled away, once again reminding myself that I wasn't being fair to Sean. I knew I shouldn't encourage him this way. But he was such a sweet guy and really hard to resist. I sighed as he ran out to his car.

Mom and Dad were talking quietly when I walked back into the kitchen. I made a pot of tea and sat down with them.

As we sipped our tea, we were quiet. I was thinking about Randi and the details we hadn't shared with the Chief. Mom was probably thinking about her disaster-prone daughter.

I had withheld things from my mother before, which, in retrospect, had not been a good idea. I knew I had to call Randi later and tell her things that would make her unhappy, but right now I needed to tell Mom and Dad the whole truth.

"Mom, Dad, I should tell you some things we didn't tell the Chief. I think I need your advice." They looked up, frowning.

"Before you get mad at me, you have to know I thought I had good reason for omitting certain details. So just hear me out, okay?"

Mom sat back, took a deep breath and nodded in agreement reluctantly. For my mother, not asking questions immediately required real self-control. Mom had never been known for her patience. My father was frowning.

"The whole reason those men and the young kids with them attracted our attention was because I saw Randi's car parked where they were standing on South Street. But we didn't see Randi. Remember, she left for Greenville after lunch because she had a date with Joey, the guy she's been dating."

Mom nodded. "Yes, I remember her mentioning him. I also remember you didn't seem too enthusiastic about her date."

"No, I didn't like the guy from the first time I saw him. He was rude and acted like he owned Randi. So when we saw him in town with Randi's car, we were suspicious. Sean and I walked down the street to ask him where Randi was, and he was, as usual, rude, telling us to mind our own business. Sean recognized the young boys standing there with Joey and told them to go home. They all know Sean from school. He has a lot of influence with the younger kids. They took off, which was when the older guy got out of Randi's car with a knife in his hand. You know the rest."

"Well, why did you leave out the details about Randi's car? Joey obviously borrowed it without telling her where he was going or why." My father nodded, still frowning.

"We were afraid the police would think Randi was involved with drug dealers, simply because it was her car they were using. Chief O'Donnell knows us, but the police in Greenville don't, and they don't know anything about Randi, who lives with her party-girl aunt now. Maybe we were wrong, but we thought it best to leave her out of it, which meant leaving her car out of it too."

My parents looked at each other, Mom shaking her head.

"Cara, I think withholding these details from the Chief was a mistake."

Frowning, she added, "These things usually come back to bite you on the butt, you know."

I had to admit she was right.

"I have to call Randi now. This won't be fun."

I went up to my room and plopped on my bed where Ralph was already sleeping.

When Randi answered her phone, she sounded surprised to hear from me. She also sounded upset.

"What's wrong," I asked.

"Two things, Cara. When I got home from your house, Joey was waiting for me. He was mad that I'd been away for two days. He had no right to be, of course. He was having Thanksgiving with his family, but he hadn't invited me to join them.

"When he got through yelling at me, he said he needed my car. I wasn't in a good mood at that point, so I refused. Of course, then he decided to be nice and said if he could borrow my car for a few hours, he'd take me out for dinner. My aunt wasn't home, and I didn't really want to spend the evening at home alone. I gave him my car keys.

"It was late when he got back, too late for dinner. He didn't even apologize, just handed me the keys and took off.

"Cara, you can imagine the mood I was in. I decided to take myself out for dinner. I was starved by that time. But when I got in my car, I found blood on the front seat, on the door handle, even on the floor mat. No explanation from Joey, of course. He's never getting my car again, trust me."

At least she wouldn't be in tears when I told her where Joey had been. If anything, she'd just be angrier. Which, in my opinion, would be a good thing.

"Randi, Joey was in Thornewood with another guy tonight. When Sean and I left the Grille, we saw your car parked on the side street but we didn't see you, so we walked over there to investigate. Uh, I hope you're sitting down.

"Joey was with a known drug dealer, apparently trying to drum up business with a group of young kids that Sean knows. Sean sent them all home, and that's when the other guy, a man named Nick Romanov, pulled a knife on him. I, uh, intervened and threw my own knife at Romanov. My knife pierced his hand; that's where all the blood came from, I'm afraid."

There was dead silence on the phone for about ten seconds.

Her voice was faint. She sounded like she was in shock.

"I guess I shouldn't be surprised. I've seen Joey with Nick, who is definitely not a nice man. I had a feeling they were up to something, but I never imagined drugs."

Silence again.

"I don't know what to do. I guess blood in my car is the least of my worries."

I explained that we'd talked to Chief O'Donnell but that we hadn't mentioned her or her car. "Randi, I think that was a mistake."

She sounded panicky. "Cara, the police will think I'm part of their drug business if they know Joey was using my car."

"No, they won't. We know Chief O'Donnell. I don't believe he'll jump to that conclusion. After all, all you did was loan your car to your boyfriend."

She snorted. "Yeah, some boyfriend." Pausing, she said, "Uh-oh. Do you think Nick will come after me? I'm not worried about Joey; I outweigh him by twenty pounds. But Nick's a scary dude."

"Yeah, he is. I certainly don't want to run into him again.

"Randi, you need to be here in Thornewood where we can protect you. Your aunt's no protection; she's never home, is she?"

"Not really. She comes home to change her clothes; that's about it. I've got to call my dad. Maybe he'll reconsider and let me come home. Uh, by the way, why do you carry a knife?"

I groaned. "Long story, Randi. I'll explain next time you come over. And by the way, you can come here any time you want, do you understand?"

"I do, Cara. Thanks. Your family has been so nice to me. I hope you know how lucky you are."

"Yeah, I do. Please call your dad now and let him know he can talk to us if he needs more information. My mom knows everything."

"Okay. I'll call you back after I talk to my dad. I just hope he's reachable and not on a plane right now." I heard her sigh.

We hung up and I went back downstairs. My father was still sitting at the table with Mom. They must have been discussing my lack of complete honesty with the Chief.

He didn't look pleased.

I knew I was in for a lecture.

"Cara, I'm disappointed in you. Chief O'Donnell has always been a good friend to us. I don't think you had any reason to tell him less than the whole truth."

I sighed. "I know, Dad. I realize that now. Sean and I were both afraid the police would think that Randi was involved in her boyfriend's drug business. All she did was loan him her car, but the police in Greenville don't know her, or us. We thought we should try to protect her."

"The police in Greenville do know Chief O'Donnell, Cara. I'm sure they'll take his word for what happened." My father looked at me, frowning. "I want you to go down to the police station and talk to the Chief. And this time, don't leave anything out."

"Okay. Do you want to go with me?" The thought of walking into the police station alone was unnerving.

He nodded, still looking stern. "Of course. I'll go in with you, mainly to make sure you tell him *everything*." I sighed.

Mom said, "Cara, you'd better call the station first to make sure Tommy is still there. It's getting late; he may have gone home already."

When I called, the policeman who answered the phone said the Chief had gone out to get some dinner but that he'd be back in an hour. I asked him to let the Chief know that I'd be coming in to speak to him.

"Dad, we'll have to wait until the Chief gets back from dinner."

"That's fine. We can wait." He was still looking very serious.

My phone rang. Randi again.

"Cara, I just spoke to my dad. He's in Chicago but he's flying home tonight. I have a key to his condo, so I'll be going there as soon as I finish packing. He won't make me live here any longer."

"That's good news, Randi. Uh, I hope you won't be upset, but my parents think we should tell Chief O'Donnell about seeing your car earlier tonight. Sean and I left that part out because we thought we should try to protect you. My dad thinks we made a mistake. The Chief has always been a good friend to us. I don't think you have anything to worry about. You didn't do anything wrong."

She didn't say anything right away.

Finally, she said, "I'm not sure the Chief will believe me. He knows me, Cara. I had some problems last year and had to go in and talk to him twice. He probably sees me as a major troublemaker."

"Oh." That wasn't good. "Well, you straightened yourself out. I'm sure he can verify that with Principal Weiss at school. You haven't been in any trouble in Greenville, have you?"

"No, of course not. Before school ended in June, I had a few sessions with a psychologist which was really helpful. That was Principal Weiss's suggestion. I just hope Chief O'Donnell believes that I've turned my life around. I did some really stupid things at school last year."

I chuckled. "Yeah, I remember." Randi had been so jealous, she'd been threatening every girl Sean spoke to, especially me.

"Randi, if you're willing, you could go to see the Chief with us. My dad's going to the station with me in about an hour. You'd have the perfect opportunity to tell the Chief about Joey and how he's been using your car, without telling you where he was going with it."

She hesitated. "Yeah, maybe. I'm leaving for Thornewood now. My aunt's not home, of course. I'm leaving her a note. I don't think she'll care that I've moved out. I'll think about what you suggested on my way over. If I decide to go with you, I'll come straight to your house, okay?"

"Okay. It's up to you. We'll talk later. Be careful."

We were getting ready to leave for the station an hour later when there was a knock at the door. I opened it to find Randi in tears and sporting a black eye.

"Oh, my God," I took her hand and pulled her inside.

Mom heard me and rushed to the door behind me. My father was right behind her.

"I'm so sorry, Randi," Mom said. "Do I have to guess who did this to you?"

Still holding her hand, I led her into the kitchen. "Can you tell us what happened?" I asked.

Mom put a box of Kleenex in front of Randi. After she'd wiped her tears and blown her nose, she said, "I had just put the last of my bags in my trunk when Joey came running into the parking lot. He tried to tell me I couldn't leave, but I told him I was moving back to Thornewood to live with my dad. He started yelling at me, like how could I leave him, didn't I care about him, stuff like that. Finally I said I didn't want any part of people dealing drugs. That's when he hit me. When I saw Nick walking toward us, I jumped in my car and sped out of there. I'll never go back there again."

She started crying again, soft sobs, the kind of crying you do when you know you've been an idiot and something has ended.

When I looked up at my father, I was shocked to see the anger on his face.

"Cara, please dial the Chief for me and then hand me the phone."

When the Chief picked up the phone, my father said, "Tom, the matter Cara wanted to talk to you about just became more complicated. I'm sorry to impose on you again, but would you please come over here before you go home. There's a young friend of Cara's here who's been beaten. She needs to speak to you too."

The Chief was at our front door in less than ten minutes. When he walked into the kitchen, he stopped short, clearly surprised to see Miranda Ross sitting at our table with a black eye.

He said, "Hello, Miranda. I heard from John Weiss that you were doing better before school ended in June. Obviously, that report was misleading."

Mom said, "Don't jump to conclusions, Tommy. Miranda's done nothing wrong. She's the victim here."

My father was sitting next to Randi, looking concerned. He patted Miranda on the back and said softly, "Don't worry, Randi. Chief O'Donnell is a fair man and a friend."

It was time for me to come clean.

"Chief, when we spoke earlier, I left out a few things. I'm sorry. I just didn't want Randi to get hurt when she'd done nothing wrong."

I explained that it was seeing Randi's car on South Street that prompted us to approach Joey, Miranda's boyfriend, to ask why her car was there.

Randi added, "Joey borrowed my car a couple of times, saying he had business to take care of and he'd bring it right back. I didn't feel I could refuse, since we were dating. Honestly, Chief, I had no idea what kind of business he was doing. But when he brought my car back tonight, there was blood in the front seat. I haven't cleaned it up yet.

"Cara told me what happened downtown. That explained where the blood came from. Joey didn't say anything when he brought my car back, just gave my car keys back and ran off."

Watching Randi closely, the Chief nodded and said, "And the black eye? When did that happen?"

"After I talked to Cara, I called my dad. He's on his way home now. He knew I hated living in Greenville with my aunt, and after I told him what I suspected Joey was doing with my car, he said I could move back to Thornewood and live with him."

The Chief said, "You haven't told me how you got the black eye, Miranda."

"Yeah, I was getting to that, Chief." She explained what happened when she was packing up her car to leave Greenville.

"I left when I saw Nick approaching. There was no way I wanted to deal with him."

"Randi, is that your car outside? I'll need to have samples of that blood collected so we can verify Cara's story. Did she tell you she threw a knife at Nick?"

"Yes, she did. Because Nick pulled a knife on Sean, which I totally believe. He's a real creep, dangerous too."

"You've never gone with them when they've been out doing business?"

"Of course not. I don't like Nick. In fact, I wasn't aware he was with Joey when he borrowed my car. If I had, I don't think I would have let him take it."

"Miranda, do you want to file charges against Joey? You have a right to, you know."

"No, Chief. Then I might have to go to court. They'd bring up my past problems. I'd really like to forget I ever knew Joey, if that's possible."

"Well, that may not be possible. But I'll call Chief Russo in Greenville and let him know what happened. Nick Romanov is known to the Greenville Police. They suspect him of selling drugs, but apparently haven't caught him in the act yet. I'll need more information on Joey."

Randi gave him Joey's last name, address and phone number, and the Chief left for the station. My father walked out with him.

Miranda asked, "Do you think the Chief believed me? I hope I did the right thing talking to him. Cara, his past experience with me hasn't been the best."

Mom got up to take an ice pack out of the freezer. Handing it to Randi, she said, "Put this on your eye. Don't worry, dear. Tommy O'Donnell is an old friend of mine and has always been fair. More than fair, to be honest. He's a good man. And you haven't done anything wrong, other than pick the wrong kind of boyfriend."

I knew that being forced to move to a new school for her senior year, where she knew no one, was responsible for everything that had happened to Randi. If her father cared about his daughter, he'd understand that too.

When my dad came back in the house, he suggested that Randi call her father again and let him know she'd be staying with us that night. "The Chief doesn't want you alone tonight since your father probably won't be arriving until very late. You can join him in the morning."

I thought that was a good idea. Randi really needed company right now. It was too bad I didn't have any of Kathleen's herbs for Randi's black eye, which was already very colorful.

After she phoned her dad, we went upstairs to my bedroom where Randi put her head down with the ice pack pressed to her face.

"I know it's still early, Cara, but I'm really tired. The past couple of hours have left me feeling like a rag doll that lost its stuffing." She yawned. "There's so much I wanted to talk to you about, but I'm just too tired. Sorry."

"Don't worry about it. We can always talk tomorrow."

Within minutes, she was asleep.

The next morning, Randi's dad phoned to thank us for taking care of his daughter, and to let her know he was home and wanted to take her out for breakfast.

Despite the black eye, Randi seemed a lot happier. Her dad was home and she knew she'd be living in Thornewood again. Hopefully, Joey was history.

"Cara, we still have a lot to talk about. I hope we can get together again soon. You and your folks have been great."

Mom was on her way to the bookstore, but she stopped to give Randi a hug and assure her she was always welcome at our house. When my father left for his camp, he'd told Randi not to be a stranger and surprised her with a kiss on the cheek.

When they were both gone, Randi turned to me somewhat starry-eyed and said, "Cara, I love your parents. Your dad is . . . amazing."

I laughed. "Yeah, I know. He has that effect on everyone."

The Chief had already stopped by to take samples of the blood spilled in Randi's car and had released the BMW to her, along with a list of people he called "cleaners" who could get the blood stains out of her upholstery.

I walked her out to her car, hugged her, and watched her drive away. With a little luck, I'd see her in school on Monday.

It was a warm but cloudy day so drawing in the forest wasn't an option. Instead I gathered up all my drawings and sketches, placed them in a large folder and took them out on the back porch. I'd been meaning to go through my work from the past few months to see which pictures would be good candidates for watercolors. Francis Sullivan was giving me an incredible opportunity, and I didn't want to waste any more time now that my sprained wrist had healed.

My favorites were the Elf drawings I'd done over the summer. I'd drawn all the beautiful woodland scenes I loved with just a hint of an Elf hidden somewhere in each picture. The views of the majestic forest landscapes were dramatic, while the hidden Elves were like a secret only a few would notice.

I smiled as I went through them, remembering the friendly young Elves who had volunteered to pose for me, none of whom had any idea how incredibly beautiful they were.

I was so intent on the watercolors I wanted to paint for Francis Sullivan's art shows, I'd forgotten about the sketches I'd done of Adam. When I came across the first one, my heart almost stopped. There he was, tall and slender, his shaggy black hair the perfect frame for his perfect face, the sculpted cheekbones, full lips, and those slightly slanted cobalt blue eyes that seemed, even on paper, to be looking into my soul.

When I was able to breathe again, I felt hot tears in my eyes and a dull ache where my heart was supposed to be.

My eyes felt glued to Adam's picture. I tried to look away but something wouldn't let me. For a few seconds I think I was in another world, a world where Adam Wolfe smiled at me, held my hand, and called me "love." A world I'd taken for granted a few months ago. A world that was closed to me now.

I knew I would have to hide those sketches somewhere I wouldn't be coming across them all the time. Seeing them was like rubbing salt in a wound.

I got up, went upstairs and opened the door of my closet. I took down the box my last pair of boots had come in, placed all my drawings of Adam in it, and shoved the box in the back of the closet. I shut the door and took a deep breath, unaware there were tears running down my face until I glanced in the mirror. I told myself to get a grip.

Wiping my tears, I went downstairs to gain some distance from those pictures I'd put away. If only I could put my feelings away too. Maybe ice cream would help. Then, of course, I remembered making ice cream sundaes for Adam and the other bodyguards.

Nope. No ice cream. Desperate for a distraction, I picked up my phone and called Amy and got her voice mail. I called Kevin. More voice mail. I had a hunch they were out together, which depressed me even more.

What could I do? I knew I had to do something. I was tempted to call Sean, but that wouldn't be fair to him. I'd just be using him again, like a pill to make the pain go away for a little while.

My long-time refuge lay at the end of our back yard, beautiful even on a cloudy day. I pulled on my old boots, threw on a sweatshirt, and left the house.

The air had been fairly calm earlier, but as I walked through my backyard, gusts of wind blew my hair into my face, actually pulling strands out of my ponytail and whipping them into my eyes. It almost felt like anger. Or desperation. Perfectly in tune with my emotions.

I started running as I entered the woods and didn't stop until I reached the stream, where I stared at that flat rock, the one constant in my long-time refuge. No matter the season, it never changed.

I stood there for uncounted minutes, so many memories flashing through my mind as the winds continued to batter me. Suddenly I heard my father's voice in my head.

Cara, sweetheart, I know what you're feeling. It's your emotions that are driving these winds. Take some deep breaths and try to calm down. Come to my camp. There's someone here I want you to meet.

I was causing these winds? I groaned. One more Blackthorne gift had just made itself known, as if I needed another Elven gift. I shook my head, once again telling myself to get a grip.

Conor had placed a wide wooden plank across the stream for times when I was unable to make the leap without getting my feet wet. I walked across it and headed for my father's camp, only a half mile farther. As I walked, I began to feel calmer. And so did the wind.

I trudged into the camp and spotted my father and Smoke right away. There was another grey behind Smoke, but I couldn't get a good look at him. I looked around but didn't see another rider.

A few Elves I only knew by sight looked out of their tents and smiled at me. I nodded at them. At the moment, I had no smiles for anyone.

As soon as my father saw me, he left the horses and strode to me, wrapping his arms around me.

He spoke softly. "What happened, Cara? What upset you? You know I always feel what you're feeling. But I think this is the first time your emotions were strong enough to affect the wind."

He led me to the campfire where there were a group of camp chairs placed in a semi-circle. This was where he'd been meeting with his men. I saw one of the younger Elves lead the two greys away. I recognized Evan, the teen who had been taking care of Pigeon for me. Of course, Pigeon was back in Elvenwood now, no longer mine since she'd panicked during the last storm.

We sat down and he poured me a large mug of the forest's sweet water. I took a deep drink, still trying to quiet my emotions. It was still a bit windy.

My father watched me, sympathy clear in his green eyes. "Feeling a little better now, sweetheart?"

I nodded. "A little, Dad."

"What was it that set you off? You seemed fine this morning when I left you having coffee with Randi."

I took a deep breath. "I was going through all the drawings I did during the past several months, trying to choose a few to recreate in watercolors for Francis. I guess I'd forgotten about all the sketches I did of Adam last summer. When I came across them, I felt like my heart was being torn out of my chest."

"I thought you were feeling better, Cara." He began running his hands through his hair the way he always did when he was frustrated. "I wish there was something I could do to take that pain away."

I shrugged. There was nothing he could do.

He stood suddenly. "I told you there was someone here I wanted you to meet. Come with me." He smiled down at me. "This may cheer you up."

He took my hand and led me to an enclosure that had been built for the greys stabled at his camp. The heads of half a dozen beautiful horses went up as we approached. I'd always thought the greys must be part human because of their intelligence, as well as the affection they could show to those they cared about. And they were discriminating animals. They didn't take to everyone and usually made their feelings clear.

Smoke trotted up to us, snorting and nodding his big head. He greeted me, bending down to place his nose on my shoulder, then raising his head to blow my hair off my face. It was the most affectionate greeting I'd ever received from my father's huge horse.

I murmured into his ear, "I'm glad to see you too, Smoke." He whinnied, nodding at me again.

Smiling, my father said, "Smoke knew you needed another grey to ride, so I left the selection up to him."

Surprised, I said, "Smoke picked another grey for me? Really?"

My father nodded, and another large grey trotted up to me. He stood very close to me and stared into my eyes. Unlike the other greys, this horse had light gray eyes, filled with intelligence. He snorted softly, blowing on my hair.

"Hello," I said. "You're a handsome fellow. Polite too." He was dark gray, not quite black, with a much lighter gray mane and tail.

I turned to my father. "What's his name, Dad? He's a beauty."

He chuckled. "I'm almost afraid to tell you, dear. But I think you'll admit it fits him. Cara, I'd like to introduce you to Storm. He's yours."

"*Storm*? You must be kidding!" My shock quickly turned to amusement as the dark gray horse began to snicker. It was obvious he was laughing at me.

I had to laugh too. This beautiful horse was in on the joke. I said, "Okay, you're a very smart horse, and you even have a sense of humor, which is a real plus. But how am I supposed to get on and off your back? You're twice Pigeon's size."

He snickered again, then folded his legs beneath him and rested on the ground next to me. He turned his head, looking me in the eye, and whinnied, sounding pleased with himself.

I was amazed. I couldn't reach his height, so he came down to mine. I think my mouth must have been hanging open, and I could hear soft laughter all around me. Every Elf in camp had come out to see if Storm and I would suit each other.

When I noticed that my padded saddle was already on his back, I climbed on. Storm slowly but surely stood up, hardly jostling me at all. I was thrilled. This horse was a dream come true, and I told him so. I heard his laughter again as I stroked his neck.

My father was already mounted on Smoke and I could see how pleased he was. He grinned and said, "Would you like to ride to Elvenwood and have lunch with me?"

I was glad he would be with me for my first ride on Storm. I prayed I'd never fall off because it was a long way down.

I smiled at him. "Absolutely. Storm is exactly what I needed. Thanks, Dad."

Smoke whinnied in a satisfied way and we left for Elvenwood.

Storm's gait was so smooth, I wasn't being bounced around at all, and we kept a fast pace all the way to the gateway. It was exhilarating! My new grey was the perfect antidote for a serious case of the blues.

THE JOINING TREE

In the weeks that followed, Storm and I spent a lot of time together. There were days when I simply wanted to be alone, with only my grey for company. We'd ride through the forest, on paths I'd never seen before, and sometimes not on any path. Storm always seemed to know where he was going and I trusted him. Apparently, my father trusted him too and never seemed to worry about my solitary rides.

As we rode through the forest, I talked to Storm and I knew he understood every word. Sometimes he'd whinny in response, sometimes he'd snicker, sometimes he'd just nod his big head up and down to let me know he agreed with something I'd said.

I'd never known I could have such a close bond with an animal. But the Elven greys were a great deal more than just animals.

Like so many things in Blackthorne Forest, the greys were pure magic.

In addition to riding Storm as often as I could, I continued to speak to Rowenna most nights. She knew how depressed I'd been, and she understood the reason. For some reason, she insisted that Adam would return some day. But I remembered that she'd also been waiting for her mate to return for many years.

Rowenna was an optimist. I wasn't.

CHAPTER 7

I had finished the artwork for the class yearbook and turned it in to Miss Burrows. I was also doing my best to concentrate on my classes, spending more time reading and studying than I ever had before. Keeping my mind occupied and staying busy was my way of fighting the depression that always threatened.

Finding those pictures I'd drawn of Adam had been like a knife to my heart. Providing I still had a heart. The jury was still out on that subject.

It was getting close to Christmas, a time of year I'd always loved. But this year it seemed like just another holiday to get through. My friends were full of Christmas spirit, shopping for gifts and planning family get-togethers.

Amy was trying to get a group together to go caroling. She knew better than to try to recruit me this year, instead muttering "humbug" whenever I was near.

Kevin seemed happier than usual, which I attributed to Amy, although neither one would admit that their relationship was anything more than good friends "hanging out." They weren't fooling me.

Mom had already started decorating our house for the holidays, a few new decorations appearing every few days and the air in the house scented with wintergreen and pine from the candles she'd placed in every room.

My father was enjoying all the decorations, which were a completely new tradition to him. Despite all the handcrafted items the Elves made for the outside world, I was surprised to learn that they didn't actually celebrate Christmas. It was a human holiday, not an Elven tradition. But that didn't spoil his enjoyment of our human traditions. He admired every decoration Mom set out, which pleased her enormously.

We were enjoying an unusually mild winter, which pleased me enormously.

Until it began to snow, I could continue riding Storm. But once winter set in with snowstorms and below freezing temperatures, Storm would be returned to Elvenwood's surprisingly warmer temperatures and enclosed stable with the other greys. There would be very few Elves stationed at my father's camp until spring, although Conor and Gavin would still be working in the forest to care for trees and wildlife as much as weather permitted. Their method of transport? Skis and snowshoes.

THE JOINING TREE

Sean and I still sat together in four classes, five days a week, but he no longer called me every night. He seemed to have the blues too. Maybe my depression was contagious.

His face brightened considerably when basketball season began. Sean and Dion were Thornewood's star basketball players, and Sean made me promise to come to their games.

"Basketball is a lot easier to understand than football, Cara, trust me. Come with Amy and Kevin. I think you'll enjoy it," he said with a smile. I hadn't attended any basketball games in previous years, but I figured I owed him that much.

Laughing, Amy said I'd be sure to enjoy the sight of athletic boys in shorts running around the gym, even if I didn't enjoy the actual game. She was pleased to see me smile at that comment. Despite my best efforts, I had never become a football fan, but maybe there was some hope for basketball.

Waves of disappointment swept over the Thornewood High student body when it was announced that there would be no Christmas dance this year. Since basketball season was about to start, the floor in the gymnasium needed to be refinished, and the work could only be scheduled for the week before Christmas, which was when the dance was normally held.

In previous years, the refinishing had always been done during Christmas vacation, the week between Christmas and New Year's. Apparently, that wasn't possible this year.

Our senior class president, Dion Washington, suggested renting the Pizza Palace for one night and having a party there. He knew that the restaurant had a banquet room behind the dining room, so there would be room for everyone who wanted to attend. And the old jukebox would provide music we could dance to. Everyone loved the idea, and the owner of the restaurant was happy to accommodate us.

At our usual table in the lunchroom, we all agreed that Dion's idea was brilliant. No one wanted to leave for Christmas vacation without a fun celebration beforehand. And we didn't think anyone would mind the cost of the pizzas.

Sean looked at me hopefully. "How about it, Cara? Will you go to the party with me?"

Amy and Kevin glanced at each other, both obviously waiting to see if I'd been able to drum up any holiday spirit at all.

My friends had put up with my moodiness for the past several months. I couldn't disappoint them now. Looking at Sean, I smiled and said, "It'll be fun. Dancing and pizza! Perfect combination."

A big smile on his face, Sean looked at Amy and Kevin. "If you two are going together, we can make it a double date. Okay with you?" he asked them.

They looked at each other and nodded, smiling.

That finally gave me the opening I'd been waiting for. "Amy, Kevin, be honest now. You two *are* dating, right?"

Kevin turned a deep shade of red and wouldn't look me in the eye. Amy, on the other hand, laughed and said, "Kev, I think we've been outed."

Looking at me, she said, "Sweetie, the three of us have been best friends forever. We were both afraid you'd feel that we'd left you behind. You haven't been yourself lately. That's the only reason we've kept it quiet."

Kevin finally looked at me. "Short stuff, we both love you. We're still here for you, just like we've always been. You know that, right?"

I looked at my two best friends since kindergarten. "Of course it's okay. I'm happy for you. Really!" I rolled my eyes. "This is not something you had to keep from me."

Sean just watched the three of us, shaking his head. "I've always been a little jealous of the three of you. You have something really special."

"We're family, Sean," I said with a smile. "We just have different parents."

Amy and Kevin both nodded in agreement. Amy added, "I think we should include Sean in that family." She glanced at all of us. "After all, we've been through a lot together."

Understatement of the year.

Since we'd be dancing to the oldies at the Christmas party, Amy suggested a trip to the thrift store downtown in search of 1950's vintage clothing we could wear. Amy loved nothing more than shopping, and since I'd agreed to go to the party with Sean, I decided to be a good sport and do one of my least favorite things—go shopping.

A few days before the party, I picked up Amy after school and we headed to the thrift shop. The store, called "Gone But Not Forgotten," was one of Amy's favorite haunts. The shop was in the seedier end of town, an area I usually avoided. Amy, of course, paid no attention to the small groups of men hanging out on the corners in that neighborhood. When it came to shopping, she was totally single-minded. I tried to find a place to park close to the shop, but we still had more than a block to walk, past one of those corners where we were subjected to a barrage of catcalls.

"Just ignore it," Amy muttered. The best I could do was look straight ahead, ignoring them.

The store was a pleasant surprise on the inside. The walls were full of old movie posters from the "golden age" of Hollywood along with old record album covers from the age of vinyl. The big band sound blared from speakers in the corners. The owner looked like a refugee from that golden age, a platinum blonde dressed in a shoulder-padded outfit that had to be from the 1940's. When we told her what we were looking for, she led us to one side of the shop where Amy immediately dove into a rack of vintage clothing, squealing in delight.

After more than an hour, Amy had found a white poodle skirt decorated with turquoise embroidery and a fitted turquoise sweater that matched perfectly. The owner told her all she needed were ballet slippers and a small strand of pearls. I had to admit, Amy looked great. Very retro.

The owner assured me that my small size wouldn't be a problem because most teens in that era were considerably smaller than today's teens. She asked if she could pick something out for me, and I was only too happy to agree. Looking around at all the vintage clothing, I had no idea where to start.

She found a black pencil-slim skirt, a wide black belt, and a short-sleeved white sweater with a black Peter Pan collar. "Try this on, dear. Tuck in the sweater. I think it will be snug, but that's the look we want."

When I came out of the dressing room, Amy gasped and the owner was all smiles.

"Perfect, Cara. Your ponytail and those bangs are exactly right!"

The owner said, "You remind me of Betty Page, but with more clothes!"

I asked, "Who's Betty Page?"

Grinning, Amy said, "She was a famous pin-up model from the 1940's and 50's. And you do look a little like her, Cara. That outfit is just perfect on you."

The owner nodded, smiling. "You must wear red lipstick with that outfit, dear."

She packed up our purchases, told us to have fun at our Christmas party, and we left the shop.

When we approached the first corner, the men who had leered at us earlier paid no attention to us now. They were clustered around another man and it appeared some kind of business was being conducted. When one man walked away, I got a good look at the man in the center of the group and immediately knew what kind of business it was.

Amy whispered, "Isn't that the same guy Randi was dating?"

I nodded, tensing up. If he recognized me, I might be in trouble.

"Walk faster," I muttered to Amy.

Too late. Joey looked up and spotted me, his eyes narrowing. "You!" he shouted.

I stopped, Amy next to me, looking curious. Sean and I had never told our friends about our confrontation with Joey and his drug dealer friend.

He walked toward us, leaving the others behind. To say that he looked angry is putting it mildly.

I whispered to Amy, "Let me handle this. Don't say anything."

"What are you doing here?" he practically spit at me.

I looked him in the eye and said, "Shopping."

He said, "You're lucky Nick isn't with me today. He can't wait to return your knife to you."

"Are you threatening me?" I asked.

"Listen, kid, I'm a nice guy compared to Nick. You really don't want to run into him again. But I'm not happy with you either. You broke up me and Randi." Grabbing my arm, he said, "You need to be taught a lesson."

I heard Amy gasp. She started forward and I reached out and pushed her back behind me.

I had one weapon she'd never heard before."Let go of me, now." My voice was deeper, echoing a little." Amy gasped again.

Joey dropped my arm, looking confused.

I spoke again, using *Vox*. "Go back to Greenville. Don't come to Thornewood again.

Leave Randi alone. You want to find a safer way to make a living. If you come here again, you're going to jail. Do you understand?"

He nodded, his face blank, the anger gone.

"You can go now," I said, my voice still echoing.

He turned and walked down the street to where a white SUV was parked, got in, started the car, and drove away as the group of men on the corner started grumbling.

I took Amy's arm and hurried her to my car, got in quickly, and drove to Main Street, where there was more traffic. Pulling over in front of The Grille, I got out my cell phone and called Chief O'Donnell.

Amy started talking, and I held up my hand. "Give me a minute and then I'll explain, okay?" She nodded impatiently.

When the Chief answered the phone, I told him that I'd just seen Joey and where he'd been doing business. I explained that he'd threatened me and that I'd used *Vox* to make him leave town. I described the vehicle he'd been driving, but I hadn't written down the license plate number. He said he'd take care of it and thanked me for calling. Then he added, "*Vox*, huh?" I said yes and heard him sigh.

I turned my phone off. "Okay, Amy, I know you have questions."

"Well, probably not as many as you think. Kevin told me about *Vox*, and how you scared the you-know-what out of him the first time he saw you use it. He said it only happens when you feel threatened, right?"

"Right. If Joey hadn't grabbed my arm and threatened me, I might not have been able to use it. I think *Vox* is a kind of hypnosis."

"Okay, understood. That was awesome, Cara. But who is Nick, and why does he want to return your knife? What's going on with those guys?"

I described what happened when Sean and I had seen Joey with Randi's car, and what happened when Nick threatened Sean with a knife. She was shocked when I told her how Randi looked when she arrived at my house later that day.

"Oh, that poor girl. So that's why she's back in Thornewood now. As far as I know, she hasn't told anyone why her dad let her move back here."

"Would you, if your boyfriend turned out to be a physically abusive drug dealer?"

"Of course not, Cara. That whole thing must seem like a nightmare for Randi. Now I understand why she's been telling the girls what a great friend you've been."

She grinned. "Of course, I've known that for *years*! But from now on, if I have to go into that part of town, I want you with me."

"No problem!"

She looked around. "Well, since we're in front of The Grille . . ."

I finally had to laugh. The perfect antidote to stress: Burgers and milkshakes.

But I knew I'd be looking over my shoulder for Nick Romanov for the foreseeable future.

Our school's holiday party was the Friday before Christmas, the last day of school before our Christmas vacation. Since I'd agreed to go to the party with Sean, he'd been in a great mood all week. He'd even called me every night the way he used to.

I enjoyed resuming my late night talks with Sean, and he had a lot to do with my new and improved mood. I think my parents were ready to pin a medal on him. They hadn't said anything about the gloom I'd been projecting. They'd been very patient with me.

Sean was thrilled when I told him about Storm and begged me to introduce him to my new grey before the horses had to return to Elvenwood for the winter. I promised to take him to my father's camp on Saturday, the day after the Christmas party. I think he was more excited about that than he was about the party.

But either way, his good mood was rubbing off on me, and I think everyone was grateful.

Apparently, Amy and I weren't the only ones who decided to go with the 1950's theme. When I opened the door to Sean, I was surprised to find a James Dean lookalike standing on my front porch. He'd slicked back his blond hair and was wearing a red windbreaker jacket over a white t-shirt and dark jeans. I had always thought the actor James Dean was gorgeous, when he was alive sixty years ago, but I thought Sean was even better looking. Amy was going to love the way he'd dressed.

We had planned to meet Amy and Kevin at the restaurant. Main Street was completely lined with cars; the Pizza Palace had no parking lot. We decided to park behind Mom's bookstore. That was about as close as we'd be able to get to the restaurant. I didn't mind walking a few blocks. It was a beautiful, clear night with temperatures only in the forties. Winter hadn't arrived yet, much to my relief.

As we walked down Main Street, Sean said, "I like your retro outfit. It's kinda tight, you know, but very sexy." He was grinning. I rolled my eyes.

The sign on the restaurant's front door read, "Closed for Private Party." When we walked in, there were Christmas decorations everywhere, even on the bar, which, according to a sign, would only be serving root beer.

We found Amy and Kevin in one of the red vinyl booths near the jukebox in the dining room. Judging by the crowd of kids that had already arrived, Kevin and Amy must have come really early in order to grab one of the prized booths.

At the rear of the dining room was a door I'd never noticed before. It was open to a large banquet hall, which was now full of chairs, tables, Christmas decorations and at least a hundred teenagers. The mouth-watering smell of pizza filled both rooms.

When we reached Amy and Kevin's table, my mouth dropped open. I had already seen Amy's 50's outfit, but Kevin looked amazing. I knew Amy must have worked on his hair, taming his curls into a greased-back ducktail. He was wearing a white t-shirt with rolled-up sleeves, jeans and motorcycle boots, and there was a black leather motorcycle jacket hanging from the back of the booth.

I couldn't help laughing. "Kev, you look like you walked out of 'Grease!' This must have been Amy's idea, right?"

He nodded, an embarrassed smile on his face. "Yeah, Amy can be extremely persuasive."

We sat down as four frosty mugs of root beer were set on our table and the waiter took our pizza orders. He also informed us that the root beer would be on the house for the night.

Our pizzas were delivered quickly. The owner must have hired extra help for our party because there were servers dashing about, efficiently delivering pizzas and root beer in both rooms. There were already couples dancing to the oldies playing on the jukebox, and we could see we weren't the only ones who'd dressed for the 50's era.

As we finished eating, I looked up and was surprised to see Dion and Randi dancing.

Amy said, "They look great together, don't they? Cara, did you know they were dating?"

"No, Randi just said she had a date for the party, but she didn't say who it was with."

Randi looked over and waved at us. Dion grinned and waved us over.

Smiling, Sean took my hand and asked, "Ready?"

"Sure." We stood up and joined the crowd on the dance floor. I looked back at Amy and Kevin. Kevin was, of course, still eating. I think he was working on his second pie. Amy was looking a little impatient, but she knew better than to try to separate Kevin from his food. It was a well-known fact that Kevin had a hollow leg.

We all danced a lot that night, only stopping for root beer breaks. Everyone seemed to be enjoying the old Rock 'n Roll records on the jukebox. We traded partners frequently, and I danced with Dion, Kevin, Sandy's boyfriend Danny, and Matt, who I'd always liked despite his chronic foot-in-mouth disorder.

Matt hadn't changed. When he was finally able to get his eyes off my chest, he said, "I think I understand why Sean's so crazy about you, Cara."

I rolled my eyes. "Thanks, Matt." I vowed to leave the tight sweater in my closet in the future.

Amy and Kevin had been close enough to overhear that exchange, and Kevin had pushed her face into his shoulder to stifle her giggles. Fortunately, Sean rescued me a minute later.

Around ten o'clock, most of the younger kids left, their parents double-parked outside to take them home. The lights in the dining room were dimmed, and the atmosphere became noticeably more romantic.

The records being played now were mostly ballads. Sean and I got up to dance and didn't sit down again. "Sincerely," "Earth Angel," "Eddie my Love," "Put Your Head on My Shoulder," "Good Night My Love," and my mother's favorite, "In the Still of the Night."

I had to keep reminding myself that it wasn't right to take advantage of Sean, but dancing close to him, his arms around me, and the sandalwood cologne I'd always liked—well, there were times when I wanted to toss those good intentions out the window.

I'm not sure why, but that night I really needed to be held by a young man who cared for me and wasn't afraid to say so. I needed Sean. There were so many things about him that I admired, respected, and just plain liked.

When he drove me home and kissed me good night, I responded with more warmth than I should have; I knew that. But I liked kissing Sean, even if the earth didn't move under my feet. Maybe I'd have to learn not to wish for the unattainable. Maybe dreams were just that . . . dreams.

The next morning Sean arrived at ten o'clock. He was looking forward to meeting Storm at my father's camp, and I couldn't wait to introduce them.

As we walked through the backyard and into the woods, he asked, "I was wondering how you manage to get on and off your new grey. Pigeon was the perfect size for you, wasn't she?"

I smiled. "Yeah, she was. But Storm has some skills you won't believe."

After we crossed the stream, Sean took my hand, squeezing it gently, and grinned at me.

I was afraid last night had convinced him we were back together. I didn't have the heart to tell him any different.

My father wasn't in camp when we arrived, but I saw Gabriel taking care of the horses. He wore a big grin.

"Hey, Cara, Sean, good to see you. Your father's not here, Cara. Will I do?"

I gave him a hug and Sean grinned at his former bodyguard.

"I wanted to show Sean my new grey, Gabe. And maybe we could take a ride while we're here."

Grinning, Gabe said, "I'll get your grey, Sean; prepare to be surprised!"

When he led Storm and Cloud back to us, Cloud immediately nuzzled Sean, clearly happy to see him again. Sean stroked her neck and whispered to her. She whinnied in delight. I snorted. Typical female.

Storm trotted up to me, resting his nose on my head and snickering. I told him how glad I was to see him and he nodded his big head, clearly agreeing with me.

Laughing, I said, "Storm knows how much I like him. I think he's a little conceited." The dark gray horse nodded again.

Gabe and Sean were laughing at Storm's method of communicating with me. He seemed to enjoy their laughter.

Gabe saddled both greys for us. I walked up to Storm, stroked his nose, and said, "Down." He folded all four legs and lowered himself to the ground, looking up at me and snickering.

Sean looked amazed. "Wow. I've never seen a horse do that!"

I smiled and climbed on Storm's back. Once I was situated, he unfolded his legs and stood, whinnying and looking proud of himself. "Good job, Storm," I whispered.

Grinning, Sean shook his head, mounted Cloud and said, "I'll follow you."

The greys trotted along the path, eventually veering off and following a path only they could see. I looked over my shoulder at Sean who was smiling. "This is an adventure, right?" he asked.

"Yeah. I think Storm knows every square inch of the forest. He knows where he's going, even if we don't. Might as well relax and enjoy the ride."

The December air was crisp and cool, not the frigid, icy air common this time of year. There were still a few red-gold leaves on the trees, although most of their leaves had fallen. I inhaled the sharp tang of fallen leaves and felt the cool wind playing with my long hair, grateful for winter's delay.

I sighed. I knew there wouldn't be much more riding so close to Christmas.

The greys took us all over Blackthorne Forest until they seemed ready to return to camp. As the horses trotted into camp, I realized I was shivering in my denim jacket. The temperature had dropped dramatically while we were in the woods.

Sean climbed down from Cloud, and Storm folded his legs and sat on the ground while I dismounted. I thanked him for a lovely ride, stroking his neck, and he stood, raising his head and whinnying. Cloud joined him, moving closer and snorting. When I looked up, I realized why.

It was snowing.

Sean and I hadn't dressed for snow, so we said goodbye to Gabe and the greys and jogged through the woods back to my house, arriving laughing and out of breath.

He shrugged off his snow-covered jacket and sat down at the kitchen table, rubbing his cold hands together.

"I think we need coffee," I said, as I filled the coffeemaker and started a fresh pot.

I tossed my lightweight jacket on a chair, pulled on Mom's old sweater from the back of the rocking chair and sat down at the table with him.

Smiling, he said, "Well, that was a surprise. Looks like we'll have a white Christmas."

My lack of enthusiasm was obvious.

"You really don't like winter or snow, do you?" he asked.

"Nope. I don't like being cold, having the wind turn me into a popsicle, slipping on ice, or being bundled up in three layers of clothing. It makes me look like the Michelin Man," I grumbled.

He laughed. "You don't know what you're missing. Ice skating, Hockey, Skiing, Sledding, there's so much to do!"

"Well, you can enjoy it. I'll stay home where it's warm."

I poured our coffee, got out cream and sugar, and sat down. Time to change the subject. I really hated cold weather.

I asked, "Will you be home with your family for Christmas?"

"I think so. Mom hasn't said anything about another trip to Boston, thankfully. I forgot to tell you. I gave my parents the picture you drew for their anniversary. I'd had it framed. They really loved it and wanted me to thank you."

"I'm glad they liked it." I smiled. "I had a great model."

He rolled his eyes, blushing.

"Uh, Cara, I didn't know if I'd see you again before Christmas. I've got something out in the car for you." He stood, throwing his jacket on. "Be right back."

When he ran back in, his dark blond hair was already covered with snow. Laughing, I threw him a towel. After he dried his hair, he handed me a small silver box with a big bow on top.

"I hope you like it, Cara. I had it made for you." There was so much love in his eyes, I had to look away.

"You don't want me to wait 'til Christmas to open it?"

"No. Please open it while I'm here."

I took a deep breath and lifted the lid of the small box. On a delicate silver chain, there was a beautifully fashioned horse inside a narrow silver circle, like an open pendant. I loved it. I immediately fastened it around my neck.

"Sean, it's beautiful. How does it look?"

His voice was soft. "Perfect. Just like you."

I looked up into his warm brown eyes. "Thank you. I love it."

He got up, came around the table to my chair and bent down. "I love you." He kissed me, smiling.

Two could play this game. "Hang on, I have something for you too." I ran up to my bedroom and came back downstairs with a gift bag, stuffed with tissue paper.

I handed the bag to him and he sat down next to me.

Grinning, he said, "Ah, a bag full of paper. Just what I needed."

"Dig a little deeper please."

Reaching in, he brought out a white cable knit crew neck sweater I'd picked out for him.

"Whoa. This is really nice," he said, holding the sweater up against his chest.

"I think it'll fit. Are you sure you like it? I can always exchange it, you know."

"Cara, it's a great sweater. Really. I like it."

He laughed, clearly pleased. Leaning forward, he kissed me again, putting his hands on either side of my face.

Holding my face that way triggered a memory so painful, I couldn't breathe for a few seconds. I gasped, tears filling my eyes.

He let go, looking surprised and worried. "What's wrong? What did I do?"

I took a deep breath, desperately trying to control myself and hold back the tears.

"Nothing's wrong. I'm okay. Really."

He didn't look convinced. He looked upset.

"Cara, you looked like I'd just hurt you. It's not okay."

I tried to laugh. "Pay no attention to me. I just got over-emotional for a minute. The holidays, I guess."

He wrapped his hands around mine. His voice was soft. "I'd never hurt you. I hope you know that. You're everything to me."

I just nodded, unable to look him in the eye.

Squeezing my hands, he took a deep breath. "Cara, I know you don't feel the same way I do. But I think you're attracted to me, aren't you?"

I took a deep breath too and nodded again, looking up at him.

He smiled, kissed me again and whispered, "Good. Because I'm not giving up."

He turned to look out the window. "Hey, it's still coming down. As much as I'd like to stay, I should get the car home before the roads get any worse."

Standing, he pulled me out of my chair and wrapped his arms around me, holding me close, kissing my neck, and sending goose bumps down my body.

"You feel so good," he whispered. His lips traveled from my neck to my face; he left tiny kisses all over my face, ending at my lips. He felt good to me too, and I couldn't help kissing him back, running my hands through his thick hair.

He was right. I was attracted to him. What girl wouldn't be?

But as someone once pointed out to me, being attracted to someone wasn't the same as being in love.

A few heart-pounding minutes later, I walked him to the front door, got one last hug, and watched him jog carefully through the snow to his car, which was already covered in at least two inches of snow. Brushing the snow from his windows quickly, he jumped into the car and started it. He turned his lights on, and pulled away, with a short beep of the horn.

After I watched his car move slowly down the block, I shut the door and walked back into the kitchen, wrapping my arms around myself to warm up.

The snow continued all day, all night, and into the next day. I was glad I'd finished my Christmas shopping so I wouldn't have to go out in the cold, icy mess. Yuck.

I still hated shopping, so I was thrilled I'd been able to get it all done downtown at Van Horn's, Thornewood's only department store. A makeup collection for Amy and a dark green crew neck sweater for Kevin that I thought would bring out the green in his hazel eyes. Not that I'd tell him that, of course.

I'd made a few more gifts as well. I'd painted a small watercolor landscape of the evergreen trees I could see from my bedroom window for Miss Burrows, my Art teacher. For my parents, I'd painted a portrait of the two of them, the way I remembered them best, sitting at the kitchen table, smiling at each other, my father leaning toward Mom.

They looked like two people in love, happy being together. The way they were always meant to be.

Usually, during the holidays, Kevin, Amy, and I would be spending time with each other, in one house or another, but not this year. Thanks to the weather, we kept in touch by phone right up until Christmas Eve, when it finally stopped snowing. All the enthusiasm about a white Christmas was completely lost on me.

If I wanted to leave the house, it meant two pairs of socks, heavy waterproof boots, layers of warm clothing, my warmest parka, gloves, and a knit cap. Therefore, I wasn't leaving the house!

The snow didn't seem to bother my parents. Mom still managed to open the bookstore every morning, and my father had no problem stalking through three feet of snow to get from his camp to our house. Fortunately, he had boots that came up to his knees, as well as a heavy poncho-like cape. There were only two greys left at his camp, both hardy enough to handle the cold, although he assured me they were both wearing heavy blankets.

My father admitted that there wasn't nearly as much snow once you got closer to Elvenwood. It was cold there, but not frigid.

Kevin joined us for dinner on Christmas Eve, since his mother was still out taking care of real estate business. However, she promised him she'd be home on Christmas Day and had arranged to have a holiday dinner delivered by the classiest caterer in town. She had also invited a few friends who had no family locally to join them. I think Kevin was relieved it wouldn't just be the two of them on Christmas.

On Christmas Eve Mom lit all our Christmas candles and we had dinner by candlelight. She'd made lasagna because it was one of Dad's favorites, and we cracked open one of the bottles of Elvenwood's homemade wine. I think Kevin and I were both a little tipsy by the time dinner was over. We were both giggling and couldn't seem to stop.

Looking amused, my father said, "I think that wine was more potent than I realized, Alicia." And, of course, that just set us off again.

I'd discovered that alcohol was an excellent anesthetic for pain.

CHAPTER 8

It was our first Christmas together as a family, and my parents seemed happily content. Mom made pancakes for us before starting our traditional Christmas dinner. The kitchen was full of good smells and quiet laughter as my father tried to help Mom prepare dinner. Well, he mostly tried not to get in her way.

In the past, spending Christmas with both my parents would have made me deliriously happy. But this year, someone was missing.

Amy called around noon, thrilled with the makeup assortment I'd given her. We had opened our gifts after breakfast, and I was delighted with the watercolor paper she had given me. Good quality watercolor paper wasn't cheap.

A little later I heard Kevin's usual knock on the front door. Clad in a puffy parka, he almost suffocated me when he hugged me.

"Merry Christmas, short stuff! I come bearing gifts."

Kevin was in a very good mood and hardly stopped smiling for the next hour. He gave my father a pair of fur-lined leather gloves saying, "My dad said you might need these, Mr. Blackthorne." Which was when I realized my father never wore gloves.

My dad was delighted. "Kevin, that was really thoughtful. Thank you, son."

Kevin gave my mother a pair of antique candlesticks that matched the beautiful porcelain bowl his mother had given my parents for a wedding gift. Kevin's mom said the bowl was an antique, but Mom filled it with fruit and kept it on the kitchen table.

Smiling, Mom said, "I think there will be more candlelit dinners in our future, Kevin. Thank you, dear."

Handing me a large box, Kevin said, "I hope you can make use of these, short stuff."

Inside the box there were different kinds of watercolor paints, some in tubes, some in solid cakes, and an assortment of watercolor pencils and ink pens.

"I wasn't sure what kind of paints you like using, so I got every kind they had at the art supply store downtown. I hope the kind you like are in here."

"Wow. Kevin, you've outdone yourself. I have a small assortment, but with all of these paints I can mix more colors to get the shades I want." I kissed his cheek. "Thanks, Kev."

He was beaming, happy we all loved our gifts.

"I have one for you too. Don't move."

I ran upstairs, got his gift, and ran back downstairs. Being Kevin, he didn't waste any time tearing off the wrapping paper. He opened the box and took out the dark green sweater with a big smile. "This is great, Cara. Amy's been telling me I should wear more green, that it brings out the green in my eyes." He rolled his eyes and I had to laugh.

He hugged me, immediately pulled off his sweatshirt, and pulled on the green sweater. Mom and Dad both told him how good he looked. I grinned and said, "Amy's gonna love it!"

My father said, "One more thing, Kevin." He got up, went to the coat closet and came back to the kitchen with a large object wrapped in a sheet. The shape was familiar, and as Kevin pulled the sheet off of it, I saw a beautiful, handmade bow.

Dad added, "I thought you might like the kind of bow all my Elves use. We make our own and no two are alike."

Kevin looked awestruck as my father handed the beautiful bow to him.

"I don't know what to say, Mr. Blackthorne. I'm honored to have this. Thank you."

My father smiled. "I think you've earned it, Kevin. You've become as good an archer as your father. He wanted you to have it."

Kevin just smiled, apparently speechless for once.

After we all exchanged rib-crushing hugs, Kevin gathered up his gifts and left for home.

I was helping Mom with dinner preparations when Sean called.

"Merry Christmas, beautiful! We're having an early dinner, but I could stop over later if it's okay with your parents. How about it?"

"Let me check with Mom, Sean. I'm not sure when we'll be eating, although you're welcome to join us."

My mother said we'd be having dinner at four o'clock, but she asked if Sean wanted to join us for dessert.

He did, joking that dessert was his middle name, and that he'd be over around five.

After we'd done justice to the turkey Mom roasted, filled up on orange-glazed sweet potatoes, green beans in a butter and almond sauce, hot biscuits, and a cranberry and orange salad, there was still an apple pie and a cheesecake waiting for us. We thought it would be wise to take a brief break from eating until Sean arrived. Dad was sure the chair he was sitting in was about to collapse from the strain of holding him.

Laughing, Mom made a pot of tea and I took Ralph out in the backyard to play in the snow for a short while. I loved my dog, but there was no way I wanted to be out in the cold for more than ten or fifteen minutes. Ralph, of course, loved playing in the snow and was reluctant to come back in.

I had that weird feeling that we were being watched from the woods. I pushed it out of my mind, telling myself I was just being silly. There was no one out there.

After Sean arrived, Mom served the apple pie and the cheesecake. Apple pie had always been my downfall, which my father was well aware of.

He told Sean, "Cara ate so much apple pie in Elvenwood last summer, we all thought she'd explode."

I rolled my eyes. What could I say? I had no will power when it came to apple pie. Unfortunately, that reminded me of all the times Adam told me apple pie looked good on me. I had too many memories to deal with today.

We were all still at the table when Mom got up and said, "Cara, we have a few more gifts for you." She went to the coat closet and brought back a slim box, beautifully wrapped. I opened it to find an assortment of watercolor brushes, flat ones, wide ones, fine-tipped brushes, a complete assortment. Knowing my mother, she had bought only sable brushes, which I knew were expensive.

"Mom, these are perfect. I'll make good use of them." I got up and hugged her. Between Mom, Amy, and Kevin, most of my art supplies had been taken care of.

Dad smiled and walked over to the same closet, pulling out something else wrapped in a sheet. Was I getting a handmade bow too?

"Cara, I know you'll need this eventually, but maybe not until spring," he said with a smile. He set it in front of me and pulled the sheet off. It was a free-standing easel, the kind I could fold and carry with me.

"It's perfect, Dad. I haven't seen anything as nice as this at the store. Was it made in your wood shop?"

"Yes. Garrett made it himself after receiving a few suggestions from Francis Sullivan. He knew you'd need it."

Naturally, that reminded me of someone else who had worked in the woodshop with Garrett. Today reminders of Adam were everywhere. I sighed as I ran my fingers over the wood. It had been sanded until the wood was like satin.

"I love the easel, Dad. Please tell Garrett he did a great job on it. It will be getting a lot of use."

With all the art supplies I'd received, I had even more incentive to master watercolor painting. I could play with all the paints and brushes to find techniques that suited my kind of art, and learn how to mix the vivid colors I loved.

My artwork would keep me from dwelling on what I'd lost. Adam was out of my life, wherever he was. If he'd just stay out of my dreams at night, I might survive.

The day after Christmas it snowed again. And again, right up until New Year's Eve. I had spent the week at home, experimenting with my paints and brushes. I was so focused on my painting, I didn't think about that box on the top shelf of my closet. Well, not much.

The decision to paint in my bedroom might not have been the best idea, but the living room was too dark, and there wasn't anywhere else for me to set up my easel and paints.

I was doing my best not to think about Adam.

Dion had planned a New Year's Eve party, but if the snowplows didn't clear most of Thornewood's streets by tonight, it might have to be cancelled. I didn't really care one way or the other, but I knew Sean would be disappointed. He'd already told me he wanted to start the New Year with me in his arms.

Amy kept calling to update me on the snowplow's progress. She and Kevin were really looking forward to Dion's party. They had officially become a "couple," to no one's surprise. Beginning a new year together meant something special to them.

Finally at four o'clock, Sean called to say the roads had all been plowed and he'd pick me up at seven. Amy called immediately after that to ask what I was wearing.

"No idea, Amy. I didn't even think we'd be going. What are you wearing?"

"Well, I think the weather and the four feet of snow out there has made that decision for me. My favorite little black dress is out. My mother insists I wear something warm, which is probably what everyone will do. Ski pants, boots, and turtleneck sweaters will be popular tonight, Cara. You might as well do the same. Tonight is obviously not the night to try looking sexy."

She sounded so disgruntled, I had to laugh. "Don't complain. You look great in ski pants and sweaters. If I were your height, I wouldn't mind at all."

When we got off the phone, I turned to my closet to see what I could find that might look New Year's Eve-ish.

I was definitely not a fan of winter outdoor sports, so no ski pants. Hmm. But I did have a pair of warm knit tights and a wool miniskirt. Once I added a green turtleneck sweater, I was as ready as I was going to be for a cold, snowy New Year's Eve. I put on the pendant Sean had given me and my warmest boots, and I was ready to go.

Mom and Dad were downstairs sharing a bottle of champagne, looking happy to be celebrating a new year together. Mom looked at me approvingly.

"That'll keep you warm, dear. What time will you be home?"

"No idea, Mom. We'll have to see the New Year in, so after midnight, I guess."

"Cara, I know the roads have been cleared, but they may get icy tonight, so please tell Sean to be really careful driving."

"Absolutely. You know how I feel about snow and ice."

The doorbell rang. Right on time, as always. I let Sean in and he came into the kitchen to wish my parents a Happy New Year while I put on my Michelin-man parka, and we left for Dion's.

As we made our way out to his car, I said, "Hope you're planning on driving very slowly. The roads will be icy tonight, and I'm not in any hurry."

He smiled as he helped me into the car. "No worries, beautiful. As long as we're together, I don't care how long it takes us to drive to Dion's."

And that was Sean in a nutshell. He always knew the right thing to say. He did take his time, probably driving no more than twenty miles per hour, so I sat back and relaxed.

We finally reached Dion's, where the entire street was lined with cars. And that was when I remembered the last party I'd attended here, when I'd had too much spiked fruit punch and got unintentionally drunk.

Sean had driven me home that night, and Adam had held me up until I managed to get into the house. Another memory I wished I could erase.

We had to park a block away, but Mr. and Mrs. Washington had put up lots of lights and Christmas decorations, so the area around their house looked a bit like Times Square. There were even a few reindeer on the roof, one with a bright red nose. Maybe New Year's Eve would actually be fun.

Dion welcomed us at the door, hugged me and slapped Sean on the shoulder. He led us downstairs to their big, beautiful family room, full of sports memorabilia from Mr. Washington's years playing pro football. There was a huge Christmas tree in one corner, and an expensive stereo built into a wall that also held the biggest flat screen TV I'd ever seen.

Sean whispered, "They take their football very seriously." I had to laugh.

We heard the doorbell ring again so Dion pointed us to a table of assorted sodas and dashed back upstairs. Most of Sean's football buddies were huddled together on the other side of the room; one or two had brought dates. Sean got me a drink and then wandered over to say hello.

Suddenly arms grabbed me from behind, and I turned around to see Randi with a big smile on her face. "I'm so glad you came, Cara. We're really overdue for another girls' night, you know."

I smiled. "You're right." It had been at least a month since she moved back to Thornewood.

"I guess Christmas got in the way, but let's get together again before we go back to school, okay?" she asked.

"Absolutely. You can pick the night. How are you and your dad doing?"

"It's really going well, Cara. He stayed home for a few weeks until I felt settled, but I know he has to travel for his job. I think he knows now that I'll be fine on my own when he's away. I'm even learning to cook!"

"Well, you're one up on me. I can boil water, but that's about all. Mom keeps waiting for me to express more interest in cooking, but as long as I have a toaster and the microwave, I'll never starve to death."

Dion had come back downstairs with four more of our classmates. Randi said, "I'll bet the rest of the basketball team will be here tonight. Are Amy and Kevin coming?"

"Yeah, I'm surprised they're not here yet. I think I'll give her a call." I pulled out my cell and called, but it went straight to voice mail. I called Kevin's cell and it just rang and rang. Finally, he answered, sounding strange.

"Kev, what's wrong? Where are you?"

"Cara, thank God. My car skidded off the road about six blocks from Dion's. We need help."

"What street are you on, Kev?"

"Uh, I'm not sure. I think Oak."

"Kev, I'm calling the police now. And we'll get there as soon as we can. Are you okay?"

"Uh, I hit my head, but Amy's out cold. She hit her head on the window when we rolled." His voice was slurred, which scared me.

"Kev, I'm calling for an ambulance. Try to relax. We're on our way." I hung up and called Chief O'Donnell. Thankfully, he was still working. I told him what had happened and he said he'd get an ambulance to Kevin and Amy right away and would meet us there.

I grabbed Sean. "We have to leave. Kevin and Amy had an accident a few blocks from here. The Chief is calling an ambulance but I need to be there." I must have sounded panicky because Sean said, "Were they hurt?" I nodded. "Okay, Cara. Just relax now. I'll get our coats."

We told Dion we had to leave, and surprisingly, he grabbed his coat too and said he'd come with us. "We can take my dad's car. It's got snow tires."

We followed him out of the house where a huge SUV was parked in the driveway. We piled in and Dion pulled out of the driveway.

"Kevin thinks he's on Oak, but he wasn't sure. He said he was about six blocks from here."

Dion nodded. "We'll find him. He can't be too far."

Sean's arm was around me firmly as we slowly drove up and down streets in Dion's neighborhood. When we reached Oak St., we found them. Kevin's Jeep was on its side in a shallow ditch. Within seconds we heard sirens. Dion turned on his flashers to help them find us.

Sean and I jumped out and ran to Kevin's car. I knocked on the driver's window and he turned to see us, blood running down his face. I couldn't even see Amy, she was slumped down so far.

"The ambulance is almost here, Kev." He nodded and mumbled, "Thanks, babe." Then he closed his eyes and put his head back. He was very pale.

The next twenty minutes went by in a blur. The Fire Dept. arrived and managed to get Kevin's door open and carefully brought Kevin and Amy out of the car.

All I could see of Amy was her red hair and freckles that stood out starkly against her fair skin. Her eyes were closed. That alone was frightening.

The ambulance pulled up and the EMT's got them on gurneys, immediately provided whatever first aid they needed, loaded them into the ambulance, and took off, siren blaring. I felt as though a piece of my heart went with them. I was fighting tears.

The Chief had pulled up behind Dion's SUV and spoke to the EMT's before they left. I heard him give them Amy's and Kevin's names.

"Chief, where are they taking them?"

"They'll have to go to Greenville, Cara. That's the closest hospital. It looks as though Kevin may have a concussion from the injury to his head. Amy's still unconscious, which concerns me more. I'll call their parents right now."

He walked back to his car and got on the radio. I turned to Sean, "What can we do?"

"Cara, I don't think there's anything else we can do for now." He wrapped both arms around me and held me against his chest. That was when I realized there were tears running down my face.

Dion said, "Let's go back to my house. Amy and Kevin are in good hands. You can make more calls from my house if you need to. Come on, it's cold out here."

Dion drove us back to his house and we went back to the party. I don't think many of our classmates had even noticed we were gone.

I didn't understand what I was doing at a party when my two best friends were in an ambulance on their way to the hospital.

Dion must have told his parents what had happened, because before I knew it, Mr. Washington was putting cups of something warm into our hands. "This will warm you up."

I dutifully drank it down. Hot chocolate. I took a deep breath as my insides got warmer. When I'd finished my drink, I did feel better. Both Sean and Dion looked better too.

"Thanks, Mr. Washington."

Sean and Dion were like bookends on either side of me. Mr. Washington nodded. "I'm really sorry your friends got hurt. Dion's mom and I will be praying for them."

Sean said, "It'll be a while before we know anything, Cara. I know you're in no mood for a party, but at least we're among friends."

Randi squatted down in front of me. "I just heard what happened. I'm so sorry. Is there anything I can do, Cara?"

"Say a prayer for them, Randi. They were both hurt when the Jeep slid into a ditch. Kevin was able to talk, but Amy was unconscious."

Word of the accident had apparently reached the rest of the kids at the party. The room had gotten much too quiet.

I looked at Sean. "I don't want to ruin everyone's New Year's Eve. Let's go home."

He hugged me against him. "Okay. Sorry, Dion, but we'd better go."

Dion patted my shoulder. "Don't worry, Cara. They're young and healthy. I'm sure they'll both be fine." I hoped that wasn't just wishful thinking.

We said good night, put our coats on and left to walk back to Sean's car.

Outside the air was still, no wind, but it was freezing. Sean held on to me as we made our way carefully down the icy street, away from all the cheerful holiday lights, which seemed like a bad joke now.

When we got back to my house, we found my parents still sitting in the kitchen. The bottle of champagne was now only half full and there was a bowl of little meatballs in some kind of sauce on the table.

"You're back so early." Mom said, looking surprised. My father immediately looked worried. "What happened, sweetheart?" he asked.

"Kevin and Amy had an accident on their way to the party. The Jeep went into a ditch. They're both being taken to the hospital by ambulance."

Mom looked shocked, then worried. "How are they, Cara?"

Sean and I threw off our coats and sat down. "Kevin was conscious; it looked like he'd hit his head. He was bleeding. But Amy was unconscious. Mom, she didn't look good at all." Tears started running down my face again. "I called the Chief and he sent an ambulance. He's notifying their parents."

Sean held my hand tightly. He looked worried too.

"I know there's nothing we can do, but feeling so helpless is awful."

She nodded and patted my shoulder. "I know it is. We can call the hospital in a few hours—after they've had time to get there and receive treatment. But right now you two should have some tea while you try to relax. I know you're both upset. I'm worried too."

She got up and started boiling water while she took down the teapot and filled the infuser with the aromatic herbs we always kept on hand. They came from Elvenwood, from Kathleen, Elvenwood's healer and herbalist. Her tea was both soothing and relaxing.

"Is that Kathleen's special tea?" Sean asked. He'd had it before.

My mother nodded. "Kathleen makes sure we're never without it."

She filled the teapot with boiling water. A few minutes later she poured cups for each of us. Just breathing in the scent of the herbs actually helped, and I began to relax.

While we drank our tea, Mom picked up her phone and called Amy's house. It was a brief conversation.

"Amy's parents are already on their way to Greenville. Mrs. Strauss said she'd call us as soon as she has any information. She's obviously upset."

Next she called Kevin's mom. Betty Sinclair had just received the Chief's message and was leaving for the hospital. I heard Mom ask her to let us know if there was anything she needed.

There was nothing more we could do.

New Year's Eve was a difficult night for us, and New Year's Day wasn't much better. I was relieved when Kevin called to let us know he was coming home. He did have a concussion and a nasty headache, but he was fine otherwise. His mom had spent the night at the hospital. She'd be driving him home as soon as the doctor released him.

The news on Amy wasn't as good. Kevin had spoken to Mrs. Strauss, who said that other than a lump on the side of her head, the doctor hadn't found anything else wrong with Amy. But she hadn't awakened. And they didn't know why. They'd be keeping her in the ICU until she woke up.

Sean had gone home shortly after midnight on New Year's Eve, so I called to give him the news.

"Do you want to go to the hospital, Cara?" he asked. "I think I can get the car and drive us if you do."

I really appreciated his offer. I wanted to go, but I didn't really want to drive to Greenville by myself.

Sean picked me up at noon and we drove to Greenville. We found Amy's parents in the waiting room outside Intensive Care.

Mrs. Strauss embraced me. "Liebchen, I'm glad you're here. We've been here all night, hoping our Amy will wake up, but still she sleeps." Her accent was heavier than usual.

I hugged her. "Mrs. Strauss, why don't you and Mr. Strauss go home and get some rest. We'll stay here with Amy." The poor woman looked ten years older than she did a few days ago. Mr. Strauss looked exhausted.

She looked at her husband and nodded. "Thank you, liebchen. We'll just go home for a nap and then we'll be back. The doctor says he can't find anything seriously wrong with her." She shook her head, clearly frustrated. "Why won't she wake up?"

"She will, we just have to be patient. You know Amy; she'll wake up when she's good and ready." I smiled, trying to cheer her up a little.

Mr. Strauss nodded. "Ja, that sounds like Amy. She has a mind of her own, that's for sure. Come, Susie, we'll go home for a few hours, get a little rest, and then we'll come back. If Amy wakes up, her friends will be here."

It was the first time I'd ever heard Amy's mom called by her first name. Susie. It suited the plump little redhead.

After Mrs. Strauss hugged each of us, they put their coats on and walked out of the ICU, promising to be back before dinner.

Sean and I walked up to the window looking into Amy's room. The lights in the room were low. The machine all the tubes were attached to showed her vital signs. Everything looked normal, blood pressure, temperature, heart rate all perfectly normal. Yet she continued to sleep.

Sean asked, "Is she in a coma?"

"I guess so. If it was a normal sleep, she'd wake up, wouldn't she?"

He shrugged. "The nurse said all the numbers on that machine are normal so why doesn't she open her eyes?"

"I wish we could ask her," I said.

We looked at each other sadly.

"Cara, why don't you sit down. I'll go find the cafeteria and get us something to eat, okay?"

"Okay, thanks."

He left and I continued to watch Amy sleep. If that's really what she was doing. I wondered if she was dreaming. Then I wondered what she was dreaming about. I'd have so many questions for my best friend when she woke up.

If she woke up.

I called Kevin the next morning. He sounded as though he hadn't slept.

"How's your head?" I asked.

"It's just a headache. All I need is aspirin. And news that Amy's awake. Were you at the hospital yesterday?"

"Yes, Sean drove us over after lunch. We stayed for the afternoon so that Amy's parents could go home and get some sleep. Have you spoken to them, Kev?"

"Yes. I snuck out of the E.R. and went to find them and see Amy before I came home."

He didn't say anything else right away, but I knew he had more to say so I waited.

"Cara, it was *my* fault! I should have been driving more slowly. I *knew* the streets would be icy. Amy's in a coma now, and it's all my fault." Of course he would blame himself.

"Kev, calm down. I don't think anyone blames you for the accident. It could have happened to anyone."

"But it didn't happen to anyone, Cara. It happened to me and to Amy. My fault, all my fault." His voice trailed off. He was barely whispering. "I don't know what I'll do if she doesn't wake up."

I'd never heard Kevin so distraught.

"Kevin, please don't assume the worst. She *will* wake up. The doctors can't find anything wrong with her. She has no other injuries, just a lump on the side of her head. She's young and healthy. Have a little faith, okay?

"Listen, Kev, I'm going back to the hospital this afternoon. Sean can't make it today, so I'm driving. Come with me."

He didn't say anything right away. Then, "Okay. Pick me up later?"

"Sure. Get some rest this morning. You sound like you haven't slept. I'll come by after lunch. Should I bring you a sandwich?"

"Yeah, please. We're out of groceries, as usual."

And that's how I knew all was not lost. Kevin's appetite was intact.

I drove Kevin to the hospital every day for the next week. Sometimes my mother joined us. I think she was as worried about Kevin as we were about Amy. He never smiled or joked anymore.

The rule in ICU was only family members could visit in the patient's room, but when Amy's parents went home, they asked the duty nurse to allow us to sit with their daughter.

Kevin and I sat at her bedside every afternoon. Kevin would hold the hand that wasn't hooked up to anything, and I'd talk to her. The nurse

THE JOINING TREE

encouraged us to talk to her, insisting that Amy could probably hear us. I talked about everything I could think of: New Year's Resolutions, the work that was progressing on the Strauss Bakery, the school friends who were calling daily to ask about her, the Elves who knew her and were sending their best wishes.

When I ran out of small talk, I'd nudge Kevin and he'd start talking to her. He'd describe the work he was doing on his new game, titled "Dragon Wars." The misery was so clear on his face, I couldn't help thinking that it was a good thing Amy couldn't see him.

On the weekend, Mom and Dad would come with us to visit. Mom told Amy about some new recipes she was planning to make, and she'd talk about some of her weirder customers at her bookstore, The Crescent Moon.

My father only said, "We'll be right here until you decide to open your eyes, Amy. We all love you and miss seeing your smile."

Kevin's car was finally road-worthy again. When he told me what the repairs had cost, I was speechless. Naturally, his insurance rates had gone way up. Fortunately, his paychecks for the video games he was designing meant he could afford it.

Christmas vacation was over and we went back to school on Monday. Everyone who knew Amy stopped us to ask how she was doing.

Basketball practice had begun, and Sean was tied up every day after school. He couldn't go to the hospital with me, and I know he felt he was letting me down.

"It's okay, Sean. I understand."

He shook his head. "I wish I could be with you. If there's any change in Amy's condition, please call me right away."

I said I would.

Kevin went to the hospital with me every day after school. I did the driving. He didn't seem willing to get into his just-repaired Jeep and I didn't ask why. I suspected that he didn't trust himself to keep us both safe. His self-confidence had taken a huge hit.

The following weekend Amy was still in a coma, and Kevin actually turned down an invitation to Sunday brunch. I was sitting in the kitchen with Mom and Dad, feeling as though I'd lost both of my best friends.

"Something has to change soon, doesn't it? I mean, how long can this last?"

I must have sounded desperate. My father reached for my hand. I knew he could feel what I was feeling, and it must have worried him.

"Cara, is it possible that Amy has some Elven blood?" he asked.

"I don't know, Dad. We were talking about taking her to the gateway to see if it would open for her, but we never actually did it. Why?"

He shook his head. "I can't be sure, but if Amy is one of us, I may be able to help her."

Mom asked, "How?"

My father stared out the window at the forest. Finally, he said, "If any part of Amy is Elven, I may be able to speak to her mind and let her know that she needs to wake up, that she's slept long enough."

"Dad, if that's at all possible, you have to try it. Come to the hospital with me."

I knew that the logical thing would be to ask Amy's mother if there was any possibility Amy had some Elven blood, but since Mr. Strauss was definitely not an Elf, it raised an awkward question.

"We can't really ask Mrs. Strauss about Elven blood, can we? It would mean that Mr. Strauss isn't Amy's father."

My father looked uncertain. "I don't want to offend Amy's parents. I'd better wait and see if Amy wakes up on her own."

So we waited. Another week went by. Amy still slept. I finally told Kevin what my father had said about speaking to Amy telepathically.

For the first time in weeks, Kevin looked excited. "Why is your father waiting? He has to try it. Please ask him, Cara."

That night I spoke to my dad. He hesitated, finally saying he would speak to Mrs. Strauss and get her permission. I drove my father to Amy's house and we sat down with her in their den. Fortunately, Mr. Strauss was upstairs resting.

My father began the conversation. "Mrs. Strauss, please don't be offended. I may be able to help Amy, but only if she has Elven blood."

Mrs. Strauss closed her eyes for a few seconds. She opened her eyes and nodded. She looked at me and smiled slightly. "Mr. Blackthorne, Cara, my husband knew that I was expecting Amy when we moved to America. He also knew that he was not Amy's father. But it made no difference to him. He loves our Amy the same way he would love a child of his own."

Turning to me, she said, "You may remember I spoke to you about the handsome young men from the forest near my village." I nodded.

"Well, his name was Stefan. We were both very young, and he was so beautiful and so kind." She shrugged. "Mr. Strauss knew about my relationship with Stefan. He also knew that Stefan and I could never marry. It simply wasn't allowed.

"When Mr. Strauss decided to emigrate to America, he asked me to marry him and come with him. So I did.

"Please understand. I love my husband. When Amy was born, we decided not to tell her about her biological father, but when you and I spoke months ago, Cara, I was afraid it would come out eventually."

She looked into my father's eyes. "If you can help her, Mr. Blackthorne, you have our permission to try. Perhaps it's time she learned the truth."

My father clasped her hand. "Mrs. Strauss, I'll do everything I can, I promise. Cara and I will go to the hospital tomorrow and I'll try to wake your daughter. You and your husband should be there too."

When we got home, I called Kevin and told him what our plans were. Naturally, he wanted to be there.

After school the next day, I drove us to the hospital in Greenville. It was a quiet ride. I think we were all afraid to hope that my father would succeed in bringing Amy out of her coma.

Amy had been moved out of ICU to a private room, so we were all able to be in her room at the same time. She was still hooked up to several tubes and her vital signs blinked from the machine at the head of her bed.

My father sat down next to her and placed his hand on her forehead. With his eyes closed, he began to speak to her mind. I could hear his voice in my head too.

Amy, dear, it's time for you to come back to us. Your parents and your friends miss you very much. Kevin is heartsick because he blames himself for the accident that caused your injury New Year's Eve. We know that you're a strong, healthy young woman. It's time for you to wake up and open your eyes. We're all here at your bedside, just waiting to talk to you again so we can tell you how important you are to all of us. Wake up, Amy.

The only sound in the room was the dull beep from the machine recording her vital signs. The five of us were barely breathing, our eyes fixed on Amy's pale face.

Her head turned to the side slightly, facing my father, and her eyes opened slowly.

"Hi, Mr. Blackthorne," she said, her voice scratchy. "Where am I?"

She spotted me standing next to my dad. "Cara? What happened? Where's Kev? Why do I sound like a frog?"

Mr. and Mrs. Strauss were standing on the other side of her bed, holding hands, tears streaming down their faces. At the foot of her bed, Kevin's head was down, his hand over his eyes, his shoulders shaking.

I leaned over my father's shoulder. "Welcome back, Amy. We've really missed you." My father stood and we left Amy's room, Kevin right behind us. I knew Amy needed to be with her mom and dad. They would explain to her what had happened.

Two days later, after her doctor had run more tests and determined there was absolutely nothing physically or mentally wrong with her, Mr. and Mrs. Strauss brought Amy home. Kevin and I let all her friends at school know that she had recovered from the New Year's Eve accident, and everyone sent messages home to her.

Right after school, Kevin and I drove to her house to see her. For the past two days, we'd only spoken to her over the phone. We were both looking forward to a full-fledged reunion of what we used to call "the three musketeers."

When Amy opened the front door, we were immediately enveloped in a three-way hug with Amy actually hopping up and down and laughing. Her mom was laughing too as she invited us in and promptly sat us down in the den, placing warm apple strudel in front of us.

"Cara, Kevin, you must be hungry. Please eat and I'll bring the coffee in." She bustled back into the kitchen, returning with a fresh pot of coffee. I could smell the cinnamon, her secret ingredient. Everything smelled wonderful.

Amy and Kevin just grinned at each other, holding hands until I cleared my throat. "I hate to break up this little reunion, you two, but hello! There are three of us here, you know." I couldn't help giggling; they were so transparent.

"Cara, I'm sorry," Amy said with a laugh. "I hope you know how happy I am to see *both* of you. And I know we have a lot to talk about, but first, apple strudel. Mom just took it out of the oven, so dig in!"

Despite the big smile that covered her freckled face, Amy had lost quite a bit of weight while she was in the hospital. I was sure Mrs. Strauss would get her back to her fighting weight quickly, especially if she continued to bake apple strudel.

"This is delicious, Mrs. Strauss, thank you." Kevin's mouth was too full for him to speak so he just nodded and winked at Amy's mom. She laughed and returned to the kitchen, giving us some privacy to talk.

When we were finally able to put our forks down, Amy said, "Cara, I have to thank your father. It was as though I was dreaming, one dream after another, until I heard his deep voice. When I heard his words, I knew I had to wake up." She laughed. "I guess I can finally understand how you felt when he began speaking to you mentally. His voice is so great, you know, like velvet. He is totally amazing."

"Yeah, he is. And now you know that you're a Halfling too, like Kevin and me. No wonder we've always been drawn to each other. Even at five, we must have unconsciously known we were alike."

Amy nodded. "When Mom told me about my biological father, I wasn't really surprised, you know? So many things began to make sense. But I love my dad even more now. He's loved me and taken care of me since the day I was born, even though he knew he hadn't actually fathered me. He's such a good man."

I smiled. "Yeah, both your parents are exceptional, Amy. That's why I've always loved spending time here. Well, that and your mom's baking!"

Kevin added, "You really hit the jackpot with your parents, Amy."

THE JOINING TREE

I knew he was thinking of his own situation at home, which really needed improvement. As far as I knew, his mother was still not speaking to his father, who was living in the woods at my father's camp just to be closer to Kevin.

Grinning, Amy asked, "So when can I visit Elvenwood, Cara? You know I've been dying to see the village, especially the old-fashioned kitchen with the huge fireplaces."

"Well, we might have to wait until spring, especially after all the snow we've had. But I promise to take you the first non-freezing day we have."

She was wearing an evil little smile for a minute or two. She met my eyes and then winked. I knew she was thinking of Neal, the Elven bodyguard who had ended their friendship because of his parents' prejudice against "human" girls. I was sure Kevin was aware of it too.

He glanced at me, smiling, and added, "His loss, my gain."

Amy blushed. Her voice was soft as she squeezed Kevin's hand. "He doesn't hold a candle to you, Kev."

CHAPTER 9

Amy would be back in school the following week, just in time for our mid-term exams. When she realized how much time she'd lost in school, she began to panic, but Kevin assured her he would help her catch up, starting that very day. He had all of her school books and the homework she'd missed.

"With Kevin tutoring you, you have nothing to worry about," I told her. "Remember, he's the one responsible for that "B" I got on my Trig exam last year."

Her eyebrows went up. "Yeah, that's right. You thought you were going to flunk Trig."

Kevin gave her a one-armed hug and grinned. "You're in good hands now, Red."

I just smiled. All was right with my best friends again. And that was more important than anything else.

Mid-terms would begin in exactly four days. Because of basketball practice every afternoon, Sean had to do his studying at night. I hadn't even started. Our plan had been to study together, but life—and basketball—had gotten in the way. I didn't really think I'd fail anything, but my grades wouldn't impress anyone either.

As soon as my daily trips to the hospital ended, Sean asked if I'd like him to come over in the evenings so he could help me cram for mid-terms. I agreed immediately.

Mom and Dad stayed out of the kitchen so that Sean and I could study at the kitchen table. With only three nights left before our exams would begin, I needed all the help I could get.

"You don't remember any of the recent material?" he asked, obviously surprised.

I shook my head, embarrassed. "I wasn't able to think about anything other than Amy and Kevin during our classes." I snorted. "Multi-tasking isn't one of my talents."

"Okay. My notes will help." They were, as usual, thorough and detailed.

I muttered, "I don't know how I'm gonna get through the course work in Art school without you. Your notes are so complete."

He smiled. "Too bad Barrett doesn't have a baseball team." I had to laugh.

I tried to discipline my easily distracted brain. I'd be visiting The Barrett Art Institute's Dean of Students later this month, and I didn't want her to decide that I was talented but dumb. My GPA was not going to knock her socks off.

Our mid-term exams weren't as bad as I'd expected, thanks to Sean's notes. I managed to score B's and one surprising A in Environmental Science! The A in Art was a given, of course. Mom invited Sean over for lasagna to celebrate.

Our celebratory dinner was fun, especially because Mom and Dad were so pleased with the two A's I'd received. This was not a common occurrence for me. I had to give Sean most of the credit for my better than usual grades.

When I walked Sean to the front door later that evening, his hugs were tighter, his kisses more passionate, and I realized I'd let his feelings for me go on for too long.

Despite the fact that he knew I wasn't in love with him, I suspected he might think my attraction to him would turn into love eventually.

I knew it wouldn't. My heart belonged to Adam Wolfe. That would never change.

My appointment with Barrett's Dean of Students was for the last Friday in January. Mom and Dad weren't thrilled when I insisted on going alone.

"Mom, I don't want the people at Barrett to think I'm not capable of doing anything without my mother by my side!"

"Cara, you're still only sixteen. I know how you feel about this, but you're *not* an adult yet!"

"But I want to be *thought of* as an adult when I'm studying at Barrett. I won't even be gone all day; I'll leave here before lunch and I'll be home in time for dinner."

My parents looked at each other rather helplessly.

"What if I go with you?" my dad asked.

"Dad, I'll still feel like a child. I think I can handle one afternoon away from home."

He shook his head. "But you'll be more than a hundred miles away from home. What if you have car trouble? What if it snows?"

I sighed. "I have triple-A for car trouble, and there's no snow forecast. Dad, you and Mom worry too much."

Reluctantly, they finally agreed I could make the trip alone. When I told Sean, he made the same face my father had made.

"Cara, I'd go with you if I didn't have a game Friday night."

"I'll be fine. You all worry too much. I'll have to take a day off from school, but I should be home in time for dinner. I might even make the game."

Friday I set off for Syracuse alone, feeling like an adult who was certainly capable of handling her life away from home. It was a heady feeling, and I was really excited.

At two o'clock I met with Mrs. Barrett, the granddaughter of the founder, as well as the Dean of Students. I liked her immediately. Gray-haired and cheerful, she went through my portfolio of drawings and paintings slowly, finally looking up at me.

"Cara, this is excellent work. I think our art instructors will have their hands full trying to challenge you."

"Mrs. Barrett, I've just begun working with watercolors. I have a lot to learn. Most of the work in my portfolio was done in pencil and pen and ink. The watercolors are the newest. I'm still developing my technique with paint."

Nodding, she smiled. "Well, you could make a career with just your pen and ink drawings. They're exquisite. Where were they drawn?"

"Blackthorne Forest. The forest begins where my backyard ends and I've spent most of my life in those woods."

She smiled. "You've given those woods a mystical, romantic look. They're charming. Do you have a mentor?"

"Well, yes. An old friend of my father's has taken a real interest in my artwork. Both he and my Art teacher have encouraged me to work with watercolors. His name is Francis Sullivan."

Her eyes widened instantly. Then she laughed. "Well, there's nothing like starting at the top, Cara. You couldn't have a more talented mentor. I have always loved his work."

We left her office and she took me on a mini-tour, stopping in all the various art classes, specializing in oils, watercolors, and acrylics, and then their photography studio. The instructors in each class came over and introduced themselves, all of them seeming surprised that I would be a new student in the fall, and all of them asking my age.

When we walked out of the last class, Mrs. Barrett smiled and explained, "Cara, you don't look old enough to be out of high school, but when they see your work, I think they'll quickly forget how young you are."

I hoped she was right. During the past twenty minutes, I had gone from feeling quite adult to feeling like a child!

At three-thirty I left her office and walked to my car parked behind the administration building. The sky showed a heavy gray cloud cover, and I began to worry.

At three-forty, it began to snow, my windshield becoming a solid sheet of white in seconds. I turned on my windshield wipers, which succeeded in allowing me to see only a few feet ahead. There was almost no visibility. I saw a van ahead with its flashers on so I pulled over to the curb behind it and parked, sighing deeply. My parents had been right to worry. There was no way I'd be making it home tonight.

I called Mrs. Barrett on my cell and asked if there was a decent motel nearby. She was obviously surprised at the sudden change in the weather

THE JOINING TREE

and told me to come right back to her office. Thankfully, I had only driven a few blocks from campus when I had to stop.

The van I'd parked behind turned off its flashers and pulled out right in front of my car, which at least gave me another vehicle to follow. I couldn't see further than the van in front of me so I hoped he was going in the same direction. We turned a few corners, passing houses and signs I remembered seeing on my way to Barrett, which was reassuring.

He stopped at the next corner, his headlights shining into Barrett's parking lot entrance, and I breathed a huge sigh of relief. My unintentional Good Samaritan turned left and I drove straight into the parking lot, stopping in front of the administration building. Outside my car, everything was white with only a few lights showing in the distance.

I saw Mrs. Barrett standing in the doorway waving at me, so I guessed it was okay to leave my car parked there. I got out and sprinted to her office door where a sudden gust of wind practically blew me in.

"Cara, it's a good thing you didn't get very far. I'm sure we can put you up for the night in one of our dorms. A number of our students left early for the weekend. I just hope they all made it home before this storm hit. I wouldn't want any of you out on the roads tonight. I'll go get my coat. You'd better call home and let them know you're safe."

While she returned to her office, I called Mom. The storm hadn't reached Thornewood yet, so she was surprised to hear that I couldn't make it home.

"Mrs. Barrett says I can stay in one of the dorms tonight, so I'll be fine. Please don't worry. I'll drive back as soon as the roads are open tomorrow."

Mom spared me an 'I told you so,' and just said, "Be careful, dear. Stay as long as you have to. We want you home in one piece."

As Mrs. Barrett walked me to the nearest dorm, we passed the bookstore, and I asked if I could purchase a few things I'd need overnight. She said she was sure I'd find what I needed.

The bookstore was really more of a general store, stocking toiletries, t-shirts, art supplies and stationery. There seemed to be only one person taking care of the store, but I quickly found a toothbrush, toothpaste, deodorant, and an extra-large Barrett t-shirt. I thought that would hold me for one night.

When I walked to the register at the front of the store, the young man who seemed to be the only employee looked at my items and smiled at me. "You must have been caught by our typical winter weather. Staying overnight?"

"Yes. I'll have to stay in one of the dorms tonight. I hope I'll be able to drive home tomorrow." I heard a radio in the background and asked, "Have you heard the weather report yet?"

"Yep. It's supposed to snow all night, clearing sometime in the morning. You should be able to hit the road by tomorrow afternoon."

I smiled at him. "Thanks."

We left and Mrs. Barrett led me to a dorm building situated right behind the bookstore.

We walked to the end of the hallway on the first floor, stopping to knock on the door of number 112. Mrs. Bennett turned to me and said, "While you were calling your mother, I called the S.A.—that's our Student Advisor—and asked who had left for the weekend."

The door opened and a tiny brown-eyed girl with a pale blonde pixie cut peered out at us curiously. "Hi, Mrs. Bennett. Who's this?"

"Lily, this is Cara Blackthorne. She was here for a meeting with me this afternoon, and, unfortunately, has been stranded by this unexpected snowstorm. Since your roommate left for the weekend, I hope you won't mind having an overnight guest."

The tiny blonde grinned. "Not at all. Come on in, Cara." She looked up at Mrs. Bennett. "You've brought me the perfect model, Mrs. B." Turning to me, "You will model for me, won't you?"

I shrugged. "Sure, I guess." Then I had a disturbing thought. "I can keep my clothes on, right?"

Chuckling, Mrs. Bennett said, "You must have visited one of our Life Drawing classes on your first trip to Barrett."

I nodded. She rolled her eyes.

Laughing, Lily said, "Don't worry. Of course you can keep your clothes on. I really just want to photograph your face." She moved around me, looking at me from several different angles. "Your face has a certain elfin quality, Cara, as though you might sprout wings and fly away at any moment."

I could feel my face flush slightly when she used the term "elfin." Hopefully, she hadn't noticed.

Beaming, Mrs. Bennett said, "I think I can leave you in good hands, Cara. I hope you'll enjoy spending the night with us. I live on campus so I'll be in my office tomorrow. Please stop by before you leave for home."

I said I would and she left, closing Lily's door on her way out.

Lily grabbed a few pieces of clothing off the other bed and said, "Sit. Be comfortable." As she pulled out a drawer built into one wall, she folded the clothing that had been lying on the bed and tucked it away. "These built-in drawers are how we deal with these tiny rooms. My roommate and I both have to keep our clothing to a minimum, I'm afraid. Will you be moving into a dorm when you start attending Barrett?"

"No, my parents want to rent an apartment for me off campus." I smiled. "I think the term, 'co-ed housing' scared them a little."

"Not surprised. I hope you're not as young as you look, Cara."

"Sixteen. I'll be seventeen in June."

"Ah. You *are* as young as you look. Well, that may actually protect you somewhat. Most of the guys here won't want to take advantage of someone your age, but there are always one or two with no scruples at all."

"That won't be a problem. I'll be here to work on my art, not date. I'm not really planning on having much of a social life, Lily. I plan to go home every weekend, weather permitting."

"Don't you like boys?" she asked.

"Sure I do, but only as friends, nothing more."

Looking confused, she asked, "Well, do you like girls?"

It finally dawned on me what she was getting at. I laughed. "I'm not gay. But, to be honest, there's only one man in my life, and he's not really *in* my life. I know that sounds weird, but it's just that he moved away and I think he took my heart with him. I don't want anyone else."

She nodded. "Ooh, unrequited love? Sounds like a sad story."

I wasn't sure how I got on that particular subject since it's one I usually avoided.

"I don't really think it was unrequited. Just not approved of by my mother. He's older . . . or I'm too young . . . or something." I sighed deeply.

She nodded, looking sympathetic. But then she stood up, announcing, "For me, Cara, it's out of sight, out of mind. I may try to convert you when you're here in the fall.

"Now put your coat back on, we've got to go out to the Café and get something to eat. It's dinner time!"

It was still snowing heavily, but Lily took my hand and steered me toward the Café, located in the middle of the campus. The wind was blowing the snow right into our faces, so entering the warm café that smelled of Italian food was like reaching an oasis at the North Pole.

It was spaghetti night at the Café and the food was excellent—and cheap! I knew my mother would have loved it. And being a non-cook, I also knew I'd be eating a lot of my meals here in a few months.

Lily and I chatted over dinner, becoming acquainted quickly. After dinner, she bought a bag full of cookies, made at the Café, and we fought our way through the blinding snowstorm back to her dorm.

We spent the evening munching on cookies while I posed for her and she took what seemed like hundreds of pictures of me. I gave her my email address and asked her to send me a few once they were developed.

"It will be my pleasure, Cara. You're a wonderful model. I think this group of photos will make a great display next time we have a show on campus." She giggled. "You'll already be well known by the time you get here in the fall."

"Oh! Everyone will see these pictures?" I wasn't expecting that.

"Yep. Everyone on campus. Your face will be familiar to all the students who will be back next year. Actually, it might make you feel more at home here. Everyone will be smiling at you, thinking they already know you!"

I actually got a good night's sleep when we finally turned in around midnight. The cot-size bed was comfortable and her roommate's down comforter was a blessing once the dorm's heat was turned down for the night.

The snow had stopped by the time we woke up and after we slogged through three feet of snow to get breakfast at the Café, we watched the TV there to find out about road conditions.

A few of Lily's friends drifted over to our table, introduced themselves, and joined us in checking the post-storm reports.

The young man from the bookstore asked, "How far do you have to drive to get home, Cara?"

"Normally, it's a two-hour drive, but I'm afraid it will take longer today. I have snow tires so that will help, but I've never had to drive in these conditions before."

Lily asked, "Nervous?"

I just nodded, watching the continuing reports on road conditions.

We had lunch at the café—croissants stuffed with ham and cheese, absolutely delicious—and finally, it was announced the main roads were clear with traffic moving only a little slower than normal. It was time for me to go home. I was surprised to realize I didn't really want to leave.

I thanked Lily for her hospitality, promising to keep in touch via email, and walked back to the administration building to say goodbye to Mrs. Barrett.

Although the side streets were still not completely clear of snow, once I reached the highway, I was fine. The main roads were wet but not covered with snow. I turned up the music I was playing, one of Mom's Golden Oldies CD's, and sailed home, singing along to The Four Tops, happy that I'd be returning to Barrett in only seven months.

Mom and Dad wanted to hear all about my trip to Barrett. They were obviously relieved that I hadn't tried to drive home during a snowstorm, but pleased my meeting with Mrs. Bennett had gone well and that I'd even made a few new friends.

When I told Amy and Kevin about my trip and about the surprise blizzard, they both frowned, which didn't surprise me. They both knew how much damage icy roads could do, but I reassured them that I didn't get far before I turned around and went back to Barrett.

Amy thought it was great I had already made a new friend who was studying photography. "When she sends you those pictures, don't forget to forward them to Kevin and me." She grinned. "I'm sure Sean will want to see them too."

We were sitting in the kitchen, drinking hot chocolate. Kevin always planned ahead; he had brought the marshmallows.

He said, "So the photos she took of you will be part of an art exhibition at the school?"

"Yeah. She thinks by the time I get there in August, everyone on campus will think they already know me. She said it might help me feel more at home."

Kevin added, "First day at Art school and you'll already be semi-famous!"

I rolled my eyes. "I doubt that, Kev."

He laughed, pulling on my ponytail. Which reminded me.

"Amy, I think I need your help. I definitely need a 'stylist'! Everyone I met made a point of telling me how young I look." I groaned. "How can I look older?"

This was Amy's specialty and she was immediately excited. "Finally, Cara! I've been after you to wear a little makeup for years. Makeup and a more mature hairstyle will definitely add a few years. We can work on it between now and this summer. You have so much to learn!" And Amy was in her element. I took a deep breath and simply agreed.

A lot of good things came out of my trip to Syracuse. Meeting Mrs. Bennett and hearing her thoughts about my artwork gave me an added incentive to concentrate on art rather than my social life. Sean was not thrilled with my new attitude, but I did manage to attend a few of his basketball games, followed, of course, by burgers and milkshakes at The Grille. Amy and Kevin always joined us so we weren't actually spending much time alone together.

I thought that was best, but Sean seemed disappointed. I got the feeling that he knew I was slowly pulling away, but also knew there was nothing he could do about it.

Not long after my trip, rumors started making the rounds at school about high school athletes taking drugs. No one thought that would ever happen at Thornewood High. Drugs were something that only happened at larger schools, like Greenville, right?

And then Thornewood lost its Friday night basketball game and rumors began to fly again. Sean joined us at The Grille, clearly upset and depressed after the game.

Kevin asked him if any of the rumors were true.

Sean took a deep breath. "I didn't want to believe it, but two of the guys on the team were just out of it tonight. They didn't seem to know what they were doing, or even why they were doing it. Coach called both of them to his office after the game."

I immediately thought about Joey and Nick Romanov. "Has anyone seen those two guys around town, Sean?"

"Not that I know of, but they could have decided to operate somewhere more private, rather than on street corners, especially since the police have been watching for them."

"I guess we should all be keeping our eyes open," I said. Maybe the little talk I'd had with Joey hadn't had the desired effect.

We didn't have anything to celebrate that night, so we left The Grille, which was quieter than usual, and I dropped Kevin and Amy off at Kevin's so he could drive her home later. It was still fairly early.

After we said goodnight to Amy and Kevin, Sean said, "Cara, I don't really want to go home yet. Can we go somewhere else for a while?"

"What do you want to do?" I asked him.

He was staring out the windshield. "We need to talk. Something's changed. I want to know what's happened." He still sounded unhappy, and it wasn't just about the basketball game.

"Okay." I drove downtown and parked behind Mom's bookstore. It was quiet and no one else was there at night.

I turned the car off, wrapped my parka around me and leaned against the door, facing Sean. I had known this was coming, but it wasn't going to be easy.

He leaned against the passenger door and faced me, leaving a lot of distance between us, which seemed appropriate. We were drifting apart, literally.

"Cara, things between us have been changing for months. At Christmas I thought we seemed closer, but I guess it was just the holidays or something."

His head down, he was quiet for a few minutes. I couldn't argue with anything he'd said.

"I thought Amy being in the hospital was the reason you seemed so distant, but she's fine now, and you're still distant. Yeah, we go out after the games, and we sit together in most of our classes, but something's missing. Especially since your trip to Barrett."

He looked up at me. "You know I love you, and I know your feelings are not the same, but you've got to level with me. I thought we were going to enjoy our senior year together. What's happened?"

How can I explain that I'm in love with someone else without hurting him terribly?

It wasn't going to be easy. But it was more than just Adam.

"Sean, you know that I care about you, right?" He nodded. "Well, my trip to Barrett showed me what my life will be like next year, all the art classes, and art history, living away from home, and so many things I've never experienced before. It excited me, made me want to work even harder on my watercolors. I guess that's all I've been concentrating on; not my social life, not my friends, not my parents, just my art and my future."

I paused for a few minutes. "I realize how selfish that sounds, but it's practically all I've been able to think about." I knew he wouldn't like what I'd say next, but I wanted to be fair to him, without breaking his heart.

"Sean, I think you should probably start dating other girls. You're a great guy and a great friend. You deserve so much more than I can give you."

He was silent for at least a minute. "It won't bother you seeing me out with someone else, will it?" I heard anger in his voice.

He was wrong about that. "It will bother me. I'll probably feel kind of jealous, but I know I'm not being fair to you, so you *should* date other girls. I care more about my art, my future, than anything else right now. That's the truth. But regardless, I'm still your friend. I always will be."

He nodded, turned and faced the windshield again, not looking at me. "You can drive me home now. I guess there's nothing else to say." His voice was full of the hurt he was feeling.

I turned and started the car. I looked at Sean and whispered, "I'm sorry." He didn't look at me, just stared straight ahead.

When I reached his house, he didn't say anything, just looked at me for a few seconds, then got out of the car and went into his house.

I sat there for a minute, feeling a heavy weight on my chest. Then I drove home, feeling like a totally rotten person. I didn't deserve Sean McKay. That was the truth.

When I got home, the look on my face immediately alerted my parents that I was more depressed than usual. A certain amount of depression was accepted these days.

Mom asked, "What's wrong, dear? You look miserable."

My father, always in tune with me emotionally, asked, "Why are you feeling guilty, Cara?"

I tossed off my parka and threw myself into a chair at the kitchen table. "I just told Sean he should be dating other girls. I can't give him what he wants or what he deserves. And I hate feeling like I'm using him."

My father just nodded. I knew he understood.

Mom's voice was soft. "This is still because of your feelings for Adam, isn't it?"

"Yeah, but it's also because I want to concentrate on art right now. I don't want to concentrate on being in love or anything else. I know how selfish that is, but I feel I need to put my goals first. I don't really want to spend the rest of my senior year trying to make Sean happy when I already know we'll break up before we both leave for college. There's no future for us as anything but friends."

"Sweetheart, I think being honest with Sean was the right thing to do." My father looked into my eyes, understanding clear in those green eyes. "Sean's a decent young man. You know we like him, but you know he's not the right one for you. He needed to know that too."

Mom asked, "You didn't tell him about your feelings for Adam, did you?"

I shook my head. "I couldn't hurt him that much."

She looked sad. "You're not planning on trying to enjoy your last year in high school with your friends, are you?"

"No, Mom. I'm looking ahead. My last year of high school just isn't that important to me."

What I didn't say was that if I couldn't have the one I loved, I didn't want anyone.

Rather than have Amy corner me in the morning to find out why Sean and I both looked so miserable, I called her before I went to bed.

"Amy, have you got a few minutes to talk?"

"Uh-oh. I know that tone of voice. What happened after we left you tonight?"

"Sean wanted to talk. Things between us haven't been the same. He wanted to know why."

"You didn't tell him about Adam, did you?"

"No. That would have been too cruel. Basically, I said I thought he should be dating other girls because I can't give him what he wants. I told him I knew I wasn't being fair to him."

"Even that must have been hard for him to hear, Cara."

I sighed. "Yeah. I know I hurt him. I hated to do it. But he does deserve more."

"Well, what about the rest of our senior year?"

"Amy, you and Kevin have each other. I don't think you'll miss socializing with me. A lot of things changed for me after my trip to Barrett. I got a look at what my life will be like next year, and I loved it. I just want to work toward that, focus on art, not on boyfriends."

"You know, you'll have to sit next to Sean four classes a day, five days a week, until the semester ends."

I groaned. "Yeah. That's not going to be easy. I hope we can continue to talk to each other, but that's up to him, you know?"

"I know. But if I know Sean, he'll continue to be the gentleman he's always been."

I hoped she was right.

Amy was usually right. I didn't hear from Sean Saturday or Sunday, but Monday in class he said hi, loaned me a pen when I couldn't find mine, and moved my bag before I fell over it. But he wasn't smiling. He was a perfect gentleman, as always. And I still felt heartless.

Rather than walking with me between classes, he walked with other friends we always saw in the halls, clearly leaving me behind. Of course, that attracted a few confused glances from our friends, but I couldn't blame him so I just smiled and tried to look cheerful.

I had an uncomfortable twinge in the vicinity of my heart when I realized I'd be seeing him with other girls before long, but that didn't matter. It was what was best for Sean. I really did want him to be happy.

CHAPTER 10

A week later, Randi stopped me in the hallway at the end of the school day.

"Hi Randi, how are you doing? How are things at home?"

"Everything's great at home, Cara, but I wanted to talk to you. Um, not here, but I need a ride home today. My car's in the shop for a tune up."

"Sure. I have to drop off Kevin and Amy first. Come with us."

"Perfect! Thanks. I'll meet you by the front entrance in two minutes."

She ran to her locker and I walked to the front door to wait for Amy and Kevin. Sean dashed past me, calling out, "See you tomorrow." He was out the front door like a shot, which felt kind of weird.

I didn't wait long before Amy and Kevin reached me, Randi right behind them.

"Hi guys, I'm giving Randi a lift this afternoon."

Amy grinned. "Hey, Randi. Where's your Beamer?"

Randi rolled her eyes. "In the shop for the day. I'm hoping I'll get it back tomorrow." She looked over at Kevin. "How are you guys doing?" She giggled. "Do I have to ask?"

Kevin blushed, of course, but Amy just wrapped her arm around his waist and smiled. "We're doing just fine."

They followed me down the block to my car and I drove Kevin home.

"Short stuff, you can drop Amy at my house. She wants to do a little shopping before she goes home."

"What are you shopping for?" I asked her.

She gave me a 'Mona Lisa' smile. "Oh, just a few things I think will look good on you."

"Hey, Amy, I can pay for my own makeup, you know."

"It's okay, Cara. You have no patience for shopping, but it's my favorite thing. And Kev has lots more patience than you have!" She was beaming, but I heard Kevin groan.

I shook my head and chuckled. "Sorry, Kev. I never meant to inflict this on you."

Randi asked, "What's going on?"

"I think I'm Amy's latest project. She loves projects, especially when they involve hair and makeup!"

Amy added, "Cara finally wants to find a way to look a little older before she starts Art school. And I'm in charge."

I explained. "I visited the Barrett Art Institute recently. Everyone I met asked me how old I was, as though I couldn't possibly be old enough to be out of high school. When I got home, I asked Amy for help."

Grinning, Amy said, "This is gonna be fun!"

We'd reached Kevin's house, said our goodbyes, and I watched them get into Kevin's Jeep.

I pulled away and headed for Randi's condo. "Okay, Randi, what did you want to talk to me about?"

"Actually, two things. First, Joey called me last night. It's been weeks, you know? I really thought he was out of my life. He sounded different, even apologized to me. And then he said something about some things you'd said to him, things that made him think about what he was doing with his life. Cara, when did you talk to him?"

I explained about running into him the day Amy and I had gone to the second-hand clothing store.

"It looked like he was trying to sell drugs to some of those out-of-work guys who hang out down there. Anyway, he saw me, yelled at me, and headed straight for me. He grabbed my arm and I thought he wanted to hurt me, so I, uh, talked to him, trying to make him see that he was only hurting himself."

Randi nodded and said softly, "You mean the way you talked to me the day I tried to hurt you."

"Well, yes. I was just trying to get through to him. I didn't want to be forced to pull a knife on him."

She shook her head, muttering, "Those knives again.

"Cara, we'll talk about your knives later." She hesitated. "What you did to me was a kind of hypnosis, wasn't it?"

I glanced over at her. "Yeah, you could call it that. It seemed to help you. So I tried to do the same thing with Joey. I wasn't sure I succeeded, but he let go of me and got in his SUV and left town. Maybe it helped."

We were almost out of town and it occurred to me that I didn't know where I was going. "Randi, where's the turn-off for your condo? I've never been here before."

She gave me directions and I pulled up in front of a large complex that looked really plush.

"Wow, this place is beautiful."

She directed me to visitor parking. When we got out of my car, I couldn't believe how luxurious the complex was. I saw tennis courts in the distance.

Randi saw me staring at everything and chuckled. "Come on, I'll give you a tour. This complex is really nice."

We walked around the huge Olympic-size pool. The tables and chairs were all covered for the winter, as was the pool, but I could see that this whole entertainment area probably looked like a tropical resort during the summer.

Each condo was a separate cottage, with a small landscaped backyard and individual patio. Randi's condo was farthest from the main gate. It actually backed up to the southern edge of Blackthorne Forest. Despite the trees that had dropped their leaves, this part of the woods was full of evergreens, which always reminded me of Christmas trees.

THE JOINING TREE

"Your condo has a great view of the forest. It's really beautiful out here."

"Yeah, it is. I do love living here. It's like having my very own luxury apartment." She chuckled. "My father is here so rarely, I'm not sure he's ever really seen the whole place."

We walked across her condo's patio and entered through the back door. Inside was modern, sleek, with lots of chrome and glass.

She invited me to sit down on the cinnamon-colored suede couch, and I sunk into the most comfortable couch I'd ever had the pleasure of sitting on. Laughing at the surprised expression on my face, she said, "It's hard to get out of so you might as well relax and enjoy it. Should I make coffee?"

"Yes, please. Coffee would be great."

I could see into the stainless steel and chrome kitchen from where I was sitting. It wasn't big, but it seemed very well equipped.

"Do you cook?"

She smiled. "I'm learning. Someone told me that if I could read a cookbook, I could learn to cook. However, I've found there's a little more to it than that. I've had as many inedible disasters as I've had successes, but I'm getting there."

"Tell me more about your phone call from Joey. You said he apologized."

She walked back into the living room and handed me a cup of coffee, joining me on the wrap-around couch.

"There's not much more to tell. He said he was staying close to home, that he wasn't seeing Nick anymore, which was a surprise. He used to idolize that guy. I was afraid he'd want to see me again, but he just wanted to tell me he was sorry about the way he'd treated me and said he hoped I was happier back in Thornewood." She chuckled. "But he did say he thought my 'little friend' was kind of scary."

I burst out laughing. "I've been called a lot of things, but scary? That's a first."

It was quiet for a minute or two as we drank our coffee. But I sensed there was more she wanted to talk about. It was so peaceful and so comfortable in her father's home, it was easier than usual to talk about the things I usually kept to myself. And I felt I could trust Randi.

"Cara, I've been dying to ask you this. Why do you carry knives? And where did you learn to throw them so accurately? I heard what happened at school months ago when that drive-by aimed a gun at Amy."

I told her about the kidnapping last spring and how I'd spent the summer learning self-defense skills.

"I'd made up my mind that I'd never be a victim again, and that no matter how many bodyguards I had, in the final analysis I would always have to depend on myself. And that was exactly what happened in October when Gaynes tried to kidnap me again. He's in jail now, but I still carry my knives because I feel safer with them."

She looked impressed. "You're carrying knives now?"

"Yep."

"Who taught you these skills? I'd like to learn myself. Even though Joey's apologized, as long as Nick Romanov is still on the loose, I don't feel safe."

"Uh, well, most of the men who work for my father have these skills. They use them working in the forest year round. My dad asked them to train me. Kevin trained with me too; he's a fantastic archer. It was a lot of work, but we did it together so we had fun with it too."

"When I met your father, I was practically speechless. He's so big, and so handsome, a real leading man type, you know?"

I chuckled. "Yeah, I do know, and you're right. Dad's been great. I think he understands me better than my mother does."

"Cara, I hope I'm not out of line, but your dad is . . . uh, different. Almost like he comes from another world. Maybe it's because he spends so much time in the forest. I don't know; he's just different." She looked me in the eye. "And so are you."

If she only knew. Time to change the subject.

"Randi, you said there was something else you wanted to talk to me about."

"Yes, and it's difficult." She frowned, as though she was trying to decide how to say whatever it was.

"It's about Sean."

Oh, crap.

"I know you broke up last June, but you've spent so much time together all year, it seemed as though you were back together. At least, everyone thought so. I hope you won't be mad. Sean called me Sunday, which was a complete surprise. We haven't really talked in more than a year. It seemed as though he just wanted to chat, nothing special, just friendly conversation. We talked for at least a half hour, about all kinds of things, school, college, basketball, baseball, and so on. Then he thanked me for listening and said good night."

I nodded. Sean had always loved long talks on the phone.

"Randi, I think I told you that Sean was not my boyfriend, that we were just friends."

She nodded. "Yeah, I remember."

I took a deep breath. "He wanted more than friendship. I told him, more than once, that I couldn't make that kind of commitment. Last Friday after the game we talked about all of that. I haven't been spending much time with him the past month, and he wanted to know why. I told him I want to concentrate on Art, not on relationships, and I told him I thought he should be dating other girls."

Randi looked surprised. "Ooh. So that's what happened."

I nodded. "I think the world of Sean. He's a great guy and he's been a great friend. I do care about him. But I can't give him what he wants, and I want him to be happy. I really do."

"Cara, I knew something had changed, but I didn't know what. I've always liked Sean. Of course, everyone does. What's not to like, you know? If he ever asks me out, I'd like to say yes. But I wanted to talk to you first.

I hope you know that I won't do anything to hurt you. You've been such a good friend, even though we didn't start out that way." She gave me a rueful smile.

And, of course, I knew what she meant. She'd tried to brain me with a baseball bat a year ago. A lot had changed since then.

"Randi, if he asks you out, you should go. You won't be hurting me and I think you'd be good for Sean." It hurt to say it, but I knew it was the truth.

I looked out the window toward the woods. It was getting dark.

"I'd better get home now. Thanks for the coffee. And for the tour. This place is fantastic!"

She smiled and nodded. "We'll have to do another sleep-over soon. The last one was fun. I'll walk you out to your car."

We put on our parkas and left through the back door. I loved being so close to the forest. "You should spend more time on the patio when the weather gets warm. The forest is such a special place. I've always loved it."

"Yeah, you're right. It generates a kind of peaceful energy. Maybe that's what I've sensed in your dad and you. You've done most of your artwork there, haven't you?"

I nodded.

"The pictures at your house that your mom has framed are wonderful. You have so much talent."

We'd reached the parking area and were talking about my trip to Barrett when a dark figure ran out from behind one of the parked cars and grabbed me around the waist.

I felt something cold against my neck. His voice was angry. "I've been hoping to run into you again. I've got your knife right here." He held me with one strong arm while he pressed a knife to my throat with the other hand.

Randi gasped. "Nick, let her go. I swear I'll call the cops."

I was barely breathing. The knife pricked my skin and I felt blood trickling down my neck. I couldn't reach any of my knives. I was sure he was going to cut my throat.

He laughed. "By the time the cops get out here, I'll be long gone. But before then, I'll make her pay. She ruined my right hand; it's not good for much now. And Joey won't work with me anymore, not since she talked to him. She's a menace. I just want to cut her up a little, leave her with some scars she'll have to live with, like I have to live with this useless hand."

Randi lurched forward suddenly and grabbed the arm holding the knife, pulling it away from my neck. I yanked myself away from him and pulled a knife out of my boot, but before I could throw it, I heard him grunt and saw him slowly fall forward until he landed face down on the ground.

Randi gasped. There was an arrow sticking out of his back. The forest was behind him but I didn't see anyone out there; it was too dark.

I bent down and pressed my fingers to his throat. "He has a pulse. We have to get help."

Randi nodded, still looking shocked.

I pulled out my phone and called the Chief, who arrived in minutes, an ambulance right behind him. When the EMT's had Nick secured in the ambulance, Chief O'Donnell walked over to Randi and me and just looked from one of us to the other for about thirty seconds.

Finally, he asked me, "Where'd the arrow come from, Cara?"

"From the woods. But it was too dark to see anyone there."

He nodded slowly. "Do you think it was one of your father's men?"

"Probably. They're all good with a bow and arrow."

"And you didn't see *anyone*?" he asked.

"No, I didn't, but whoever it was probably saved my life. Nick wanted to cut my throat. He was holding me so tightly, I couldn't reach either of my knives. If Randi hadn't pulled his arm away from my throat, I'm sure he would have cut me."

"How did he know you were here? Do you think he followed you?"

I shrugged. "He must have, Chief. This is the first time I've driven Randi home."

Turning to Randi, he asked, "Has Nick been here before?"

Her eyebrows shot up. "Of course not. I haven't seen him since I moved out of Greenville. He's no friend of mine." She sounded insulted.

"All right, calm down. I'm not accusing you of anything. I'm glad he's in our custody now, but I'd still like to know who shot him. Cara, will your father be home tonight?"

"I think so."

He nodded. "Okay, please let him know I need to see him. By the way, do you need medical attention? I see blood on your neck."

I reached up to feel it, but the blood had already dried. "It's not much more than a scratch, Chief. All I need is a band-aid."

"Okay, I have to go back to the station now." Looking over at Randi, he asked, "Are you all right, Miranda?"

"A strong cup of coffee and I'll be fine, Chief. My dad will be home tomorrow."

He said good night to us and walked back to his cruiser.

I took Randi's arm. "Are you sure you're okay? You're shaking a little."

She just shook her head. "I'll be fine. You should get home now."

"Randi, why don't you come home with me? I don't want you to be alone tonight. Besides, it's spaghetti night at our house, Kevin will be coming over, and I want you with us. Since your dad won't be home until tomorrow, you can stay over. It'll be fun."

She smiled for the first time since Nick appeared. "That really sounds good. Thanks. Let's go back inside so I can throw a few things in a bag and then we can leave."

Helping Randi pack a few things for overnight allowed me to avoid thinking of what my parents were going to say when I told them what had happened. I also remembered to wash off the blood on my neck and put a sheer band-aid over it.

Yep, disaster magnet. Still in perfect working order.

THE JOINING TREE

When we walked into my house, the delicious aroma of Mom's meat sauce hit us in the face, or nose, immediately.

Randi moaned. "Does your house always smell so good?"

I laughed. "Only when Mom's making spaghetti sauce. She uses Italian sausage and beef in her sauce. And lots of garlic, of course."

Kevin was already in the kitchen, doing my usual job, chopping veggies for salad.

"Well, short stuff, you decide to show up now that I've done all the work for you." He snorted and I had to tickle him.

"Stop it, please stop," he wailed. "You know how I hate to be tickled."

"Yeah, and you know how I hate to be heckled."

Randi stood in the door to the kitchen, smiling at us.

"Mom, I invited Randi to join us for dinner, and to stay over tonight. I didn't think you'd mind."

My mother, standing in front of the stove, wooden spoon in hand, turned and said hi to Randi. "Welcome back, Randi. Of course you can join us tonight. There's always plenty to eat on spaghetti night."

Kevin added, "That's actually true every night, Mrs. B. Dinner time at my house, all you can smell is pine cleaner and Comet."

Randi started giggling and I had to join in. Kevin wasn't kidding.

She said, "Your mom doesn't cook, Kev?"

He shook his head. "Nope. She's always working. But she's really good at ordering take out and delivery." He chuckled. "I have my best meals right here."

My father came in the back door smiling, obviously pleased to find the kitchen full of people. "Hello everyone! Alicia, dinner smells incredible. How soon can we eat?"

Mom laughed. "Just as soon as everyone hangs their coats up, and Cara sets the table."

Dad grabbed my coat and Randi's, along with his own, hung them all on hooks by the front door, kissed Mom on his way back, and I set the table quickly.

Mom served the spaghetti covered in thick meat sauce, put a bowl of salad and some fresh Italian bread on the table, and we all sat down for dinner. I was glad everyone would be well fed and content before I had to explain to my parents what had gone down this afternoon. Randi and I exchanged glances. She knew exactly what I was thinking. But we weren't about to let that spoil spaghetti night.

When we were finished eating, I picked up the bottle of wine on the counter and refilled Mom's and Dad's glasses. I wanted them as relaxed as possible.

Dad said, "Thanks, sweetheart," but Mom gave me a suspicious look.

"Cara, should we be bracing ourselves for some unpleasant news?"

Of course, that was when the doorbell rang.

I attempted a reassuring smile as I went to the front door to let the Chief in.

As he came in the front door, I asked, "Would you like coffee or wine, Chief?"

He looked down at me and asked, "Have you told them what happened?"

"Uh, no. We just finished eating. I was planning on bringing it up after dinner."

He shook his head. "Well, at least we won't be ruining anyone's appetite. Make mine coffee, black."

Half an hour later, we had filled in my parents, calmed them down, and the Chief had assured them that Nick Romanov was in the hospital, under police guard, in serious condition, but was expected to recover. At that time, he'd be charged with selling drugs and with the assault on me.

My father looked the most upset. He knew the arrow must have been shot by one of his men, but no one had reported it to him, which he said was surprising.

"I'll be meeting with all of my men tomorrow, Tom. I'll get to the bottom of it then. I hope you're not planning on charging one of them for trying to protect my daughter."

"No, Brian, there won't be any charges. I'll handle the paperwork the way I always do when anyone from Elvenwood is involved." He rolled his eyes.

That was when I realized how much fancy footwork the Chief always had to do when one of us was involved in any trouble. We'd written first-person reports and signed affidavits a few times, but we'd never had to go to court to testify against anyone. And that was all thanks to Chief O'Donnell.

My father nodded. "Thanks, Tom. I'll be in touch after I've spoken to my men."

The Chief finished his coffee and said good night. As I walked him to the door, he smiled and said, "I'm glad you weren't hurt this time, Cara."

Kevin was talking to Randi when I got back in the kitchen. "You're the hero this time, Randi. You took a real chance grabbing his arm when there was a knife in his hand."

She shrugged. "I wasn't thinking. I just wanted to get that knife away from Cara's throat. I feel so responsible, you know? If I hadn't been dating Joey, Nick would never have met Cara, and none of this would have happened." She put her head down, closing her eyes for a few seconds.

My dad shook his head. "Randi, you can't be blamed for any of this. Nick and Joey were responsible for their actions. Kevin's right. You took a big chance when you tried to help Cara. Alicia and I are grateful."

Randi looked at me. "You have no idea how much I owe Cara. I've never had a friend like her before." She reached out and squeezed my hand.

"I never did thank you earlier, did I? I guess seeing that arrow in Nick's back pushed everything else out of my mind. I owe you a big one, Randi."

THE JOINING TREE

After Kevin hugged all of us, he went home with a plastic container of spaghetti that he insisted he would eat for breakfast. Mom just laughed, and Randi and I went upstairs to my room with a pot of herbal tea to help us relax.

After we'd changed into our pajamas and had our tea, Randi asked, "What's Sean going to say when he hears about this? He got in Nick's face too, didn't he?"

I sighed. "Actually, Sean got in Joey's face first, but he was right there when I threw my knife at Nick's hand." Groaning, I said, "Kevin's probably calling Amy right now. Then Amy will call Sean. Sean doesn't call me at night anymore, but he may tonight, just to ask me if I'm okay. That's the kind of guy he is." I shook my head. "I really don't deserve him."

I was telling Randi about everything I'd seen at Barrett, and the cool people I'd met there, when the phone rang. Randi looked at me with a sad little smile.

Of course it was Sean.

"I'm fine, really. I just got a scratch on my neck. When Nick recovers from that arrow wound, he's going away for a while. He won't bother us again. Randi saved me today. Actually, I'm not sure what happened first; the arrow that hit him in the back, or Randi knocking Nick's arm away from my neck. I don't know which of Dad's men did the shooting, but I'll thank him when we find out.

"Yeah, thanks for calling, Sean. Good night."

I put the phone down and shook my head. "I *really* don't deserve him."

Looking thoughtful, Randi said, "Cara, I can't date Sean. He's obviously in love with you. I can't compete with that."

"Randi, he deserves someone who can return his feelings. I can't."

She chuckled. "I can't help it, Cara. You must be out of your everlovin' mind. Sean McKay is every girl's *dream!*"

And she was right. But my dreams were of someone else.

Just before we drifted off to sleep, Randi asked, "By the way, the Chief mentioned Elvenwood. What is that, Cara?"

"Oh, just the area where my father's workers stay; sort of a camp, not a real place."

Sounding half asleep, she mumbled, "Oh."

The next day my father spoke to every one of his men who had been in the forest the day before and found out who had shot that arrow into Nick Romanov's back. It was Gavin, my former disgraced bodyguard.

He'd been working in the southern part of the forest that day and was walking back to camp along the edge of the woods when he saw Randi and me walking to my car. He was about to walk out of the woods to say hello to us when he saw Romanov dash out from behind a parked car and grab me.

When Gavin saw that Romanov was holding a knife to my throat and heard his threats, he didn't hesitate. His arrow hit Romanov in the back a split second later. When he saw the police and ambulance arrive, and could see that I hadn't been hurt, he went back to camp.

My father didn't seem as surprised as I thought he'd be. "After everything that happened last year, Cara, I knew if Gavin ever had another chance to protect you, he wouldn't hesitate. He knows how much he owes you."

I'd forgiven Gavin a long time ago, a lot sooner than the rest of Elvenwood had.

CHAPTER 11

For the rest of the winter, nothing else too dramatic happened. My life was actually peaceful. Sean and I coexisted peacefully in class five days a week. Kevin and I took turns driving to school peacefully Monday through Friday, although I still had to remind him to slow down. Kevin hadn't lost his lead foot.

Valentine's Day came and went. Amy, Kevin, and I exchanged insulting cards like we did every year. Even Sean dropped a funny card on my desk that morning. It was only mildly insulting and made me laugh, which he enjoyed.

A couple of times a week, I bundled up at night and went out on the back porch to sing Rowenna's song. She wasn't out flying during the frigid winter weather, but I heard her rusty voice faintly saying, *Thank you, Cara.*

I spent my afternoons and weekends painting almost non-stop. Francis Sullivan had sent me a message through my father that he had an art show scheduled in April, and he wanted me to exhibit some of my work along with his. I was determined to have some good watercolor paintings finished in time.

Naturally, it continued to snow off and on, so there was that to deal with. I hadn't had a chance to ride Storm in months. I hadn't been able to visit Elvenwood either. I missed the village, my friends there, and especially my beautiful grey.

Finally around the end of March, the weather warmed up temporarily—I knew winter wasn't done with us yet—and I was able to ride Storm to Elvenwood for the day. My father had been riding back and forth all winter to make sure all was well in the village. His big grey, Smoke, was apparently strong enough to ride through any kind of lousy weather, even blizzards.

I had my art portfolio strapped to Storm's saddle and it was pure pleasure riding him again. He greeted me happily with snorts and whinnies, and I hugged him around his dark gray neck and told him how much I'd missed him. We were both happy to be together again. Most of the snow had melted in the forest, making it an easy ride to Elvenwood.

My father had business in the village that day, so he and Smoke were right behind us. The sun had come out, teasing us that spring might not be too far away.

When we rode into Elvenwood, I immediately felt the village's magic surround me and I began to feel happier than I had in months. Elvenwood always had that effect on me.

We pulled up in front of my father's cottage, thanked the greys for a good ride, and sent them to the stable. I carried my portfolio into the cottage and my father lit the fireplace to heat water for tea.

I had barely put down my portfolio before Roscoe barreled into me, greeting me so joyfully, you'd think he hadn't seen me for a year. Which, to a dog, is probably what these last months had seemed like. I sat on the floor in front of the fireplace with the happy dog, rubbing his ears and scratching his back. I didn't live here in Elvenwood, but at that moment it felt like I'd come home.

We had our tea together and then Elvenwood's residents began to arrive to meet with my father. After I'd said hello to everyone, I took my portfolio over to Francis Sullivan's studio.

I walked around his cottage to the studio and knocked on the door. I heard, "Come in, Cara." I don't know how he did it. He had to be psychic.

He was wiping paint off his hands as he walked to the door to greet me. Wearing a big smile, he wrapped one arm around my shoulders. "Welcome back. We've all missed you this winter, Cara."

With a twinkle in his blue eyes, he asked, "What have you brought me?"

I opened my portfolio and spread out a few watercolor paintings and some of my older pen and ink drawings on his table. "I think these are my best, Francis."

He bent over the table, examining each one closely, finally standing up with a pleased smile. "Two of your watercolors are excellent, Cara. You've painted autumn in the forest with the most glorious mixture of colors. Both of them are wonderful and I am sure they will sell, if you're interested in selling them, of course."

He walked back to my pen and ink drawings. "I believe you've been calling these your 'Elf' drawings. I've always loved them. I'd like to display four of them." He pointed to the four that were my favorites, where I'd drawn Ian up in an apple tree, Melissa in the woods, Ian hiding behind a rose bush, and, of course, my drawing of Adam leaning against a tree next to the duck pond. The Elves were mostly hidden, looking like fantasy figures within the multiple shades of the forest's greens and browns in summer.

"Cara, your pen and ink drawings are masterful, truly. Your watercolors are coming along very nicely, but these two are the only ones I think should be shown this year." He looked down at me and smiled. "I'm quite sure they will improve every year."

I told him about my visit to Barrett Art Institute. "Mrs. Barrett, the Dean of Students, said she thought I could make a career out of just pen and ink. What do you think?"

"Well, yes, you could concentrate on just pen and ink. But I really think you can do so much more, Cara. Your watercolors show real promise. The two I selected to be shown are as good as anything I've seen. I just don't want you to limit yourself. You have so much potential." He smiled. "Frankly, dear, I think you've barely scratched the surface so far."

I was floored. "Uh, thank you, Francis. I appreciate all the advice you've given me. You're really helping me stay focused."

He nodded. "Good. Now leave these six pictures with me. I'll have them framed here in the woodshop and then one of the men, probably your father, will take them to Mr. Callahan. He'll meet with my agent who will transport them to the art exhibition in April. It will be in Albany. Harry can give you all the details."

"You're not going, are you?"

He laughed. "No, Cara, I don't travel anymore. Frankly, I don't have to. My work is so well known now. But I would encourage you to be there. This will be the first public showing of your work, and art buyers and critics like to meet the artist." He chuckled. "They will all be amazed how young you are, and how very talented."

"Thank you, Francis. I'd better let you get back to work."

"I'll see you soon, Cara. Keep working on your watercolors; they're getting better all the time."

I left his studio and walked over to Kathleen's. I hadn't seen her since the first snowfall. My visit with Francis had left me excited and I guess it showed.

Kathleen greeted me with a warm hug and we sat down in her cottage, which resembled a small clinic more than a home. But since she was the village healer, that's what was needed.

"Cara, I haven't seen you for so long. I have visited your mother a few times, but you were always in school. I've missed you!"

I had missed her too. Kathleen had become a good friend during the past year.

She smiled. "Your mother has kept me up to date with what's been going on in your life, dear. And I know you two have had your problems, but all mothers and daughters go through the same thing at about your age. All part of growing up, I think."

"Yes, I guess so. Things at home are more peaceful now." I didn't add that I still held my mother responsible for Adam leaving back in October. Kathleen must have read my mind.

"Cara, I know that Adam left after your parents' wedding. And I know that was a terrible blow to you. I can guess why, dear." She patted my hand, her eyes sympathetic.

I knew Kathleen understood, but I was still determined to put it out of my mind.

"That's over and done with. I'm concentrating on my artwork now. I'll be starting art school in a few months. I don't have time for distractions."

"And isn't Francis Sullivan showing some of your work with his own this spring?"

I smiled, my spirits restored. "Yes, it's so exciting! He's giving me the kind of start that most artists don't get. I'm so grateful to him."

"Well, dear, I don't think he'd be doing it if your work wasn't exceptional."

"Thanks, Kathleen." I stood. "I'd better get back. I haven't seen Ian yet."

She laughed. "Prepare yourself. Ian has grown since last autumn."

We said goodbye and I walked back to my dad's cottage, waving at a few villagers I passed. Everyone had a smile and a "Welcome back" for me.

I was almost at Dad's cottage when a boy burst out of the cottage across the road and raced to my side, arms outstretched. It was Ian, who was now almost as tall as I was!

The last time I saw him, he almost reached my shoulder. He had apparently shot up at least four inches in the past few months.

"Cara, finally!" He hugged me, grinning hugely. "I've missed you. Actually, I think everyone in Elvenwood has missed you. Welcome back!"

I just stared at him, hardly believing my eyes. "Ian, how old are you anyway?"

Laughing, he said, "I'm eight now."

"Ian, are all eight-year-olds this tall?"

"Yes. I'm a normal height for eight. I don't think I realized how small *you* are!"

I snorted. "Don't rub it in. But it was nice being taller than *someone* for a while."

"How long are you staying?" he asked.

"Just a little longer. I came to visit Francis Sullivan and show him my latest artwork. He's invited me to show my work along with his at an Art Show next month. It's a great honor."

"I'm not surprised. Your drawings are wonderful. My parents think so too."

"Thank you, Ian. I'd better go in and see when my father wants to leave. As soon as the weather gets warmer, I'll be visiting more often."

His freckled face serious, he said, "I hope so, Cara. I've really missed you."

I hugged him and he ran back to his cottage while I went inside.

My father was alone, sorting through a stack of paperwork. "It's time for more tea, dear. Would you make some for us?"

I added more water to the pot, got it boiling, and poured it over the tea in the teapot. I carried the teapot over to the table where he was working and poured a cup for each of us.

"Thank you, sweetheart. I had to speak with so many people this afternoon, my throat is really dry.

I sat down with him and told him about Francis Sullivan's plans for me.

He looked delighted. "Cara, that's wonderful, but I'm not at all surprised. Your art deserves to be shown. Which pieces does he want to use?"

I described the two watercolors and the four pen and ink Elf drawings.

"I'm sure the public will love your work, dear."

He looked over my shoulder out the front window and chuckled. "We'd better finish our tea. It just started to snow."

I groaned and we drank our tea quickly, bundled up and left the cottage, heading for the stable. Will had saddled up our greys at the first sight of snow.

Laughing, he said, "Well, I'll have to say 'hello' and 'goodbye', lass. We'll just hope for an early Spring."

I gave Will a quick hug, we mounted our greys, and rode out of Elvenwood as the village took on the charming appearance of a Christmas card. Snow was falling softly on the picturesque cottages with their thatched roofs. It was a beautiful scene.

Storm seemed to enjoy running on new snow and took the lead back to my father's camp. Throughout the forest, the falling snow turned the scenery all around us to something magical. We saw deer run past us, seeking shelter, and I was sorry when the ride was over. Everything looked beautiful as the snow fell.

As pretty as it was right now, I was still not a fan of winter.

It wasn't long before the snow melted and we were able to exchange our heavy winter parkas for lightweight jackets and sweaters. When most of my winter clothes had been stored away, I was happy. Winter was finally over for another year.

I had finally received the photos Lily had taken of me at Barrett. She had made me look so good, I barely recognized myself. She emailed me that the photo collage she was putting together was going to be spectacular.

Harry Callahan had called to ask for a photo of me to use for the art show. It was perfect timing. When I asked Lily if we could use one of her photos, she was delighted.

The art show in Albany was only a week away and Mom decided to go with me. My dad chose to stay home because, as he put it, he attracted too much attention, which he felt belonged to me. I appreciated his thoughtfulness, so typical of my father.

We were sitting in the kitchen after dinner one night when Mom said, "Albany is a much longer drive than Syracuse, Cara, so I think we'll have to stay at a hotel and drive back the next day."

I'd never stayed in a hotel before. When I mentioned that to my mother, she just smiled. "You'll probably enjoy it."

The opening of the art show was on Saturday and would continue until the following Friday, when it would close, making room for another artist's show. As I packed for our trip, my nerves were getting the better of me. My artwork was going to be shown to the public for the first time. I had no idea whether it would be well received. Was I even ready?

Naturally, it rained on Saturday. Mom took one look out the window and asked me if she could do the driving. It was a long drive, so I said yes. She said her little compact car needed a long highway drive, which was fine with me.

Other than the rain, it wasn't a bad drive. We reached Albany a few hours before the art show and had plenty of time to check into a hotel and change our clothes.

Francis Sullivan had told me that most of the people who attended an Art show on the first night would be fairly wealthy people and would be dressed accordingly. Therefore, skirts would be required, whether I liked it or not. Mom loaned me her little black dress for the occasion so that I would look more "professional." Fortunately, it fit me. She brought a tailored black suit for herself.

Amy and I had been practicing with hairstyles that would make me look older, and we had settled on a sleek chignon at the nape of my neck. I thought it added a few years, but Mom just smiled and told me I looked lovely. In other words, in her eyes, I still looked like a teenager. She loaned me her jade earrings and I knew there was nothing more I could do.

The Art Gallery wouldn't be open until four o'clock, so we had a little time to relax at the hotel. I loved our room. It was equipped with a refrigerator, a microwave, and a coffee maker. "I could live here," I told Mom.

She laughed. "I think you'd get tired of microwaved food before long, dear."

When it was finally time to leave for the Gallery, nerves hit me. Would anyone like my paintings or my drawings? Would they wonder why my artwork was being shown alongside Francis Sullivan's well-known work?

Mom could see that I was suddenly nervous. "Relax, Cara. Your work is beautiful. Everyone will see that. Have you decided which ones you're willing to sell?"

And that gave me something else to think about. I hadn't even considered selling my artwork before. "I think I should just wait and see if anyone's interested in buying, Mom." My self confidence, at that point, was a little shaky.

We drove to the Art Gallery, parked in their lot and entered through the gallery's back door. A well-dressed woman in a blue suit, who looked older than my mother, rushed up to us.

"Which one of you is Cara Blackthorne?" she asked.

Mom pushed me forward. "This is Cara. Are you Miss Galen, Francis Sullivan's agent?"

The woman smiled warmly. "Yes, and I'm delighted to meet you. She shook Mom's hand. "You must be Cara's mother." She seemed a bit surprised when she looked at me.

"My dear, when Francis wrote me about you, I had no idea you'd be so young." My heart sank a little.

She smiled. "I'll bet you haven't yet seen your work framed, have you?"

I shook my head, and she took my hand and led me into the gallery. The first thing I saw was one of Francis' latest paintings, a large oil painting showing two young boys flying kites at a beach. It was framed in a pale wood that seemed to match the color of the sand dunes shown in the painting. It was such a joyful scene, I could barely take my eyes off of it. Then I peeked at the price and almost fainted. I immediately understood why the gallery's customers were described as "fairly wealthy."

Miss Galen said, "Isn't it marvelous? Francis' work is in such demand. But come take a look at your paintings."

She led me to the wall at one side of the gallery where my two watercolors and the four pen and ink drawings had been hung. I stood there amazed at what I was seeing. I'd never seen my artwork displayed this way before, and it all looked so much better than I'd expected.

That was when I realized that my work *did* belong here. People *would* like it. I finally relaxed. I felt like celebrating.

Miss Galen said, "Well, what do you think, Cara? Have we done justice to your work?"

Turning to her, I said, "I can't get over how good they look. They've been framed perfectly, and the way the gallery has hung them is wonderful. Honestly, I never expected my work to look so amazing."

She chuckled. "Your work *is* amazing, Cara. When the public starts arriving, I predict the display of your drawings and paintings will attract a great deal of attention. Have you given any thought to selling? Should we put prices on any of them?"

I didn't know what to say. "Mom, what do you think? Should I sell them?"

"That's completely up to you, dear."

I had to think about this. I thought I could probably bear to sell the two watercolor paintings, but the Elf drawings I'd done in pen and ink were too close to my heart. Especially one of them.

"Miss Galen, I'm willing to sell the two watercolors, but these pen and ink drawings are too personal. I'm happy to show them, but I can't sell them."

She shook her head. "I see. Well, I'll price the two paintings and we'll see what happens. I hope you'll do more pen and ink drawings in the future. They are really lovely.

"Now, I'd suggest you and your mother walk around the gallery and enjoy Mr. Sullivan's paintings. People will be arriving any minute."

As we were admiring Francis' other paintings, a tall man approached us and introduced himself. "I am Henri Jourdan. I own the gallery. It is a real pleasure to meet a new young artist, Miss Blackthorne." He had a heavy French accent, a thin mustache, and he reminded me of an old-time movie star.

Mom shook his hand and he gave me a small bow and a smile before he wandered away, gazing at all the art hanging on the white walls of his gallery. People were now coming in the front door, most well dressed and middle-aged or older. I was happy to see a few younger couples trail in along with one or two single people, who looked like artists themselves.

A well-dressed young man passed out glasses of champagne to the growing crowd. When he spotted Mom and me, he smiled, handed Mom a glass of champagne and said, "I have something special for you, young lady."

He reappeared a few minutes later with a champagne glass holding what looked like ginger ale. "For you, Miss Blackthorne. When you want a refill, just let me know. I'm Hank. Mr. Jourdan is my father." He winked at me and left to pass out more champagne.

We continued to wander around the gallery, admiring Francis' wonderful oil paintings, all of which featured children playing. I heard murmurs of "such carefree, happy scenes," "Mr. Sullivan must adore children," and "I wish we could afford this one."

When we reached the wall where my work was displayed, we were behind an older couple and overheard, "lovely, her pen and ink drawings are so delicate. Is she here? I'd love to meet this girl, too bad they're not for sale." My photo was displayed on an easel at the front of the gallery, right next to Francis Sullivan's.

They turned around and were startled to find me right behind them. We all laughed. The older gentleman said, "You must be Cara Blackthorne. We've been admiring your work. My wife has fallen in love with your pen and ink drawings. Is there any chance you'll change your mind about selling them?"

"No, I'm afraid not. They're very special to me. But I will be doing more drawings in pen and ink in the future and I might sell those."

His wife smiled at me. "Then I'll look forward to seeing them another time. In the meantime, I'd love to buy one of your watercolors. You've used the most glorious colors in this autumn scene; they remind me of the woods near my family's home in Vermont. And it's clear how much you love the woodlands you paint."

"I do. This was painted in the woods behind my house. We live next to a beautiful forest. I spend a lot of time there."

"Well, I'm so glad we had a chance to meet you, Cara," the man said. "We love to discover new artists. You have a bright future, young lady."

I thanked them and they moved away to look at more of Francis' paintings.

Mom looked at me and grinned. She whispered, "Have you noticed the prices Miss Galen placed on your watercolors?"

I hadn't. When I looked at the small price tag tucked in the corner of each frame, I gasped. My watercolors had been priced at five hundred dollars each. And one had just been sold!

"Holy moly, Mom!" I couldn't believe my own eyes.

She was laughing. "Sweetheart, I don't think the term 'starving artist' will ever be used to describe you."

By the time the crowd thinned and the gallery was ready to close, both of my watercolors had been sold, and several more requests had been made for my pen and ink drawings. Miss Galen congratulated me and asked me to keep painting because she had another Art show scheduled in June in New York City and wanted me to participate.

The gallery owner, Mr. Jourdan, gave me a much deeper bow and kissed my hand before we left. "Miss Blackthorne, I sincerely hope your paintings will grace my humble gallery again very soon. You have a bright future, cheri." He winked at me as we left.

It was after eight when we left the gallery, way past dinner time for us.

"I think we should celebrate your first successful art show, dear. I saw a nice looking steak house as we drove over here. In the mood for a steak?"

I was. Mom pulled into the parking lot at the restaurant and we entered a rather dim, rustic place that smelled wonderful. Mom whispered, "They're so busy, the food must be good."

And it was. After a thankfully brief wait, we sat down to Rib Eye steaks with baked potatoes and Caesar salads. The food was fantastic.

"Did I actually make a thousand dollars today?" I asked as I put down my fork.

Mom smiled. "Well, not quite. Both the gallery and Miss Galen get a percentage of your sales, but you'll get enough to open your first bank account. Congratulations, Cara. I'd say your career as an artist has already begun."

It was a great feeling, and for once, my mind was full of the art I hadn't yet created. This was the happiest I'd been in many months.

Mom was enjoying a glass of wine when I noticed a man at another table staring at us. He was fairly young and was dining alone. When he continued to stare at me, Mom said, "Ignore him. I'm afraid you'll get a lot of that once you're out of Thornewood. Don't stare back; you'll just encourage him."

I took her advice and studiously ignored him until we left, but I couldn't help noticing all the attention we received as we walked through the dining room on our way out. I decided it had to be for my pretty redheaded mother in her sleek black suit that fit her like a glove. She looked more like my older sister than my mom.

As we walked out to our car, I noticed that we hadn't parked in a very well-lit area. We had almost reached our car when a man came out from behind the restaurant and grabbed Mom's purse, pushing her to the ground.

I yelled, "Stop, don't move." My voice had deepened and echoed.

It was the same man who had been staring at me in the restaurant. His mouth was hanging open, and he dropped Mom's purse.

"Mom, are you okay?" The man hadn't moved.

Her voice was faint as she picked herself up off the ground, looking somewhat shocked. "Yes, Cara. I'm all right. Uh, what do you want me to do?"

"Why don't you go back into the restaurant and tell them what happened. They can call the police. I'll stay right here with him. He's not going anywhere until the police arrive."

She picked her purse up off the ground and dashed back into the restaurant.

I looked at our attacker again. My voice deepened again. "Why did you attack my mother?"

He looked at me wide-eyed. "I heard you talking inside. You said something about making a thousand dollars. I need that money bad." He was trying to move his feet but they seemed to be fastened to the ground.

He was beginning to look desperate. He frowned at me and asked, "What *are* you?"

I used *Vox* again. "You will never try to rob anyone again. Do you understand?"

Wide-eyed again, he simply nodded vigorously.

Mom and the restaurant manager rushed through the parking lot to me. I could hear sirens some distance away. I wouldn't release my prisoner until the police put handcuffs on him.

Standing next to me, Mom had that "who are you?" look on her face. She was obviously working hard to remain calm. I realized this was the first time she'd actually seen me use *Vox*.

When the police car drove up and stopped beside us, the restaurant manager pointed to the man who was still facing me. The cop asked my mother, "He tried to mug you?"

Mom said, "Yes," the cop fastened the man's hands behind him, and I said, "Go with the police, and don't ever mug anyone again. Understand?" I hoped the cop wouldn't notice my deep voice.

Our attacker just nodded as he frowned at me. I'd released him from *Vox*, and I had no idea how he'd explain himself to the police. I didn't really care. I was suddenly very tired.

I asked my mother, "Can we go back to the hotel now?"

One of the two policemen who'd answered the call took down our personal information and said they'd be in touch. Mom told him to call Chief O'Donnell in Thornewood if the police needed a reference for us. He said he would and offered to follow us back to our hotel. I think he could see that Mom was still shaken from the whole ordeal. He must have taken one look at me and dismissed me as an innocent kid. Which was fine with me!

It was after ten when we got back to the hotel. Suddenly exhausted, I took a shower and got ready for bed while Mom called home to speak to my father. While I was in the bathroom, I could hear her side of the conversation. She was having a tough time calming down my father, but it seemed to calm her down as well. I gave them a few more minutes before I left the bathroom.

Mom handed me the phone, I said hello to my dad, and reassured him that we were both okay. "We can talk more when we get home tomorrow, Dad. Please try to relax." Then I climbed into bed and was out cold in under a minute.

After we checked out of the hotel, we stopped at a coffee shop for breakfast and were on our way home by noon.

Neither one of us wanted to talk about the attempted mugging, so we talked about my success at the art show instead. I think we were both relieved when Mom pulled off the highway at the exit sign that said "Thornewood."

She smiled at me as we pulled into our driveway. "No place like home, Cara."

As soon as we got through the front door, my father grabbed us both for hugs. No one gave hugs like my dad.

Mom called to have pizza delivered, which cheered up my dad a little, and we told him all about the art show, the Jourdan Gallery, my first art sales, and ending with our rather scary experience outside the restaurant.

After congratulating me, he said, "I'm sorry now that I didn't accompany you. I won't send you off to a strange city by yourselves again."

Mom gave me a look as if to say she knew this was how my father would react.

"Dad, I had my knives with me too. But *Vox* was all I needed."

Mom added, "As frightening as the whole thing was, Brian, I now have a lot more faith in Cara's ability to take care of herself. She was wonderful, calm and collected the entire time. I'm so proud of her. You should be too."

When we'd finished eating and my father seemed calmer, I went up to my room. I was tired but I made quick calls to Kevin and Amy to let them know the art show had been a success, and that I'd fill them in on Monday.

They were both happy for me, but Amy insisted she wanted *details*! I chuckled to myself as I thought about all the "details" she wasn't expecting.

I slid under my comforter, Ralph asleep at the foot of my bed. My mind was whirling despite how tired I was. While I was thrilled with the way my artwork had been received, I couldn't help wondering if using Vox had left a lasting impression on our would-be mugger. I'd probably never know.

CHAPTER 12

It was my week to drive, so I picked up Kevin and Amy who immediately bombarded me with questions about my first art show. After I had told them everything I could remember about the gallery and the art show, Kevin wanted to know if I thought I could make a living with my painting.

I laughed. "Well, if I work my butt off creating new paintings and pen and ink drawings, maybe. I was kind of shocked at the prices my agent placed on my two watercolors."

"But as your work becomes more well known, don't you think the prices for your work will go up?" Kevin asked.

"Who knows? But I have to tell you, when I saw the prices on Francis Sullivan's paintings, I thought my head would explode. And by the time we left the show Saturday night, every one of his paintings had been sold!"

"Will you have any more shows soon?" Amy asked.

"Yeah, there's one in June in New York City. I was asked to participate, so for the next two months, I'll be spending most of my waking moments painting."

Kevin chuckled. "Do you think you'll have time to finish our senior year? Or is that not important anymore?"

"Of course it's important, Kev. I'll be in classes five days a week, but I'll still have nights and weekends for painting and drawing."

"No socializing?" Amy asked, eyebrows raised.

"Well, not much. I won't have time."

I wasn't watching the two of them while I drove, but I could imagine the looks my two best friends were probably exchanging.

When we got to school, we separated. We each had classes in different directions but we'd meet at lunch. Which was when I planned to share my other experience in Albany.

Sean was already in his seat in Science class when I sat down next to him.

"Hey, Cara. How was your show?"

"Really good. Both of my watercolors sold, and a lot of people wanted to buy my pen and ink Elf drawings, but I decided not to sell them."

"Why not? Don't you show your artwork in order to sell it?"

"Well, I didn't know whether or not any of my artwork would sell. This was really a kind of test run, Sean, to see whether my work would be well received."

He smiled. "I knew it would be, and I'm sure Mr. Sullivan knew it would be. So why wouldn't you sell those Elf drawings?"

I hesitated. "Well, I did all of them last summer in Elvenwood. They're tied up with so many memories, I just felt I should keep them. The Elves I hid in each drawing shouldn't be exposed to the whole world."

Sean nodded. "I understand. They're kind of private, right?"

"Right. But the pen and ink drawings were so popular, I'll have to do more. I just may not be adding the Elves to my new drawings."

Class had started, so Sean whispered, "You can tell me more at lunch, okay?"

Sean hadn't been sharing our table at lunch lately, so I was surprised. "Yeah, okay. I do have more to tell you about what happened *after* the show."

His eyebrows shot up. "Can't wait to hear about it."

Once Amy, Kevin and Sean were all seated, Sean asked, "So let's hear the rest of the story, Cara."

Amy looked confused. "The rest?"

"Yeah. Our day didn't end when we left the gallery," I said.

"We didn't leave until just before it closed, and we were starved."

I told them about the steak dinner Mom treated us to, as well as the man who spent close to an hour staring at me. By that time, Kevin and Sean were frowning.

"When we got out to the parking lot, the same man tried to mug us." I heard Amy gasp.

While they sat there wide-eyed, I told them the whole story, ending with the arrival of the police.

My friends all looked shocked until Kevin asked, "Had your mom ever seen you use *Vox* before?"

"No, but I had talked to her about it before." I chuckled. "That was her first demonstration. Her initial reaction was a lot like yours, Kev. She looked at me like I'd just grown another head."

He laughed. "Yeah, I remember. I felt like my best friend had just been replaced by an alien who only looked like you."

Sean and Amy were both nodding. They'd seen it too and had reacted the same way.

Amy asked, "How did your dad react? I'll bet he was sorry he didn't go with you."

"Yeah, definitely. He said he would never let us go out of town by ourselves again." I rolled my eyes. "That will have to change!"

Amy added, "At least he knows you can take care of yourself now."

Sean's attitude toward me had warmed up a little after that, but otherwise, school continued as usual—just something to get through as far as I was concerned.

A week later spring break began, giving me an entire week to draw and paint until darkness chased me indoors.

I tried not to think about last year's spring break, when Sean and I met and began our relationship. It seemed like a time of such promise, and I remembered how excited I'd been as Sean and I got to know each other. It was also a time of discovery, as I began to learn who my father was and where he'd been all my life.

So much had happened since then.

Amy and Randi both tried to interest me in senior year social activities, but I didn't feel I had time. I only had about two months before the next art show. All I really wanted to do was paint. Even my parents gave me the "all work and no play" lecture, but I was determined not to be distracted.

By the time spring break was over and I headed back to school, I had four more watercolor paintings completed, and I'd begun four more pen and ink drawings. Spring was budding everywhere and I'd had good weather so I'd been in the forest every day with my portable easel and paints. I had even been able to capture some of the forest's wildlife in my paintings, mainly deer and rabbits.

Miss Burrows was pleased with my watercolors. I had been experimenting with texture, with layering my watercolors, creating shadows and playing with my brush technique. I was enjoying it all so much, my hours painting in the woods simply flew by. Occasionally, I was aware that Conor and Gavin were near, watching me work, but they always left without a word, unwilling to disturb me.

I rode Storm to Elvenwood most weekends, working in the apple orchard as well as out in the old orchard where Rowenna visited with me. I took advantage of the apple trees and the distant mountains for my pen and ink drawings.

One afternoon after I'd sung her song, Rowenna wanted to talk.

Cara, you seem to be putting all of yourself into your drawing and painting. You haven't brought a friend to visit in a long time. You feel far away to me.

"I'm sorry. I've really been concentrating on my artwork, not on anything else. I'm preparing for another art show, trying to get as much work done as possible."

I think you are also using your art to hide the hurt I know you're feeling. You've shut everyone out, haven't you?

She was right.

"I haven't wanted to think about what I've lost. I thought it was better to put all that emotion down on paper, where I can turn it into something beautiful rather than something that makes me sad."

She nodded her big head, her golden eyes sympathetic. *You should never give up hope, my young friend. Never.*

With that final word of advice, she lifted her huge wings and rose into the sky, taking her special magic with her. I watched as she disappeared behind the purple mountains.

Never give up hope? What? I should cry myself to sleep every night for the rest of my life? No way. Adam was gone. There wasn't another man on the planet I would ever want. I had to accept it and move on. After putting all my feelings into my paintings and drawings, I had nothing left over.

There was only one more month of school left when Sean reminded me about something I'd completely forgotten.

School was over for the day and I was heading out to my car with Kevin when Sean ran up to us. "Cara, could I speak to you for a minute?"

Kevin said, "I'll wait by your car." I threw him my keys and he grinned and continued down the block. He seemed to know something I didn't.

"What's up, Sean?"

He didn't answer right away, just stood there looking unsure of himself, which was rare.

Finally, he said, "Cara, our prom is in another week." He hesitated, frowning. "I know you wanted me to date other girls, and I've tried, but our senior prom is too special. I don't think I'd enjoy it with anyone but you. Please say you'll let me take you to prom. It would mean a lot to me."

Prom. I'd completely forgotten. I'd been tuning out everything but my artwork. I realized I'd spent almost no time with my friends lately.

I took Sean's hand. "I'd forgotten about prom. And you're right. It's too special to ignore. I'd love to go with you. It's formal, right?"

He was now wearing that killer smile I'd been so attracted to a year ago. "Right. It's formal. I'm really happy you want to go, Cara. If you hadn't said yes, I think I would have stayed home."

Wow. It meant that much to him.

"Well, now I can make my mother happy too." I laughed. "She loves to get me into a dress. Thanks for asking me. I've been so wrapped up in getting ready for the next art show, I've been tuning everything else out."

With one blond eyebrow raised, he said, "I've noticed. Everyone's noticed."

I shook my head. There was such a thing as being too single-minded, I guess.

Of course, Amy and Kevin were going to prom. Amy couldn't believe I'd forgotten all about it.

"Cara, this is the pinnacle of our high school years! When will we ever have a chance to celebrate together again?"

Once Amy was sure I was on board, she asked, "So what are you wearing? Are you getting a new dress? You know, the dress you wore for your parents' wedding was beautiful. Are you going to recycle it for prom?"

I almost shuddered. The memories attached to that dress were more than I could bear. I would never wear it again.

"No, I think I'll ask Mom to buy me a new dress. You already know that I've been trying to change my style this year. Want to go shopping with us?"

"Absolutely! I already have my dress. Wait 'til you see it! But I'd love to help you pick out yours."

My mother was all smiles when I said I needed a new dress for prom.

"I was afraid you wouldn't want to go," she admitted.

"Well, Sean talked me into it. He said if I didn't go with him, he'd stay home. I couldn't do that to him."

With a sigh, I added, "I guess prom isn't an occasion I should miss."

"Good. How about Van Horn's tomorrow night? Is Amy joining us?"

I laughed. "Yes, the queen of shoppers will be with us, Mom. Can we eat at The Grille after shopping?"

My mother smiled. "Of course. That's become our tradition, hasn't it?"

Our shopping trip was a success. Since Mom still saw me as her little girl, Amy over-ruled her and picked out my dress for prom. It was a very grown-up black and white strapless number that fit perfectly. It had a black satin strapless top and a flared white chiffon skirt. Since I'm still averse to high heels, I chose white sandals with only a one and a half inch heel. I was reasonably sure I wouldn't break an ankle in them.

Amy just shook her head. "When it comes to shoes, you're hopeless."

It took my mother a few minutes to admit the strapless dress looked good on me.

"Cara, I know you're growing up. It's just hard for me to get used to. You'll understand when you're a mom." I thought she looked a little sad.

I rolled my eyes. Not much chance of that happening.

Amy had talked me into an appointment at the best salon in town for prom. She was determined to have her hair blown into a straight style, something she'd never managed to accomplish with her short, curly hair, and we both agreed that something had to be done with my long, thick hair. My mother had thrown her hands in the air helplessly when I said I wanted something as sophisticated as my strapless black and white dress.

Amy insisted we both use the same stylist, a young man Amy described as a "genius." Carlos was a short, slim man in his twenties who greeted us with a smile.

"Well, who wants to be first?" he asked us.

Amy hopped up into his chair. "Would you please straighten out these curls? I want my hair sleek and sophisticated, like Jennifer Lawrence's style from a few years ago. Know which one I mean?" she asked.

He nodded with a smile. "That will be a perfect look for you."

When he was done, Amy looked like a new person. I was so used to her curly red hair, which she'd always kept short, I couldn't believe the difference the new hairstyle made.

Beaming, Amy got out of his chair and said, "Okay, Carlos, let's see what magic you can create for my best friend."

He seated me and ran his fingers through my thick hair. Nodding, he said, "You want to wear it up, right?"

I described my black and white strapless dress and told him I wanted my hair to look as grown up as my dress.

He grinned. "Well, not too grown up, I hope. How about young and breathtaking?"

I had to laugh. "That sounds good."

After he washed my hair, he blew it dry and began pinning it up loosely. He braided a few sections and used his curling iron on all the other sections. After curling a few fine tendrils along my face, he wove the braids through the mass of curls cascading from the top of my head and pinned them in place.

When he stepped back to let me see the finished style, I was amazed.

Amy's mouth was hanging open. "Cara, you look like a princess in a romantic fairy tale. Sean will be speechless, for once!"

As Carlos helped me out of his chair, two more girls from our class came in the door, stopping short when they saw us, their mouths hanging open.

We paid a smiling Carlos, who whispered, "You two are my best advertisements. Don't forget to tell your friends who did your hair. Have a wonderful time tonight, young ladies."

Back in my car, I drove us to Amy's house where we polished each other's nails in a pearl white shade and feasted on Mrs. Strauss' just made cream puffs. Amy's parents paid us lavish compliments, insisting we both looked like movie stars.

When I got home late in the afternoon, both my parents were sitting in the kitchen, apparently waiting for me. Mom smiled approvingly, but my dad seemed to be speechless.

I smiled. "I gather you both like my transformation, yes?"

Mom said, "Sweetheart, I'm so glad you decided to go to prom. You look perfect, or you will once you put that beautiful dress on. I'll help you dress so you don't mess up that gorgeous hairstyle."

Mom knew I'd be dancing at Prom so she'd thrown together a chicken salad that was one of my favorites and wouldn't fill me up too much. And then it was time to get myself dressed for Prom.

After helping me put my gown on, she insisted on loaning me her antique pearl necklace with its matching earrings. "They're perfect, Mom. Thanks." She smiled and hugged me.

When I finally walked downstairs, my father sprang out of his chair and just stared at me. Mom chuckled behind me. "I think your father is a little overwhelmed, dear. Give him a minute. Or two."

He walked up to me, took my hand and kissed it. His voice was soft. "You make a father proud, dear."

On the dot of seven o'clock, there was a knock on the front door. I took a deep breath and opened the door to find Sean, incredibly handsome in a white dinner jacket, black bowtie, and black slacks, a perfect complement to my black and white dress. His thick blond hair slicked back and just grazing his collar, Sean looked like a model for GQ Magazine.

His warm brown eyes widened as he gazed at me, from top to bottom, and he simply whispered, "Wow."

From behind me, I heard my mother say, "You two look like a matched pair tonight. Please come in, Sean." Naturally, she had her camera ready.

My father greeted Sean, shaking his hand and smiling. "Alicia is right. You make a handsome couple."

Sean turned to me and handed me a box containing a white gardenia, just as he had a year ago when he took me to my first dance.

Mom said, "I'd suggest we pin that lovely gardenia into your hair, Cara, just above your ear. That way you can both enjoy its scent tonight." She smiled as I realized that the gardenia would be just below Sean's nose when we danced. My mother thought of everything.

She tucked the satiny white flower into the curls just above my ear, and after she took more pictures, we left.

As we walked to Sean's car, I don't think either one of us knew quite what to say. As he helped me into the car, he leaned in and kissed my cheek. "You are the most beautiful girl I've ever seen, Cara. You make me weak in the knees."

How does a girl respond to a compliment like that? I felt my face getting hot.

He came around and got in on the driver's side, still shaking his head as he smiled at me.

I couldn't help grinning. "Sean, you were made for that dinner jacket. Every other girl at Prom will be shooting daggers at me tonight." I chuckled. "Not that that's anything new, you know."

His face a bit red, he said, "I don't think anyone will be looking at me tonight."

Our Prom was being held at the Thornewood Country Club, which was next door to Randi's condo complex. I'd never been to the Country Club before; Mom and I had never traveled in such well-to-do circles.

After a uniformed valet helped me out of the car, I took Sean's arm and we walked into the Country Club's plush ballroom. It was a gorgeous place with large potted trees and plants placed on the marble tiled floor all around the room, and tiny twinkle lights threaded through the branches.

THE JOINING TREE

The level of conversation dropped a bit when Sean and I walked in, looking for our assigned table. I could almost feel the stares as we walked across the ballroom to the white linen-covered table where Amy was waving at us. She and Kevin had arrived early, as usual.

Kevin looked truly handsome in a dinner jacket. Amy must have tamed his curly hair, and as he stood up to greet us, I realized that his lean body had finally caught up with his long arms and legs. At about six feet three inches tall, Kevin was every bit as handsome as Sean, but more *Sports Illustrated* than *GQ*.

Smiling, Sean shook Kevin's outstretched hand. "Lookin' good, Kev. You really clean up well." Snorting, Kevin just said, "You too, man."

Looking me up and down, Kevin smiled. "Welcome back, short stuff. We've missed you. Oh, and by the way, you look great!" He gave me a quick one-armed hug.

When Amy stood up, I gasped. She belonged on the cover of *Vogue*. Her new hairstyle with the long, side-swept bangs was perfect with her burnt orange satin slip dress. The color was perfect with her red hair, and the satiny fabric glided down her tall, slender body like it was made for her.

"Amy, I wish my mom could see you now! You look fabulous. We've got to get more pictures taken tonight." I chuckled. "After all, we may never look this good again!"

We sat down at the table just as Randi and Dion arrived, both looking totally gorgeous. Dion had also gone the dinner jacket route, looking very cool. Randi was wearing a dark red silk off-the-shoulder dress that accented her lush curves. It was the perfect color for her dark hair and eyes.

Before long, waiters began serving salads, filling our goblets with ice water, and the band began to play background music as photographers moved from table to table, snapping pictures.

Randi whispered, "I hope the band plays some music we can dance to. I'm afraid what they're playing now would put us all to sleep."

Amy said, "I've heard the Country Club has a great band, Randi. Members of this Country Club aren't all old farts, you know." Randi giggled. "Good to know."

After a wonderful dinner of broiled salmon and rice pilaf, we enjoyed ice cream topped with raspberries.

The band took a brief break and returned, sporting sunglasses and fedoras, the "Blues Brothers" look.

Randi was all smiles as she pulled Dion up from the table. Soon most of our class was on the large dance floor, and we joined them. Amy and Kevin looked outstanding together.

Sean moved well for a big guy. He insisted I made him look good. For the record, Sean had never needed any help looking good.

As the night went on, the band played more slow songs, and the ballroom's lights were dimmed, making the already beautiful setting even more romantic. Feeling Sean's arms around me, I automatically cuddled up to him and heard him sigh. I told myself I wasn't really leading him on, I was just enjoying dancing with him. After all, it was prom.

When I felt him lean down to kiss my forehead, I realized I should have been keeping a bit more distance between us. But I hadn't been held like this, or kissed, in months, and I'd always loved the way he smelled of sandalwood and soap. I couldn't deny how good it felt being close to him.

I refused to think about that other mind-blowing kiss I'd had. After all, that man, or Elf, had left me the very next day.

We continued dancing, our arms wrapped around each other, until the lights began to blink and the band began playing "Moonlight," which was our Prom's theme.

Our magical night at Prom was ending. I had enjoyed every minute of it.

On our way out, Randi invited us over to her condo for more dancing. "We've got a great sound system and a very cool vinyl collection. I hope you'll all come over. Prom doesn't have to be over just yet!"

"Sounds good to me," Sean said with a smile. "Okay with you, Cara?"

It was still early, only ten-thirty, so I agreed. More dancing sounded perfect.

Randi asked, "Amy? Kevin? Are you coming?"

Amy looked at Kevin and he nodded. "Okay, we can stay for an hour. We already have some after-prom plans, but we're good until midnight."

Amy hadn't said anything to me about after-prom plans, so I was curious what the two of them were up to.

We took separate cars to Randi's, but as soon as we got there, I grabbed Amy to ask, "What after-prom plans? Are you two keeping secrets?"

Kevin laughed. "No, of course not. I've always wanted to see Washington, D.C. so my mom paid for a trip for me this weekend. Amy's parents agreed to let her go with me."

Amy giggled. "Of course, we both got the *'you'll have separate rooms'* lecture, but I think our parents trust us. And I've always wanted to see the Lincoln Memorial as well as the White House."

Kevin added, "We leave early tomorrow and we'll get back Sunday night."

"Cool. A whole weekend out of Thornewood? I'm jealous," Dion said with a grin.

Looking completely serious, Randi said, "After living in Greenville for several months, I'm totally happy right here in Thornewood. You don't appreciate something until you lose it, you know."

I took her hand and squeezed it. I knew how right she was.

Randi hadn't been kidding about their sound system, and the shelves of vinyl records contained something for everyone. At that point, we were all a little low on energy, so she pulled out music by Sinatra, the Eagles, and the Beatles, giving us great tunes for dancing. She also went to the huge fridge and pulled out beers for anyone who wanted one, but she and Dion were the only takers.

I still remembered how I'd been affected by some spiked punch last summer. I didn't want to embarrass myself again.

As we danced, I could see the southern end of Blackthorne Forest through the patio door. I wondered if there was anyone in the forest looking back.

Looking around, Sean said, "This is a great condo, isn't it? I heard they have an Olympic sized pool as well as tennis courts, and a fully equipped gym. Randi's really lucky to be living here."

I smiled, remembering how thrilled Randi was when her father told her she could move back here and live with him. "She thinks so too. She really hated Greenville."

He pulled me closer as we continued to dance. The Beatles' "Norwegian Wood" was playing on the stereo.

He chuckled. "I'm really enjoying that gardenia in your hair. I'll get one for you every time I know we'll be dancing."

I couldn't answer him. I didn't want him to think this would be a regular occurrence. But I was enjoying our closeness more than I should have.

Before long, Amy and Kevin had to leave and we all wished them a great weekend in D.C.

Randi put some old R&B on the stereo. The atmosphere was suddenly a lot warmer.

When I was younger and Mom would play R&B on the radio, I liked it but I never noticed how sensual the lyrics and rhythms were. I was noticing them now. The way Randi and Dion were dancing made it obvious they were really into the music too. It was a little embarrassing to watch.

Sean murmured, "I hope Randi knows what she's doing."

I added, "I hope Dion knows what *he's* doing!"

Sean snorted. "He knows exactly what he's doing, Cara."

It suddenly dawned on me what was probably going on between Randi and Dion.

"Oh. I wasn't aware their relationship was that serious."

"It isn't. But Dion and Randi are both over eighteen. I guess they both know what they're doing."

I didn't want to think about Randi and Dion. I closed my eyes, rested my head on Sean's chest and concentrated on moving along with the irresistible rhythms.

Finally, Sean moved away slightly and said, "I think we should sit down for a while." He sounded a little breathless.

When I looked around, Randi and Dion were gone. "Where'd they go?" I asked.

Sean gently pulled me down to sit on the couch next to him and said, "Uh, I guess they went into Randi's room."

"Oh. Well, maybe we should leave."

"In a few minutes. We haven't really been alone in months, Cara." Giving me a meaningful look, he wrapped one arm around me, pulling me closer, and kissed me. At first it was the sweet, tender kisses I'd always received from Sean. He'd always been so gentle with me, as though he was afraid I'd break.

I guess the music had gotten to both of us because our kisses quickly became more heated, more demanding. I'd always been physically attracted to Sean, tonight more than ever. His hands stroked the bare skin of my back and moved to my sides.

I knew where his hands would go next, and I suddenly remembered another voice telling me that being attracted to a boy wasn't the same as being in love with him. It was like a splash of cold water.

I tried to push Sean away, but he murmured, "Cara, please . . . you know I love you."

"I know, but I can't do this. It's not fair to you. I care about you, Sean. You must know that, but . . ." He let me go, his hands falling to his sides.

"But you're not in love with me, right?"

I simply shook my head. I felt so guilty, I couldn't look him in the eye.

"I'm sorry, Sean. I've never wanted to mislead you."

Running his hands through his thick hair, in a choked voice he said, "It's all because of what I did last year, right? I made a stupid, immature mistake and ruined everything, didn't I?"

I sighed. "No. I forgave you for that a long time ago."

Sounding desperate, he asked, "Then what is it? I'd do anything for you. Is there something else I don't know about?"

I saw the light dawn on his handsome face.

His voice suddenly became softer. "That's *it*. You're in love with someone else, aren't you?"

I couldn't put it off any longer. I turned to him, forcing myself to look into his eyes.

"Yes." I took a deep breath. I whispered, "I'm sorry."

I could see the hurt on his face. He closed his eyes and sat there for at least a minute while I was busy hating myself for hurting him.

Finally he stood. "I'll take you home now." He slowly wrapped my shawl around my shoulders and led me to the back door near the parking lot.

Feeling like an idiot, I asked, "Shouldn't we let Randi know we're leaving?"

Looking toward the bedrooms, he sounded unlike himself when he said, "I don't think she'd care."

He didn't say a word on the drive home. The atmosphere between us was acutely uncomfortable.

When he pulled up in front of my house, I thought he'd get out immediately but he didn't. After a few long minutes, he turned to me, his mouth tight, eyes cold.

"I have to know. Who is it?"

I had fervently hoped he wouldn't ask. But he deserved the truth.

I took a deep breath and finally said, "Adam."

Looking confused, he said, "But he's gone. He left, didn't he?"

"Yes, he's gone."

"Cara, he's at least ten years older, he left Blackthorne Forest, permanently as far as I know, and you're still in love with him?" He looked completely at a loss. "I don't get it."

I was quiet for a while. Then I said, "Elves mate for life, Sean. I've told you that before."

Sounding angry, he said, "Mate for life? What exactly do you mean by 'mate'?"

I sighed. "Probably not what you're thinking. It's not really a physical thing. In the Elven world, 'mating' is really just falling in love. Once you give your heart, it stays given."

"Well, that's just great, Cara. I think I gave my heart to you when I was only ten. And I've never wanted anyone else. I have Elven blood too. Does that mean I'll never love anyone else?" He still sounded angry. Angry and kind of lost.

"I hope not. I hope you forget all about me when you go away to college. I want you to be happy. That's the only reason I suggested you date other girls."

"Well, believe me, Cara, I'll do my best to forget I ever knew you."

He was really angry. And I couldn't blame him.

"Well, I'll always be glad I went to prom with you, Sean. I wouldn't have gone with anyone else. You've been a wonderful friend. I'll always care for you."

He didn't say a word so I got out of the car and went into the house.

I'd gone to my senior prom and broken the heart of a young man I would always like and respect.

I didn't like myself much at the moment.

CHAPTER 13

Disliking myself intensely, I didn't get much sleep that night. I kept seeing the pain on Sean's face, the look of betrayal in his eyes.

I was so glum when I went downstairs for breakfast, my father retreated from the back door he had been about to open and placed one arm around my shoulders. Leaning down, he looked into my eyes and asked, "What's wrong, Cara? What happened?"

"I finally told Sean the truth, that I'm in love with someone else. He didn't take it well. And I hate myself for hurting him. He's such a great guy, and he's been a really good friend."

"I'm sorry, Cara. But it's always best to be honest, even when it hurts. I like Sean, but you did the right thing. He'll get over it eventually."

After giving me a comforting hug, he said, "I'm on my way to Elvenwood. Why don't you come with me?"

I decided to skip breakfast, grabbed my easel and paints and followed my father to his camp where our greys were waiting for us.

Just riding Storm again cheered me up. As we rode into Elvenwood, the magic of the hidden village surrounded me and I was finally more at peace. Glancing over at me as we rode through the gateway, my father sensed my mood and smiled.

That weekend in Elvenwood set the pattern. I'd be in school Monday through Friday and in Elvenwood every weekend.

My birthday came around, and my parents, Amy, Kevin, Conor and Arlynn helped me celebrate. Finally I was seventeen. The year I spent being sixteen seemed a lot longer than just a year. I was glad it was over.

I'd told Amy and Kevin what happened after prom. They guessed something dramatic had occurred when Sean stopped talking to me at school. He no longer ate lunch with us either.

Kevin said, "Well you almost made it through senior year with Sean. But I guess he deserved to know where he stood with you. Don't beat yourself up, short stuff. You had to tell him the truth sometime."

Nevertheless, I think we all missed Sean. He'd become such an integral part of our group.

We were getting close to Graduation, but first, we had to get through our final exams. Without Sean's help, I didn't expect to sail through finals.

One morning in Science class, he surprised me by dropping copies of his class notes on my desk, muttering, "These may help."

THE JOINING TREE

I looked up to thank him, but he just sat down and looked in another direction. I leaned over toward him and whispered, "I really appreciate this, Sean. Thank you."

He nodded, not looking at me, as usual.

At lunch one day, Kevin told me that Sean had received two scholarship offers, both for athletics, specifically football, and that he'd chosen to attend Penn State.

I was a little surprised Sean hadn't told me himself. "I'm happy for him," I said. "What was his other choice?"

"UCLA." Kevin added, "He didn't want to move to California. Besides, his living expenses out there would have been too high." He chuckled. "I guess he prefers snow to sunshine."

I said, "Well, he told me he didn't want to be too far from home, but since a lot of things have changed recently, I thought he might have changed his mind about that."

He'd said he wanted to forget he ever knew me. That thought brought on a sigh, drawing understanding looks from both Amy and Kevin.

Using Sean's excellent notes, I studied hard the week before exams, hoping for no grades worse than a B. I knew I'd receive an A in Art; I always did.

When we'd all finished taking our finals, the three of us celebrated at The Grille, our traditional end of term celebration. It seemed kind of weird, with only three of us.

Amy said, "Last year there were six of us, remember? That was really fun."

Kevin chuckled. "Yeah, we had fun with our bodyguards. That was the night Adam got all possessive . . ." He stopped, looking guilty as he glanced at me.

I gave a deep sigh. "Yeah, I remember. And it was also the night my mother warned him off, telling Adam he was too old for me."

Amy reached over and patted my hand. "I'm convinced he'll be back one day."

I snorted. "I won't hold my breath. If that was his plan, I think he would have told me before he left. I think I'm better off concentrating on my art. After all, that's something that will never leave me."

Amy and Kevin just looked at each other and said nothing.

I resumed painting after school every day, barely noticing when my final grades arrived.

Amy called when she got home from school and found the email with her grades on her laptop. She was thrilled with a mixture of A's and B's. "I can thank Kevin for coaching me and helping me study." She laughed. "I think these grades are more his than mine, but I'll take them!"

I congratulated her and she asked if I'd seen my grades yet.

"No, I'd kind of forgotten all about them. I'm working on my last painting for the show in New York City. I'll barely have time to have it framed and sent off."

"Well, Cara, look them up now! I'll wait."

"Okay." I turned on my laptop and opened my email. I couldn't speak for a minute.

"Well, what did you get?" she asked impatiently.

"Uh, this can't be right," I said. "These grades must belong to another student. They can't be mine."

"Cara, is your name at the top of the email?"

"Uh, yes."

"Then they're your grades!"

I gave an Amy-like screech. "Holy crap! I got A's in Science, English, History, Art and P.E. And a B in Economics! It's a miracle."

She was laughing. "This really deserves a celebration. Mom just made a cherry pie. I'll bring it over after dinner, okay? And I'll bring Kevin too!"

Still somewhat in shock, I said, "Okay. I have to invite Sean even though he might not want to come. His notes get all the credit."

"Cara, I get why you want to ask him, but don't be surprised if he turns you down. Okay?"

"What do you know that I don't?" I asked.

"He's started dating a Junior. They're spending every spare minute together. I'm surprised you hadn't noticed."

"Oh. Okay. Well, maybe I'll just email him to let him know how valuable his notes were. And to thank him again."

"That's probably best, Cara. I'll be over around seven, okay?"

"Okay. See you later." I put my phone down feeling like I'd just been punched in the stomach. What was I expecting? Of course Sean was dating someone else. I had wanted him to date. So why the heck did it hurt?

I no longer felt much like celebrating, but I knew my parents would be thrilled with my final grades and that cheered me up a little.

I decided to wait until bedtime to email Sean. Maybe at that hour he wouldn't feel he had to answer. I had to be honest with myself. I didn't want to hear his voice, cold and unfeeling the way it had been the last time we exchanged any words. The coldness really hurt.

When Mom got home from work and Dad came in for dinner, I told them about my amazing final grades and collected hugs and kisses from both of them.

When I told them that Amy and Kevin would be arriving around seven with a cherry pie, Mom grinned and simply said, "Perfect. We're so proud of you, honey. Good job."

Smiling, my father said, "You really are a wonder, dear."

I didn't feel I deserved that much praise. I knew most of my success in school was due to Sean's painstaking notes, which he'd so generously shared with me. With that thought, my stomach started to ache again.

I soothed the ache with my dad's favorite meatloaf dinner, after which Amy and Kevin arrived with a cherry pie just oozing with cherries and juice. Amy insisted a celebration was in order because she had received an amazing B in Calculus, thanks to Kevin's tutoring.

Kevin, of course, had earned a 4.0 GPA and had already received his acceptance letter from NYU where he planned to major in Computer Science. We all knew Kevin would be successful, no matter what he chose to do in the future. Amy and I were both happy he wouldn't be any farther away than New York City.

The "three musketeers" would still be together, at least part of the time.

After Kevin and Amy left, Mom and Dad continued to sit at the table with me, talking about the Barrett Art Institute, where I'd be spending most of the next three years.

"After Graduation, dear, we really should drive up to Syracuse to look at apartments for you. Mrs. Gardner did say that June was the best time to see what's available to rent."

"Okay, Mom, but I have that Art Show in New York City after Graduation to get through first."

"I think I'd like to join you this time," my dad said.

I actually liked that idea. "Sure, Dad. Maybe we could do both at the same time. We'd only have to be at the art show overnight, and then we could drive up to Barrett to look at apartments."

Mom was obviously thinking about that plan. "Cara, I don't know if I can get someone to cover the bookstore for that many days. Would you mind if I didn't go with you this time?"

She looked at me, then at my dad.

He shrugged. "What do you think, Cara?"

I smiled. "It might be fun, Dad. I think you'd find the art show interesting. As far as finding an apartment in Syracuse, I don't think I'll need much help deciding where I'd like to live. I already know what I'll need."

Mom's eyebrows went up. "Really? What do you have in mind?"

"Well, something like we had at that hotel where we stayed in Albany, plus some well lighted space for drawing and painting. And a place close to campus, of course."

She nodded. "Okay. I'm sure your father can handle this, dear." She winked at my dad and said, "We can talk more about this later."

When I couldn't stay awake any longer, I said goodnight and went to my room. It was time to send that email to Sean. I'd put it off as long as possible. I was such a chicken.

I forced myself to sit down at my desk and turn on my laptop. It was almost eleven p.m. so I didn't think he'd answer tonight. If he answered at all.

"Sean, I have to thank you again for sharing those class notes with me. When I received my grades today, I was sure they were someone else's. I actually got A's in everything but Economics. I got a B in that class. This never would have happened without your help.
I also want to congratulate you on receiving not one, but two scholarship offers! Kevin says you've chosen Penn State. I know you'll do well there. Congratulations!
Again, sincere thanks.
Cara"

That completed, I breathed a sigh of relief and got into bed. For a few minutes, I waited for the little bell signaling receipt of a new email. But it didn't ring. I finally fell asleep, feeling sad about the friend I'd lost.

The weekend before Graduation, I rode to Elvenwood with my last watercolor to show to Francis Sullivan. A few weeks earlier, I'd taken two other watercolors to him along with four new pen and ink drawings, which I'd done inside the Elven village. I hadn't inserted any Elves into my drawings this time, just the beauty of nature in the rose garden and apple orchard with the tall pines and the misty mountains in the distance. I had inserted a thatched roof cottage in one background, which I thought appeared more imaginative than real. Hopefully.

My newest watercolors depicted three of the oldest Victorian houses in Thornewood, my attempt to depict days of old in our small town. Of course, since I'd painted them during the spring season, nature was at its best with flowers everywhere. I hoped Francis would like them.

When I knocked on the door of his studio, I heard him call out, "Come in, Cara!" I finally decided to ask him how he always knew it was me.

I walked into his studio and before he could ask me what I had brought him, I asked my question. Francis laughed, the usual sparkle in his blue eyes.

"My dear, you don't just use your eyes when you paint, do you?"

I was confused.

"Cara, you have your sense of smell, your hearing, even the sense of touch which, whether you realize it or not, all find their way into your artwork."

He smiled. "When I hear a knock on my studio door, I always know who it is because no two knocks are the same. Your knock, for example, is light, almost delicate."

I had to laugh. "I thought you were psychic."

"Well, I have to admit to a little of that sense as well, Cara." He winked at me.

He had all my paintings and drawings spread out on his table, examining each one closely. I was beginning to feel a bit nervous.

Finally, he straightened and turned to me. "It's hard for me to realize that you haven't even begun art school yet, Cara." He shook his head but I thought he looked pleased.

"I think you should exhibit all of these at the New York show. The watercolors will be popular, I'm sure. They're excellent. Your technique has improved beautifully. And, as you were already told, your pen and ink drawings are exquisite. I recognize all the settings in your drawings." He chuckled. "I doubt anyone will think they're real, just that they're delightfully imaginative. I see you decided against adding any Elves to these drawings." He nodded. "Probably a wise choice.

"Leave these with me. I'll have them framed and delivered to Mr. Callahan. The next time you see them, they'll be hanging in the Madison Avenue Gallery in Manhattan."

When I asked him how many of his paintings he was going to show, he said, "Four for this show. This gallery will be showing the work of one more artist, I believe. It should be a popular show. I think you and your father will enjoy it." His eyes twinkled.

"Thank you, Francis. I don't think I would ever have gotten this far without your advice and encouragement."

He smiled. "Just keep painting, Cara."

It was a cloudy day, and when I left Francis' studio, the clouds had become darker, so I decided to forgo visiting other friends and head home before it started to rain. I was riding alone today and didn't want to take any chances.

I shuddered when I remembered the last time I'd been caught in a storm on my way home from Elvenwood.

As I rode past Ian's cottage, he came outside and waved, but when I pointed to the dark clouds above, he nodded and waved me on.

Naturally, I didn't make it home before it began to rain. But this time, I was riding Storm, who had no problem with rainstorms. He kept a steady pace and didn't react at all when peals of thunder began rolling across the sky.

I had been a little nervous, but Storm was so calm my tension relaxed within minutes. As we rode into my father's camp, he came out of his tent with a smile on his face.

"I think we found the right horse for you this time, Cara." He rubbed Storm's nose and thanked him for taking good care of me. The big grey snorted proudly and proceeded to fold his legs under himself so that I could dismount.

When my feet were solidly on the ground again, I hugged Storm's neck and told him how wonderful he was. He obviously enjoyed the praise, snorting and whinnying and blowing at my hair.

Before I knew it, it was Graduation day. My mind was so full of drawing, painting, art shows and moving to Syracuse, graduation didn't seem as important as it had a year ago.

Amy, of course, thought my whole preoccupation with my future, rather than with our high school graduation, was ridiculous.

I realized her situation was somewhat different from mine. Amy wasn't going on to culinary school this year. Instead, she'd be staying in Thornewood to help her parents reopen and expand the Strauss Bakery, which had been closed for almost a year. She would be running their new catering department, which I knew she'd excel at.

The weather was warm and sunny as we lined up in rows on Thornewood High's football field. I was surprised when Kevin was called up to the podium to give a speech. He was our class Valedictorian, which I should have known, but hadn't.

Once again, I'd been too wrapped up in myself to notice everything that was going on around me. I was so busy mentally beating myself up, I didn't hear much of his speech, but judging from the enthusiastic applause, it had gone over well.

Red-faced, Kevin accepted Mr. Weiss' congratulations and left the podium to take his seat with the rest of the class.

One by one, we were called up to receive our diplomas to scattered applause from friends and family in the audience.

It wasn't long before the long-awaited event was over. Well, long-awaited by most. Soon the audience of family and friends had filed out of the stands to congratulate and hug the new graduates, smiles and tears everywhere.

My parents, accompanied by Conor and Arlynn, found me quickly, and I was immediately wrapped up in my mother's arms.

"Congratulations, sweetheart. We're all very proud of you."

My father, beaming but more reserved than most of the proud parents, put one arm around me and dropped a kiss on my head. In my head I heard his voice. *This is just the beginning, Cara dear.*

Conor and Arlynn both hugged me and said, "Congratulations, Cara."

I learned that this was the first high school graduation the Elves had ever attended, and Mom admitted the only one she'd attended had been her own, eighteen years earlier.

Amy dragged her parents over to us and more hugs were exchanged. Mr. Strauss was all smiles, saying, "Our girls have done so well. Susie and I are very proud."

I spotted Kevin across the field with his mother, and some people I assumed were his grandparents. We waved at each other, but there were too many families between us so I knew we'd have to wait until later to talk. Unfortunately, Kevin's father was nowhere to be seen.

THE JOINING TREE

As Mom and Dad were talking with Amy's parents, I saw the McKays nearby, talking with the parents of some of Sean's friends. Sean was staring at me through the crowd. When I smiled at him, he looked away. I sighed.

Conor must have heard me because he said softly, "He'll get over it eventually, Cara. I have a feeling that you and Sean will always be friends."

Arlynn didn't say anything, but I saw the sympathy on her face. I knew her sympathy was more for my loss of Adam than it was for Sean. I nodded to her to let her know I understood the things she wasn't saying.

Mom invited everyone back to our house where she had prepared several salads for a Graduation day lunch.

She had made lemonade and iced tea to go along with the tray of veggies and dips, fruit-kabobs, and a ham and cheese tray. I helped her set it up in the kitchen. Everything looked wonderful and I realized how hungry I was.

The kitchen had become a little crowded, so Amy and I filled our plates and went out to sit on the back porch. That was when I realized I'd been avoiding the back porch ever since the weather became warm. There were too many memories of sitting out there with Adam last year.

Amy must have read my mind.

"Cara, you look sad. I think I can guess why. You spent a lot of time out here last year, right?"

I nodded. "Too many memories. This porch is where Sean and I got to know each other, and where Kevin, Sean and I used to talk about the possibility that my dad wasn't human." I smiled at those memories.

I shook my head. "Later, Adam sat out here with me quite often."

She chuckled. "I remember the night we introduced our bodyguards to Ice Cream Sundaes."

That memory brought a smile to my face. "Yes. I think I should invite the boys over for Sundaes sometime soon. They were all so good to us, all through the summer and into autumn."

Amy grinned. "We still have to make that trip to Elvenwood, Cara. I'm dying to see the village, and I'd like to see Neal's face when he finds out I'm a Halfling."

"I'm surprised Kevin hasn't taken you already. He can borrow a grey anytime and ride to Elvenwood. Oh, you don't ride, do you?"

She shook her head. "Afraid not. And it sounds like a long hike on foot."

"We'll speak to Conor. I'm sure he or someone else can let you hitch a ride into the village. Maybe you could even ride behind Kevin. I'm surprised he didn't think of that."

Amy raised one eyebrow. "Cara, I think Kevin's been awfully busy the past few months. He helped me study for finals, he had one video game to finish and then started working on the design for another one. He really hasn't had much spare time lately. Plus, we had that weekend in Washington, D.C., remember?"

I slapped my head. "Oh, I'm sorry, Amy. I never even asked you how that weekend went. As usual, I've been too wrapped up in my own problems. Did you enjoy yourselves that weekend? How much of D.C. did you see?"

She gave me a dreamy smile. "Cara, it was a wonderful weekend. We had a great time. We walked all over the city, saw the White House, Congress, the Washington Monument, and spent as much time as we could in the Lincoln Memorial. That place is so special. It has an awe-inspiring atmosphere. I may be crazy, but I really felt Lincoln's spirit in there."

I grinned at her. "Amy, did you and Kev observe the separate rooms rule?" I couldn't help giggling because it was so obvious that they hadn't.

She just rolled her eyes and groaned. "Well, we did have separate rooms. But Kevin didn't spend much time in his. Don't get the wrong idea, Cara! All we did was fall asleep together."

Now she was smiling. "Having so much time alone together was really great because after we got home, Kevin got so busy, I haven't seen much of him. But we talk on the phone every night. Everything's cool."

"I'm glad. You and Kevin were made for each other, you know?"

She nodded, grinning. "Yeah. That's what I keep telling him!"

My dreams that night had nothing at all to do with graduating from high school. Probably because it just didn't seem very important to me. Instead, I saw those deep-set brown eyes staring at me disapprovingly, followed by a familiar pair of dark blue eyes in a face that was no longer as clear in my memory.

The golden boy and my dark knight, as Christina had called them last year. Somehow I'd managed to lose both of them.

CHAPTER 14

My high school years were finally over. Now I could concentrate on art school and my future with no distractions. The art show in Manhattan was next on the agenda, and I was both excited and nervous. After all, New York was a much larger city than Albany. There were many art galleries there, and I suspected that the art-loving public might be more discriminating.

Rather than driving into New York City, Mom suggested we take the train. Although passenger trains don't run through Thornewood, we weren't far from a train station in another slightly larger town.

After checking hotel rates in Manhattan, Mom thought we should take the train back the same day. Dad whispered to me, "Money is really not a problem, Cara, but we should probably humor your mother." He winked at me and I had to stifle a laugh. We both knew that my mother was the practical one.

We took a taxi from Penn Station to the Gallery on Madison Avenue. Although I'd taken taxis with Mom before, it was a new experience for my father.

"People actually live here?" he asked me as he looked out the taxi's windows at the teeming city. "There are no trees, just these huge buildings everywhere. And so much noise. How do they stand it?"

The cab driver chuckled. "It ain't easy. This your first trip to New York?"

I hastened to explain. "I've been here before, but my father hasn't. There are a lot more trees where we live. And it's a lot quieter."

When the taxi arrived in front of the gallery, my father preceded me out onto the sidewalk, attracting the usual amount of attention his height and amazing looks always seemed to command.

Oblivious to the stares, he simply gazed around the busy street. "Unbelievable," he muttered.

I paid the cab driver and he sped into traffic. Smiling, I took my father's hand. "Come on, Dad. I see Miss Galen inside. I'm sure she's waiting for us."

The agent was wide-eyed as my father and I walked through the gallery's front door.

"Hi, Miss Galen. I'd like you to meet my father, Brian Blackthorne."

It took her a minute to regain the power of speech as she gazed up at my father. "Welcome, Cara. It's very nice to meet you, Mr. Blackthorne." She sounded slightly breathless.

My father smiled at her. I could almost hear her purr. I sighed. I should probably be used to it by now.

I nudged her. "Why don't you show us around the gallery. It's a lot bigger than the one in Albany, isn't it?"

"Yes, indeed it is," she said. Finally looking at me, she said, "Cara, for a new, young artist to be included in a show at a gallery like this one is practically unheard of. Art lovers here in New York are rather different than those you met at the show in Albany."

I must have turned a bit paler than usual because she quickly added, "Don't worry, dear. Your work speaks for itself. I think these new watercolors are even lovelier than the last ones. I'm sure they'll sell." She hesitated. "That is, do you want to sell these?"

I nodded. "Yes. Everything I'm showing today can be sold if there are buyers who like my work."

"They will, Cara, trust me." She smiled. "Why don't you and your father take a tour of the gallery? Mr. Sullivan's paintings are to your left, and another new young artist is showcased at the rear of this room. He's not a client of mine, but he's very talented."

After we'd admired Francis Sullivan's big, beautiful oil paintings, we moved on to the wall where my work had been hung. On the bright white wall, under the gallery's lighting, I was again amazed at how good my watercolors and the pen and ink drawings looked.

"Cara, your work belongs in settings like this one," my father whispered. "Do you have any idea how proud of you your mother and I are?" He smiled and dropped a kiss on my head.

I felt my face turning red, wondering if I'd ever be able to accept a compliment calmly. "Thanks, Dad."

He chuckled. "There are people arriving. Let's move on to the rear of the gallery and take a look at the other new artist's work."

The other artist's work was all in oils, large street scenes of poorer neighborhoods filled with the fascinating people who lived there. It was a microcosm of city life, the good and the bad, the hardworking and those who skirted the law. It was all there in each of his paintings. I could spend hours just examining each person, each element he'd included on each canvas. I thought it was wonderful.

"Dad, this is great work. I love it. I wonder if the artist is here today? I'd like to meet him." The small signature in one corner of the canvas was simply signed, "Win."

A tenor voice behind me said, "Winthrop Mason, at your service. I heard what you said. Thank you."

I turned to see a young man, not much taller than me, smiling. "I hope everyone who comes into the gallery today likes my paintings as much as you do, Miss."

I smiled. "I'm sure they will. Is 'Win' the name you go by?"

He laughed. "Well, Winthrop is pretty stuffy, so yeah, you can call me Win."

I put out my hand. "Cara Blackthorne. I'm really pleased to meet you. I was telling my father I could spend hours examining every element in your paintings. I've never seen anything like them before."

He looked up at my father. "Your father. I should have known." He smiled. "You have the same eyes." He put out his hand and my father shook it.

Win asked, "Who's this other young artist the gallery is featuring today? Those pen and ink drawings are wonderful."

Once again, I felt my face turning pink. "Uh, those are mine."

Win's eyes got bigger. "Seriously?" He laughed. "This is my lucky day. I'm honored, Miss Blackthorne." And he bowed to me.

He said, "The gallery is getting crowded. Let's find a corner where we can see and hear without drawing too much attention. Uh, Mr. Blackthorne, I'm afraid you will always draw too much attention. Maybe you could find another corner."

It was said with such good humor, my father laughed. "You're quite right. I think I'll simply circulate. They're serving champagne up there." He looked at me, "Sweetheart, no champagne for you, I'm afraid."

And with that he drifted away, as every head turned in his wake.

Win looked at me with a smile. "Your father has what we call 'presence.'"

I rolled my eyes. "Yep, he practically stops traffic wherever we go."

We found a quiet corner not far from where his paintings had been hung and chatted about art shows in general. He was surprised to learn this was only my second show.

"You have a top-level agent, Cara. Miss Galen is very well known in art circles. How did she find you?"

"Francis Sullivan is a good friend of my father's. He's been my mentor for the past year."

Win's eyes widened again. "Wow. That's a real stroke of luck."

Blushing, I said, "I know. Without his help, it might have been years before my work would ever be shown in a gallery like this one."

He shook his head with a smile. "I doubt that. I really like your work. You have such a delicate touch, both with a brush and with the pen. I would almost call your pen and ink drawings 'magical.' They have that feeling, you know?"

Laughing, he said, "You're blushing again. How young are you, Cara?"

"Seventeen. I keep hoping I'll outgrow this tendency to turn pink. It's embarrassing."

He smiled. "It's charming. I hope you keep it. Where are you studying?"

"I'm starting at the Barrett Art Institute in September. Are you still in school?"

"I just graduated from Massachusetts College of Art and Design. I can now add B.F.A. after my name. That pleases my parents more than me. I've heard good things about Barrett. Your first time away from home?"

"Yes. I'm really looking forward to it. My father and I will be driving up to Barrett next week."

We could both see a respectable sized crowd around his paintings. But we were too far from where my work hung to see if it was getting much attention.

An older man approached us. "Win, I have a client who'd like to meet you. Can I drag you away from your beautiful companion for a few minutes?"

I patted Win's arm and whispered, "Good luck." He grinned at me and walked over to the crowd of people clustered around his paintings.

My father reappeared with two glasses. One was acceptable for a seventeen-year-old. "Thanks, Dad. Let's take a walk over near my work."

Several people were discussing my work. One lady was telling her husband, "I really want these watercolors, dear."

He asked, "All of them?"

"Yes, definitely," she said. "I have the perfect place for them. The artist's approach is so nostalgic. Her signature is 'Cara.' Is she here? I'd like to meet her."

Miss Galen was right behind me and drew me over to the couple. "I'd like you to meet Cara Blackthorne."

They turned around and looked surprised. The woman said, "You're Cara?"

"Yes. It's nice to meet you."

"It's lovely to meet *you*, Cara. You're very young to show such skill. I love the way you painted these Victorian homes. They remind me of my childhood. I grew up in a house like this one." She pointed to one of my paintings.

I smiled. "So did I. In fact, that's my mother's house. She grew up there."

After telling me again how much they liked my watercolors, they moved on. The gallery was crowded now, so I tried to stay out of the way as I watched and listened to the conversations of the obvious art lovers. I noticed that all of my watercolors had "Sold" stickers on the frames. Two of my pen and ink drawings were wearing the same stickers.

I couldn't stop smiling.

About an hour later, after a few encouraging words with Miss Galen, my father and I left the gallery. We didn't want to miss the last evening train to Somerville, which was only ten miles from Thornewood.

"I'd say you had an extremely successful day, Cara," my father said as we returned to Penn Station in another taxi.

Still smiling, I had to agree. "Miss Galen said she was sure the last two pen and ink drawings would sell during the week. I'm thrilled so many people liked my work. And, last but not least, my bank account will get a little fatter."

He laughed, shaking his head. "Seventeen and a financial success. It doesn't seem possible."

As we rushed through the train station to our platform, I thought I saw a familiar face, but not one I'd ever wanted to see again. The man rushed past us on his way out of the train station. When he spotted me, his eyes narrowed.

I'd stopped short when I saw him and stared at him. Nick Romanov. I had thought he was in jail.

From right behind me, my father asked, "Who was that? He seemed to know you. I didn't like his looks, Cara."

Romanov had continued out of the station after giving me a dirty look.

"That was Nick Romanov, the drug dealer, the man who tried to cut my throat. I have to call the Chief when we get home. I want to know why he's out of jail."

My father's face had turned to stone for a few tense minutes.

By the time we got home, it was late and we were starved. Mom had waited up and must have started making sandwiches as soon as she heard my car pull in.

After we told her how successful the art show had been, I asked, "Is it too late to call the Chief?"

She looked startled and obviously curious, but she said, "You can probably leave a message on his phone, Cara. Did something happen today?"

"In Penn Station tonight I saw that drug dealer, Nick Romanov. You know, the one Gavin shot in the back." I snorted. "He looked pretty healthy to me."

My father added, "He was not pleased to see Cara. We both thought he was in jail. That's why she wants to call Tom."

Mom was frowning. "Did he say anything to you?"

"No, he just gave me a dirty look. He might have said something if he hadn't seen Dad with me."

Mom said, "Well, go ahead and call Tommy and leave a message. I'm sure he'll call you back first thing tomorrow."

"Tomorrow's Sunday, Mom."

"Cara, our Police Chief works seven days a week, I'm afraid. Other than the police force, I don't think Tommy has a life."

I felt kind of sorry for the Chief, but I called him anyway. I left a message on his machine, asking why Nick Romanov was out of jail.

With that out of the way, I ate a sandwich and had a bowl of Mom's delicious homemade split pea soup. It had been simmering on the stove when we got home.

When we'd finished eating, I realized that I was too tired to stay up any longer.

I rinsed out my dishes and put them in the dishwasher. Hugging my father, I said, "Thanks for going with me today, Dad. It was fun."

"It was my pleasure, sweetheart. I enjoyed the art show, but New York City was a shock. I still can't believe people actually live in that crowded, noisy environment."

Mom was trying not to laugh, but I agreed completely. It was obvious to me that Elves did not belong in the city.

Early Sunday morning, Mom woke me to say the Chief was on the phone and wanted to ask me a few questions. I groaned. "The Chief starts his day too early," I grumbled.

I staggered out of bed and went downstairs to the house phone in the kitchen.

I yawned. "Morning, Chief."

He chuckled. "Too early for you, Cara?"

"A little. I was in Manhattan yesterday and got back late. That's why I called you last night."

"Your mother tells me you saw Romanov in the city yesterday. Did he say or do anything to you?"

"No, he just glared at me and kept going. But I thought he was in jail. How come he's out?"

"Cara, his trial isn't scheduled until August. He's out on bail until then. Someone with a lot of money paid his bail, which I didn't expect. His bail was set very high."

"You mean he's on the loose until August? Judging by the look he gave me, he'd still like to cut my throat."

"I understand your concern, but he hasn't been seen in Thornewood, and his only restriction is not to leave the state. Maybe you should ask your father to assign a bodyguard for you until after Romanov's trial."

My heart sank a little. I didn't want another bodyguard.

"I don't think so, Chief. I'm out of school now and other than a trip to Syracuse, I'll be sticking close to home until I leave for Art school the end of August. By that time, Romanov will be in prison, won't he?"

"As far as I know, he will be. The State has a good case against him for drug distribution, as well as his assault on you. But I'll let my men know that they need to keep their eyes open in case Romanov is dumb enough to come to Thornewood. They know he's a threat to you. You'll just need to be totally aware of your surroundings. You know what to do if you see him."

"Yes. I'll call you right away."

"Good girl. I've got to get to work now, Cara. Give some thought to a bodyguard, okay?"

"Okay. Thanks, Chief."

There would be no bodyguard. Not unless the situation became desperate.

Mom was sitting at the kitchen table and had heard my side of the conversation.

"Why isn't that man in jail, Cara?"

I told her what the Chief had said. "It's not likely he'll come back here, Mom." I chuckled. "He probably knows he might get another arrow in the back if he shows his face around here."

THE JOINING TREE

"Maybe so, but I think it's best if your father and I both go to Syracuse with you to help you find an apartment."

"Okay. That sounds good." For obvious reasons, driving up to Barrett by myself had temporarily lost its appeal.

I left for Syracuse with Mom and Dad bright and early Tuesday morning. Mrs. Gardner had given me addresses and phone numbers of houses we could check out.

Mom and Dad were in a great mood, as though they were playing hooky from school. Their high spirits kept me smiling all the way to Syracuse.

Of course, Mom normally spent all her time either at the bookstore or at home. And Dad traveled between Elvenwood, his camp, and our home. Except for my art shows, my parents never went *anywhere*! No wonder they were enjoying themselves so much.

We'd taken my car because it was roomy, something my father's long legs appreciated. Traffic wasn't heavy and we made it to Syracuse in under two hours.

All morning we drove through the neighborhoods that surrounded the Barrett Institute, stopping at several houses to see available apartments. The apartments were small, which I expected, but they all lacked one thing: a separate room with good light where I could paint. We stopped at a coffee shop for lunch and then continued looking at apartments.

The last apartment was no different than those we'd already seen, and I was feeling discouraged. The homeowner was a middle-aged lady who noticed the unhappy look on my face as we left the upstairs apartment.

She said, "This doesn't seem to be what you're looking for. If I knew exactly what you need, I might be able to point you in the right direction." She looked at my father, who smiled and said, "I think my wife can give you better answers than I can."

Mom said, "Well, like most of your tenants, my daughter is an artist. She needs some extra space for painting, but so far we haven't seen any apartments with enough room. All the apartments we've seen are quite small. Do you know of any larger places?"

The lady smiled. "I think I can solve both our problems. Having an upstairs tenant is rather noisy, mainly due to them running up and down the stairs day and night." She laughed. "Students are constantly in and out, of course. My downstairs apartment is much larger than the one I rent out upstairs. It may have the space you need, and living upstairs would give me the peace and quiet I need."

Mom looked at me and I nodded.

"Can we see it now? We're only in Syracuse for the day."

"Of course. Come on in. I've got coffee made if anyone's interested," the lady said.

"By the way, my name is Laurie Williams. The house belonged to my parents originally. It's mine now. They converted the upstairs to an apartment while I was away at college."

She poured coffee for all of us and invited me to look around. After I finished my coffee, I walked through her apartment, which was larger than the upstairs unit. It had a generous living room where my parents were sitting, a modern, fully equipped kitchen with a breakfast nook, a small bedroom with attached bath, and a larger room in the rear with three generously sized windows that let in a lot of light. It was currently set up as a guest room.

It was perfect. When I returned to the living room, Miss Williams nodded when she saw the smile on my face.

I looked at my parents. "It's perfect. That back room is big and sunny, and the rest of the apartment is bigger than anything we've seen today. If Miss Williams is willing to give it up, I'd love to live here."

Mom asked if she could take a look, and no more than two minutes later, she returned to the living room smiling. "Cara's right, this apartment is perfect for her. I think she'll be very comfortable here."

With that settled, Miss Williams said she'd need a month to move upstairs, which worked out perfectly since I wouldn't be starting at Barrett for two more months. She gave us a one-year lease at what I thought was a reasonable rate and told me she'd call me as soon as her downstairs apartment was painted and ready for me. She also offered to leave some of her furniture for me so I wouldn't have to buy everything.

"Thanks so much for everything, Miss Williams," I said as we were leaving.

Mom added, "You've been very generous. We do appreciate it."

Smiling, Miss Williams said, "Last year I had two young men upstairs. I had to use ear plugs at night! I'll talk to you soon, Cara."

As we drove out of Syracuse, Mom said, "That's a lot more apartment than I thought we'd find for you, Cara. You could live there comfortably for the next three years. As soon as you hear from Miss Williams, let's drive up again to see what you'll need in the way of furnishings." She grinned. "This is really exciting, isn't it?"

I had to laugh. "Doesn't sound like you're going to miss me very much, Mom."

"Of course I will, sweetheart. We'll both miss you, but you said you'd be coming home most weekends, so I don't think we'll forget what you look like!"

My father added, "I've only had about a year to enjoy having a daughter, Cara. I'll be missing you a great deal." He was totally serious which took the smile right off my face.

I hadn't even thought about my father's feelings. What was wrong with me?

THE JOINING TREE

After dinner that night, I asked him a question that had been on my mind.

"Dad, will we still be able to talk to each other mentally when I'm away at school?"

He raised one eyebrow. "I've never tested the ability from such a distance. I guess we'll find out."

My ever-practical mother added, "There's always the phone, Cara. The world won't come to an end if you and your father have to communicate the same way we humans do."

We both looked at her to see if she was teasing us. She was, a smile on her face.

My father added, "Cara, as you pointed out, you'll be home every weekend. I'll be looking forward to that."

He smiled at me with the same warmth I'd been taking for granted.

I didn't think my father realized how important he'd become to me. I had to find some way to let him know. Words simply weren't enough.

As I lay in bed that night, waiting for sleep to claim me, I suddenly realized what I wanted to do for my father. I fell asleep as I was making my plans.

Since my thoughts while still awake often coincided with my dreams, I found myself dreaming of the day a year ago when I got my first look at my larger-than-life father.

With that unusual mental ability he had, he'd inserted himself into a drawing I was working on in the forest. I hadn't noticed it until I got home when Sean pointed it out to me.

Leaning against one of the tall pine trees I'd drawn was a tall, well-built man with long dark hair. His high cheekbones and green eyes seemed familiar, and he was smiling at me.

In my dream, I knew instinctively that I was looking at my father for the first time.

CHAPTER 15

I spent my summer working on the project I planned to give my father. Amy and Kevin made sure I wasn't turning into a total hermit by collecting me every Friday afternoon and taking me out to either the Pizza Palace or The Grille. I hoped we wouldn't run into Sean, and so far we hadn't.

"You've been drawing and/or painting non-stop, Cara," Amy said. "Is this for another art show?"

I shook my head with a smile. "No. This is a personal project of mine, something I'm making to give to my father before I leave for Barrett."

"Well, are you going to show us what you've done so far?" Kevin asked.

"Nope. No one sees this until it's finished. I've never done anything like it before. To be honest, I'm a little nervous about it. My father knows nothing about it. I don't want to disappoint him in case it's an artistic disaster!"

She laughed. "Not possible, Cara."

Amy was working with her parents on the final stages of reopening the Strauss Bakery. It had a brand new kitchen and the building had been expanded to make room for a catering office that Amy would be running.

"How's the bakery coming along?" I asked her. "When's the grand opening?"

She was grinning. "Two more weeks. I'm putting a big ad in the Thornewood newspaper to let everyone in town know we're back. I'll also be serving free samples at the catering desk during the grand opening."

Glancing at Kevin, she added, "Keeping Kevin from the samples will probably require all of my energy." She laughed. "But I hope you'll take some time off from your artwork to come to our grand opening. Bring your mom and dad too, okay?"

"Absolutely."

"Your father has been great, Cara. He's helped out a lot since my folks finally decided to rebuild instead of retiring."

For a while, Mr. and Mrs. Strauss were so freaked out by the arson fire that had destroyed the bakery's kitchen, they had considered retiring. I think my parents finally convinced Amy's parents how important the Strauss Bakery was to Thornewood.

Kevin had already finished his last computer game, "Dragon Wars," and was now working on something he was calling, "Return of the Alien." I refused to think about what had inspired that title.

He'd already given us our preproduction copies of Dragon Wars, but I hadn't taken the time to play mine yet. Amy said she and her father were having a ball with it. Unlike me, they were both avid gamers.

THE JOINING TREE

Kevin was doing extremely well financially, thanks to the diabolical computer games he was designing. The manufacturing company he was under contract to paid well. Kevin already had the expense of his first two years of college paid for.

The generous college fund my father had set up when I was born would pay for all three years of the Barrett Art Institute, including my living expenses in Syracuse, with money left over. Where fathers were concerned, I'd been blessed—one more reason for the project I was working on.

I had decided that my project should be done mostly in pen and ink, with just a touch of watercolor as an accent. I'd been working on it daily for three weeks when I ran out of India Ink. Of course, I'd known I was getting low and should have replaced it sooner, but I'd procrastinated. Right now, I could go no further until I bought more ink.

Annoyed with myself, I pulled on a pair of sandals and drove downtown to the art supply shop. Naturally, they were completely out of India Ink, but the owner assured me he would receive a shipment in three or four days. I didn't want to wait that long.

"Do you know of any other stores that carry it locally?" I asked the manager.

"Only the Artist's Corner in Greenville. Let me call them for you before you drive over there."

Fortunately, that store had India Ink in stock. Unfortunately, Greenville wasn't a place I particularly wanted to be since Nick Romanov was still out of jail, awaiting trial. I wondered if I could talk one of my friends into going with me.

Amy was waiting for the new stove to be delivered to the bakery, and Kevin's phone went to voice mail. My father was in Elvenwood for the day. I knew Randi wouldn't be caught dead in Greenville, probably for the same reason I didn't want to go there. I couldn't call Sean. Who did that leave? I couldn't go for days without ink!

In my opinion, my need was urgent, so I left the house and jogged through the woods to my father's camp, hoping to find one of my former bodyguards there.

I was in luck. Gabriel walked out of a tent, spotted me and headed for me with a big smile on his good-looking face.

"Cara! This is a nice surprise. What brings you here today? Your dad's in Elvenwood. In the mood for a ride on Storm?"

"Maybe later, Gabe. I need someone to ride to Greenville with me. I ran out of ink."

I was a little breathless. Gabe raised one eyebrow, looking a bit confused.

"Uh, Gabe, I'm working on a project for my dad, a picture I want to give him before I leave for art school. I've got a few more weeks, but it's a difficult project, the kind of thing I've never done before. I ran out of ink today and the store downtown won't have any more for several days, but the store in Greenville has it in stock."

He nodded. "You don't want to drive to Greenville alone? Is that the problem?"

"Yes. That drug dealer is out on bail. I know he blames me for his arrest. I saw him in New York City a few weeks ago when my dad and I were there. I know he hates me. I'm lucky my dad was with me."

"Okay, Cara. I'll have to change my clothes and let the other Elves know I have to leave camp for a while." He pointed at the camp chairs around the campfire. "Have a seat. This won't take long."

I sat down, relieved that I'd have a big, strong young man with me. If I ran into Romanov, he'd think twice before tangling with Gabe.

Within minutes, Gabe was back, dressed in what the Elves called "human clothes," jeans, t-shirt, and tennis shoes in place of the green tunics and slacks they normally wore.

I couldn't help smiling. They must have stocked up on "human clothes" last year while so many were playing bodyguard for my friends and me.

With their Elven features glamoured, dressed in the predictable jeans and t-shirts, the Elves looked like human teenagers, but noticeably better looking. They couldn't help it. The Elves, male and female, were a beautiful race.

"Okay, Cara. Let's go."

As we walked through the woods, Gabe said, "This will be a real treat. I've missed my bodyguard days almost as much as I miss football." He was grinning. "I've never had so much fun. I know it was a huge relief to you when Gaynes was put in jail, but I was sorry to see it end." He chuckled. "Purely selfish, of course."

I rolled my eyes. "Huge relief is putting it mildly. That monster wanted to kill me. If it hadn't been for a certain dragon, along with my knives, he might have done it."

"Cara, your skill with knives has saved your life twice now. Don't let yourself get rusty. You should keep practicing."

Gabe was grinning as we got into my big, black car. "I love your car. It looks powerful. Any chance we'll get to race it today?"

"Hate to disappoint you, but I doubt there will be any reason to race it. The speed limit is 65, and I'm not planning on going any faster than that."

I heard him mutter, "I can always hope."

It was early afternoon and traffic on the highway was light. We made it to Greenville in under thirty minutes. I only had to exceed sixty-five mph once when I had to pass a car doing fifty in the fast lane. To Gabriel's delight, I got the car up to seventy-five for a few seconds, before slowing down to sixty-five again.

"It's a good thing you'll probably never have a car," I said to him.

"I think I would be a very good driver."

"A very fast driver," I added. "Lots of speeding tickets."

He just laughed. He was smiling the entire trip. Gabe really loved being in a car.

THE JOINING TREE

We found Artist's Corner on a side street and went inside to buy my ink. It was a much larger store than the art supply store in Thornewood, and I decided to spend a little time browsing. Gabe stayed at my side, just looking around, occasionally asking me to explain what something was used for.

We stayed there for almost an hour before I decided I'd go broke if I stayed any longer. I'd purchased some large sheets of watercolor paper, a supply of heavy backing cardboard, several additional cakes of watercolor paint, and a few bottles of India Ink.

As soon as I'd paid for my supplies, we left.

I talked about watercolor painting as we walked back to where my car was parked, about a block away. When it came into view, I froze.

Leaning on my fender with a nasty smile on his face was Nick Romanov.

He took a few steps toward me, but when Gabe stepped toward him and got in front of me, Romanov stopped short, dropping the smile.

He sneered, "What's the matter? Did you lose your knife?" Slowly he pulled what looked like my knife out of his back pocket.

Within a split second, Gabe and I were both holding our knives in front of us, ready to throw, which Romanov clearly wasn't expecting. For a split second, I saw fear on his face.

He backed up, tossing my knife on the ground in front of me. "Just returning this, little girl. That's all." He sauntered away, looking over his shoulder at us until he reached the corner.

When he'd disappeared from sight, Gabe reached down and picked up my knife.

He looked at me. "Is this really yours?"

I nodded. "The last time I saw it, it was sticking out of Romanov's hand."

Gabe's eyebrows went up. "Oh, I see. I'm guessing he would have done more than return it to you if I hadn't been here."

I took a deep breath. "Yeah. Let's go home."

On the drive home, Gabe wanted to know more about my history with Romanov. When I'd finished describing my previous run-ins with the man, Gabe was quiet for a while. Finally, he asked, "Why hasn't your father assigned a bodyguard for you?"

I immediately shook my head. "Because I don't want another bodyguard, Gabe. And I think my father's too smart to force one on me."

I realized I sounded angry, and I didn't want Gabe to think that my anger was directed at him.

His voice was softer than usual when he said, "It's okay. I think I understand."

I looked over at him and found him watching me carefully.

"Cara, most of us were shocked when Adam left. But a few of us understood why he did."

That surprised me. "Why do you think he left?"

"It was clear to me that you and Adam had become close. Even though Brian had assigned him to be your bodyguard, we all realized his devotion to you went beyond duty."

His words were making my heart pound as I realized that my relationship with Adam had not been a secret. Not to the other Elves.

"Yes, we did become close. But why did he leave? I depended on him and he left without even a word." I knew I sounded angry again.

Gabe said, "Cara, I think the closeness between you was too much for Adam to handle. You weren't a child to him, you know."

I had reached home and we were parked in front of my mom's house.

I didn't say anything right away. After a few quiet minutes, I asked, "Do you think he'll ever come back?"

"Do you want him to come back?"

I hesitated. "I don't know."

I was making good progress on my pen and ink project when Miss Williams called from Syracuse a week later. She had moved into the upstairs apartment, the downstairs rooms had been painted, and I was welcome to come up to Syracuse any time.

When I passed this information on to Mom, she looked pleased. "Well, we can drive up to furnish your new apartment whenever you're ready. We'll have quite a bit of shopping to do. I know you hate to shop, dear, but I think it will be fun. Your first home away from home, Cara. Aren't you at least a little excited?"

I nodded, still a bit unsure about all the shopping. "Maybe Amy will have time to go with us. That would speed up the shopping considerably."

My mother laughed, shaking her head. "Yes, the queen of shoppers. I know she'll enjoy the whole process more than you will. Call her tonight. I know she's been spending her days at the bakery, getting ready for their grand opening."

Amy was, of course, delighted to help me shop. "I can get away on Thursday. We're not expecting any major deliveries that day, so Mom and Dad can handle anything else that's going on. Shopping for your first apartment, Cara! This will be such fun. I can't wait!"

On Thursday Mom actually closed the bookstore for the day, something she rarely did, so I knew how excited she was about getting me situated in Syracuse.

"Remember, Cara, I never had a chance to go to college, so I'm enjoying it vicariously. It's not that I won't miss you when you're away, it's more that I'm really happy for you. And when you're home on weekends, you can tell me all the wonderful things you're doing." She sounded wistful as she added, "The next best thing to being there myself."

Before we left, I hugged her, something I didn't do very often anymore.

Amy and Mom chattered all the way to Syracuse. We'd taken my car, so I was perfectly happy to listen to them while I concentrated on driving.

Amy described all of her plans for the new bakery, and Mom made a few suggestions.

Amy wanted a complete description of my apartment in Syracuse. She had tons of ideas for furnishing it; I only had one or two ideas of my own.

When Amy asked, "What's our budget?" Mom simply smiled.

"Brian wants Cara to have whatever she needs to be comfortable and happy, so I guess we don't have to look too hard at price tags," Mom said with a chuckle.

"Cool!" Amy said. "This is really gonna be fun!"

We arrived at Miss Williams' house two hours later. I rang the bell and my smiling landlady let us in, promptly handing me a key for the front door and another key for the door to my new apartment on the ground floor.

I unlocked the apartment door and we walked inside with Miss Williams.

"I want to see how you like the paint job as well as the pieces of furniture I left for you. I can remove anything you won't need, Cara."

"Thanks, Miss Williams. The paint is a perfect shade, a warm off-white."

We were standing in the cozy living room that featured one whole wall of built-in bookshelves and three windows on the wall that looked out on the street. There was a small table against the wall next to the doorway, and the floor was a highly polished hardwood that looked like oak. I'd need either a couch or a couple of armchairs, and maybe a coffee table.

"I love this room," I told Miss Williams. "Those bookshelves will come in handy. And I won't need much furniture."

She smiled. "You'll just need something to sit on. Now come and take a look at the kitchen. I think it already has everything you'll need other than silverware, dishes and maybe a pan or two. Do you cook?"

Mom laughed. "Cara uses the toaster, the microwave, and a coffee pot. That's a very nice stove but it's unlikely it will ever be turned on."

I rolled my eyes.

The kitchen was also equipped with a built-in L-shaped breakfast nook that would seat four. There were thick gingham cushions on the seats. Mom said, "This looks comfortable."

Amy said, "Didn't you say there was a café on campus?"

I grinned. "Yep. That's probably where I'll get most of my meals. I'll survive."

From the kitchen we walked into the bedroom and bath, small rooms but roomy enough for me. There was a double bed and a small dresser, so I wouldn't have to buy those either.

"Miss Williams, thanks so much for leaving so much furniture for Cara," Mom said. "We won't have to buy nearly as much as I'd expected."

My landlady smiled. "No problem, Mrs. Blackthorne. They're all pieces I don't need upstairs. I'll leave you now. Have fun shopping!"

There was one more room I wanted to inspect—the large room in the rear of the house that would be my studio. To me, it was the most important room.

I walked through the bedroom into the larger room behind it. Three large windows let in the afternoon sun, and there was a sliding door closet at one side of the room. That would be perfect for storing my art supplies. Instead of the hardwood that had been used in the other rooms, the floor was an attractive black and white checkerboard vinyl tile.

Mom said, "I think there was carpet in here when we visited before. Miss Williams took it up and replaced it with vinyl because you said you needed this room for your painting. Cara, your landlady has thought of everything."

I was beaming. My mother was right. I looked at Amy. "What do you think, Amy? Do you like it?"

Amy hadn't said a word since we arrived. "This apartment is wonderful, Cara. It's even partially furnished. All it needs is some color!"

She was wearing a big grin and I knew she couldn't wait to be let loose in a department store.

Mom and I looked at us and smiled.

"Let's go shopping, girls!"

Three hours later, we'd stopped for lunch and come close to maxing out Mom's credit card at the huge department store near the Barrett campus. Fortunately, they were holding a "Back to School" sale.

In addition to linens, towels, plates, coffee mugs, and silverware, I had picked out a plush, comfy couch covered in some kind of velour that felt just like velvet, and an easy chair in the same style. The couch was a pale smoky gray, and the chair was a deep blue that reminded me of someone's eyes. I couldn't help it. The chair looked perfect with the couch. Amy thought so too. On a more practical note, I found an adjustable office chair to use in my studio. Everything would be delivered the next day, and Miss Williams would be there to let them in.

Since Amy was our resident "decorator," she dashed through the store grabbing throw pillows, blankets, a down comforter, shower curtain, place mats and matching napkins which I insisted I wouldn't need, and an ultra-modern coffee maker that looked like it could operate itself with no help from human hands.

Practical Mom had taken over the kitchenware department. Despite my arguments, she insisted I might need a few pans some day. I threw my hands in the air and left her there, perusing the sleek stainless steel sets of cookery and the expensive implements that would rarely if ever be used, obviously enjoying herself.

After I'd picked out colors for all the items Amy had found, we filled two shopping carts and returned to my mother who was still in the kitchenware department, debating the merits of two frying pans.

"Mom, you know I'm not going to fry anything. Fear of flying grease, remember?"

She snorted. "How could I have forgotten? In that case, I'm buying you one of these." She picked up a small electric frying pan with a lid and placed it in my hands.

Before I could complain, she said, "You're not too likely to get splattered if you use one of these. You can set the temperature nice and low, and put the cover on while you're cooking. You'll be safe from flying grease."

I decided to go along with her. It was easier than trying to convince her I would never fry anything.

I peeked into her shopping cart and saw the electric frying pan, a 4-slice toaster, one sauce pot, two spatulas, a large spoon, a bottle opener, a set of kitchen knives, four potholders, a cookie sheet, a round pizza pan, a set of measuring cups—*like I'd be measuring anything*—and an electric can opener.

"If you find you need anything else," she said to me, "you can always pick it up later. But I think you've got the basics now."

I just shook my head while Amy tried to hold back giggles. "Yep. You know, I'll probably only use the bottle opener, a kitchen knife, a potholder, and the pizza pan."

She gave me the one-eyebrow raised, mother-knows-best look and said, "We'll see."

On our way to the cashier's station, I saw a standing brass coat rack, old-fashioned in style, and grabbed it.

Mom looked surprised. "There's no coat closet in the living room," I told her.

She nodded, smiling. "You *can* be practical on occasion. Good thinking, Cara."

Amy tried to stifle a giggle.

The cashier was wide-eyed when she saw our three overflowing shopping carts. Then she smiled. "Had fun today, didn't you?"

I had to laugh. "Yeah, we did."

After we unloaded all the stuff we bought into my new apartment—I'd get organized on my next trip—we asked Miss Williams if she'd take care of the furniture delivery the next day. She said she'd be happy to. I told her I'd be back a week before classes started to get settled, and she said she was looking forward to seeing me then.

As we walked to my car, Mom said, "Since it's getting so close to dinnertime, why don't we find a nice restaurant and have dinner before driving home."

Amy and I thought that was a splendid suggestion.

As I drove down the street I'd be living on in a few weeks, I noticed an old green van parked a few houses away. It reminded me of the van that had been an unknowing Good Samaritan the day of the snowstorm, leading me safely back to the school. I recognized it by the dark green curtains covering the van's rear windows.

The memory made me smile. I'd have to thank the van's owner if I ever saw him. Apparently we'd be neighbors.

With everything at Syracuse fairly well settled, I could concentrate on my pen and ink project again. There were only two weeks left before I would leave for Barrett, and my project was almost finished. It had turned out better than I expected, which was a huge relief. I hoped it would show my father how much he meant to me.

Late Friday afternoon Kevin and Amy stopped by to collect me for our usual Friday night dinner. This had become a fixed point in my week over the summer. Without it, I doubt I would have known what day it was.

This week they had chosen the Pizza Palace for our get-together. My growling stomach told me it was a perfect choice. As we sat in a booth after placing our order, Kevin was pretending to be deafened by the noises my stomach was making.

"When was the last time you ate?" he asked me.

"Hmm. I'm not sure. Maybe breakfast?"

He shook his head. "You do get lost in your artwork, don't you?"

"Yeah. Occupational hazard, I guess."

"How's your big project coming?" Amy asked.

I smiled. "Almost finished. I'm happy with it. I think it says what I wanted it to say to my father. I hope he likes it."

"I'm sure he'll love it," she said.

Looking toward the entrance, she whispered, "Uh-oh," and looked over at Kevin. She wasn't smiling. His eyebrows went up slightly.

When I turned toward the door, I understood. Sean had just walked in with the girl he was now dating. She was tall, blonde, and blue-eyed, all the things I wasn't.

He spotted us, Amy smiled and waved, Kevin said hi, and Sean nodded at them. He wasn't smiling and he didn't look at me.

Our pizza was brought to our table, but I already had heartburn. I couldn't take even one bite.

Amy slid closer to me in the booth and said, "Sorry. I guess we were bound to run into him eventually."

Kevin, being Kevin, simply said, "If you've lost your appetite, I can eat your pizza."

Amy elbowed him and gave him one of those *"You insensitive idiot!"* looks.

Kevin put down his pizza to say softly, "Come on, short stuff. You knew he was dating, right? You told him he should date, and you told him you didn't want a relationship with him. Am I right?"

I nodded. He was right, but seeing Sean with another girl hurt. And I knew it was my own fault. I was the one who ended things when I told him I was in love with Adam.

Kevin ate most of my pizza while I sipped at my root beer. My appetite had left town.

I tried not to look at Sean and his date while we told Kevin about my apartment at Barrett. We talked about my almost-finished project too.

Kevin grinned. "I can't wait to see it, babe. Knowing you, it'll be brilliant. When will the unveiling take place?"

"I've been planning on giving it to my dad the night before I leave for school. Maybe you two could join us for dinner that night."

"Ask your mom to make it spaghetti night and we'll have a 'Bon Voyage' party for you," Kevin said. After a few seconds, he added, "I'm really gonna miss spaghetti night."

Groaning, Amy elbowed him again. "Pay no attention to him, Cara. I'll bring the cake."

Kevin chuckled. "Oh, I'll miss you too, short stuff. You know that, don't you?"

I finally had to laugh. "Other than my parents, I think I'll miss you and Amy the most, Kev."

Behind me, I heard coins dropping into the old jukebox and my heart broke a little. I knew Sean and his date would get up to dance, something I really didn't want to watch. It was definitely time for me to leave.

Her eyes on my face, Amy knew exactly what I was feeling. She told Kevin to take the last piece of pizza with him and got up to pay the owner up at the bar in the front room. I was right behind her. Kevin followed me, grumbling a little, but he wrapped his free arm around my shoulder and gave me a brief hug anyway.

When we were outside on the street, I said, "Thanks, guys. Sorry I made you rush out of there. I couldn't sit there and watch Sean dancing with someone else."

Amy nodded, putting her arm around me. "I know. It may not be as hard the next time you run into him." I didn't want to think about a 'next time.'

We got into Kevin's Jeep and they took me home.

She nodded. "Call us if you need us, Cara."

She gave me an encouraging smile and they drove away.

When I walked in the door, I could hear my parents talking in the kitchen. I'd hoped to say good night to them and go straight to my room, but sharp-eyed Mom could see that something was wrong.

"You look upset, honey. What happened?"

I gave a deep sigh and sat down at the table with them. "We saw Sean and the girl he's dating now at the Pizza Palace. It hurt more than I thought it would."

Mom looked sympathetic. My father simply reached for my hand.

"Did you know he was dating someone new?" Mom asked.

"Yeah. Amy told me a few weeks ago. It wasn't a surprise." I snorted. "After all, I told him I thought he should be dating other girls."

My father squeezed my hand. "Cara, you were honest with Sean. You did the right thing, even if it's hard to deal with right now. It will get easier with time."

"I guess."

I stood. "I think I'll go to bed. Good night." I dropped a kiss on Mom's cheek and hugged my dad.

They were silent as I trudged up the stairs, but I was sure they'd be talking about me as soon as they heard my bedroom door close.

I filled a hot bath with herbal bath salts that smelled like the forest and soaked until the water cooled. I thought it might relax me so that I could sleep. But after I dried off and got into my pajamas, I was still too awake, imagining Sean dancing with his blonde, even though I'd left before I'd been forced to see it.

So many times I'd wished that I'd fallen in love with Sean. He was such a good person, decent, honest, kind, considerate. . . I could spend the next hour listing all of his good qualities. He was always there when I needed him. But I'd sent him away because I was in love with someone else.

Had that been a mistake?

For the next week, I didn't leave the house except to sing for Rowenna from the back porch a few times. She never landed in the yard, but she always let me know she could feel what I was feeling. She was sorry I was depressed but let me know that she believed in listening to your heart.

It never lies, she told me.

Did she mean that my heart knew that Adam was the one I would always love? Or that my feelings for Sean were more important than I'd believed?

I went inside, more confused than ever.

I spent the entire week working on my pen and ink project. By Friday morning, I knew it was finished. There was simply nothing else to add.

Standing back several feet from my easel, I tried to look at my drawing the way others would. I had to smile. It was my father, his warmth, his humor, and his love reflected in his eyes, the quirk of his lips, his body language, the way he held his head and shoulders.

I'd drawn him leaning against a tall pine, his arms crossed in front of him, just the way he'd looked in the simple line drawing that had appeared in a drawing of mine more than a year ago. He had put that sketch of himself in my mind, without my knowledge, and I'd unknowingly added it to the picture I'd drawn. I had decided later that it was his way of saying hello, since I wasn't supposed to meet him until I turned sixteen. It had happened a few weeks before my birthday.

His friend Conor had admitted that I looked a great deal like a good friend of his, but he didn't identify the friend, and he couldn't say more. He and my father were both bound by a promise my father had made to my mother when I was born. Getting that brief look at my father had meant so much to me.

THE JOINING TREE

Even though I wasn't allowed to actually meet my father, for weeks before my sixteenth birthday he had done everything he could to let me know he was nearby. I think I loved my father more than he realized.

And that was why I'd done this portrait of him. I wanted him to see himself the way I saw him.

I was at loose ends for the rest of the day. My father's portrait was finished, I'd covered it up, leaving it on the easel. I had nothing more to do until late afternoon when Kevin and Amy would pick me up and take me out for dinner.

The phone rang when I was in the kitchen. I was surprised when I heard the Chief's voice.

"Cara, I'm glad you're home. I have some news I'm afraid you won't like."

"What's going on, Chief?"

"Nick Romanov's trial is next week. I had thought we could keep you out of it, but the D.A. isn't sure she can convict him of drug distribution with the evidence she has. She's decided that there's a much better chance of convicting him for his attack on you."

"Does that mean I'll have to testify against him?"

"I'm afraid so, Cara. I know you've never had to go to court before, but I think you can handle it. Just to play it safe, I'll have a patrol car parked in front of your house for the next few days. I'll take you to the Courthouse in Greenville myself on Monday. We'll get you in and out quickly. It shouldn't take long."

We said good night, and I made a pot of herbal tea. We would all need a little help relaxing tonight. I'd have to tell my parents about the Chief's phone call before I went out with Kevin and Amy.

I sincerely hoped my father wouldn't insist on a bodyguard for me.

Mom got home right after she closed the bookstore, shortly after five, and my father returned from Elvenwood by five thirty. When they found me in the kitchen with a fresh pot of tea, they knew something was up.

Mom just shook her head, not surprised. "I was hoping Tommy could keep you out of this whole thing, but that man did attack you, and you should testify against him. I hope the penalty for attacking a girl with a knife is tougher than the penalty for selling drugs."

My father said, "Cara, should we be in court with you? Would it help you?"

I thought about it for a few minutes. "I think it would, Dad. If you wouldn't mind being there."

Mom said, "I'll close the store for the day. I think we should both be there, honey."

"Okay, thanks." Seeing my parents in the courtroom would make me less nervous.

As I was getting ready to go out, my phone rang. It was Kevin.

"Hey, babe. I took Amy shopping this afternoon, and, no surprise, we're still in Greenville. Only one store in Greenville carries the shoes she just *had* to have."

I laughed. Kevin sounded totally out of patience with Amy's shopping habits.

"Okay, Kev, so you're going to be late picking me up?"

"Actually, since The Grille will probably be busy at dinner time, why don't you drive over there in about twenty minutes and get us a booth. I'm already starved and I don't want to stand on line waiting for a table. Would you mind?"

"No problem, Kev. I'll see you there. Now tell Amy to make up her mind so you can get out of the store!"

He snorted. "Yeah, right. Piece of cake, short stuff." The sarcasm was hard to miss.

Mom came to the door as I left, and sure enough, there was already a police car parked in front of my house. I walked over to the cop to let him know where I was going, and he responded with a smile.

"Good choice, Cara. I can pick up a burger too."

McNally was one of the officers I'd met previously when Donald Gaynes had been trying to have me killed.

He followed me to The Grille, parked his vehicle, helped me out of my car, and escorted me into the restaurant. I explained that I was meeting two of my friends, and he took a seat at the counter.

Good thing Kevin asked me to get a booth when he called because The Grille was filling up quickly and I got one of the last booths.

I ordered a soda while I waited for Amy and Kevin, hoping Sean wouldn't walk in while I was there. If that were to happen, I think I would have left without eating. His coldness toward me had left a pain in the vicinity of my heart.

Twenty minutes later, Amy and Kevin finally walked in and joined me. By that time I was on my second soda and getting dirty looks from all the people who were waiting for a table.

"Sorry, sorry, Cara," Amy said. "I never thought my shopping would take this long." Glancing at Kevin, "Kev's annoyed with me too." She rolled her eyes, looking guilty.

"Well, did you at least find the shoes you were looking for?" I asked.

She grinned. "Yep. Navy blue stilettos. They make my legs look fantastic. Definitely worth the trip to Greenville. Now I just need the dress to go with them!"

Kevin rolled his eyes, his chin resting on his hand. "I'm starved, ladies. Can we just order now?"

We placed our orders and Amy looked around the restaurant. "The coast is clear tonight, isn't it?"

THE JOINING TREE

I nodded. "Honestly, Amy, sitting here alone, if Sean had walked in with or without a blonde, I would have left."

Kevin just watched me, understanding in his eyes.

Amy grinned. "I see that cute Officer McNally is in the house tonight."

"Yeah, he's actually with me," I said.

Kevin and Amy both gave me curious looks. I explained about my court appearance on Monday and the Chief's decision to provide some protection for me, "just in case."

"The Chief called to let me know the D.A. decided she'd have a better chance of convicting Romanov for assault than for selling drugs. So I have to testify. I've never had to go to court before. To be honest, I'm a little nervous."

After our burgers, fries, and milkshakes arrived, I tried to change the subject.

"I finished my pen and ink project. I think it turned out well."

"Congratulations," Amy said with a grin. "I'll bet it's gorgeous. I'm guessing it's a picture of your dad, right?"

I couldn't help smiling. "Yep. It's the first portrait I've ever done. I think it's pretty good."

Kevin chuckled. "Pretty good? Short stuff, I'll bet it's great."

We talked about our college and art school plans. I asked Kevin when he was leaving for NYU.

"I'll drive down to the city a few days before Labor Day to get my assigned dorm and get settled. Mom actually took the time to shop for all the dorm stuff I'll need." He snorted. "She even bought me some men's cologne." We all knew Kevin hated cologne and never wore it.

"But she got me linens and towels, soap, shampoo, an electric shaver, and a coffeemaker. What else will I need?"

Amy was laughing. "I can think of a few things, but at least she got you the basics, Kev."

"Yeah," he said, "I was really surprised that she made time to go shopping for me."

Amy added sarcastically, "Now if you could just teach her to shop for groceries."

Kevin chuckled. "I won't hold my breath."

I said, "Kev, I think she's going to miss you. Really. She'll be coming home to an empty house every night. You've always been there. But you won't be anymore."

Kevin looked up at me and nodded. "Yeah, you're right. I'm afraid she's gonna be lonely."

Amy asked, "When are you leaving for Barrett, Cara?"

"One more week. I want to spend at least a few days getting my apartment organized, stocking up on some groceries, walking around the campus, getting to know where everything is."

"Well, at least you'll be here for the bakery's grand opening next week. The old shop has been completely transformed, all sleek and modern now," Amy said.

Kevin grinned. "We'll be there, won't we, short stuff?"

I grinned back. "You bet. I've got to keep you from devouring all the free samples, don't I?"

We were all in a good mood when we got up to leave.

I paid our check—it was my turn this week—and we approached the front door of The Grille. Officer McNally saw us coming and jumped out of his patrol car to open the door and follow me back to my car.

I was on my way back to my house with the police car right behind me.

I can't describe what happened next, it was so sudden. One minute I was driving through the Main Street/Oak Street intersection on my way home, and the next minute I heard an incredibly loud crash and felt the passenger side of my car being slammed and I was pushed to the other side of the street.

The airbag hit me in the face, my hands came off the steering wheel to protect my face, I couldn't see anything in front of me, my heart was pounding, my ears ringing, which I later realized was the police car's siren behind me.

I guess I was in shock. I couldn't move and I didn't even know if I was hurt. I sat there in a kind of trance with my heart pounding until I realized someone was tapping on my driver's side window. I tried to turn my head, but the airbag was pressed to my face and I began to panic. I heard McNally's voice.

"Don't move, Cara. An ambulance is on the way. They'll get you out of your car safely, so just sit tight. I'm right here with you."

I think I said, "Okay" as I tried to calm down by taking deep breaths and telling myself I was okay, which I wasn't really sure about. That was when I realized my head was pounding like a drum, keeping time with the beat of my heart. I remembered this same kind of headache and hoped I wouldn't have to vomit into the airbag.

Where was Adam? I needed Adam *now*.

I obviously wasn't thinking clearly.

I vaguely remember someone forcing the door open, cutting my seatbelt off and lifting me out of my car. I remember the ride in the ambulance more clearly. They'd fastened a cervical collar around my neck, gave me oxygen through that little plastic thingy in my nose, checked my blood pressure regularly, and asked me questions I can't remember now.

By that time I realized I'd been in an accident. My car had been hit as I was driving home. I do remember wondering what kind of shape my car was in. I was more worried about my car than I was about my own injuries, whatever they were.

They took me to the Greenville E.R., where I'd been treated before, so they already had my records, insurance info, etc. An E.R. nurse checked me out and sent me to Radiology for X-rays. By the time I was brought back to the E.R., my mother was there, speaking to Officer McNally who, for some reason, had stayed at the hospital with me.

Mom rushed over to me when I was wheeled back into the E.R.

"Cara, how do you feel, sweetheart?" She had that worried look on her face I'd seen too many other times.

"I think I'm okay, Mom, no broken bones at least. But I have a killer headache and my neck is really stiff."

The E.R. doctor walked up to us, looking at a tablet he carried. "Mrs. Blackthorne?"

Mom nodded.

He smiled in what seemed a reassuring way. "Cara will be fine in a week to ten days. She's suffering from a kind of whiplash, involving a great deal of muscle pain, which is why she should keep that collar on, and she has abrasions and contusions. So, Cara, you'll be stiff and sore for at least a week. Don't get upset when you look in the mirror. Your face is bruised too, but the bruises will fade. Here's a prescription for pain for the next few days." He handed it to Mom. "If you begin to feel worse, come back in right away. Go home and get some rest now."

He handed Mom some papers to sign, and we walked out to the waiting room where Officer McNally still sat.

Mom whispered, "Do you know why he stayed here?"

"He was there, when I had the accident. He was right behind me. I'm not sure why he stayed."

We walked over to the young policeman and Mom asked, "Officer, it was good of you to stay with Cara. Is there some reason you're still here?"

He'd taken off his hat, and I got a good look at the young officer for the first time. He was blond and blue-eyed with a young, boyish face. I was guessing he was still in his early twenties.

He looked rather embarrassed.

"Mrs. Blackthorne, when Cara was stuck in her car, before the Fire Dept. got her out, she was asking for Adam. She kept saying she needed Adam." He turned red. "My name is Adam, so I thought I should stay with her." He shrugged.

Oh. I closed my eyes and felt my bruised face get hot. I opened my eyes and looked at the young man. "Officer McNally, I'm so sorry. I wasn't thinking clearly at the time. I must have been thinking about another Adam. But it was really sweet of you to come to the hospital and stay with me. I'm very grateful."

McNally was at least six feet tall. I stood on my toes and kissed his cheek. He promptly turned even redder.

"You're welcome, Cara. I'm glad I was able to help, even if I'm the wrong Adam." He smiled, put his cap back on and left the E.R.

My mother held my hand and stood there for a minute, just looking at me with sympathy. "Let's go home, sweetheart. Your father is probably frantic. I left him a note when I left for the hospital. I'd better call him before we leave."

I could hear her trying to calm my father over the phone, which didn't seem to be working, so I took the phone out of her hand and said, "I'm okay, Dad. Please don't worry. We'll be home in about a half hour."

"Are you able to walk, Cara?" he asked, obviously still upset.

"Yes, I can walk, Dad. I didn't break anything, honest. Please try to relax."

I handed the phone back to Mom, and we left for home.

I hadn't yet looked in a mirror.

CHAPTER 16

When we got home, my father was waiting on the front porch. It was dark so he didn't get a good look at me until I'd climbed the stairs and was standing in front of him. The look of dismay on his face told me all I needed to know.

He put his arm around me.

"How are you feeling, Cara?" His voice was so soft and full of sympathy, I knew I probably looked worse than one of Kevin's zombies.

"Believe it or not, Dad, I'll live. Although when I finally get a look at my face, I may not want to!"

"Let's get inside, Brian. I know she's in pain, although she hasn't complained. I have pain meds for her that I'm sure she needs."

He led us into the kitchen where I was surprised to find Amy and Kevin waiting for us. The looks on their faces could only be described one way: Utter horror.

I groaned and closed my eyes. "I know I'm a mess, you guys. No need to rub it in. And why are you here anyway?"

Kevin said, "We were only a few blocks away and we heard the crash. Something told me it was your car. I drove over to Main and Oak and when I saw your car, I wasn't sure you were still alive. Cara, we were scared to death. We watched the ambulance take you away. We were already here when the police called your mom."

Mom added, "The phone rang while Kevin was telling me what your car looked like. I was absolutely sick until the police assured me you were alive. I left a note for your father, but I don't think Kevin and Amy were able to calm him down at all!"

She got up and handed me a glass of water along with a pill. "Better take this now, dear. Those sore muscles and bruises may hurt even more later tonight."

My dad said, "All I knew was that you'd been hurt in a car crash and had been taken to the hospital. I had no idea how badly you'd been hurt, sweetheart."

His face still showed the strain. I'm sure my bruised appearance wasn't helping much.

I got the pain pill down and went into the bathroom. I closed my eyes while I was taking care of business, but I knew I'd have to look at the damage sooner or later. When I stood up, I braced myself, faced the mirror and opened my eyes.

Everyone in the kitchen must have heard me use a popular four-letter word.

I heard Mom on the other side of the bathroom door. "Cara?"

"You should have warned me, Mom!"

I opened the door and we both went back to the kitchen. My head ached, of course, and now I knew why my face ached even more. I sat down, praying the pain pill would kick in quickly.

Every part of my face above my chin was either bruised, swollen, or both. It was mostly red and purple, which were not complementary colors. The cervical collar was the perfect touch. I wanted to put my face down on the table, but it would have hurt too much.

Amy and Kevin just watched me sadly. They had no idea how to cheer me up.

My words were a little slurred when I said, "Anyone got a bag I can wear over my head for the next two weeks?"

My father was stroking my hair. "Sweetheart, the main thing is you weren't seriously hurt."

I turned my swollen face toward him and said, "You don't consider this *serious*? And what about my poor car? Where is it? Can it be repaired? I'm supposed to leave for Barrett in less than two weeks."

Mom reassured me, "Cara, your car has already been towed to the mechanic who maintains all the police vehicles. We weren't aware of this, but Officer McNally told me your car was structurally reinforced. Which is what saved you from more serious injury. It can be repaired."

Kevin added, "That's probably why you can still walk and talk, short stuff. The SUV that hit you was totaled."

"What about the driver?"

"That cop was taking down all his information when we left. He was obviously the one at fault, Cara. He ran right through a Stop sign doing at least fifty."

Kevin's eyebrows suddenly shot up. "Do you think this accident had anything to do with you going to court to testify against Romanov?"

I closed my eyes.

Amy said, "It's a horrible thought, but it would have been one way to keep you from testifying."

I tried to nod, but the cervical collar wouldn't let me so I ripped it off. "I can't tolerate this thing any longer. To answer your question, Kev, I'm beginning to think you're right. I mean, that driver had to have seen the police car right behind me. I'd like to know who he was."

Mom frowned at me. "Cara, put the collar back on, at least for the next few days. You can take it off when you go to bed, but you need it on now."

I rolled my eyes and put the uncomfortable collar back on.

Mom picked up her phone. "Getting back to the identity of the driver who hit you, I'd like to know too. I'll ask Tommy."

We couldn't tell much from her side of the conversation. When she hung up, I asked, "Well, what did he say?"

She wore a dissatisfied expression. "Tommy had the same suspicion, but without further research, he can't tie that driver to Nick Romanov. He's trying to check him out more thoroughly."

Amy looked at me. "Sweetie, we've got to go, but we'll keep in touch. I can't tell you how relieved I am that you weren't hurt more seriously. Those bruises will fade quickly and you'll be as beautiful as ever. Please don't worry about that."

Kevin stood and leaned over to hug me gently. "Call me if there's anything I can do, short stuff." His voice was rough. "Awfully glad you're still in one piece, babe." He dropped a kiss on the top of my head, the one place that wasn't bruised.

Mom walked them to the door, and I heard her talking to them as they left. They asked her to call them if there was any change in my condition.

When she came back into the kitchen, she looked at the clock. "Is anybody hungry? It's been hours since you ate, Cara."

She made sandwiches and heated up some soup for us. I wasn't sure I could get anything down, but my parents had to be starving. They hadn't even had dinner.

The pain pill had finally taken over and dulled the pain. As I forced myself to nibble on half a sandwich, the doorbell rang. My father got up to answer the door and I heard him say, "Relax. She'll be fine in a few weeks. Come in. She's in the kitchen."

When my father stepped out of the kitchen doorway, I was shocked to see Sean, white-faced and carrying a bouquet of flowers. Of course, when he got a look at me, his eyes got so huge, I wanted to crawl under the table.

Mom looked from me to Sean and back to me. "Sean, she's badly bruised but she'll be fine."

His horrified eyes still glued to me, Sean said, "From what Amy told Sandy, it sounded like she was at death's door." He took a deep breath. "To be honest, Cara, you look like you should be. Are you really okay?"

A little buzzed from the pain pill, I muttered, "I didn't think you cared."

His face got red. "Of course I care," he said softly. "I think I'll always care."

My father was sitting next to me. He looked at us, stood up and said, "I think you two need to talk to each other." With a raised brow, he added, "Cara's present state may be a bonus, Sean."

He took Mom's hand and led her upstairs. "We'll watch some TV for a while."

After what seemed like five minutes of silence, I said, "Well, you know, I care too. Having you stare at me coldly, or refuse to look at me at all, and not even speak to me has been killing me. It really hurts, Sean."

At that moment, I was surprised to feel tears running down my face. I didn't plan on doing *that*. I realized later that the pain meds had bared all my feelings, with no filters to speak of.

He looked pained. Pulling his chair closer to mine, he took my hand and raised it to his lips.

He kissed my hand, then reached out and very gently wiped the tears from my bruised face. "I'm sorry, Cara. I've been hurting too. Just seeing you was painful." He looked down at the floor. "So I did the only thing I could and tried not to look at you."

I couldn't seem to turn off my tears. "Can't we still be friends? I sort of love you, you know. My feelings go way beyond liking you. I really do want you in my life, Sean."

Still holding my hand, he closed his eyes. I think he was fighting tears too.

"Cara, we're being totally honest today, right?"

I nodded.

"You said you're in love with Adam. How do you think I felt when you told me that?"

"I know. I never wanted to hurt you, but I felt I had to be honest. The thing is, I love you too."

He took a deep breath. "Cara, if Adam comes back, I'll be history, right?"

I closed my eyes. He was right. I opened mine and looked into his warm brown eyes.

"Sean, there has to be a way to resolve this, without cutting each other out of our lives. We *are* good friends. Trying to ignore each other is hurting both of us."

He looked away, shaking his head. "I don't know how to handle this, Cara. I really don't."

He took my hand again and kissed it. "I think I should be going."

I mumbled, "We haven't resolved anything, Sean."

He looked sad. "I know. I love you, Cara."

I swallowed hard. "I love you too, Sean."

"Then I guess we'll have to leave it at that for now. I'll call you tomorrow."

When my parents heard the front door close, they came back downstairs.

Mom was carrying the bottle of pain pills. "It's time, honey."

She handed me a glass of water and another pill. It only took about ten minutes before my head started to spin.

My mother asked, "Did it help to talk to Sean?"

"We haven't settled anything, but I don't think he'll ignore me anymore."

"You two will work it out, Cara. You're both too good not to," she said.

"But right now, I think you should be in bed, dear." She helped me up the stairs, got me out of my clothes and into my p.j.'s. I sank into my mattress and pillow, feeling completely boneless.

I was out for the night. No dreams, no nothing. Just a deep, deep sleep.

The next day wasn't much better. My head ached badly until I finally gave in and took a pain pill. Of course, I got loopy again, and Mom and Dad were

THE JOINING TREE

laughing at the things I was saying. Whatever I was saying, I really don't remember. At least I was able to amuse them.

Sean and Amy both called as soon as I was up. I have no idea what I said to them, but I remember they were laughing. I guess I didn't say anything too offensive.

Since it was Sunday, Mom made her normal Sunday brunch. Kevin called to ask if it was safe to come over. Mom told him it was, that I was reasonably coherent. Which wasn't entirely true.

When Kevin arrived, there was a big stack of pancakes on the table and Mom was frying sausages. We had decided to omit the fresh-squeezed orange juice for the foreseeable future, or until I was able to handle the job again.

There was a soft tap on the back door. Dad opened it to Kathleen, who'd arrived in response to a message I was sure my father had sent her.

"You're just in time for brunch," Dad told her.

"Very kind of you, Brian. Alicia, your kitchen smells divine." She sat down next to me.

"How are you feeling today, Cara? Any better?"

I shook my head. "I hate taking these pain pills, but it's the only way I can stand the pain. Please tell me you have a remedy for my swollen face."

"Of course I do, dear. I'll make a poultice out of these herbs and they will take a good deal of this swelling and bruising away. I think an ice pack on the back of your neck will help with the neck and head pain. You'll need to be lying down for these treatments."

"I have to go to court on Monday, Kathleen. Will I be healed up by then?"

"Not exactly, dear. Your face is so badly bruised, it will take a bit longer. However, my herbs do offer another benefit. A cup or two of this particular herbal tea will leave you completely calm, almost serene. You won't worry about a thing."

"Hmm. That might be helpful when I go into court, as long as my head's not pounding as badly."

Mom said, "Chief O'Donnell called this morning before you were up, dear. He just wanted to see how you were feeling. He has promised to take you to court tomorrow and get you in and out in record time. You can even take one of your pain pills on the way home. Now how about a pancake? I've got real maple syrup."

Kevin had already chowed down on half a dozen pancakes along with a couple of sausages. I barely managed half a pancake before my stomach rebelled.

"Sorry, Mom. I can't eat. But I'd love a cup of tea."

She'd made a large pot of tea and poured out cups for Kathleen, Dad, herself and me. Kevin was sticking to coffee, as usual.

Later, after Kevin left, I gave in and went upstairs to take a nap with Kathleen's herbal poultice covering the worst bruises. By the time I woke up, it was night and time to go to bed again after Mom reapplied the poultice.

But thinking about my court date the next day kept me awake for quite a while.

Mom woke me early, earlier than I would have liked. I was in a lot of pain, all the muscles above my waist were letting me know they'd been badly strained, but I couldn't take another pain pill.

"Mom, I'm gonna need that herbal tea Kathleen brought yesterday just as soon as you can boil the water. My pain pill must have worn off while I was sleeping."

While she was downstairs, I sat in the bathroom bathing my face with cold water and trying some deep breathing, telling myself I only had to get through the morning. My head throbbed horribly.

A few minutes later, Mom brought me a king-size mug of the herbal tea and I starting sipping it immediately.

After I finished in the bathroom, she helped me dress. I wasn't a skirt or dress person—even for court—so it was jeans, boots, and a loose shirt

"No ponytail today. I just want to look neat, not stylish.

I finished my tea and actually began to feel calmer, not nervous at all. My head still throbbed dully, but I knew I could handle it. Three cheers for Kathleen's herbs!

I was about to go downstairs when my phone rang.

"Hi, beautiful."

I'd always loved that greeting.

"Kevin told me you'd be going to court today to testify against that dirtbag, Romanov. I had no idea that might have been behind your accident. How are you feeling today?"

"Well, Kathleen's herbs must have some kind of magic because I'm perfectly calm, even with the pain in my head. I think I'll be okay in court."

"Cara, I think you're very brave to go through with this, especially in your condition.

I'll be in court too, just for moral support. I think Kevin's planning on being there too."

I had to smile. "My parents are going too. I have an incredible support system, Sean. I really appreciate it."

"Well, good luck, Cara. I'll see you there."

"Thanks. You're one in a million." And he was.

When I got downstairs, I found the Chief sitting in the kitchen with my dad, enjoying a cup of coffee. He looked surprised when I walked into the room.

"Cara, you're looking much better than I expected. How are you feeling?"

"I'll be okay, Chief. Kathleen brought me some herbs for tea and I'm feeling very calm. I can do this."

"Good girl. Let's leave now. Court will begin in about a half hour, and I promise to get you out of there and back home as quickly as possible."

My dad added, "Alicia and I will be right behind you, sweetheart. Don't worry about anything."

He hugged me gently, and I left with Chief O'Donnell.

The ride to the Courthouse in Greenville was actually kind of fun when I could forget about the pain in my head for a minute or two. The Chief ran his lights without the siren, so it was a fast ride. Other motorists got out of our way quickly. We walked into court in less than a half hour.

We sat behind the prosecutor's table. She smiled when she saw me and asked how I was feeling. I said I was okay. There wasn't time for more conversation since the judge had just entered the courtroom.

Naturally, Romanov pled "Not Guilty," the defense and prosecution gave their opening statements, and it wasn't long before I was called to the stand.

The prosecutor was a middle-aged brunette, tall and thin, plain-faced until she smiled. She smiled at me.

"I know you were seriously injured just two days ago, Cara, so I'll try to keep this brief."

She asked me to identify the man who attacked me months ago. I pointed to the defendant, who was glaring at me. It was one of those "if looks could kill" looks.

Then she asked me to describe the events leading up to the attack and the attack itself. I did.

"Do you know who shot the arrow into Mr. Romanov?"

I said, "No, but I wish I did." The Chief had agreed to leave Gavin out of these court proceedings.

She asked, "Why?"

I said, "Because I'd like to thank him. I think he saved my life."

She said, "Do you know who drove into your car two days ago, causing your injuries?"

I said, "No."

She said, "Don't you find the timing suspicious?"

I didn't answer because the defense attorney objected and the judge agreed with him.

The prosecutor thanked me for coming to court despite my injuries and said she'd have no further questions for me.

The judge asked the defense attorney if he had questions for me. I guess I looked pathetic up there in the witness box because the defense attorney said, "No." But he stated he might want to recall me later. The bruising and swelling on my face wasn't winning any points for the defense.

The judge dismissed me and I stood, but the effect of the tea must have worn off because I was suddenly woozy.

Within seconds, Chief O'Donnell was at my side, holding me up and helping me out of the witness box, leading me through the courtroom and out of the building, my parents right behind us.

I had to sit down on the steps in front of the courthouse to catch my breath. Mom put a cup of water and a pain pill in my hand. I got it down and rested there until I began to feel better.

I looked up to see Kevin and Sean standing over me with my parents. They looked as worried as my parents did.

"Hey, guys, I'll be okay in a few minutes. Don't look so worried."

My father said, "Sweetheart, you did what you had to do today, but now I want you off your feet and resting." With that, he picked me up and carried me to the Chief's car.

Mom said, "Tommy, we can take her home, you know."

The Chief grinned. "Not as fast as I can, Alicia. I have lights and a siren."

I heard Kevin laugh. Even my father and Sean were smiling.

Mom said, "Okay, you win. We'll see you at home."

Dad placed me gently in the Chief's car, fastened my seat belt, and leaned in to kiss my cheek. "We'll see you at home, sweetheart. And I want you to know I'm extremely proud of you."

He shut the car door and the Chief pulled out into traffic, lights *and* siren on.

Needless to say, we made it out of Greenville in record time. But to be honest, the siren wasn't doing much for my headache.

The Chief helped me out of the car and into my house where I sat down in the kitchen.

"Chief, if you want coffee, I'm afraid you'll have to wait until Mom gets home. Sorry. But I did enjoy the ride home. It was kind of exciting." I smiled at him.

He chuckled. "Glad you liked it. You know, I'm as capable of making coffee as you are, and I have the same kind of coffeemaker at home. Just point me at the coffee."

I told him where we kept the coffee, and he had a pot made by the time my parents got home.

Kevin and Sean arrived at the same time and followed my parents into the house.

Sean said, "I won't stay long. I know Cara has to rest." He sat down next to me. "I just wanted to tell you how impressive you were on the witness stand. The jury will find him guilty and I hope he'll get the longest sentence possible. When you were describing his attack on you, every person on that jury was frowning."

Kevin said, "Yeah. Those twelve people all looked ready to lynch him. You were terrific, short stuff."

There was a knock on the front door. Mom let Amy in. She never came empty-handed.

"How'd it go, Cara? You obviously survived. And I brought some peach turnovers Mom made this morning. I couldn't be in court this morning, but I was thinking of you."

I was already feeling a little dizzy from the pain pill. "It went fine. Kevin and Sean both think they'll throw the book at Romanov. I hope when they lock him up, they lose the key. And since I haven't had anything to eat today, I'll take one of those turnovers *now*."

Mom got down plates and silverware and passed the turnovers around the table.

Like all of Mrs. Strauss' pastries, they were fantastic. My appetite had returned. I ate two.

After I'd stuffed myself, my eyes started to close.

"Thanks to all of you for being there for me this morning. I love you all. But I'm about to go face down on this table."

My father picked me up and carried me up the stairs. I don't remember anything else. I was out cold before I hit the bed.

I didn't wake up until Tuesday. After another large cup of herbal tea, I began to feel more like myself.

I was still in bed because Mom insisted I stay off my feet and rest. I wasn't going to argue with her, especially after she told me the doctor had wanted to keep me in the hospital for another week. I hadn't been aware that it was against doctor's orders that they took me home.

My father explained that Elves don't usually do well in hospitals. He'd already told me that he felt I was more Elf than human, and Mom agreed. Kathleen was on call if I needed her.

So I stayed in bed and watched movies on my laptop—when I could stay awake. Ralph spent part of every day, and all night, of course, at the foot of my bed.

Sean came over every day to sit with me. We talked about college, how we felt about leaving home, how different our lives would be, and how much we'd miss each other. We both knew we were running out of time.

Kevin stopped in whenever he had a few minutes. He brought me a sample of his latest game, "Return of the Alien," and asked me to test it for him. Since I wasn't a gamer, he felt I'd be a good person to find any flaws. I played it at night when I couldn't sleep. Since Kevin had designed it, I never found any flaws.

The Strauss Bakery had its grand opening without me. Mom and Dad went over to the bakery for an hour and said the whole establishment was impressive. Mom was sure Amy's catering department would draw in a lot of new customers. She brought me some of the free samples. Amy had made little sandwiches of all kinds, just like the ones everyone enjoyed at Mom and Dad's wedding. They were delicious.

Dad's friend, Dr. Costello, who was also a Halfling, came to the house twice that week to check on me.

He pronounced me healing well, but said I needed at least another week of rest. That cut into the time I'd planned to spend in Syracuse getting acclimated to my new home. I was disappointed about the delay, but I knew the doctor was right. I had very little energy, and my parents refused to let me make the move until I was completely well.

Kevin would be leaving for NYU in another week, and Sean would be leaving for Penn State on Friday. Amy would still be in Thornewood and promised to make a pastry run to our house whenever I needed a sugar lift.

Our group was finally breaking up, maybe permanently, and that was sad. Sure, we'd get together during holidays and school vacations, but it would never be the same again.

CHAPTER 17

By the end of that week, I was feeling much better. The swelling on my face was almost gone, and Kathleen's herbs had healed most of the bruising. I was looking human again.

My parents wanted me to wait until the middle of the following week to leave for Syracuse. That would only give me a few days before classes started, but I agreed.

I spent more time with my friends. We all knew time was getting short, so we spent part of each day together at my house. We made Thursday night spaghetti night since Sean was leaving on Friday for Penn State.

We played music, we danced, we remembered our most embarrassing moments at Thornewood High. We laughed a lot.

After dinner that night, Sean said, "I feel so close to the three of you. It makes me wonder if I'll ever have friends like you again."

I said, "Of course you will. You'll make so many new friends at Penn State, you'll probably forget all about us by Christmas." I smiled and winked at him.

He snorted. "I doubt that. Sure, we'll all make new friends, but I read somewhere that 'old friends are the best friends because they knew you *when*.'"

Amy looked sad. "Remember, I'll still be here, just waiting for you guys to come home. I'll probably miss you more than you'll miss me. I mean, you'll all be so busy with school and the new friends you'll make. Makes me wonder if you'll ever think of me."

"Of course we will," I said. "I don't know how I'll get along without you. Who's gonna haunt me about my clothes, or my hair, or the makeup I don't wear?"

We all laughed. But the feeling of impending loss was really strong that day. I think we were all wondering how we'd get along without the strong, reliable friendship we shared.

Thursday night we stuffed ourselves with spaghetti and the cannoli that Amy

brought. Mom and Dad had spent dinner laughing at our teasing conversation, and nothing was sacred.

Kevin laughed off his earlier reputation as head nerd at Thornewood High.

Sean looked embarrassed but couldn't help smiling as we all reminded him how the girls at school had always drooled and groaned when he sailed past.

Amy had to agree with a grin when we kidded her about her inability to resist a guy with a pretty face. And, of course, we listed all the pretty boys she'd dated during our four years of high school as her freckled face turned redder.

Kevin added, "Well, her taste has finally improved." We all agreed with laughter and applause.

When they got to me, Sean gave me a gentle smile and described the little girl with the big green eyes who never met anyone's eyes, never spoke to anyone but Amy and Kevin, and just attended school silently, as though she was the only person there.

I rolled my eyes. "Yeah, I know. I felt like an alien who had landed on the wrong planet." I looked over at Sean with a smile. "Fortunately, Sean changed all that. He made me an offer I couldn't refuse: an invitation into the human world."

It was quiet for a few minutes while we looked at each other with the very real affection we all felt.

And then it was time for everyone to leave. Sean would be leaving for Penn State in the morning. His dad would be driving him since Sean didn't have a car of his own yet.

Sean said, "Dad's still looking for a car for me, something that will make it from Pennsylvania to Thornewood in one piece. I'm hoping he'll succeed by Thanksgiving."

Kevin would leave on Sunday, two days before his classes would start. He hadn't decided yet whether to take his Jeep or leave it home and take the train. Cars weren't necessary in the city.

I was still playing it by ear. I'd leave for Syracuse sometime the following week. It all depended on how how good I felt.

Amy would be holding the fort here in Thornewood, getting her new catering business off the ground. And missing us *a lot*, she insisted.

After Kevin and Amy left, I stood at the front door with Sean, saying goodbye.

"Promise me you won't fall in love with anyone while I'm gone," he said.

I was already in love with someone, but it didn't seem necessary to remind him about that.

"Don't worry. I'll be happy to see you whenever we both get home," I said.

I was planning on coming home every weekend, but it would probably be Thanksgiving before Sean got home again.

After several warm kisses and some breathless hugs, Sean left reluctantly.

As much as I liked being physically close to Sean, the ground beneath my feet didn't move when he kissed me. That only happened with Adam, despite the fact that I tried not to think about him. I wasn't always successful.

I stood at the door until Sean drove away with a wave out the window and a brief beep of the horn. I really would miss him, but more as my good friend than anything else.

I walked back into the kitchen where my parents were still sitting.

THE JOINING TREE

My father said, "You've been blessed with good friends, dear. But you'll make more good friends at Barrett, I'm sure. Your life is really just beginning, Cara."

I nodded. He was right. In my opinion, it was my *adult* life, which was just beginning. My mother might not agree, but I would no longer be *too young* for anything.

I spent the next few days alternately resting and packing. I had just one suitcase on wheels and a large duffle to pack. There was no way I could take everything, so it was a mixture of art supplies and some clothes that I had to cram into the two bags. But since I'd be coming home every weekend, that wouldn't be a problem.

Kevin came over before he left for New York City. "I might be home for a weekend before Thanksgiving, but I'm not sure right now. I will expect frequent emails from you, short stuff." He hugged me until my still-sore ribs objected. He didn't know how much I'd miss him.

Amy stopped by several times, as her work allowed. She joined us for dinner Tuesday night. I was leaving on Wednesday.

"Cara, you'd better call or email—I know you hate texting—but you have to promise to keep me in the loop. I want to hear all about Barrett, including all the cute guys you'll be meeting!"

I rolled my eyes. "No cute guys, Amy. I'll be concentrating on art, nothing else."

She laughed and shook her head. "Listen, young lady. There *will* be cute guys, have no doubt. And I know they won't be able to resist those big green eyes and that pretty face of yours. Promise me you'll *at least* be friendly."

"Okay, okay, Amy. I'll be friendly. But that's it. I'm not planning on dating, or parties, or any of the things you're interested in. I think you know why."

It was her turn to roll her eyes. "Yeah, I know. Your missing bodyguard." She shook her head. "It's been almost a year, Cara. Without any word from him. It might be time to accept that he's gone and might not return. Don't waste your life waiting for him, sweetie. You deserve more."

There was no sense arguing with her. She wouldn't understand how committed, or "mated," I already felt. Which made me wonder why she didn't feel the same things for Kevin. Maybe it just hadn't happened to them yet.

I decided to give my father his portrait later that night, when it was just the three of us.

After Amy left, I said, "I have a gift for Dad in my room. Would you both come upstairs with me please."

They followed me up to my room, my father looking curious.

When we were all standing in front of my easel, I looked at Mom.

"Mom, we've been together for over seventeen years. I think you know how much you mean to me. I know I don't say it often enough, but you're a wonderful mother, as well as a great friend."

I turned to my father. "Dad, you've become such an important part of my life, I often forget we've only been together for about fifteen months. A few weeks ago, you reminded me of this when you said that I've only been part of *your* life for a year. And that's not very long. I don't think I've ever told you how much you mean to me. So, before I leave for Art school, I wanted to find a way to *show* you."

I pulled the cover off the pen and ink drawing I'd done of my father and heard two gasps from behind me.

This picture was much larger than most of my drawings, measuring about nine by twelve. I thought it was the best work I'd ever done.

I'd shown my dark-haired, green-eyed father leaning against a pine tree, his arms casually crossed against his chest, and a loving but mischievous smile on his handsome face. It was a more detailed version of the picture he'd mentally sent to me, which I'd unknowingly drawn into the landscape picture I'd been working on that day more than a year ago.

The love he felt for me was clear on his smiling face, and so was the fact that he knew he was taking liberties with the promise he'd made to my mother when I was born. I hadn't had my sixteenth birthday yet, and he'd promised my mother to stay out of my life until I was sixteen.

Mom was looking at my father, with a knowing smile on her face. My father's eyes were glued to his portrait. He finally looked at me, his smile full of understanding as well as his love for me.

His voice was soft. "My Cara, what a splendid gift you've been all your short life, and especially these past fifteen months. Thank you for this incredible portrait." He held his arms out to me and I walked into them. No one gave hugs like my dad.

By Wednesday morning, I was packed and ready to go. Mom made pancakes, of course, and after breakfast, Dad loaded my bags into the trunk of my totally repaired car. The Chief had told the body shop to pull out all the stops in getting my car repaired, and its black paint gleamed, not a ding or a dent in sight.

After hugs and kisses from my parents, as well as the usual advice from Mom about getting enough rest and eating healthy, I got in my car and headed for Syracuse. I finally felt that I was really, finally on my own. My heart was, in equal parts, both elated and sad. There would be no memories of Adam to haunt me in Syracuse.

THE JOINING TREE

There was no sun that day, but I hoped the rain would stay up in the clouds where it belonged. The weather cooperated and I made it to my new home before it started to rain.

I pulled up in front of the yellow house on Birch Street around lunchtime. Miss Williams must have been catching up on her gardening because all of the shrubs and flowers that bordered her front yard looked neat and beautiful, with lots of gold and orange tones complementing the house's cheerful yellow paint. It had looked a little overgrown the last time I'd been here. Today the colorful flowers were like a welcoming smile.

Using the front door key Miss Williams had given me, I lugged in the wheeled suitcase and unlocked the door to my apartment, wishing the duffle bag still in the trunk had wheels too.

I was about to go back to the car for the duffle when I heard my landlady coming down the stairs from the second floor.

She was smiling. "Welcome, Cara."

I invited her in and we both sat down on the brand new couch and chair that had been delivered while I was still in Thornewood. Miss Williams had the delivery men place them in front of the wall of bookshelves, where they looked perfect.

After we'd chatted for a while, I jumped up. "I've left my car's trunk open and the bag holding most of my clothes is still out there. I forgot all about it while we were talking."

I rushed to the front door only to find my duffel bag sitting in front of it. I looked out at my car and saw that the trunk had been closed.

I looked at Miss Williams. "I wonder who my Good Samaritan was this time?" I explained about the van that had led me through a snowstorm in January.

She chuckled. "I have some very nice neighbors, Cara. We do little favors for each other all the time. It was probably one of them who brought your bag up to the door."

As she got up to leave, I complimented her on the beautiful garden in her front yard.

She smiled. "I just had some gardening done last week. There's a young man who's been working in this neighborhood recently. He did gardening for my next-door neighbor a few weeks ago. He came over and asked if I'd like to have my yard worked on. It obviously needed it, so I agreed. He did a marvelous job, didn't he?"

"Absolutely. All these cheerful flowers were like a welcome sign when I pulled up in front of your house. Your yard looks great."

"Thanks, Cara. That young man obviously has a very green thumb. A lot of these plants looked dead, but he brought them back to life."

"When will you be starting school?" she asked.

"There's an orientation on Friday. Classes start next Monday." I grinned. "I'm really looking forward to it. I've dreamed of Art school for years."

"It's nice to see a student so enthusiastic about starting school. I'll leave you now to get settled. Don't forget to call me if you need any help."

She went upstairs to her apartment while I looked around the neighborhood from the front door. It seemed quiet now, but I realized that would change once school started next week.

The chore of putting everything away, including my purchases from weeks ago, which were still sitting on the floor in the kitchen, seemed overwhelming at that moment. My stomach growled and I realized it was past lunchtime. I hadn't eaten since breakfast and there was no food in the apartment. The obvious solution was to walk across the street to Barrett's campus and find the Café. I hoped it would be open since school hadn't officially started yet.

The house on Birch Street faced the rear of the Barrett campus. In the distance I could see the dorms on one side of campus. I couldn't see the Café from where I stood, but I didn't think it would be more than a ten-minute walk.

Walking across campus was enjoyable with all the leafy trees, green grass, and some fall flowers already blooming along the brick walkways. It took only ten minutes to reach the Café, which thankfully was open.

When I walked in, the place was empty. I only saw one girl behind the counter. She was scrubbing something vigorously and didn't see me.

"Hi," I said as her head popped up. She was obviously surprised to see me.

She looked a little annoyed. "Sorry, we're not open for business yet. Someone left the grill filthy and I haven't cooked anything yet. But there's coffee, if you're interested." She waved at a table in the corner where there were two coffee pots on warming stands.

"One's decaf. The other is fully leaded," she said. She looked up at me again, her eyes widening as she got a good look at me.

"You're the girl in the photo collage." She finally smiled. "Cara, right?"

I nodded. "Lily warned me everyone would recognize me when I got here." I chuckled. "She wasn't kidding."

She stuck out one wet hand. "I'm Ginger. Welcome to Barrett."

When she realized her hand was wet, she wiped it on her apron and stuck it out again, laughing. I shook her hand, laughing with her.

"Thanks. I just drove in a little while ago and haven't stocked up on groceries yet. I was hoping I could get a bite to eat here. I'd be glad to make myself a sandwich if you've got bread and something to put on it."

She pointed at a box on the rear counter. "We've got bread, cheese, peanut butter, and even some bacon. Help yourself." She smiled and began scrubbing the grill again.

When I looked in the box on the counter, I was delighted to find bagels and bacon.

Ginger must have read my mind. "Look in the fridge back there. I think there's some lettuce, a few tomatoes, and some cream cheese."

She was right. "I can make bagel sandwiches with what's here. Would you like one?"

THE JOINING TREE

She nodded, grinning. "Sounds perfect, Cara. It's always more enjoyable when someone else does the cooking."

I put bacon wrapped in a paper towel in the king-sized microwave, popped two bagels into a big four-slice toaster, sliced up tomatoes, and proceeded to make two Sunrise Specials. When I handed one to Ginger, she wiped off her hands and looked surprised.

"Cara, this looks great. I may start offering these to our starving students for breakfast. What should we call them?"

"I've always called them Sunrise Specials, but you can call them whatever you like."

We sat down at the counter with our bagels and I could hear satisfied sounds coming from Ginger as she enjoyed her lunch.

When she'd finished, she smacked her lips and asked, "Do you cook too?"

I shook my head and laughed. "To my mom's continued disappointment, no, unless you consider using a toaster and a microwave 'cooking.' The stove and I really don't get along. Although I have recently mastered boiling water," I said with a smile.

We chatted over lunch. She told me the students who worked at the Café were all volunteers, receiving their meals free while they worked there.

"For a lot of us, this is a great deal. Have you priced groceries lately?" She groaned.

"Not yet, but I have to find a grocery store this afternoon. My cupboards and apartment fridge are completely empty."

"Well, prepare yourself for a shock. You won't believe what bacon costs!"

She gave me directions to the most reasonable grocery store in the area. "Family Foods isn't a chain store. They use produce from local growers when it's available, and I think everything else is bought from a distributor who specializes in goods nearing their 'Sell by' dates. It's the only place I shop. By the way, where are you living? Obviously, not in a dorm."

When I told her which house I was renting my apartment in, she grinned. "Lucky girl. That's a nice house, although the owner is kind of fussy about who she rents to. You're probably her ideal tenant, one girl rather than a group. You'll love it there, Cara. It's a short walk to anywhere on campus."

I was ready to leave so I thanked her for lunch and for all the information.

"I'm here three days a week for lunch and early dinner, so stop back anytime." She grinned. "Don't be surprised to see your Sunrise Special on our breakfast menu!"

I continued along the brick walkway toward the dorms, passed them and headed for the Administration building. I wanted to say hello to Mrs. Barrett if she was working today.

When I reached the Administration building, I peeked in the window and saw Mrs. Barrett at her desk. I went inside and tapped on her open door.

She greeted me with a smile and waved me into her office. "How are you? Have you moved in yet?"

I told her where I would be living, gave her the address and my phone number, and said I was on my way to a grocery store. "I just wanted to say hi. I know you must be busy with classes beginning next week."

She nodded with a tired smile. "Yes, it's always a little frantic this time of the year. But thanks for stopping in, Cara."

I left and walked back to the yellow house on Birch Street. I definitely had to get to a grocery store this afternoon. As appealing as it was, I couldn't eat *all* my meals at the Café.

Down at the end of the block, I saw a green van parked at the curb. I stopped. Of course, there were plenty of older green vans around, but I didn't think there were many with dark green curtains hung over the rear windows. I'd seen this particular van before.

I couldn't help smiling. Was the owner of that van my Good Samaritan? If I ever saw him, I'd have to ask!

By mid-afternoon, I got back to my apartment with more bags than I expected to bring home. I had forgotten about all the condiments, paper supplies, and cleaning products I would need in addition to food. My checking account had taken a huge hit.

I put the kitchen and cleaning stuff away quickly, but still had my clothes to unpack. Since I'd need clean clothes the next day, I couldn't put it off. But I could take a quick break. I made a pot of coffee in my new coffeemaker and sat down with a cup. The coffee actually gave me a little burst of energy, which I really needed. I couldn't help thinking how much fun this would be if Amy was with me.

Sighing, I finished my coffee and trudged into the bedroom to empty the duffel bag, quickly realizing I'd need a larger dresser. The one Miss Williams had left me was too small.

Maybe I could find one second-hand.

The dresser had filled up quickly so I stacked up the rest of my foldable clothes on the top. The bedroom closet wasn't very big, but I didn't have a lot to hang up. Once I'd lined up my boots and shoes on the floor, I was finished.

I'd already hung the colorful shower curtain in the bathroom, put out clean towels, and put my few toiletries away. It was a very warm day, and I'd worked up a good sweat while I unpacked. A semi-warm shower might restore me.

Once I was clean and dried off, I put on shorts and a tank top and padded into the kitchen to see what I might be able to make for dinner. It didn't take long to discover I had plenty of food for breakfasts and lunches, but unless I wanted soup or a sandwich for dinner, I'd have to go back to the Café.

Living alone was going to take some getting used to.

CHAPTER 18

I could have skipped Orientation on Friday. I'd already had a tour of the Barrett campus, including the classrooms. But it was pleasant walking around the campus with a crowd of other first-year students, listening to their excited comments.

Most of them were living in the dorms. Many of those comments were irritated rather than excited, the lack of living space the complaint heard most often.

As we passed the various studios, the door to the photography studio opened and I spotted Lily walking with a short, heavyset young man. She was speaking excitedly, waving her arms around, repeatedly smacking her companion in the gut. Then she spotted me in the crowd.

"There she is! I've been waiting for you, girl," she called out as she waved me to her. I made my way out of the crowd, delighted to see her. With a huge smile, she hugged me quickly and announced, "This is the person responsible for that A+ I received for second half!"

She was so excited, I couldn't help laughing. "I doubt I'm fully responsible for that impressive grade, Lily," I said.

"That photo montage I created for the Barrett Yearly Art Exhibit is what got me that A+," she told me. "And without you as my model, I doubt I would have gotten better than a B. I didn't tell you but I used your name, "Cara," as the title of the montage. So everyone now knows your face and your name."

"Yeah, I wondered how Ginger knew my name when I walked into the Café at lunchtime today."

She looked at the young man next to her. "Sorry, where are my manners? Cara, this is my good friend, Freddy. Actually, Frederick Van Wyck the third, to be accurate. But he'll answer to Freddy. He's one of the few students here at Barrett who's interested in someone other than himself. Artists are a strange lot, in case you didn't know."

I hated to admit that I didn't know any others, other than Francis Sullivan, and he wasn't strange at all. Unless you considered Elves strange.

"It's nice to meet you, Freddy," I said to the smiling young man. He took my hand and kissed it, bowing in a courtly manner. I giggled, feeling like an idiot.

"The pleasure is all mine, Cara, and I truly mean that. Really." He grinned at me.

Lily asked, "Do you have plans for dinner? I'm meeting Freddy and a few of the more interesting students at the Café for dinner tonight. Join us."

"I'm glad you suggested it. I don't cook so the Café will probably see me for dinner every night while I'm at Barrett," I said.

"Great! Come over around five and we can catch up. See you then, Cara. Come on, Freddy, I have some shopping to do and I'll need your car."

Freddy looked at me with a rueful smile. "She only loves me for my car. But I adore her so I don't care."

I was still laughing as they strolled away. I smiled to myself as I jogged ahead to catch up with my Orientation group. By the time I left for my apartment, I knew where everything was on campus, and there was no way I'd get lost.

I had to change my clothes before I went back to the Café to meet Lily and Freddy. The weather was still hot enough for shorts, but I needed boots to hold my knives. I wouldn't give up carrying them just because I now lived in Syracuse.

However, my boots were not the kind that looked good with shorts. I sighed and took out the softest pair of jeans I owned. Leaving the tank top on in deference to the summer weather, I tucked a pair of knives into my boot sheaths, brushed my hair back into the loose bun that I'd hoped would make me look older, added the lip gloss Amy had given me, and I was ready to go.

After I tucked some cash into my back pocket, I left the house. As I crossed the street to the campus, I looked down the block but there was no green van in sight.

The sun was low as I walked through the campus, but the heat hadn't let up much. I was enjoying the way the sun was shining through the branches of the trees, creating a much different atmosphere on campus than there'd been earlier in the day. It was a more mellow, end-of-day mood and I felt myself relaxing.

When I walked into the Café, I heard Lily's shout. "Over here, Cara." I followed her voice to a corner table near the wide window overlooking the treed side of campus and found her, the guy I'd met in the book store in January, Freddy, and another girl with dark brown hair streaked with gold in no discernible pattern.

Lily grinned at me. "Everyone, this is Cara. I'm sure her face is familiar to everyone who was here last term. Cara, you've already met Joel." The young man from the bookstore smiled and nodded. Lily added, "And the young lady with the interesting hair and the big brown eyes is Paula. She's a first-year student like you." Paula gave me a friendly smile and a wave, and I sat down with them.

Lily looked me up and down. "I didn't even notice earlier. You've got a little bruising on your face that wasn't there last year. You haven't taken up kick-boxing, have you?"

I laughed. "No, just an auto accident a few weeks ago. The airbag did some damage as it was saving my life."

THE JOINING TREE

Ginger was once again behind the counter and waved at me. I smiled and called, "Hi, Ginger." Looking around the table, I asked, "Is everyone having dinner here tonight?"

Lily looked at everyone and said, "I think so." They all nodded.

Joel said, "Since school hasn't officially started yet, this week the menu is basically whatever can be found in the freezer and fridge. Ginger hasn't even written it on the board tonight.

"Hey, Ginger. What are we eating tonight?" he called over his shoulder.

"Tomato soup and grilled cheese sandwiches." She grinned at me. "I'm saving the bagels and bacon for breakfast tomorrow."

I laughed. "Thank you!"

Lily looked confused. "What did I miss?" she asked me.

Ginger winked at me. "You'll find out tomorrow morning. You'll love it, Lil."

She counted heads. "Are you all having the tomato soup and the grilled cheese?"

"Sounds good to me," I said.

Joel nodded. "Me too."

Lily and Freddy looked at each other and Lily said, "Okay with us."

Paula said, "Just the soup for me, please. I don't eat bread. Or cheese." She shrugged, then asked, "Do you have any lettuce?"

Scratching her head, Ginger asked, "You want lettuce with your soup, or *in* your soup?"

I couldn't help laughing. Freddy and Joel were grinning, each shaking his head. Laughing, Lily said, "Paula lives on salads. Ginger, can you make her a salad?"

"Oh, sure. I've got a few tomatoes in the fridge, but that's all. Just lettuce and tomatoes, is that okay?"

Paula was smiling, looking relieved. "Sounds good. Thanks."

We were all looking at her so she added, "I don't want to gain any weight. They say your first year in college, you're bound to gain twenty pounds. I can't let that happen!"

Lily rolled her eyes. She said, "Paula's from my home town, folks, so we know each other fairly well. I don't think she's ever weighed more than a hundred pounds."

About fifteen minutes later, Ginger brought a big tray to our table. We all had soup, and the grilled cheese sandwiches looked delicious. She wasn't stingy with the cheese.

Paula was happy with her soup and salad and a bottle of Ranch dressing. She used so much of it on her lettuce and tomato, Freddy said, "You know, you probably have as many calories in your salad dressing as you would have had from a grilled cheese sandwich."

Paula stopped eating and thought about it. "Maybe, but I still think I'm safer with a salad. Bread makes you fat. I refuse to get fat."

Lily chuckled, shaking her head.

When we'd all finished eating, we carried our dishes to the counter and Lily brought one of the two pots of coffee back to our table with her. Once we all had our coffee, we started talking about art and the new school year. Joel asked me what medium I was working in. I said, "Watercolors and pen and ink. How about you?"

"Oils, only oils," he said. Freddy said it was watercolors for him, and Paula said she'd been working strictly in pen and ink. "My specialty is cartooning, especially political satire. I'd love to work with an on-line publisher and poke fun at our major political figures," she said with a grin.

Lily laughed. "Back home, Paula did a satirical cartoon that featured our fat-cat mayor. The local paper loved it and printed it, and the mayor threatened to have her arrested!"

We were all laughing about the political cartoons that were so popular during the last election, when I looked up to see a good-looking man wearing a well-tailored suit come in the door. He looked around the café, obviously searching for someone until his eyes met mine.

He approached our table, saying, "I'm looking for Cara Blackthorne. That would be you, wouldn't it?" His eyes pierced mine, and I guessed denying it would be useless.

All conversation at our table stopped as everyone turned to stare at the very attractive man who appeared to be in his late twenties or early thirties. His hair was that bronze shade, neither brown nor red, cut short at the sides and back, longer on top. His eyes were a very light blue, almost gray. I felt as though they could see into my brain. It was not a good feeling. He had to be a cop.

"I'm Cara. Who are you?" My tone of voice let him know he'd better have a good reason for tracking me down here.

He lowered his voice and smiled. "Sorry, I didn't mean to upset anyone. I'm Lieutenant Fox of the Syracuse Police Dept. My Captain spoke to Chief O'Donnell in Thornewood recently. They asked me to introduce myself as soon as I had time to get over here."

He glanced at the curious faces around the table. "Cara, is there somewhere a little more private where we could talk?"

"May I see your badge and I.D. please." After all, how did I know he was with the Syracuse Police?

He nodded, serious now, pulled his badge and I.D. out of his inside pocket and handed it to me.

It certainly looked legitimate. His full name was Aidan Fox. "How did you know where to find me?" I asked him.

"I went to your house on Birch Street first. Miss Williams told me I might find you here." I nodded. I was sure she would have checked his I.D. too.

I looked around the café, but all the tables were close to each other. Through the window on the other side of the room I could see a few small tables and chairs on an outside patio. It was so warm, no one was out there, but the group I was sitting with would be able to see me while I was sitting with him. I pointed to the patio and he followed me outside.

THE JOINING TREE

Lily stood and asked, "Is everything okay, Cara?"

I looked back at her, smiled and said, "It's okay. Nothing to worry about." Of course, I could see by the looks from my table, no one actually believed me.

Lieutenant Fox and I sat down at a small table on the patio. I waited for him to speak.

"Cara, have you recovered from that accident I heard about?"

"Almost. There's still a bit of bruising, and some sore muscles, but I feel fine. I'm guessing Chief O'Donnell called you."

He nodded, sat back and smiled. "You're not quite what I expected, Cara."

That surprised me. "What did you expect?"

"Well, you don't look like the kind of girl who would tangle with a drug dealer, stab him, survive a serious auto crash, have the guts to go to court injured and testify against him, and still be willing to leave home by yourself to start college away from everyone and everything you know. Oh, and carry knives with you that I understand you're highly skilled at throwing." He raised both eyebrows.

"I wasn't expecting a small, delicate looking girl who doesn't look any older than sixteen."

"I'm seventeen."

He chuckled. "Yes, I know. That's still very young, Cara."

There were obviously a few things he didn't know about me.

"Lieutenant Fox, I was kidnapped twice last year. That's why I developed my skill with knives. I don't ever want to feel like a victim again."

His eyebrows popped up again. "Twice? I wasn't told about that."

"It was a tough year. So I had to get tough to survive."

"Okay, Cara. I think what you're telling me is not to underestimate you. Am I right?"

"Yes."

He said, "Okay, I won't. But Chief O'Donnell is still concerned about you and asked us to keep an eye on you. Have you seen anyone suspicious since you got to Syracuse? Any weird phone calls or anyone following you?"

"No, nothing that set off my internal alarm. That drug dealer is in prison now, so I'm not expecting any trouble."

"Do you have any knives with you now?" he asked.

"Yes."

"May I see one of them?"

I pulled a knife out of my boot and handed it to him.

He looked it over, felt it for weight, and handed it back to me. I tucked it back into my boot.

He pulled out a business card and handed it to me. "My cell phone is listed on the back. If you suspect anything at all, even if it's just an uneasy feeling, call me. You've probably learned to trust those feelings, right?"

I nodded.

"Every cop learns to trust his instincts, so don't hesitate to call, okay?"

"Okay."

"I'll be checking in with you regularly, Cara, and your neighborhood will be patrolled more often than usual. Chief O'Donnell hasn't established a connection between that drug dealer and the driver who caused your accident, but we're taking this seriously. Call me anytime."

We stood, and he shook my hand. "A pleasure meeting you, Cara Blackthorne." He gave me an appraising look, smiled and left for the parking area.

Before I walked back into the Café where people were waiting for me, I had to decide how to explain the Syracuse P.D.'s interest in me.

I returned to our table to a group of expectant faces, all of whom looked eager to learn what business the police department had with me.

Lily gave me a conspiratorial smile. "Tell the truth, Cara. Is your face on a 'Wanted' poster somewhere?"

The looks on the other faces told me they were considering it too.

I sat down, shaking my head. "It hasn't been proven, but the auto accident I had might have been a deliberate attempt to prevent me from testifying in court against a local drug dealer."

Everyone gasped and stared at me, even Lily. I thought Lily could handle the truth, but I regretted the fact that Lieutenant Fox had found me when I was with a group of people who didn't know me.

I sighed and shook my head. I explained about the problems I'd had with the drug dealer and how he'd tried to cut my throat.

Paula said, "But the drug dealer is in prison now, right?"

I nodded. "Thornewood's Police Chief still suspects my accident might have been set up deliberately. He contacted the Syracuse Police so they'd be aware of the history since I'm now living here."

Joel said, "We can all keep our eyes open for any strangers on or around campus. I don't know about the rest of you, but if I see anyone who doesn't belong here, I'll call your Lieutenant Fox right away. I think we all should."

Freddy added, "Absolutely. Five pairs of eyes are better than one, Cara."

Lily and Paula were both nodding. I was relieved that no one seemed taken aback by my weird history. Of course, they didn't know the weirdest part of it, which was just as well.

"Thank you. It's always a good idea to have your eyes and ears open, something I've learned the hard way."

By that time, there weren't any other people in the café, other than Ginger. She came over to our table and said, "I couldn't help overhearing, Cara. I'll keep my eyes open too. Just give me that cop's number before you leave."

I made sure all my new friends had the Lieutenant's number before they left for their dorms. I seemed to be the only one lucky enough to have an apartment off campus. Of course, that meant I might be more at risk too.

During Orientation, we'd been given our first semester class schedules. Mine included four classes each day: "Principles of Drawing," which I didn't think I really needed, "Watercolor Painting," which I knew I did need, "Art History," which I was really looking forward to, and "Oil Painting and Mixed Media." I couldn't wait to get started on Monday.

Meanwhile, I had the weekend to get through. I hoped Lily would be around, but after talking to Lieutenant Fox, I was tempted to simply stay in my apartment. That felt cowardly.

Finally I decided I didn't want to feel like a coward. I would do a bit more shopping. I wanted a TV for my living room. Even though I wasn't in the habit of watching TV often, I knew there would be weekends during the winter when I'd be unable to get home. A TV would be a good thing to have for those weekends. It might be fun to invite my new friends over if they were stuck on campus too.

By eight o'clock, I pulled a more modest t-shirt over my tank top and went out. I'd seen a big electronics store about a half mile away, so I hopped in my car and drove over there.

It was a well-known chain store, and there were a lot of people in the store, which helped me relax. I wandered around the TV department, comparing prices and features, grateful there was no salesman on my heels.

Prices had come down so much, I decided to buy a larger TV than I'd originally planned. I had plenty of space in my living room for a big flat screen. I finally chose a forty-inch Smart TV and looked around the store for a salesman. When I turned around, my eyes met a pair of amused pale blue eyes I'd looked into just a few hours ago. Instead of his well-tailored suit, he was in jeans and a blue polo shirt. He looked good in those too.

"Hi, Lieutenant. Are you shopping for a new TV?"

"Yes. Against my will, I promised my sister a bigger TV last Christmas and she won't let me forget it." His face turned serious. "I was surprised to see you here. I've been watching you for a while."

"Why? I can assure you I plan to pay for my new TV, not steal it."

Suddenly he laughed, which changed his whole look. Unsmiling, he had a stern appearance even though he was a good-looking man. But when he laughed as he had just done, he was drop-dead gorgeous, as Amy would say. I wasn't sure how to respond.

"Cara Blackthorne, you're one of a kind. I think I understand why Chief O'Donnell is so concerned about you." He was clearly trying not to smile.

"Well, you're probably wrong, Lieutenant. Chief O'Donnell went to high school with my mom. They're good friends."

He got serious again. "What I wanted to say is that you shouldn't be out shopping at night alone. Next time you want to leave campus, I'd suggest you bring a friend, or even several friends. It would be safer."

"Oh. I wasn't thinking about that." I took a deep breath. "You're probably right. I guess it's a good thing I ran into you."

"Yes, it is. And since you're here, how would you like to help me pick out a TV for my sister?"

It would certainly be better than shopping alone.

"Sure. How big a TV are you looking for?"

It seemed his sister was a football fanatic and also liked to catch up on certain TV shows by streaming them. He would need a Smart TV too, a big one.

A relaxed Lieutenant Fox was actually a very pleasant shopping companion, and he finally settled on a fifty-five inch TV that he thought his sister would love.

When I complimented him on his choice, he snorted. "Maybe now she'll stop bugging me about it."

"How old is your sister?"

"She's twenty going on thirty-five, in my opinion."

"Oh, a lot younger than you."

He turned to look at me. "I'm not an old man, Cara." He sounded insulted.

"Of course not. Um, how old are you?"

One eyebrow went up and he gave me what I have to call "a look."

I shrugged. "Well, you know how old *I* am."

He sighed. "True. I'm twenty-eight, which isn't old."

I nodded. "Okay. It isn't old." I tried not to smile. He sounded a bit defensive.

He finally found a salesman, indicated the TV's we had each picked out. He had to arrange to have his behemoth of a TV delivered, but I said I wanted to take mine home with me.

The salesman nodded, but looked surprised. Lieutenant Fox asked, "How are you going to get it into your house?"

"Well, I don't think it's very heavy, and Miss Williams can help me. I'd like to set it up tonight."

I heard a heavy sigh and looked at him. One eyebrow was again raised, an amused expression on his face. The expression was familiar. Where had I seen it before?

Oh. Adam used to look at me just that way when I amused him. *No, not going to think about Adam.*

He wrote a check and I used the credit card Mom had given me, after a lengthy lecture on the use of credit cards.

The salesman brought my TV out in a big box and I balanced it on a shopping cart. If I was careful, I was sure I could get it to my car safely.

There was a firm tap on my back and I turned to see a disapproving look on the Lieutenant's face.

"How do you expect to get this *into* your car?"

"I have a big car. I'm sure it'll fit, either in the trunk or in the back seat."

"Hope you're right. Let's go. Lead the way."

He pushed the cart through the store carefully and outside into the parking lot. When we reached my car, he looked surprised. "This looks like a police car."

"It was. Now it's my car. When Chief O'Donnell ordered new cars for his department, my parents bought this one for me. It was the Chief's. He took very good care of it." I smiled. "I love it."

THE JOINING TREE

I thought I heard him mutter, "An appropriate vehicle for you."

He put my TV on the back seat. "I think it's a good idea if you drive slowly, Cara. I'll be right behind you."

When we got to the yellow house on Birch Street, Lieutenant Fox carried the large box into my living room, set it leaning against the table I planned to place it on, and turned to me. "How do you plan on setting it up?"

"Uh, well, I'll need help. Maybe one of my friends . . ."

He shook his head, again looking amused. "I'll set it up for you."

"I really appreciate all your help, Lieutenant. Are you hungry? Would you like a snack?"

He was kneeling on the floor, opening the TV box, and looked up at me, clearly surprised. "A snack would be great, Cara. What'd you have in mind?"

I smiled. "I call it the Sunrise Special, but it's just as good at night. It'll be a surprise."

He chuckled. "I'll look forward to being surprised."

As he carefully removed the TV from the box, I went into the kitchen, got out the bacon, bagels, tomatoes and cream cheese, and made two Sunrise Specials. I put them on two plates, took two sodas out of the fridge, and set them on the table in the kitchen nook.

When I went back into the living room, the new TV was sitting on the table Miss Williams had left for me, and the Lieutenant was plugging it in and connecting it to the cable that stuck out of the wall. I remembered that Miss Williams had her TV in the same place. Maybe she'd left the cable turned on.

He turned it on and we had a picture. It was beautiful. Our old TV at home that sat in Mom's bedroom didn't look nearly as good as this did. I'd have to thank Miss Williams.

"It looks fantastic! Thank you, Lieutenant. I know this isn't part of your job but I really appreciate all of your help tonight."

He grinned. And once again, he almost took my breath away. The man was totally gorgeous when he wasn't in cop mode.

"Okay, Cara, you're very welcome. Now where's my snack?"

"In the kitchen. Follow me."

Needless to say, he loved my Sunrise Special. Of course, everyone did. While we ate, he talked a little about his family. It was just his sister and his mom since his dad passed away from a heart attack at the age of forty.

"What about your family, Cara? Any siblings?"

"No, I'm an only child. My parents just got married last year." I had to smile at the shocked look on his face. "It's a long, strange story, but they've loved each other for the past nineteen years, just never got married. They were finally able to resolve their issues, and they got married in October last year. Their wedding was in our back yard with about a hundred people there to witness the occasion. It was lovely. And they're very happy."

"Sounds as though it made you happy too."

I smiled. "Yes, incredibly happy. I didn't meet my dad until I turned sixteen. He's a wonderful man. We made up for a lot of lost time this past year. I told you it was a rough year."

He nodded.

"I'm not sure I would have made it through the year without my father."

He was watching me carefully as I spoke. Finally he smiled. "I'd like to hear that long, strange story one of these days. It must be interesting."

He stood up. "But now I'd better get home and let my sister know she'll have her new TV tomorrow." He grinned again. "Maybe now she'll stop nagging me."

I walked him to the door, thanked him again, and watched him walk to his car, parked behind mine.

Tonight had certainly been unexpected. I'd enjoyed his company. Maybe because I'd felt completely safe with him. No, it wasn't just the safety issue. Aidan Fox was a good man. His good looks were simply icing on the cake. I wondered why he wasn't married. Of course, it was possible he had a girlfriend. In my opinion, he deserved one.

Before I closed the front door, I looked up and down Birch Street. I had to smile when I saw an old van parked at the far corner. I couldn't see its color from this distance, but I was sure it was green.

I shut the door and went to bed, feeling completely safe.

The next day was Saturday, but I didn't plan to drive home for the weekend since I'd only been in Syracuse for three days. Lily called to ask me to meet her in the Café for lunch, and I agreed.

There was a different student behind the counter. Lily said he was a third-year student and an excellent cook. The menu board listed two things: Ham and Cheese Omelet, or Ham and Cheese Sandwich on Rye. There must have been a sale on ham and cheese.

I could always make myself a sandwich at home, so I ordered the omelet. Lily did the same. Over excellent omelets, we talked about the rest of the weekend.

She said there were always parties at Syracuse University, a few miles away. She was trying to recruit a few girls to go with her. It sounded like she had her eye on a guy she'd met the previous year.

"I'm not a party girl, I'm afraid. Most weekends I'll be going home. It's not a long drive and I want to see my parents and a few friends as often as possible," I said.

"Cara, don't you want to meet some new people, specifically guys?"

I snorted. "No thanks, Lily. I'm only here to study Art, not to do more than make a few new friends. Emphasis on *friends*."

Her eyebrows almost hit her hairline. "Oh, that's right. You're still carrying a torch for the guy who got away, right?"

I shook my head. How did I explain being mated to an Elf who had taken my heart with him when he left?

"It's a bit more than carrying a torch, Lily. It's hard to explain."

"Well, try. It sounds more like a punishment, if you ask me. Which you haven't!"

She smiled sympathetically.

"Okay. All I can tell you is that I never knew what falling in love meant . . . until he kissed me. The ground beneath me moved. There was a roaring in my ears like surf hitting the beach. The rest of the world simply went away. Even though there were dozens of people nearby, nothing mattered but the feeling of his lips on mine and his arms around me. As though we were all alone in the universe. Have you ever experienced anything like that?"

Her eyes were big as she stared at me. "Uh, well, no, I can't say I have. But I don't think I've ever fallen in love myself. I've fallen 'in like' several times, and 'in lust' once. Haven't you ever had feelings for anyone else?"

"Well, yes. He used to be my boyfriend, the first guy I ever dated. And I even love him in a certain way. He's a great guy. But I knew I wasn't in love, even before I fell for Adam. It would be so much easier if I was in love with Sean. But I'm not."

Lily looked fascinated. "So you're not even going to date while you're at Barrett? Three years of not dating? No guys to snuggle up with? You must be nuts!"

I had to laugh. "Maybe I am, I don't know. I just want to focus on art, on perfecting my craft, nothing else."

After we finished lunch, Lily left to round up a few second-year classmates to accompany her to the Syracuse campus Saturday night.

After she left the Café, I stayed to finish my coffee, glad I had my new TV to keep me company.

When I returned to my apartment, I went to the back room that I'd already named my "studio" to see what kind of view I had from the rear windows. Since I was just slightly above ground level, it was almost like being in Miss Williams' backyard where there was a well-tended flower bed full of summer and fall flowers, and two white birch trees to remind me of the stream I enjoyed sitting next to in Blackthorne Forest. The best part was the wooded area behind the backyard. I thought it might be part of a public park, although I didn't see any people back there. I looked forward to painting this new view. It would also be a good idea to hang some curtains! I didn't need an audience when I was drawing at night.

Since it was a sunny day, I decided to set up my easel and get started. The various views on Barrett's campus would also be excellent for painting. I wanted to make the most of them before winter arrived.

I got out my watercolor paints and lost all track of time until the sun went down. After dark I began to feel a little lonely, so I called my parents and Amy and spent time chatting with everyone. I tried to call Kevin too but just got voice mail so I left him a message.

Both my parents told me how empty the house seemed without me.

Mom said, "Ralph hasn't eaten much since you left. I've had a hard time just getting him off your bed. I think he's waiting for you to come home."

My heart dropped. I hadn't realized my being away at school would be so hard for Ralph.

My dad wanted to take Ralph to Elvenwood to meet Roscoe, his father, but Ralph wouldn't cooperate, refusing to leave the house for more than the few minutes necessary to take care of his doggy needs.

"Cara, you might have to bring Ralph to Syracuse with you. Why don't you check with Miss Williams to see if she'd mind having a well-behaved dog in the house," Mom asked.

I said I would. Ralph's behavior had me worried. Although he loved everyone he met, I knew he considered himself *my* dog, no one else's.

Sunday morning I climbed the stairs and knocked on Miss Williams' door. She answered the door, still in her robe, but with a smile for me along with an invitation to come in for coffee.

After she'd asked me if I'd settled in yet, and I thanked her for leaving the cable turned on in my apartment, she grinned as she added, "I saw that handsome police lieutenant bringing in your TV. He hooked it up for you too, didn't he?"

I admitted he had.

She shook her head. "If I were twenty years younger, Cara . . ." She laughed. "I wonder if the rest of the police force is as good looking and as gallant as our Lieutenant Fox. I may have to stop in at the Syracuse Police Department and find out."

I grinned. "You should, you know. He can't be the only gorgeous man on the force."

She asked, "Isn't he a little too old for you, Cara? I'm only speaking as a mother, you know."

"Miss Williams, I'm not planning on *dating* the Lieutenant. But I think we're becoming friends. He's just keeping an eye on me at the request of my Police Chief back home."

She nodded. "I see. I did wonder. After all, he's a handsome man. You're a beautiful girl. Stranger things have happened." She looked at me, her eyebrows raised.

I shook my head. "Not gonna happen, trust me."

We'd finished our coffee. It was time to get to the reason for my visit.

"Miss Williams, how do you feel about dogs? Have you ever had one?"

She gave me a sad smile. "I had a Golden Retriever when I was younger. When she died, I was heartbroken. I didn't think another dog could ever take her place. Why do you ask?"

I explained what my mom had said about Ralph and that I was worried about him.

"Mom suggested I bring him up here to stay with me. But I know not everyone wants a dog in their house. Ralph is really well behaved, housebroken, and very friendly. He's also a good watch dog."

"What kind of dog is he, Cara? Small, yappy dogs drive me crazy."

"Ralph's a Boxer, and bigger than most Boxers. He weighs about seventy pounds. He never barks unless someone comes to the door, or if he hears someone outside."

"He does sound like a good watch dog. If you'll clean up after him, take him out for the walks he'll need, we can give it a try. It might be nice to have a dog around. And the backyard is fenced, fortunately."

I was so happy, I started bouncing up and down in my chair. "I actually have time to drive home, get Ralph, and drive back today. Would that be okay with you?"

She chuckled. "If you're willing to do all that driving, Cara, go right ahead. I'm looking forward to meeting Ralph."

"Thank you so much, Miss Williams. Ralph will thank you too!"

I rushed downstairs, pulled my boots on, and called Mom. She and my dad were just sitting down to Sunday brunch.

"I'm driving home to get Ralph, Mom. Miss Williams said okay to having him here. I should be home in about two hours. But I'll have to drive right back. Classes start tomorrow."

"We've missed you, sweetheart, probably more than you realize. You can take time to have a quick bite to eat, can't you? Of course, Ralph will be overjoyed."

"I'm on my way, Mom. See you soon. And tell Ralph I'm coming home for him, okay?"

She said she would, and I ran out to my car and began the drive to Thornewood. It was only mid-morning, so I didn't have to rush. But I was anxious to see my dog and hug him so he would know he hadn't been forgotten.

I still had a couple of Mom's Golden Oldies CD's in my car, so I sang along with the Beatles until I pulled into Thornewood and arrived in front of my house.

It seemed strange. I'd only been gone four days, but it seemed longer.

Mom was waiting at the front door and greeted me with the mother of all hugs. My father was standing in the kitchen doorway with a big smile for me.

"This house hasn't been the same since you left," he muttered as he wrapped his arms around me and dropped a kiss on my head.

I couldn't stop smiling. I loved my home. Nothing would ever take its place in my heart.

I tore up the stairs to my bedroom to find Ralph standing up on my bed, his nose pointed at the doorway. He must have recognized my footsteps because he launched himself at me as soon as I came through the bedroom door. Which put me flat on my back on my bedroom floor, laughing as Ralph licked my face, his little tail wagging like mad.

"I missed you too, Ralphie," I told the ecstatic dog. "You're coming back to Syracuse with me. I won't leave you again, I promise." I rubbed his velvety ears and hugged him as he wagged his entire body. I was sure he understood every word.

When I was able to get up off the floor, he followed me downstairs and went straight to his food dish, emptying it in less than thirty seconds.

Mom was smiling. "I think Ralph will live. His appetite is back to normal. I'll pack up his food and treats for you. Can I interest you in a few pancakes? I've already got the batter ready to go on the griddle. I think your dad will help you eat them."

"Thanks, Mom. Pancakes sound great. I'll have to leave in about an hour, maybe two."

There was a knock at the front door. When I opened it, Amy practically tackled me. "Your mom called to let me know you'd be home for an hour or so. You know I had to stop over!"

I hugged her back. "I've missed you too, Amy. But I'll be home every weekend, weather allowing."

"Thank goodness. Kevin won't be home until Thanksgiving. Nothing's the same without you guys." She sounded a little sad.

She sat down and helped us eat pancakes while Mom drank coffee and smiled at our chatter.

Mom asked if the Syracuse police had been in touch with me. I assured her they had.

"Amy, I wish you could meet Lieutenant Fox. He's gorgeous and single!"

"Maybe I'll come up for a visit," she said with a laugh. Of course, I knew the bakery would be keeping her too busy to take much time off this year.

Before long, it was time for me to leave. Amy gave me another bear hug at the door and made me promise to call her frequently.

I had to hunt for Ralph's leash. It wasn't something we used often since he got his exercise in the backyard and in the woods. I finally found it in the pantry and clipped it to his collar. He gave me a confused look until he realized he was getting into the car with me, then his tail went crazy again, and I swear he was smiling.

I kissed Mom and Dad goodbye and said, "See you next weekend!" A few minutes later I was back on the highway with a happy dog in the back seat, busy looking out all the windows he could reach. He didn't even mind wearing the harness I'd attached to the seat belt.

When we got back to Birch Street and into my apartment, Ralph examined every room, every nook and cranny, tail wagging happily, until there was a knock on my door. He started barking immediately, stationing himself in front of the door. I opened it to Miss Williams, who knelt down to greet Ralph.

"Ralph, this is Miss Williams, who owns this house. She belongs here, so be a gentleman," I told him.

He sniffed her for a few seconds, then sat and held out a paw to her. She smiled and shook his paw.

She looked up at me to say, "Cara, he's beautiful, one of the best-looking Boxers I've ever seen. And he has lovely manners." She stood. "Let's introduce him to the backyard. And in case you didn't notice, there's a doggy door in the back room, tucked into the corner."

I hadn't noticed, but it solved the problem of how to let Ralph out when I was at school. I showed Ralph the doggy door and we followed him out through the back door, located at the rear of the entrance hallway. He stood there, waiting for us, and then ran from one end of the yard to the other, christening the trees and anything else he thought needed to be marked, finally returning to me, tongue hanging out in the typical Boxer smile.

As long as Ralph was happy, I was happy too.

CHAPTER 19

Classes started the next day. Ralph seemed confused when I left the house, but since I planned to come home for lunch, I was sure he'd get used to the routine. Miss Williams assured me she'd keep him company when she saw him out in the backyard.

As I walked across campus to my first class, Fundamentals of Drawing, other students either smiled or said hi. It seemed Lily was right. They recognized me from Lily's photo display last spring. I didn't feel like a stranger.

Although Lily and I didn't have any classes together, we waved at each other in passing. I was happy to find that Paula and I had every class together. As I got to know her, I enjoyed her quirky perspective on life as well as her rather painful honesty. No matter how hard she tried, her drawings inevitably turned into cartoons, much to her despair. Our drawing instructor just shook his head, although he couldn't help smiling at her work. He finally admitted, "Paula, it's a gift. Don't knock it." Which cheered her considerably.

I loved my class on Watercolors. The instructor was excellent, showing us how to layer colors, without making them muddy, and how to use shading and texture to increase the drama in a painting. I'd figured a lot of it out by trial and error, but the finer points were new to me.

As the instructor, Mr. Roth, was looking over my shoulder at my work one day, he said, "I remember seeing similar technique at an Art Gallery in Albany last spring. I think the artist's name was . . . Cara." He frowned at me.

"That was your work, wasn't it?"

I admitted it probably was since I had exhibited two watercolor paintings in Albany.

"Why are you in school, Cara? I would expect any artist whose work actually sells to be painting full-time, not studying a craft she has already mastered."

"Mr. Roth, I haven't mastered anything yet! There's so much more I want to learn. I don't know anything about painting with oils, I think my watercolor painting still needs work. The only thing I'm really confident about is my pen and ink drawing."

He raised his eyebrows and stared at me. Finally, he nodded. The man rarely smiled. "Well, you're an unusual first year student. You could probably teach this class." He walked away, looking over the next student's shoulder.

That student looked over at me, wide-eyed. Once Mr. Roth had passed by, he asked, "Your paintings already sell?"

THE JOINING TREE

I nodded. He moved closer to look at my work. "I can see why." He put his hand up for a high-five, grinned and said, "By the way, I'm Tim."

Unfortunately, my oil painting class was my undoing. I struggled, day after day. I tried round brushes, flat brushes, thin brushes, but the effect I was trying to achieve continued to elude me. Mixing oil paints wasn't the same as watercolor paints. Maybe Francis Sullivan could tell me what I was doing wrong. The class instructor, Miss Alvarez, couldn't. I didn't really think she was doing *any* actual instructing.

Since my oil painting class was my last class of the day, I usually left campus feeling discouraged as I walked home to spend time with Ralph before dinner. If the weather was nice, I'd take him for a walk. Sometimes that was enough to cheer me up.

A few weeks into the semester, I was leaving the house with Ralph when Lieutenant Fox pulled up at the curb. He got out of his car, clearly surprised to see Ralph with me.

"When did you get a dog?"

I smiled. "Seven years ago. I've had Ralph since he was a puppy. He didn't like being left behind when I moved here. My mother said he'd stopped eating, so I decided to bring him to Syracuse if Miss Williams would allow it."

He nodded with a smile. "Obviously, she did." He bent down to say hello to Ralph, who was sitting, watching the Lieutenant alertly.

It took Ralph a few minutes to decide that the Lieutenant was a friend, finally offering his paw.

Lieutenant Fox smiled, scratching under Ralph's chin. When he stood, he said, "I hope he's a good guard dog, Cara. He looks big enough to defend you, if it's ever necessary."

"He is, Lieutenant. I know I can trust him. I was about to take him for a walk. Care to join us?"

"I wish I had the time, but I'm due at headquarters. I just stopped by to check up on you. Everything's okay?"

"Everything's fine as long as it doesn't involve oil paints," I said, shaking my head.

He laughed as he climbed back into his car. "Can't help you there. Sorry."

A group of us met for dinner at the Café most nights. There were Lily, Paula, Joel, Freddy, Tim from Watercolor class, and Ginger, when she wasn't on duty as the Café's cook. The menu that night was Spaghetti and Meatballs, everyone's favorite. I'd been missing our traditional spaghetti night at home with my parents and Kevin.

I'd had a few emails from Kevin, who said his classes were keeping him so busy, he barely had time to eat. He still had to find time to work on the video games he was contracted to design. Apparently, his studies didn't allow him much free time. As a result, he wasn't sure he'd be coming home for Thanksgiving. I knew that would make Amy unhappy.

I emailed him back to remind him he could design his video games at home as well as in his dorm. As an added incentive, I promised that Mom would be happy to fatten him up.

My dinner group was always lively, including complaints about second year instructors as well as my ongoing fight with oil paints. Tim couldn't understand how someone who had my deft hand with watercolors could have such a hard time with oils.

I would have to find time to ride to Elvenwood to see Francis Sullivan before I gave up on oil paints entirely.

One night as I was walking through my neighborhood with Ralph, about three blocks from my apartment, I saw the old green van again. It was parked away from the nearest streetlights, so I didn't recognize it at first. As we began to walk past it, Ralph pulled hard on the leash, obviously finding something about the van interesting, trying to get close enough to sniff the at the back doors. I tried to pull him back since it was possible someone was living in the van. Miss Williams had already told me it didn't belong to any of her neighbors.

"Come on, Ralph, leave it. There's nothing for you here." I yanked hard on his leash until he gave up and returned to my side, his head still turned toward the van. As we continued down the street, his head kept turning back toward the van. I wondered what it was that he found so fascinating.

My parents were celebrating their first wedding anniversary in October and I knew they wanted me to be home that weekend. Their wedding day was also the last time I saw Adam Wolfe. He'd left Blackthorne Forest early the next day, leaving my heart in pieces.

Working up the necessary smiles and cheer was not going to be easy. But I knew my father, who was usually tuned in to my emotional state, would be aware of how I was feeling and would understand.

I drove back to Thornewood with Ralph on Saturday morning. It had been raining for two days, and it showed no sign of stopping. The weather was totally in tune with my mood. Due to the storm, I took my time driving home, wishing all the other drivers would do the same. Naturally, there were a few who thought doing eighty miles per hour in the pouring rain was a good idea. Idiots.

When I allowed myself to think about this day a year ago, I remembered the excitement I'd felt when Adam finally broke down and kissed me for the first time. And I remembered the heartbreak followed by the deep, dark depression that had never totally left me after he was gone.

I was doing my best to push those memories out of my head so I could at least try to be happy for my parents. Their wedding and their love, after

THE JOINING TREE

sixteen years of estrangement, deserved to be celebrated. I couldn't wear a gloomy face this weekend.

Despite the rain—and the blues that might be with me forever—we had a fun anniversary celebration for Mom and Dad. Amy joined us for dinner Saturday night, and Conor came over for Sunday brunch. Good food, cooked by my mother, of course, and good company raised my spirits.

Unfortunately, I wasn't able to ride to Elvenwood to see Francis Sullivan. Thanks to the third day of constant rain, the forest was too muddy to be safe enough for me to ride. I'd have to wait one more week and hope everything would dry out by then.

Over dinner, Mom surprised me by saying she'd spoken to Lieutenant Fox.

"Tommy O'Donnell stopped by to let us know he'd been in touch with the Syracuse police. He said your case had been referred to Lieutenant Aidan Fox, who knew the history of the case and would be keeping an eye on you, Cara. Has he been in touch with you yet?"

"Oh, yeah. The Lieutenant has actually become a friend." I grinned. "I ran into him shopping one night, and he helped me get my new TV home and even set it up for me."

Amy looked interested. "What's he like? Is he good looking? How old is he?"

I laughed. "Calm down, Amy. Lieutenant Fox is 28, single, and when he smiles, he's drop dead gorgeous."

She gasped. "I have to come up for a visit. Soon!"

Mom was chuckling. "And when he doesn't smile?"

I thought about it. "He looks very stern when he's in cop mode. But I can usually make him laugh." I smiled. "He and Ralph have become friends."

As usual, my father sat quietly, apparently enjoying our conversation, just smiling and occasionally chuckling. It was at times like this that I remembered he was an Elf, not a human like Mom. And Amy and I, both raised in the human world, probably acted more like humans than the Halflings we really were.

The only thing missing tonight was Kevin. "Amy, has Kevin decided whether or not he's coming home for Thanksgiving?"

She rolled her eyes. "Cara, we need to talk."

Uh-oh. Trouble in Paradise.

"Let's go out on the back porch for a few minutes. I owe Rowenna a song."

We left Mom and Dad in the kitchen, enjoying their wine, and stepped out on the porch. It was still raining, but I didn't want to neglect my dragon friend.

I began to sing her song, hoping Rowenna would hear me over the rain. We didn't see her in the sky tonight, but when I was finished, I heard her voice in my head.

Thank you, Cara. I can hear sadness in your voice. Next time we'll talk about it. My song sounded beautiful. Thank you for coming out in the rain to sing for me. I'll see you next week, yes?

"Yes, my friend. Next week."

I looked over at Amy, who was staring at me with a bemused expression. "Rowenna's song is lovely, but kind of eerie. Every time I hear you sing it, I get goose bumps."

"Do you want to talk out here, or upstairs in my room where it's warm and dry?"

"Your room please."

We went back inside and headed for my room, after pouring coffee to take with us.

Mom smiled at us. "It's so nice to see you both here, Amy. Brian and I miss you girls, and Kevin too." She chuckled. "My grocery bill is smaller since he left for school."

Amy didn't even smile, so something was obviously very wrong.

When we got up in my room, Ralph was already asleep at the end of my bed. I pulled my desk chair over and invited Amy to sit while I curled up next to Ralph, who wagged his little tail a few times and went back to sleep.

"What's going on between you and Kevin?"

She sighed. "I thought I could deal with his being away at school. He promised to call me every night, send funny texts like he used to, and come home for weekends as often as possible. But it's not happening. I haven't talked to him in over a week, and that last phone call lasted a whole minute.

"Cara, I know he's busy with his classes. He's said they're harder than he expected, but his whole attitude toward me seems to have changed. Like I'm barely an afterthought, you know? I don't feel like I'm his girlfriend anymore, more like a friend he's outgrown."

I felt bad for her. I knew that people often changed when they went away to college, but it'd only been about six weeks.

"Amy, maybe you should email him and be honest about this. Let him know exactly how you feel and see what he has to say. I hope you're wrong about his apparent lack of interest, but if he's really changed that much since he started school, you need to know."

She nodded. "Yeah, you're right. I'm just afraid he'll tell me it's over, that we have to go back to just being good friends."

"Are you in love with Kevin? Did you think he was your mate? Was it that serious?"

She thought about it and then shook her head. "Not exactly, but close. Is the mated thing something that hits you all at once, or is it a more gradual thing?"

"Well, I'd have to say it's gradual, like the way my relationship with Adam developed while he was my bodyguard. He became a close friend, someone I totally trusted. But when he kissed me at Mom and Dad's wedding, it almost felt like an epiphany, like something I'd wanted badly, without being aware

THE JOINING TREE

I wanted it. You know? I knew immediately that everything between us had changed. I knew I was in love with him, that I'd never want anyone else."

"It's been a year, Cara. Do you still feel the same way? Hasn't anything changed for you?"

I snorted. "The only thing that's changed for me is that he's not here anymore. I'm really angry that he left, but I'm still in love with him. If he came back, I'm not sure whether I'd want to hit him or throw myself into his arms. Maybe both."

I could see she was thinking about it. "I wouldn't describe my relationship with Kevin that way. Maybe we're not mates. Maybe we're just good friends who discovered we're physically attracted to each other. Maybe it's a case of out of sight, out of mind."

She said she'd email him this weekend, and we went back downstairs. She had borrowed her mom's station wagon and needed to get it home.

"Mrs. Blackthorne, Mr. Blackthorne, thank you so much for inviting me for dinner. It was really great seeing you both. Please invite me again!"

Mom smiled and got up to hug my best friend. "Of course, Amy. You're always welcome here. Stop in any time. We miss you too."

Dad smiled and kissed her on the cheek, which always left her blushing.

I walked Amy to the front door and she hugged me tightly. "I really do wish I had a free weekend now and then so I could come up to Syracuse and visit you. I'm envious."

She giggled. "I'm also curious about that handsome cop!"

"I'll tell you what. Any time you aren't tied up with bakery or catering business, call me and come on up. I'd be willing to stay at school for the weekend if you were visiting. It would be fun."

"I'm going to work on that, Cara. Just keep those emails coming. I look forward to them *a lot*, you know."

She ran down the steps in the rain and jumped into her mom's car as quickly as possible, tooted her horn and took off. I felt badly that Amy wasn't happy. She deserved to be.

When Conor came in the back door to join us for brunch the next morning, he wore a big smile and gave me a warm hug. "Cara, I've missed you. Are you enjoying Art school?"

Conor was one of my very favorite Elves. He considered himself my "big brother" since he'd been watching me grow up since I was a toddler. He was always available to me, whether I needed answers to questions, or a shoulder to cry on. And I'd done a lot of both with Conor.

"School's great, Conor. I really enjoy most of my classes."

I told Conor and my parents about all of my classes and instructors. Including my present difficulty with oil painting. They were all surprised that I didn't like working with oil paints.

"I don't think it's my medium. I much prefer watercolors and pen and ink drawing."

My father said, "I'm sure Francis can help you with oils. You'll just have to be patient until the weather clears. Even I haven't been able to slow down this constant heavy rain."

I was surprised. My father had an unusual affinity with weather, sometimes controlling both wind and rain. But apparently, not this time.

Mom had made pancakes and my favorite quiche. I stuffed myself because I knew I wouldn't be eating quite this well at school. The various students who cooked for the Café were good, but not as good as my mother.

By the time we'd cleared the table, the rain had become lighter and I thought it would be a good time to drive back to Syracuse.

We said our goodbyes and exchanged hugs, my father holding on to me longer than usual. He finally whispered, "I know how you've been feeling, sweetheart. I'm sorry you're still in pain. I wish there was something I could do to help."

But, of course, there wasn't, not unless he knew where Adam had gone and could bring him back to us.

I fastened Ralph into his harness and we ran through the rain to my car. Once I had him hooked to a seat belt, I waved goodbye to Mom, Dad, and Conor and drove away.

The trip back to Syracuse took longer than usual, thanks to the non-stop rain. By the time I pulled off the highway, my neck was stiff again and I knew I'd need an icepack when I got in.

When I reached the yellow house on Birch Street, I was surprised to find Lieutenant Fox parked in front. I got out with Ralph and walked to his car window.

"What's up, Lieutenant?"

He got out of his car. "Chief O'Donnell called me while you were on the road so I decided to come over and wait for you. How was the drive?"

He sounded anxious.

"It was fine; just very wet. Let's go inside. Sounds like you've got some news I won't like, and I'm already wet enough."

We entered my apartment and I headed into the kitchen. "I have some really great herbal tea that relaxes me. Would you like some?"

He stood in the doorway to the kitchen. "Herbal tea? Sure, I'll try it. My mom thinks I drink too much coffee."

I boiled the water, poured it into my new teapot and added the tea leaf infuser I'd brought from home. "Have a seat, Lieutenant. The tea will be ready in about five minutes."

He sat down in the kitchen with me, looking unusually serious.

"Okay, why did the Chief call you today?"

He looked like he was trying to figure out how to explain something he knew would upset me.

"Come on, Lieutenant. I'm tougher than I look, remember?"

He smiled, giving me an apologetic look. "Yes, I remember, Cara. Okay, here it is. The driver of the car who hit you has disappeared. He seemed to check out, his I.D. was genuine, it was verified that he was an accountant from another town, just visiting friends in Thornewood. But when the Chief tried to contact him with a few more questions, no trace of him was found. The house is furnished, his damaged car is in the garage, but his clothes are gone and no one has seen him for a week."

That did sound weird. "What do you and the Chief think happened to him?"

"The police can't prove it, of course, but the Chief guesses the driver was paid to cause your accident, and decided it would be healthier for him to leave town once he'd completed that job. We don't believe he has stuck around to cause any more trouble for you."

"Cara, I think all I can do is have police patrol your neighborhood. I think you're safe at school. The man who hit you is middle-aged. He'd really stand out on campus."

I poured a cup of tea for each of us. My tension level had risen a bit, and my head was beginning to ache. I needed to relax.

When we'd finished our tea, the Lieutenant stood up. "There will be a patrol car in this neighborhood at night, and it would be a good idea to avoid going out alone. You'll always be safer with your friends. These are just sensible precautions."

I followed him to the door. "I'll be in touch, Cara." He smiled down at me. "Stop frowning. We don't want those creases on your pretty face. Have a little faith in the Syracuse police, okay?"

I tried to smile. "Okay."

I watched him dash down the steps to his car and drive away. Then I realized it would probably be a good idea to shut the door instead of standing there like a target.

After all the stress from last year, I really thought I could handle anything.

I might have been wrong.

CHAPTER 20

The next morning as I was getting ready to leave the apartment for my first class, there was a knock at my door. Ralph sat in front of the door, whining but not barking.

When I opened the door, my mouth fell open. Standing there with a huge duffle bag over his shoulder was a very tall, slim young man with pale blond hair, blue eyes, and a shy smile. He didn't look as though he was too sure of his welcome.

"Good morning, Princess."

"Gavin!"

"Cara, your father sent me. He believes you need a bodyguard." His face became serious, all traces of a smile gone.

I shook my head, groaning on the inside. "Please come in, Gavin. I wasn't expecting anyone from home, that's all."

I would need to have a few more words with my father about the bodyguard issue.

"I'm here to provide more protection for you. And I'll be in class with you too."

I was about to ask how that could be arranged with the Barrett Institute, when he smiled. "Your father spent most of last night on the phone with Chief O'Donnell, Lieutenant Fox, and Mrs. Barrett. Everyone knows about the other driver who has disappeared, and everything has been arranged. You'll just have to tell your landlady why I'm staying here with you."

My mouth fell open again. "You're staying here . . . with me?"

"Of course, Princess. Where else?"

"Um, there's only one bed. I can sleep on the couch; I don't take up as much room as you do." My mind was whirling, worrying about sheets, towels, groceries, and only one bathroom. I was also beginning to get irritated. Why was my father doing this to me?

"I don't need a bed, Princess. I brought an excellent sleeping bag." He smiled. "Conor donated it. It's by far the thickest sleeping bag I've ever seen. I'll be quite comfortable."

My brains still felt a little scrambled when there was another knock on my door. Ralph stopped licking Gavin's hand long enough to return to the door, whining again. He obviously knew who was out there.

Just as I reached for the doorknob, Gavin immediately inserted himself between me and the door. I opened the door, peeking around Gavin to see Miss Williams, who looked surprised at the sight of the tall young man, but smiled anyway.

"Good morning, you two," she said. "Cara, your mother called me late last night to explain about your roommate, who seems to be very protective." She smiled up at Gavin.

"I'm Cara's landlady, Laurie Williams, and you must be Gavin, Cara's cousin. Welcome."

My mother had definitely filled her in regarding my "cousin's" presence.

He bowed to her. "Thank you, Miss Williams. I promise not to cause any problems for you while I'm here. Cara can tell you that I'm generally very quiet."

He was indeed. Gavin had never been what anyone would call talkative.

She smiled. "No worries. We all want to keep Cara safe. If you need anything, don't hesitate to ask."

She left for her apartment upstairs, and I gathered up my messenger bag.

"You'll have to unpack when we get back, Gavin. My first class is in fifteen minutes."

He nodded, following me out the door, a large manila envelope under his arm.

I pointed to the manila envelope. "What's that?"

He blushed. "It's some of my artwork. I'll show you when we get to your class."

His artwork? "I didn't know you were interested in art, Gavin. What do you like to draw?"

"Uh, well, plants, flowers, herbs, birds, the small things in the forest that some people never see. Not the big, showy stuff like trees, roses, lilies. I like to draw the lesser-known plants. They have their own beauty."

"I can't wait to see what you've done. I had no idea there was another artist in Blackthorne Forest."

He smiled shyly. "Actually, there are a few others as well."

This was news to me. No one had ever shared his or her work with me, other than Francis Sullivan, of course. I felt immediately guilty. I'd make it a point to meet all the other artists in Elvenwood as soon as possible. Why had no one told me before?

As we walked across campus to my Drawing class, we attracted quite a bit of attention. Actually, Gavin attracted all the attention. He was a very good-looking young man with his pale blond hair and dreamy blue eyes. Being at least six feet four didn't hurt either.

Lily's eyes almost popped out of her head when she spotted us, and her arm started waving like mad immediately. "Cara, wait up." She ran over to us, stopped short in front of Gavin and said, "Who's your friend?" Nothing shy about Lily.

Naturally, Gavin immediately turned pink as he looked down at the tiny blonde. Lily was one of the few people smaller than me.

I introduced him, saying, "Gavin's my cousin, and he'll be studying Art here with me."

Even though Lily and my other new friends knew about my accident, they didn't know the other driver had disappeared. I didn't think sharing that information was necessary, and I didn't tell her that Gavin was sent as my bodyguard. It was better if everyone just considered him another art student.

She actually got Gavin talking, which never happened with strangers, and they chatted right up until we reached my Drawing class.

"My class is in the next building so I'll see you both later," she said, grinning. She was going to be late for her class, but she seemed to feel it had been worth it.

We walked into my Drawing class and the instructor obviously expected Gavin. He directed him to another easel set up next to mine. When we got to our work space, I pointed to his manila envelope and he opened it, setting a group of drawings up on his easel. They were really good, like illustrations from a botany textbook. Every detail was perfect.

Our instructor, Mr. Russell, came over to take a look at Gavin's drawings. "You're an excellent draftsman, Gavin. I'd like to see you turn these into much larger drawings, into real art, so they don't look like illustrations."

He said, "These small plants have their own beauty, you know, but they'll have a great deal more impact once they've been blown up. Let's see what you can do with them."

Gavin nodded, looking eager. He immediately went to the supply table for a larger piece of art paper and fastened it to his easel. Looking over at me, he grinned. "I'm going to enjoy this class."

The same thing happened in my other classes as well. The instructors all seemed to be expecting Gavin and they were all complimentary about his drawings. He would be learning to recreate them in both watercolors and oils. I wondered if he'd have the same problem I was having with oil paints.

As we walked between classes, Gavin's eyes scanned the groups of students carefully. He seemed to be looking for anyone that didn't "belong." He was so tall, his visibility was far better than mine, and I was suddenly glad he was with me.

I remembered how good he was with bow and arrow. I wondered if he was equally as skilled with a knife. Maybe my father's decision to send Gavin to stay with me wasn't such a bad idea.

We went back to my apartment for lunch. Gavin played with Ralph while I made sandwiches. He assured me he was accustomed to preparing his own meals, so we agreed to take turns. I would supply the groceries.

Since Gavin was a Halfling, like me, he was familiar with grocery stores. He'd grown up in Elvenwood, but had spent weekends in Thornewood with his mother until her untimely death. Gavin was much more accustomed to life in the human world than most Elves were, which made life simpler.

After our afternoon classes, we returned to the apartment to take Ralph for a walk. Gavin thought it reckless of me to be walking Ralph by myself. When I thought about it, I had to admit he might be right. I stayed in the apartment while he walked Ralph, who didn't seem to care who was at the other end of the leash. Since he could no longer run loose in the forest, these daily walks were all-important to Ralph.

Gavin was accustomed to cooking over a campfire, not a gas stove, so he agreed we should continue to have our dinners at the Café. The first time I joined my usual crew for dinner with Gavin by my side, everyone made him welcome, especially Lily and Freddy, both of whom barely took their eyes off my tall, blond "cousin."

Lily immediately made room for Gavin next to her, much to Freddy's disappointment. I couldn't help smiling at their reactions, especially since Gavin was obviously aware of Lily's tactics and was already blushing.

I introduced Gavin as my cousin who'd been forced to start Barrett late in the term because his family had been traveling and had just arrived home. Naturally, Lily wanted to know where he was living. When he answered, "With Cara," I thought her eyes were going to pop out of her head.

"You're *living* together?" Everyone at the table looked interested in that piece of news.

Gavin again turned red, and I had to assure the group that Gavin and I were like siblings, nothing more. "Gavin has an extremely comfortable sleeping bag," I told them. Joel and Tim looked amused, Freddy kept staring at Gavin longingly, Paula and Lily both looked fascinated by the living arrangement I was describing.

No one said anything until Gavin added, "I can't afford to live anywhere else. Cara is doing me a big favor." He looked around the table. "I hope no one misunderstands. That wouldn't be fair to Cara."

Everyone nodded and seemed to relax. Conversation returned to a couple of second year instructors no one liked, and we all enjoyed a Pasta Salad Ginger had put together. It was full of ham, salami, olives, tomatoes, and chunks of cheese with an oil and vinegar dressing. Gavin went back for a second bowl, bowing his thanks to Ginger, who looked as though she'd give him as many bowls as he wanted, no charge.

Paula nudged me and winked. I smiled, shaking my head. I hoped the interest in Gavin would die down quickly.

When we returned to my apartment, Gavin unrolled his sleeping bag and placed it directly in front of my door.

"It's so early. Are you actually going to bed now?" I asked him.

He shrugged. "We go to sleep early in the forest, mainly because we're up at or before dawn. Your schedule is probably quite different," he said with a smile.

"Well, yeah. In the evening, I might read one of my Art History books for class, watch TV, or email my friends. I don't go to bed until around ten o'clock. I'm usually up by seven thirty. Will those hours work for you?"

"I'll try to stay awake. I'm sure I'll get used to your schedule in a few days." He smiled a little sadly. "I used to enjoy watching television at my mom's house. Can we watch something now?"

"Sure." I handed him the remote. "Go ahead and see what's on. You can figure out how to use the remote."

I curled up at one end of the big couch, and Gavin made himself comfortable in the blue easy chair. He seemed fascinated by all the buttons on the remote, figured out which one turned the TV on, and started smiling as he learned how to use the other buttons.

He kept the volume low so I was able to write and answer some emails on my laptop.

I'd received a few emails from Sean, telling me all about Penn State, his classes and, of course, the punishing football practices. He said he missed me and was looking forward to coming home for Thanksgiving. I didn't mention the current problem, saying I'd see him during Thanksgiving break and told him to take care of himself. After all, I wasn't even sure it was a problem. I was trying to convince myself that the Chief and my father were simply making mountains out of molehills, one of Mom's favorite expressions.

I didn't like keeping things from Amy and Kevin, but I hoped the current problem—if there was one—would be resolved by Thanksgiving, so I didn't tell them that I again needed a bodyguard. I kept my emails light and focused on my Art classes, but I did confess I was frustrated with oil painting.

It was a very pleasant evening, with Gavin chuckling occasionally as he sat in front of the TV. Ralph was curled up at my feet while I was on my laptop. My apartment no longer felt empty, which was an improvement. I hadn't really gotten used to living alone.

The rest of the week was calm. Gavin fit in so comfortably, it was as though he'd always been there. He was the perfect roommate. I refused to think of him as a *bodyguard*.

At lunch in the Café every day, he was quiet and polite. Lily constantly tried to engage him in conversation, finally asking him if he'd go to a party with her Saturday night. He thanked her for the invitation but explained that he'd be going home to Thornewood with me for the weekend.

Clearly disappointed, she muttered, "You two certainly spend a lot of time together."

He politely pointed out that his family was in Thornewood too.

Lily stopped pouting, looking a bit embarrassed. "Of course. I understand."

It was a real temptation to tell Lily the truth, but something held me back.

As soon as classes ended Friday afternoon, Gavin and I packed up and headed for home. Gavin hadn't ridden with me before and was fascinated with my big car.

It occurred to me that I didn't know how Gavin had traveled to Syracuse a few days ago. "How did you get up here? I never asked."

"Mr. Callahan was driving to Albany. He made a detour to Syracuse to drop me off. He sent you his regards. I'm sorry. I was nervous and forgot to tell you."

"Why were you nervous?"

He hesitated. "Well, I wasn't sure you'd like having me dumped on you. You've always seemed to value your independence, Cara. I knew your father hadn't consulted you before he sent me here. I was afraid you'd be angry."

"To tell the truth, I'm glad you're here. Living alone, once I learned that other driver had disappeared, made me a little nervous. I'm more comfortable now."

"Ah. That's a relief." He smiled. "Being here at school with you has been wonderful! I'm enjoying your classes. I like your friends too." I heard him chuckle. "Especially Lily. I think she likes me. Under other circumstances, I'd certainly accept her invitation."

I had to laugh. "Yeah, she likes you all right. Do you have a girlfriend at home?"

He shook his head. "No. Most of Elvenwood is friendlier now than they used to be, but no one is *that* friendly. Boys outnumber girls, so unattached girls are too few and too young. I doubt I'll find an Elf to mate with. Besides, I'm more comfortable in the human world."

This was interesting. Maybe Lily actually had a chance with Gavin. It was too bad that Gavin had to stick so close to me.

We arrived in Thornewood two hours later. Seeing the "Entering Thornewood" sign put a smile on my face.

It was great being at home with Mom and Dad. Gavin had dinner with us before leaving to see Conor in the forest.

After Gavin's mother was killed, Conor had sort of adopted Gavin, training him to work in the forest with him. It was a good decision for both of them.

I called Amy after Gavin left and asked if she'd have time to come over Saturday. She said she'd make time and that she needed to talk to me. She didn't sound happy.

My father decided that Gavin should stay with us whenever we were home for the weekend because he didn't want me going anywhere alone.

He finally asked, "How are you and Gavin getting along? Do you think he's an effective bodyguard?"

"Gavin's great, Dad. He's very protective, and a good roommate too. If you had to send anyone, Gavin was a good choice."

He nodded, looking pleased. "Well, I know that Gavin's devoted to you. I trust him to do whatever is necessary to protect you. I'm glad you're getting along well."

There was no sense telling him I didn't really need a bodyguard. Besides, I kind of liked having Gavin with me.

I was tired so I went to bed early, after putting a load of laundry in Mom's washer. I'd have to remember to tell Gavin I'd do his laundry too. Miss Williams had a washer and dryer, but I didn't want to take advantage of her generosity any more than I already did.

Climbing under the covers of my own comfy bed felt wonderful. Ralph was curled up at the foot of my bed, snoring softly. I left one of my windows open and I could smell the forest. I'd missed this.

I'd slept well for the past few weeks without any disturbing dreams. But my subconscious was overactive that night. In my dream I saw a huge SUV barreling toward me, smashing into my car again. I heard the awful sound of metal crashing against metal, screaming sirens, and felt pressure against my face, taking my breath away.

I must have actually called out because I woke up to find Ralph licking my face and whining. "It's okay, Ralphie. I just had a bad dream."

Amy came over Saturday morning after we'd had breakfast. All she wanted was black coffee. She looked miserable.

After Gavin went out on the back porch to do some drawing, my father left for his camp, and Mom left to open the bookstore. Amy and I had the kitchen to ourselves.

After staring into her coffee for a few minutes, she looked at me and said, "I can't get any real communication out of Kevin. He keeps saying he's busy, he's got a ton of studying to do, he's working on his video game, yada, yada, you know? I don't know how he feels about us, or if he feels anything at all. I took your suggestion and wrote him a long email." She sighed. "He never answered it."

"Thanksgiving is only a couple of weeks away. Has he said whether he's coming home?"

"No. I can't get him to commit to anything. I don't know where I stand. I don't know what else to do." She sounded so hurt. I hated seeing Amy like this. She'd always been so upbeat, so positive about everything.

"Amy, do you want me to talk to him? Frankly, I'm ready to read him the riot act. I can't believe he's treating you this way."

"Please, Cara. Maybe he'll talk to you. Maybe you can find out what's going on with him. If it's time for me to move on, I want to know."

"Okay. I'll call him as soon as possible."

She nodded, finished her coffee and looked out the kitchen window. "Hey! Who's that on your porch?"

"Uh, that's Gavin. Remember him? He's attending Barrett too. I never knew that he's into Art, but he's very talented. We've been commuting together."

She looked genuinely surprised. "Didn't you say your father sent him to work with Conor in the forest after his mom died?"

"Yes. He loves working with Conor, but he also has a lot of artistic talent. My dad is sending him to Barrett too."

Amy looked suspicious. "And when did all this happen? You never said a word about Gavin being at school with you."

THE JOINING TREE

I took a deep breath. There had never been any way to keep anything from Amy. "Gavin's only been at school with me this past week. My father sent him after the driver who hit me suddenly disappeared. The Chief and my dad suspect the accident was set up to hurt me so that I couldn't testify against Romanov."

Her eyes got big. "They think you're still in danger?"

"Well, they think it's possible so they don't want me out of town alone."

"Well, crap, Cara! So Gavin is actually your bodyguard, right?"

"Yes. But he's also a talented artist. He's really enjoying our classes. Outside of class, though, he sticks to me like glue." I giggled. "One of my friends at school is finding that extremely frustrating. She invited Gavin to a party, but he had to turn her down. She has no idea why, of course. They were also surprised to learn that he's living with me!"

Her mouth dropped open. "Living with you? In that one-bedroom apartment?"

"Relax, Amy. We introduced Gavin as my cousin. He has a nice warm sleeping bag. He unrolls it in front of the apartment door every night."

"Well," she whispered, "he is awfully nice to look at. I kind of envy you."

I whispered back, "If he could hear you, he'd be blushing like mad. It's one of his charms. Lily really has the hots for him."

At least I'd given Amy something else to think about besides Kevin. She talked about the bakery, and the few catering jobs she'd already received. Apparently, Thornewood was delighted to have the Strauss bakery open again. They were doing record business. And my cousin Jason was once again a regular customer for the doughnuts Mrs. Strauss made every day.

She looked at her watch and groaned. "I've got to get back, Cara. Cakes to bake, etc. Just let me know if you're able to talk to Kevin." She got up from the table, hugged me, and left for the bakery.

As I was washing our cups and cleaning off the table, Gavin came back in. "I thought you and Amy would appreciate some privacy. She looked upset. Is she okay?"

"Well, not really. She and Kevin are having some problems. They're my best friends. I don't like seeing either one of them unhappy."

"Amy and Kevin are together, like girlfriend-boyfriend?"

"Yeah. Kevin's away at college now. It sounds like he's lost interest in his relationship with Amy. She's miserable."

He looked shocked. "How could anyone lose interest in that lively, beautiful girl? When I was your bodyguard last year, she was always joking and laughing with Neal. I thought he was really lucky he got to spend so much time with her."

I nodded. "Well, it's Neal's loss. His parents didn't approve of him spending time with a human girl. That was before we found out that Amy's a Halfling. Her mother had never told her."

His eyebrows hit his hairline. "She's a Halfling too?" He thought about that for a few seconds, then said, "Cara, if she and Kevin break up, please let her know that I'd welcome a chance to get to know her better."

"Okay. I'm sure that will cheer her up immensely." I grinned at him, and he blushed, naturally.

Before we went to bed that night, Gavin came out on the back porch with me. He'd heard the other Elves talk about Rowenna, and he wanted to meet her.

"I never dreamed dragons were real, Cara. I think it's wonderful that you and she have become friends."

"I think so too. She's already saved my mother's life and mine too when Gaynes snatched me last year."

"Yes, I heard about that." His voice changed to a harsher tone. "I think it's a shame you didn't kill him. He doesn't deserve to live."

Since Gaynes had killed Gavin's mother, I understood how he felt. I even agreed with him.

I began singing what I'd always called the Dragon's Song. It wasn't long before I heard her large wings above us, and felt her magic surrounding us like a soft blanket.

She landed in the backyard. In the dark, all we could see were her golden eyes, and the glitter of her scales in the moonlight.

Good evening Cara. You have a new friend for me to meet. Hmm. He's a very handsome young man with his pale hair. I can read his heart, you know. He would give his life for you if it ever became necessary. A good friend to have.

I didn't think Gavin was telepathic, so I spoke out loud.

"Hi, Rowenna. I'd like you to meet Gavin, a good friend and at present, my bodyguard as well."

Why do you need a bodyguard now?

"My father and our Police Chief both believe my auto accident was deliberate. The other driver has disappeared. They're afraid I may be at risk."

I'm sorry I can't help you when you're at school, my friend. But I am glad you won't be alone. If you need my help at any time, please call me.

"Thank you, Rowenna. I value your friendship."

She chuckled. *You have many friends, Cara.*

I could barely see her as she rose into the night sky, her huge wings moving the air with such strength. Her magic swirled around us for a few seconds more and then left us.

Gavin promptly sat down hard in one of the deck chairs.

"That was amazing," he said. "By the way, I could hear what she was saying to you. Her voice is distinctive, rough like gravel. She loves you as one of her own."

I sat down next to him. "You're telepathic? I didn't know that."

He laughed. "I didn't either. This was the first time I heard another's voice in my head. It was a very strange sensation."

THE JOINING TREE

The next morning we were all downstairs in the kitchen very early, which was my father's idea.

"Cara, we feel it would be a good idea to vary your schedule, leave for school a lot earlier one week and later the next. Just in case you're being watched. Your mother has agreed to make breakfast early this week so you and Gavin can eat before you have to leave."

Mom was already at the stove, scrambling eggs and frying ham. She turned to say, "I think your father's right. Sorry we had to wake you so early, but this way you can leave by nine o'clock and return to school before noon."

We'd been up late last night so I was still tired, but my parents' plan was a good one. "You're probably right. I may have to do the same thing in Syracuse; leave for classes either earlier or later."

After we'd had breakfast, I hugged Mom and Dad. "I'll keep in touch by phone."

Mom added, "And I'll be in touch with Lieutenant Fox as well."

It wasn't even nine o'clock when we left Thornewood, our clean laundry safely tucked into the trunk.

We were only about ten miles outside of town when Gavin said, "I think we're being followed. The same gray car has been behind us since we got on the highway. I'm keeping an eye on him through your side-view mirror."

I glanced in my rear-view mirror. I could see the gray car two cars behind us.

I sped up and the gray car sped up. I slowed down, pulling into the right hand lane, and the gray car slowed and followed us.

"I think you're right. Use my cell phone and just press "5". I've got Lieutenant Fox on speed dial."

He got the Lieutenant on the phone and put the phone on speaker. I heard the Lieutenant's voice. "What's up, Cara?"

"We're on our way back to Syracuse. We're on Route 9 and I think we're being followed. There's a gray sedan behind us, speeding up and slowing down when we do. We just passed the Foster's Mill exit."

I heard some garbled conversation on the phone, then the Lieutenant said, "I've notified the Highway Patrol, Cara. They'll put two cars on the road in your vicinity to keep an eye on your car and the gray sedan. I'll be in constant touch with them. Call me back if there's any change."

I glanced over at Gavin. "Well, I feel better now."

"I hope the Syracuse Police will pick up where the Highway Patrol leaves off. I'd like to know who's driving that gray sedan," Gavin said.

The rest of the drive was more relaxed. I could still see the gray sedan behind us, but two Highway Patrol cars were behind us as well. We left the highway at the second Syracuse exit, but the gray sedan kept on going, Highway Patrol still behind it.

My cell phone rang. Gavin put it on speaker again. "Cara, where are you now?" the Lieutenant asked.

"We just got off Route 9 headed for Barrett."

His voice sounded a little sharp. "We?"

"I have Gavin with me. He works for my father who decided I needed a bodyguard."

I heard the Lieutenant chuckle. "Can't say I disagree, Cara. That gray car didn't follow you off the highway, did it?"

"No. But I'd still like to know who was driving that car. It stayed too close to us all the way to Syracuse."

"I know. Highway Patrol will pull it over at the next rest stop. We'll find out who the driver is and check him out. But I still don't want you and your bodyguard to take any chances. Stay indoors as much as possible. By the way, your mother called me. She wants you to vary your schedule every day, which is a good idea."

"I know. We will. I just pulled up in front of our house."

"Okay, I'll stop by later. I want to meet your bodyguard and give him some instructions. Is he armed?"

"Only with knives, Lieutenant."

"Oh. Not as effective as a gun would be. Well, I hope he's at least bigger than you."

Gavin and I both laughed. "Yeah, he's bigger than me. Much bigger."

"Good. I'll see you later, Cara."

Gavin got out of the car first, telling me to wait. He walked to the driver's door and let me out, staying close behind me as I unhooked Ralph from his seat belt and then pulled our bags of clean laundry out of the trunk.

I think we were both a little tense until we were inside my apartment.

"I'm making a pot of coffee." "Good idea, Cara. I'll take Ralph's harness off so he can go out in the backyard. He really enjoys car rides, doesn't he?"

I smiled. "Yeah, he loves going anywhere with me. He's just not fond of being left at home. But he has the doggy door so he can run around in the backyard whenever he wants."

We were sitting in the kitchen over coffee when there was a knock at the front door.

"That's probably the Lieutenant," I said as I got up and headed for the door.

"Wait, Cara. Let me answer the door." Gavin put his hand on my shoulder to keep me in my seat and went to the front door. He returned a minute later, followed by the shorter Lieutenant Fox.

The Lieutenant sat down with us and I poured him a cup of coffee. "Lieutenant, this is my cousin, Gavin Blackthorne. Well, he's my cousin as long as he's here at Barrett with me. Gavin, Lieutenant Fox."

They were trying to be subtle as they checked each other out, but I thought they were fairly obvious.

THE JOINING TREE

The Lieutenant said to Gavin, "Cara says you're armed with knives. May I?" He reached out one hand. Gavin pulled two knives out from his waistband and handed them over.

"You only carry two knives?"

Gavin smiled and pulled two more from ankle holsters, handing them over too.

Examining them carefully, the Lieutenant nodded and handed them back. "A gun would be more effective, but Chief O'Donnell already asked me to issue Concealed Carry Permits for both of you for your knives." Looking at Gavin seriously, he said, "I sincerely hope you won't have to use them."

Gavin nodded.

"What have you heard from the Highway Patrol, Lieutenant?" I asked.

He smiled. "The driver was a sixty-five year old grandmother on her way to Schenectady to visit her children. There's no way she's the person we're looking for."

I wasn't so sure. "She was awfully careful the way she followed us, Lieutenant."

He grinned. "She thought you were the police—she recognized your car—and decided she'd be perfectly safe if she stayed behind you. When she saw the Highway Patrol, she was sure she was right."

I was relieved, but I was still worried about the driver who'd gone missing.

The Lieutenant and Gavin discussed police methods for protection, how to vary my schedule to and from school, what to watch for outside the house, etc.

"Do you have an answering device on your phone?" he asked me.

When I said I did, he suggested I let it pick up all my calls. "No sense letting anyone know when you're home and when you're not. A legitimate caller will leave a message."

He finished his coffee and stood. "I think that's it for now. I'll be stopping by regularly and there will be more patrol cars in the neighborhood for the time being. Actually, a few days ago, one of my men found a man living in his van, parked a block away. He was told to stay out of this neighborhood. Transients are not welcome here."

The Lieutenant left, and Gavin and I returned to the kitchen. We were both hungry so he offered to make sandwiches. He grinned. "My turn. Groceries are getting low. We'll have to go shopping soon. Dinner at the Café tonight?"

"Yeah. But we shouldn't go at the same time we usually do. We should go earlier, just in case we're being watched." He agreed.

To relieve some stress, I went into the back room to do some painting while Gavin turned on the TV and found a football game to watch. I set up my easel for the first time since I'd moved in, unpacked my watercolors and a large sheet of textured paper. After taping the paper to a piece of rigid cardboard, I got a tiny cup of water and placed it on the easel's shelf.

Hoping I'd find something worth painting in the backyard, I raised the window shade and looked out. I reminded myself to speak to Miss Williams about curtains.

There was a lovely small maple tree in the backyard. It was so young, I was sure Miss Williams had planted it herself. The leaves were shades of red and gold, perfect for painting. I began mixing those colors on my palette.

An hour later, Gavin wandered in to see what I was doing. "Those colors are wonderful, Cara. You've captured them perfectly."

Looking at the three windows next to my easel, he said, "You're awfully exposed with the window shades pulled up, Cara. Curtains would be a better idea."

"Yeah, I know. I've been meaning to ask Laurie if she has any I could use."

He reached up and pulled the shades down. "Sorry, but keep them down for now. I'll run upstairs and ask your landlady about curtains."

He rushed out and I heard the apartment door open and close.

Ten minutes later, he was back, with what looked like several pairs of textured beige curtains over his arm. He was grinning. "Miss Williams said these were over the windows before she took them down when the apartment was being painted. The curtain rods are still there. Let's put them up now."

Once the curtains were up, the room wasn't as bright, but I couldn't be seen from outside either. I simply peeked out at the little maple tree I was painting. It was the next best thing to actually being outside in the yard.

I was beginning to resent the need to "hide," because that's exactly what it felt like, but I knew there was always the slight chance that I wasn't as safe as I'd assumed I was.

However, I hadn't been having that familiar, creepy feeling of being watched. I wondered why.

CHAPTER 21

One of the first things I had to do that week was call Kevin and find out why he seemed to be avoiding Amy. I tried—unsuccessfully—to reach him on the phone several times. Finally, out of total frustration, I sent him a blistering email, accusing him of dropping both of his best friends as though we were yesterday's news. He finally called me back late Saturday night while I was at my mother's house.

"Cara, that email you sent practically set my laptop on fire. What's going on?"

"Kevin, it's been over a month since we talked. You haven't been answering your phone, and Amy feels as though you've ended your relationship with her out of lack of interest. What's going on with *you*?"

There was silence on the phone. Finally, he said, "My workload here at school is killing, I overestimated how much I could handle and I'll have to drop a couple of classes. I've only been getting two or three hours of sleep at night. I don't mean to sound callous or uncaring, but I don't have time for a relationship right now."

"It didn't occur to you to alert Amy to these facts? She feels like you've dumped her, without even an explanation."

I heard him sigh. "Cara, college isn't anything like high school. There's no time for anything, not even enough sleep. I guess I've just been avoiding the Amy issue. And I know how bad that sounds."

"Well, I don't think you can practice avoidance any longer, Kev. You should come home for Thanksgiving and lay it out for her. Either she'll decide to live with your absence and total lack of attention, or she'll decide to move on."

He sighed again. "Yeah. You're right. It's not fair to Amy. She needs a guy who's gonna be there for her. I can't be right now.

"By the way, short stuff, are you all healed up from your accident?"

"Yeah, Kev. But the driver who hit me seems to have disappeared."

"Wow, I've really been out of the loop. I'm guessing the police found that suspicious, right?"

"Right. That's when my father decided I needed a bodyguard again and sent Gavin to stay with me at school. He's attending classes with me. It turns out he's a talented artist himself. He's a great roommate so it's working out well."

"Holy crap, babe, you're *living* with another Elf?"

"Yes, Kevin. Get your mind out of the gutter. And Gavin's a Halfling, like us, in case you forgot."

"Platonic, right? No funny business?"

I sighed. "Of course it's platonic."

More softly, he asked, "Still carrying a torch for the missing bodyguard?"

I sighed more deeply. "Yeah. I guess you could call it that."

"Oh, babe. Well, at least your life's not boring."

"Kev, will I see you at Thanksgiving? Please say yes. I really miss you."

"Miss you too, short stuff. I'll do my best to get home."

Now I had to talk to Amy. It wasn't going to be pleasant.

It was late, but I'd be going back to school the next day, so I called her around eleven o'clock. She needed to know what Kevin had said.

"Hey, Cara, this is a late call. What's wrong?"

"I just got off the phone with Kevin. He wasn't answering his phone so I sent him an email that practically set his hair on fire. We talked for a while. He's being forced to drop some classes. Apparently, he took on too much this semester."

"Well, Cara, I gathered that much. He's always been an over-achiever. I guess he didn't realize how much tougher college would be. Be honest with me, is he breaking up with me?"

I hesitated. "I think that will be up to you, Amy. I've convinced him to come home for Thanksgiving so you two can hash it out. He admitted he doesn't have time for a relationship right now. He knows it's unfair to you. I don't think he'll blame you if you decide you want to move on."

I heard her deep sigh. "I guess I have until Thanksgiving to make that decision. Of course, once I see him that may change too. Cara, what would you do?"

I snorted. "You're asking *me* that question?"

She chuckled. "Yeah, I almost forgot. You'll wait forever for Adam to come back, won't you?"

"I don't think I have a choice."

I continued to drive home every weekend, knowing that when winter set in, there would be fewer chances to come home. And then it was Thanksgiving and we had a four-day weekend. Even students who lived far away flew home for the holiday.

We got home the night before Thanksgiving. Gavin came in to say hello to my parents but then left for Blackthorne Forest, my father's camp, and Conor who'd become like a surrogate parent. Mom made Gavin promise to bring Conor and join us for Thanksgiving dinner on Thursday.

Kevin actually did make it home on Thursday, pounding on our door around noon, wrapping me up tightly in his long arms, resting his chin on top of my head, which he knew I hated.

THE JOINING TREE

He wouldn't let go, and I was laughing when my father came to the door to see what was going on. Grinning, he said, "Welcome home, Kevin. I hope you're planning on staying because I invited your father to join us too."

"Mr. Blackthorne, this house and all of you feel like home to me. Thanks for the invitation, and I'm glad you're including my dad. My mom, of course, is working."

We all rolled our eyes. Kevin's mother was a workaholic, even on holidays.

When he finally made it into the kitchen, he practically lifted Mom off her feet.

"I've missed you, Mrs. B," he said as she laughed and insisted on being put down.

"Well, it wouldn't be Thanksgiving without you, Kevin," she said. He'd had Thanksgiving with us since he was a little boy, and she was right. It wouldn't be the same without him.

Later, my father, Conor, Gavin, and Kevin's dad, Kelly O'Rourke, went out on the back porch while Mom, Kevin, and I got our Thanksgiving dinner on the table. It had become a tradition, one we didn't want to give up. Kevin reached things on the top shelves, helped with the chopping, and generally did whatever we asked of him.

Thanksgiving dinner was fantastic, as always. We all stayed at the table talking and laughing, long after we'd all stuffed ourselves. It was Gavin's first ever Thanksgiving dinner. The Elves celebrated Harvest in October, which he'd missed. Blushing like crazy, he told Mom it was the best food he'd ever had in one place, at one time, which made all of us laugh. Mom really put on a spread for holidays.

After we'd polished off an entire pumpkin-cheesecake pie, the doorbell began ringing. I got up to answer it while Mom, Kevin, and Gavin loaded the dishwasher. The older men had gone out on the back porch with their coffee.

I didn't even have a chance to see who it was before I was practically tackled, wrapped up in a pair of strong arms, my nose against a chest that smelled of sandalwood and soap. Sean was home, and apparently extremely glad to see me!

To be honest, I was just as glad to see him. I hadn't been hugged or kissed with that kind of affection since August, and I'd missed it. I'd also missed his smile, his "hello, beautiful" greeting, and the affection I'd always kept at arm's length. Maybe it was time I let him get a little closer.

After all, I didn't know if Adam would ever come back.

Sean and I spent most of that Thanksgiving weekend together, either at my house, his house, the Grille, where he ran into many of his high school buddies, the Pizza Palace, where we danced to the oldies until we needed some air, or my car, where a lot of affection was shared.

I couldn't ignore or deny the physical attraction between us, and I was no longer pushing him away. I'd missed him. I'd missed the closeness, the long talks, and the knowledge that I was loved. Sean was everything I should want. Why did I have to want someone I'd probably never see again?

We would both be going back to school on Sunday. "It's only another few weeks until Christmas break," he said on Saturday. "You'll be home for two weeks, right?"

"Yeah, unless I get snow-bound," I told him. "But I'll be home for as much of that two weeks as possible. However, I'll have to spend some time painting. I've been invited to exhibit at another Art Gallery in Manhattan in February, and I have to get a lot of work done while we're on vacation."

He had his arm around me as we sat in Mom's living room. The bookstore was open and we had the house to ourselves, although I knew my dad was apt to pop in whenever he needed to warm up. Our fall weather had finally turned frigid. I was hoping there wouldn't be any snow until we got back to school.

After nibbling on my neck for a few minutes, he pulled me closer and asked, "At least save your evenings for me while we're home, okay? I'll try not to disturb your painting time too much." He smiled mischievously and whispered, "But you know I can't resist you." More nibbling ensued. I wasn't complaining. Soon I was nibbling on one of his ears until I heard the back door open and close. My father was home.

We looked at each other. Alone time was over. Somewhat regretfully, we got up from the couch and wandered into the kitchen to greet my father, who took one look at my flushed face and shook his head at us. "I think it's time we all took a coffee break, Cara."

I chuckled. "Yeah. Would you like me to make the coffee, Dad?"

He agreed, I got the coffee pot going, and we all sat down at the table. I knew he wasn't mad at us. My father and I had had a short but emphatic talk the previous night about relationships. I had admitted that Sean and I shared a physical attraction, but that I wasn't about to go too far with it.

He'd asked me if my feelings about Adam had changed in the past year. I said they hadn't, and I could see the sadness in his eyes. "So he's still the only man you want, Cara?"

Despite feeling torn between Adam and Sean, I nodded.

He only had one piece of advice for me. "I like Sean, you know that. It's obvious he loves you. Don't take advantage of him."

I said I wouldn't, but I knew I was probably close to doing exactly that already.

Sean stayed and had dinner with us Saturday night. When I drove him home around nine, we had a hard time saying goodbye. We'd had a really good weekend together and were both looking forward to seeing each other at Christmas. After one last kiss and a bone-crushing hug, he got out of my car and waved at me as he walked inside.

THE JOINING TREE

As I drove back to my house, I asked myself if I was being fair to Sean. I had been honest with him last summer when I told him I was in love with Adam. I couldn't deny that I loved Sean too, but it wasn't the same. I told myself that he knew that. Selfishly, I didn't want to give up the comfort and affection he gave me, but I felt guilty.

I had to call Amy to find out if she and Kevin had worked things out, but he was probably still at her house, so I waited until bedtime to call her.

Her voice sounded defeated when she answered her phone. Obviously, things hadn't gone well.

"Amy, you don't sound happy. What did you and Kevin finally decide?"

"We're over, Cara. Kevin doesn't love me, except as a friend. He's more interested in college and his future. I think he got carried away with graduation, our trip to DC, and having time to relax over the summer. But that's all it was. He was never in it for the long haul, I realize that now."

My heart hurt for her. I knew how she felt, probably the same way I felt when Sean broke up with me at the end of our junior year. That feeling of "being dumped" was devastating.

"I'm so sorry, Amy. Is there anything I can do? You were there for me when my heart was broken, both times, and I'm totally here for you."

She snorted. "Yeah, have you met any cute guys at school who'd be perfect for me?"

I remembered what Gavin had said. "Well, yes, actually. I mentioned to Gavin that you and Kevin were having problems, and he was shocked that anyone couldn't see how wonderful you are!"

"Wonderful? He called me wonderful?"

"Actually, I think his exact words were "beautiful and lively." He thinks Neal made a terrible mistake. He also said he'd love to have a chance to get to know you better."

"But, Cara, you're taking him back to school with you tomorrow!"

"Yeah, but Christmas break is only a few weeks away. Shall I set you up with my tall, blond and handsome roommate?" I couldn't help smiling.

"Yes! Definitely! Please tell Gavin I'm really looking forward to seeing him again. You are a friend, the best kind of friend, Cara. Thank you for caring so much."

I think we were both smiling when we hung up.

I had one more call to make. It wouldn't be as pleasant.

Kevin picked up his phone with, "Hey, short stuff. If you're going to yell at me, do it now and get it over with. I already feel like a sack of shit. I never wanted to hurt Amy, you know. I care about her almost as much as I've always cared about you. You fall into the 'sister' category, after all."

"Kevin, you did hurt her, and I hate that. And I really believe you'll live to regret it. There aren't many girls like Amy, you know."

His voice was dull as he said, "I know, Cara. But I've set this goal for myself at school, and maybe even longer if I go for my Master's. If every year is as tough, or tougher, than this one, I won't have anything to give anyone for years to come. Amy needs and deserves a lot more. I couldn't ask her to wait for me."

"Well, good thing because Gavin wants a chance to get to know her. He thinks she's beautiful—which she is, of course—and I'm going to set them up."

Silence on the phone. Then, "Wow, Cara, you really know how to twist the knife, don't you?" His voice sounded choked.

I immediately felt guilty for hurting my other best friend. "Sorry, Kev, but it's what's best for Amy. Now you can go back to school and devote all of yourself to your studies. I thought that was what you wanted."

I heard a deep sigh. "Yeah. I guess it is. Do you think Amy will still be willing to be friends? Are *you* still my friend?" He sounded beaten.

"I think Amy will be, eventually. Not right away, though. As for me, I'll always have your back, Kev. I love you like a brother. Which means I can still smack you when you get out of line, you know."

He finally chuckled. "Yeah, I know. Listen, have a safe trip back to school, and please keep emailing me, even if I don't have time to reply. At least I'll know you're out there and still thinking about me."

I agreed and we said good night. He'd be taking the train back to New York City the next day.

The next morning, Mom made my favorite Quiche for Sunday brunch, accompanied by home fried potatoes and baked apples. Gavin joined us, curious what Sunday brunch was all about. Conor had assured him he'd love it. Quiche was also new to him. He loved everything Mom put on the table and thanked her profusely, after apologizing for making a pig of himself.

I'd already packed up our clean laundry and stowed it in my car. By noon, we'd had as much coffee as we thought we'd need, I gave Mom and Dad big hugs, said I was hoping to be back the following weekend, depending on weather, and we hit the road.

Once we were out of town and back on the highway, I told Gavin that Amy and Kevin had broken up.

"You mean I have a chance with Amy now?" he asked, a big smile on his face. He added, "Not that I wish any hurt for either Amy or Kevin, you understand."

I chuckled. "I know. When I spoke to Amy last night, I asked her if she'd like to see more of you. She said yes, absolutely. She remembers you from last year when you and Gabe were in school with me."

When I looked over at him, he actually looked excited.

"So I figure you and Amy can get together over the Christmas holiday when we're home for two weeks. Maybe you could double-date with Sean and me."

"Cara, that sounds great. Thank you."

Gavin wore that smile all the way back to Syracuse.

THE JOINING TREE

The weeks until the Christmas holiday went by fast. I still struggled with oil painting but all my other classes were going well. The cold weather kept us indoors most of the time, so I had to pull out some of my older drawings to paint or recreate in pen and ink. When Miss Galen, who was now my agent as well as Francis Sullivan's, had called me to ask if I would like to participate in the February Art Show in Manhattan, she said she was especially interested in exhibiting more of my pen and ink drawings, so that's what I was working on.

Some nights Gavin got bored with television and came into the studio—which now held his sleeping bag—and just watched over my shoulder, the way Adam used to.

"Cara, these pen and ink drawings tend to look as though they were drawn in another era. I think that's what makes them so appealing."

No one had ever said that before. I began to look at my work a little differently.

"From another era, huh? That's interesting." I smiled at him. "I think I like that. Thanks."

Occasionally, Gavin wanted to go to bed earlier than I did, so I would move my easel into the living room and put it in front of the window that looked out on Birch Street. One night as I gazed out the window, I saw the old green van drive by slowly. It was dark so I couldn't see the driver, but since I still suspected he was the Good Samaritan who led me out of last year's blinding snowstorm, his van was always a welcome sight. I wondered if I'd ever get a chance to thank him.

By the following Friday it was snowing. Big, white flakes coming down like a curtain, the same way last year's unexpected snowstorm had fallen. Gavin and I looked out the window together, duffels packed for the weekend but going nowhere.

I called home and let Mom know we'd be staying in Syracuse for the weekend. She commiserated but said she was glad I wasn't going to try to drive home. It was snowing in Thornewood too.

Gavin and I bundled up and only went out to struggle through the snow to the Café because we'd run out of frozen dinners to make in the microwave. We were both craving something more appetizing for dinner.

As we left the house, I saw the green van again, slowly driving along Birch Street. When it caught sight of us standing on the curb, it sped up and disappeared around the nearest corner. Once again, thanks to the heavy snowfall, I couldn't see who was driving.

When I told Gavin I thought that same driver had led me back to Barrett the year before in another snowstorm, he said, "Yeah, maybe. I've seen that guy when I take Ralph out for a walk."

"Oh? Does he live nearby? I've been wanting to ask him if he was my Good Samaritan last year, but I never see him."

Gavin hesitated. "He always waves when he sees me and Ralph, but he's always in his van. He must live somewhere nearby."

We may have been stuck in Syracuse for the weekend, but we both used the time as productively as possible. Gavin curled up on the couch with one of our Art History textbooks—he was a huge fan of the Renaissance artists—and I worked on more pen and ink drawings for the Manhattan Art Show. And it kept on snowing.

We'd be fine as long as we didn't run out of coffee.

We had snow every weekend until Christmas. There was no choice but to stay in Syracuse.

Gavin and I both got a lot of reading completed. He was now almost an expert on Renaissance artists, and I was becoming addicted to the Impressionists.

I'd completed ten pen and ink drawings, some small, some larger, and I was sure Miss Galen would be pleased. It was time to return to watercolors, although finding something pleasing to paint in our almost pure white landscape would be a challenge. And I hadn't yet found the key to painting with oils.

I was definitely ready for Christmas break.

We drove to Thornewood after our last class a few days before Christmas, more than ready to leave Syracuse. Being away from home for a week wasn't a problem, but being away from home for the past month had made me homesick. Gavin confessed he'd begun feeling like a prisoner.

Mom and Dad greeted us as though we'd been away for a year. My mother had been cooking and baking, preparing for Christmas. And, like last year, the house was fully decorated with the things she'd collected for years. Candles smelling of pine and cinnamon were everywhere.

I had grown up enough to realize that these memories of my parents and our home during the holidays would be memories I'd treasure for the rest of my life.

After a welcome-home dinner, Gavin returned to the forest to spend a few days with Conor and Arlynn. He promised to return for Christmas dinner and would bring Conor with him. In return, I promised him I'd call Amy and arrange to get the two of them together, which put a big smile on his face.

Ralph was, of course, beside himself with joy, running circles around Mom and Dad, obviously thrilled to be home with his favorite people. He followed me upstairs to my room, planting himself on the foot of my bed while I called Amy. She was delighted we'd finally made it home. She'd be over sometime on Christmas to deliver gifts and meet Gavin. She sounded as excited as he had.

Next I called Kevin, hoping he'd be home. But when he answered his phone, he was still at school finishing up a project he'd been assigned.

"Kevin, don't tell me you're not coming home for Christmas."

"Calm down, short stuff, I'll be home by Christmas Eve. You and your mom are expecting me, right?"

"Of course, Kev." We always had Christmas Eve together. I was relieved this year would be no exception.

"I'll be coming home on the train. Can you pick me up at the station?"

"Absolutely. Just call me and let me know what time the train will get in."

He said he would, but he needed to get back to work so he'd be able to come home with a clear head.

As soon as I hung up, my phone rang. I answered it and heard, "Hi, Beautiful! Are you home yet?"

Laughing, I told Sean I was and invited him over. My Christmas holiday was shaping up to be fun. Everyone I loved would be home.

With one exception I was trying hard not to think about.

Two weeks later, I had to admit it had been a great Christmas. Mom and Dad were both in excellent spirits. With an affectionate smile, my father admitted my being home might have something to do with it.

On Christmas Eve, Kevin and his father, Kelly O'Rourke, joined us for dinner. Kevin had lost weight and had circles under his eyes. It was obvious he'd been working too hard at school. He admitted he'd underestimated how difficult college would be and had over-estimated how many classes he could handle. We all insisted he take an easier schedule for his second semester. He tiredly agreed. I hated seeing my best friend so worn out. College was turning out to be more of a challenge than Kevin had anticipated.

Amy arrived on Christmas day, loaded with gifts for everyone, including Gavin, which made him blush bright red. They stood in the kitchen staring at each other until Amy grinned and gave him an unexpected hug. I never knew a face could get that red.

They sat together over coffee and talked quietly until Amy invited him to take a ride with her. Dinner was a few hours away so they left together, both smiling, obviously happy.

Laughing, Mom asked, "When did you become a matchmaker, dear?"

"When I had an unhappy best friend and a lonely roommate. It seemed like the perfect solution, Mom." I grinned, delighted with my meddling.

"And what about you, Cara? Are you happier now?"

I hesitated, unsure how to answer her question.

"Well, I'm okay. I love school, as long as I can get home most weekends. I love my friends, I love spending Christmas with you and Dad. I'm not sure I would describe myself as happy, but I'm doing what I always dreamed of doing, Mom."

She nodded, but she wasn't smiling. "But something's missing, isn't it?"

"Yes. I think I'm as content as I can be under the circumstances."

She looked down, frowning.

"Please don't worry about me. I'm good."

There was nothing else I could say. We both knew exactly what was missing.

Sean and I spent less time together than I'd expected. He and his dad went skiing for several days, which was probably a good thing. I didn't want Sean to expect too much from me. I was really trying to be fair to him. We were good friends, but that was all. Spending so much time apart while we were both at school had clarified that fact for me.

I used to wish I could be in love with Sean, but I now knew that could never be. I didn't want him to think it was a possibility. I would always care about him and miss him, but he needed to move on.

By the end of our Christmas break, I think he knew it too.

CHAPTER 22

Near the end of my time at home, the snow finally stopped long enough for my father to ride to Elvenwood with me. He didn't want me to go by myself because more snow was forecast.

I desperately needed some guidance from Francis Sullivan about my oil painting. I also wanted to show him the pen and ink drawings I'd completed for the February art show.

Surprised that I was having so much trouble with oil painting, my father went to Francis' studio with me.

When my father knocked on Francis' studio door, we heard, "Come right in, Brian." I had to smile. Francis obviously recognized my dad's knock. It was a lot louder than mine.

We walked in and Francis smiled when he saw me. "What a nice surprise, Cara. I wondered when I'd see you again. Nice to see you too, Brian."

My father said, "Cara needs your help, Francis. If you have time, I'm hoping you can solve some problems she's having."

I put my portfolio on his table and drew out the pen and ink drawings I'd done for the February show. "I wanted to show these to you first. What do you think? Should I show them?"

He examined each one carefully, nodding and smiling. "Cara, these are excellent. They will sell quickly. The mood you set in these drawings is nostalgic, very appealing. Now tell me, what is it you're having trouble with?"

I explained how I'd been struggling with oil painting, always unhappy with the results. Francis smiled, nodding.

"Cara, I think you're expecting your oil painting to look a great deal like your watercolors. They won't. It's a completely different medium."

He led me to a blank canvas already set up on one of his easels and showed me how to prepare the canvas, explaining as he worked on it.

Over the next half hour, he showed me so many things my instructor at Barrett hadn't taught at all.

"Perhaps your instructor assumed you already knew the basics of painting with oils, mainly because you're already so proficient in the other media. You'd never touched oil paints before, had you?"

"No, I didn't have a clue. I was just dabbing paints on the canvas, trying to get the same look I get with watercolors, and it wasn't working."

He chuckled, then showed me all the various tools he used to create the effects and the textures on his own paintings. It had never occurred to me to scrape off paint that went on the canvas too thick, which by itself could create an interesting effect. He explained his own technique and suggested I could adapt it for my own landscape paintings.

Over the next half hour, he demonstrated many different techniques, telling me to play with all of them until I began to get an effect I liked. "No two artists paint the same way, Cara. With experience, you'll find your own methods. Don't get discouraged. Oil painting may never be your favorite medium, but I would encourage you to work with it until it begins to feel as comfortable as your pen and ink drawing and your watercolor painting.

"Your artwork is delicate, feminine, and quite detailed. I find painting with oils to be a bit more abstract. I don't think I could create pen and ink drawings nearly as beautiful as yours. However, in time you may find the key to your own oil paintings and surprise yourself. You have so much potential, my dear, and so much natural talent."

He gave me a paint knife before we left, which I couldn't wait to use on my own canvas at school. Overly thick paint in spots was one of my problems. In a half hour, Francis taught me more than my instructor had in the past four months.

My father thanked Francis for giving me so much help and so much of his time.

I couldn't resist hugging him, much to his surprise. "Francis, I can't thank you enough."

He chuckled and hugged me back. "Glad I could help, Cara. Please remember I'm here whenever you need me." He glanced back at my pen and ink drawings. "And you can leave these drawings with me for framing. Are you going to exhibit any watercolors at the next show?"

I had to laugh. "Well, the landscape has been nothing but white for the past month, so I haven't been sure how to make a painting interesting without more color."

He smiled, his blue eyes twinkling. "I think you can find color if you simply look for it. If you do come up with a watercolor or two before the February show, I'd like to see them."

We thanked Francis again and walked back to my father's cottage. I felt as though many of the windows in my brain had been opened, and bright light was pouring in. I couldn't wait to get back to the oil painting I'd left on my easel at school.

After sharing tea at my father's cottage, we got our greys from the stable and rode home. My father looked as pleased as I did after our productive trip to Elvenwood.

***

I'd left things kind of up in the air with Sean, simply promising to keep in touch. Neither of us said anything about getting together during spring break.

New Year's Eve he'd invited a few friends to his house for an informal get-together, which was fun. Later in the evening he asked me if I still thought I was in love with my former bodyguard. When I said yes, he simply nodded, as though he'd expected that answer. He'd kissed me at midnight, but it was the kiss of a friend, not a boyfriend.

Gavin and Amy had happily spent a lot of time together and were looking forward to seeing more of each other whenever we got home for weekends.

The next day we packed our baskets of clean laundry into the trunk of my car, secured Ralph in the back seat, and drove back to Syracuse. The sky was gray, and it was very cold. I knew what that meant.

By the time I parked my car on Birch Street, it was snowing again.

Not long after we were back in classes, signs went up announcing the Barrett Art Institute's Yearly Spring Art Show. I'd been Lily's model last year, but this year she asked Gavin if he would agree to be her model for another photographic montage. He said yes, much to Lily's obvious delight. I was quite sure she would be doing more than just photographing him. Lily was nothing if not tenacious.

Armed with so many new ideas about painting with oils, I began to enjoy those classes, almost as much as I'd disliked them a few months earlier. I was taking Francis' advice and trying all the various techniques he'd shown me. The paint knife he'd given me was getting a lot of use as I played with it. He'd also shown me how to use tissue paper on larger areas to remove excess paint, which created a gauzy effect. Even my instructor looked impressed with the effects I was getting. I couldn't help wondering why *she* hadn't shown the class these same techniques.

I also remembered Francis' advice to look for the colors that would brighten up a snowy landscape. In our back yard, I saw vivid red cardinals, the green branches of pine trees peeking out from beneath their snowy coats, occasional patches of blue in the cloudy skies, the golden rays of the sun as it sank into the western sky. There were small bursts of color everywhere, and I captured all of them on canvas.

I still hated winter, but I'd finally made peace with it.

Between snowstorms, Gavin and I made it back to Thornewood for weekends as often as possible. He and Amy were spending every Friday and Saturday night together. I'd never seen Gavin so happy. The once serious young man smiled all the time, which made him even more handsome.

Poor Lily. She didn't stand a chance.

When it was time for the February Art show in Manhattan, my father again wanted to accompany me, insisting that New York City was not a safe place for me.

I simply smiled and agreed. I loved going places with my dad. His reactions to the human world always made me smile. Of course, the human world's reaction to my father was always interesting too.

We took the train into the city, as we had the last time, and a taxi to the Manhattan Gallery. Miss Galen greeted us happily, clearly pleased to see my handsome father again.

After she was able to drag her eyes away from my father, she said, "Cara, I'm in love with your pen and ink drawings. I predict every one of them will sell quickly. And the two watercolors of winter scenes are charming. I'm raising the selling prices on all of your work."

Her eyes sparkled. "I don't know if you saw the New York Times review of the last show you exhibited here." I shook my head. "Well, the Times Art reviewer hailed you as, and I'm quoting, 'an exciting and gifted young newcomer to the Art world.'

"That review is worth big money, Cara. And the Jourdan Gallery in Albany has actually *requested* another showing of your work in the spring! Mr. Jourdan tells me that a few of his best customers have asked for more of your work."

She beamed at my father. "Mr. Blackthorne, your daughter is really on her way in the Art world!"

My father simply nodded and smiled.

Miss Galen led us to the area where my work had been hung. When I saw my pen and ink drawings and the two watercolors framed and under the gallery's lights, my mouth dropped open.

She smiled. "And since you gave us a dozen pieces of your work this time, they decided to give your art the premier wall. Cara, being your agent is pure pleasure, believe me." She looked back at the front door. "You and your father should circulate. Your public is arriving."

She left us to speak to a few people she knew, and my father and I walked away to check out the art being displayed on the other white walls. Within minutes, a young man handed my father a glass of champagne, and handed me what I assumed was ginger ale.

I took a sip and felt my eyebrows rise. It wasn't ginger ale, but some kind of sparkling white wine. It was delicious.

My father laughed and said, "Maybe you should give that to me, dear."

I looked up at him and grinned. "I don't think so, Dad. I like this. One glass won't kill me, right?"

He raised one eyebrow. "Well, just one, Cara. Make it last."

I giggled and took another sip.

During the next few hours, Miss Galen introduced us to a lot of very well-dressed people, as well as a youngish-looking, well-tanned man she introduced as an Oscar-winning director from California.

Taking my hand, he confessed he was buying both of my winter watercolors. "May I call you Cara? I fell in love with those two paintings the moment I saw them." He chuckled. "After all, that's as close to snow as we get in Beverly Hills."

I smiled. "If you really miss snow, you should spend some time in upstate New York."

He laughed. "Seeing your paintings on my wall will be close enough, Cara. You should really show your work on the West Coast some day. You'd gain a lot of new fans."

I thanked him and Miss Galen led him away to talk to someone else.

A few hours later, my father whispered, "Cara, I can see 'Sold' stickers on most of your work already."

He grinned. "I'd say today has been a success. Let's find Miss Galen. I think it's time to go home."

After saying goodbye to Miss Galen, we caught a cab back to the train station.

By the time we found our seats on the train, I realized how tired I was and had to admit that the glass of wine was probably responsible.

My father chuckled and put one arm around me. "Why don't you take a nap. I'll wake you when we're almost home."

I leaned against my father's broad chest and closed my eyes. The next thing I knew, he was helping me up and leading me off the train. Mom's car was in the parking lot flashing its lights at us.

On the way home, Mom asked me how much of my art had sold.

With a laugh, my dad said, "All of it. Miss Galen slipped me a piece of paper as we were leaving. Cara made almost $15,000 today." Smiling, he added, "She'll be able to support us soon, Alicia."

That woke me up in a hurry. I had no idea how much I'd made in sales.

Mom said, "What are you going to do with all your money, dear?"

Still stunned, I said, "I have no idea."

My father said, "Harry Callahan and I were talking recently, Cara. I remember you saying something last year about wanting to open your own art gallery here in Thornewood, both for your artwork and for local artists. Harry thinks it's an excellent idea. Are you still interested?"

I was surprised he'd remembered. "Absolutely. When I've finished school two years from now, opening a gallery here in town would give me something to do that I'd really enjoy. And I think it would be great for Thornewood, especially when we have so many visitors from the city during the autumn months."

"Well, if you keep on selling your artwork the way you did today, in two years you may be able to open your gallery, with a partner or two, of course."

"Partners?"

He smiled. "Harry and I would both be interested in investing in an art gallery with you. Harry feels it would be very good for other businesses here in town, which would benefit everyone."

I loved the idea, and it would give me a definite goal to work toward, something solid to dream about that didn't feature those impossible to forget dark blue eyes.

The next day Gavin and I returned to Syracuse. Thankfully, it wasn't snowing.

With the Manhattan show behind me, I needed to figure out what to do for Barrett's Spring Art Show. The only rule was that it had to be work done in school this year. I had two months to come up with something new since all of my recent work had been sold the previous weekend.

I decided to try to paint something in oils worthy of exhibiting. A few days later my brain kicked into gear. I remembered the pen and ink drawing of my father I'd done before I started school. It had turned out really well. Perhaps I could recreate it in oil paints on a larger canvas.

But I couldn't forget about the next show in Albany either. Remembering how many people had wanted to buy my original pen and ink "Elf" drawings, I had to find time to create at least a few more. And I was hoping I would have one or two oil paintings worthy of exhibiting.

The next few months would be busy ones. So busy, I hoped I would fall into bed at night, too tired to dream about what was missing in my life.

When winter ended and we were finally enjoying warm Spring temperatures, I began setting up my easel on campus where I could enjoy the great work of Barrett's gardeners, whoever they were. Red roses were blooming all around the red brick Administration building, the sunny patio outside the Café was lined with yellow daylilies, and even the dorms were surrounded by flowering shrubs I hadn't noticed before.

Some of our drawing and painting classes were being held outside, giving me much needed time to create new artwork for the upcoming Art Show in Albany. At the same time, I was working on the oil painting of my father that I wanted to exhibit in the Barrett Art Show.

I took my easel and paints home every weekend. Work had become my middle name, and despite invitations from Amy to join her and Gavin on some of their weekend dates, I declined so I could paint. The weather was beautiful most of the time, allowing me to spend time both in Blackthorne Forest and in Elvenwood.

The "Elf" drawings I'd refused to sell had been so popular, I created some new ones with Ian's help. It was a real pleasure being out in the apple orchard finding places for him to partially hide while I was drawing.

This time he'd been so well hidden, if anyone did spot him, he'd appear to be purely imaginary. I was sure Mr. Jourdan in Albany would be pleased with this new collection.

One night, a week before the Barrett Art Show, I was sitting in the Café with Gavin and our usual crew when a familiar figure in a suit and tie came through the door and headed for our table. I hadn't seen him in a few weeks. I guessed the search for the missing SUV driver had been moved to a back burner.

"Hey, Lieutenant Fox, where have you been keeping yourself?" I asked with a smile.

His pale blue eyes lit up, crinkling at the corners as he smiled and asked if he could join us.

Lily grinned and said, "Good-looking members of Syracuse's Police Dept. are always welcome at our table, Lieutenant. Have a seat."

He shook his head, trying not to smile, and pulled over a chair from another table. "I'm glad you're all here tonight. I was just in Mrs. Barrett's office. You'll be hearing an announcement from her very soon, but I thought I'd deliver the news personally."

His face had become serious. His voice carried, and all conversation at other tables stopped.

"We're searching for a predator, a young man who has been stalking girls on school campuses all over Syracuse. So far, no one has been assaulted, but based on the way he's been behaving, it's just a matter of time. He picks his victim, stalks her to her dorm or her home off campus, then tries to break in.

"So far, the girls have been able to call the police before he's managed to enter their rooms, or homes, but sooner or later, he'll get in. He follows a set pattern, following the girl of his choice for a few days, making sure she's alone." He ran his hands through his short hair. "We want to grab him before he hurts anyone."

I asked, "How about a description, Lieutenant?"

He nodded. "He's probably late teens, or twenties, quite tall, probably six foot two or more, thin, but always wears a dark hoodie so all we know is he's white. No one has gotten a good look at him. I've asked Mrs. Barrett to make sure that you all walk in pairs, at least, until we catch this guy. *Do not be outside alone, okay?*"

We all nodded. The guys agreed to make sure none of the girls walked to their dorms alone.

The Lieutenant said, "Okay. Good. Spread the word. Mrs. Barrett is sending emails and leaving phone messages for everyone on campus. I was over at Syracuse U. earlier. Other officers are visiting the smaller schools in our area. We want everyone aware of this guy."

He stood. "Be safe, folks. Cara, can I see you outside for a minute?"

I got up and joined him outside the Café door. "What's up?"

"Are you still carrying your knives whenever you leave your apartment?"

"Yes, Lieutenant. I never go anywhere without them. Is that a problem?"

He shook his head, again looking serious. "Not a problem. I hope you won't have to use them. Just keep your roommate with you, okay?"

"I will. Don't worry about me." I smiled. "But thanks for paying us a personal visit, Lieutenant."

He nodded. "Get back inside now, Cara." I could see the real concern in his light eyes. "I want you safe."

When I went back to our table, Paula said, "Cara, you seem to get special attention from the handsome Lieutenant." Both eyebrows were raised as she asked, "Anything going on that we should know about?"

Every pair of eyes at our table was suddenly pinned on me. I thought I heard Gavin snicker.

I groaned. "No, you guys. I haven't even seen Lieutenant Fox since before Christmas."

Lily chuckled. "Too bad, Cara. He's gorgeous! Those eyes . . ."

"Yeah, yeah, I know. He's a friend, but that's all."

Lily and Joel looked skeptical. Lily simply said, "Well, we believe you . . . sort of."

Paula and Tim grinned at me but didn't say anything.

Freddy had a hopeful look on his face. "Do you think there's any chance the Lieutenant is gay?"

I smiled. "I don't think so, Freddy."

The next day everyone on campus was talking about the alleged stalker, but in the week before the Barrett Art Show, there were no reports of anyone on our campus being followed. Nevertheless, no one walked alone. We all had escorts to and from classes.

Gavin had attached himself to me with one arm draped across my shoulders, as though saying to any possible stalker, "Make my day!" He had once again appointed himself my bodyguard and couldn't understand why I was smiling. He was such a sweetie.

I tried very hard not to think about the bodyguard who was missing.

CHAPTER 23

Classes were cancelled the day of the Barrett Art Show to allow us time to set up easels, tables, painted wooden room dividers, hooks and wire hangers, everything necessary for outdoor art displays. The school's landscaped campus created an inviting outdoor setting.

And just in case the weather didn't cooperate, the school had canvas canopy covers erected everywhere art would be displayed. Apparently, all art lovers in Syracuse looked forward to Barrett's Art Show every year. I was told it always drew a crowd.

There were photography displays, paintings of still life, landscapes, seascapes, portraits, abstract paintings, graphic art, and Paula's collection of political cartoons, which I was sure would be popular. Our current President wouldn't have been pleased, but I doubted he'd show up in Syracuse for our art show.

Gavin hadn't wanted me to see what he was working on, so once my oil painting of my father had been set up and displayed, I searched the area for Gavin's work. When I found his small display, I was amazed.

He had been drawing all the wildlife that lived in Blackthorne Forest from memory, and his drawings were fantastic. There were beautifully rendered pictures of deer, rabbits, chipmunks, squirrels, birds, even a skunk. I almost expected them to walk off the paper they were drawn and painted on. The year Gavin had spent working alongside Conor in the forest hadn't been wasted. Some of his pictures were done in pen and ink, and some were finished in watercolors.

I knew Gavin was talented. But I hadn't known *how* talented! I looked around but didn't see him anywhere. I thought maybe I'd find him over at Lily's photographic display, but when I got there, Lily was there but no Gavin. When I saw her photographic montage, it was obvious why he was probably in hiding.

"Lily, I had no idea you would be photographing Gavin in the *nude!*"

She was smiling but looked just a little guilty. "Well, Cara, I didn't *force* him. After I took a few sample shots, I could see how beautifully he photographs. He's even more photogenic than you! I simply suggested that I'd prefer to photograph him *without* clothes, and he shrugged and took his clothes off. Like it was no big deal, you know?"

I was in shock as I gazed at her photos of my blond roommate. They were tasteful, nothing overdone or in bad taste, but they were amazing. Gavin was a beautiful man, from head to toe. And I was sure every girl on campus would be hunting him, as well as a few of the men.

"Lily, did you tell him how many people would actually be seeing these photos?"

Once again, she looked rather guilty. "Uh, I may have neglected to mention that part."

"Do you know where he's hiding? I haven't seen him anywhere since we got here this morning."

She chuckled. "He's probably sitting out the show in my dorm room. He asked me to let him know when everyone was gone. I think he's a little annoyed with me, Cara. But aren't these photos of him gorgeous? Be honest. Granted, I had a great model, but I am an *awesome* photographer!"

Yes, she was, but I couldn't help feeling she had taken unfair advantage of my rather naïve roommate. There was no doubt she had enjoyed every minute of it.

I sighed, shook my head, and returned to my own display. Much to my surprise, my parents were standing in front of my painting, with looks of genuine pleasure on their faces.

"Mom, Dad, I didn't know you were coming up today." I threw my arms around both of them. "It's so good to see you! What do you think of my painting?"

Mom was wearing a big smile. "Sweetheart, I think you've finally mastered oil painting. You know, we both love the pen and ink drawing you did of your father. Brian had it framed and it's hanging in our bedroom."

She looked up at my oil painting. "But this, it's incredible, Cara. I think you captured his very spirit here. It's wonderful."

I looked at my father. Shaking his head, he said, "I'm simply honored that you see me this way." He looked down into my eyes. "You've made me look like a hero."

"Dad, you've been my hero since the day we met. Painting this was a labor of love."

Mom asked, "What are you going to do with this painting when this show is over?"

I smiled. "Well, I'll never sell it. It will hang in my apartment until I've finished school. Then it will hang wherever I live. But I hope, by that time, I'll have done a painting of you as well so they can hang side by side."

My father smiled down at my petite mother. They really made a beautiful couple.

My father said, "Where is Gavin's artwork displayed? I'd really like to see what he's done."

I led them to the area where Gavin had set up his wall of drawings. "Dad, I'm guessing Gavin learned more than forestry while he worked with Conor."

My parents were amazed at what Gavin had accomplished. My father said, "I had no idea he was so gifted."

Mom admired every one of Gavin's wildlife drawings. "Cara, if he ever wants to sell any of these, I'll be first in line. They're wonderful."

"Where is Gavin?" Dad asked. "We haven't seen him since we've been here. I really want to compliment him on the fine work he's doing."

THE JOINING TREE

"Uh, I'm not sure. I haven't seen him since he set up his artwork." I thought it best to keep them away from Lily's display.

Mom said, "Well, if we don't get a chance to talk to him, please tell him how much we like his work. We won't be able to stay much longer, dear. I have to get back to the bookstore to lock up for the day. Christina is covering for me today."

"Okay, I'll be sure to tell him. Before you leave, how about joining me for lunch at the Café? We didn't have time for breakfast this morning, and I'm starved."

They agreed and I led them to the Café, making sure to avoid the Photography display.

Today's lunch specialty was my Sunrise Special, which someone had renamed "Cara's Bagel Sandwich." Mom laughed when three of them were delivered to our table.

"I can see your influence on the Café's menu, dear. I'm sure these are popular."

I grinned. "Yep. Everyone loves them."

After we'd finished our lunch, I walked my parents to Mom's car on Birch Street.

"When we got here this morning, we stopped in to say hello to your landlady. She's such a nice person. She seems to like having you here, Cara."

"Yeah, I really lucked out with my landlady, Mom. We get together for tea once in a while." I looked around. "She's probably somewhere in the crowd on campus by now. She said she always attends the yearly Art Show."

That was when I realized that Miss Williams would probably see Lily's photo montage of the very nude Gavin. I shuddered slightly. Maybe living across from the Art Institute all these years had broadened her mind. Hopefully. But I wasn't sure how my parents would have reacted.

I hugged both of them and they left for home, after again telling me how much they liked my painting. As they drove down the street toward the highway, I couldn't help a sense of relief. I knew Gavin would have died from embarrassment if my parents had seen those photos.

Returning to the Art Show, I wandered around the campus, enjoying all the lovely paintings on display, although I didn't understand the abstract paintings at all.

Most of Barrett's instructors were present, many of them congratulating the students on their work. I was surprised to find Miss Alvarez, my oil painting instructor, standing in front of my painting, with a slightly confused look on her face.

She turned and saw me. "Cara, who is this?" she asked.

"That's my father. I did this same picture in pen and ink before school started. Once I became more comfortable working with oils, I recreated it for this show."

She shook her head. "I remember that you were having difficulty with oil painting until recently. But this painting? It's really good, Cara. What changed?"

I explained that my art mentor at home had spent some time helping me learn the techniques he used.

"Is your mentor a teacher?"

"No, just a good friend, a successful artist who's always encouraged me."

She snorted. "Well, if he was able to get you to this point so quickly, he should be teaching."

I felt like telling her that he had taught me all the things she hadn't, but I bit my tongue. No sense pissing off my instructor.

"If he comes to our Art Show, I'd really like to meet him," she said.

"Francis doesn't travel anymore, Miss Alvarez. He's an older man who does all his painting at home."

"Francis? Is he someone I might have heard of?"

"I'm sure you have. His name is Francis Sullivan."

Her mouth dropped open. "*The* Francis Sullivan? He's your *mentor*?"

"Yes. He's a good friend of my father's."

She began to look annoyed. "Well, Cara, I don't know why you're even taking my class. He's taught you techniques that I only teach third-year students."

"Why wait so long, Miss Alvarez? I was getting really frustrated with my work in oils. I *needed* to learn those techniques!"

She was frowning. "Perhaps I could show a few of them to first-year students. I'll have to think about it."

She looked at my painting again. "Well, this is excellent work, Cara. I wish I could take credit for teaching you." She nodded and walked away.

I sighed. I was pretty sure I'd pissed her off.

The crowds on campus were beginning to thin. Paula waved me over to her display.

"I got an eyeful of Gavin's photos earlier today. Wow!" She giggled. "He must be hiding somewhere. I haven't seen him all day."

"Yeah, he's hiding. I don't think he had a problem posing for Lily, but I guess he freaked a little when he found out how many people would be seeing the photos."

She looked as though she felt sorry for Gavin. "Lily didn't tell him how many people would be here for our Art Show, did she?"

"Nope. She'll never get a date with him now!"

She laughed. "Serves her right. Will you be at the Café later for dinner?"

"Yes, but I'm not sure Gavin will be with me."

"Well, please let him know we all think he's gorgeous and very brave to pose for Lily. I predict he'll have a lot of new friends on campus tomorrow." She giggled.

I chuckled as I walked back to where my painting was on display. Some students were already taking their artwork down and returning them to their classrooms. I was surprised to see that Gavin's drawings were already gone. Maybe I'd find him inside one of our classrooms.

THE JOINING TREE

I searched each of our classes but didn't see him. He must have been moving at top speed, undoubtedly anxious to put his work away and go home. I decided to take my painting home with me. I'd hang it in the living room.

When I got back outside, I saw people scattered here and there around the campus, but no one I knew personally. Gavin had apparently gone home without me. The sun hadn't set yet, and the campus wasn't actually deserted. I felt safe enough to walk home, my painting under my arm. If I wasn't carrying a canvas, I would have jogged home, but it was too awkward.

I looked around, but there was no one near me. By the time I was halfway across the campus, I could see the yellow house on Birch Street. I felt perfectly safe, even though Lieutenant Fox's words echoed in my mind. I walked a little faster.

When I reached the sidewalk in front of our house, I heard Ralph barking from the backyard. He sounded frantic and I began running. I had almost reached the steps to my front door when I thought I heard someone behind me. My keys slipped out of my hand and as I bent to pick them up, I glanced over my shoulder to see a figure in a dark hoodie swing something at my head. Darkness swallowed me before I hit the ground, Ralph's frantic barks echoing faintly in my ears.

When I opened my eyes, I was lying on my living room couch with something ice cold pressed against the side of my head. Gavin was leaning over me with a guilty look on his face. He whispered, "I'm so sorry, Cara. I was upset and I wasn't thinking..."

I heard Lieutenant Fox's voice. It sounded as though he was on the phone.

Gavin was pushed aside by a young man in a uniform who was fastening a blood pressure cuff around my arm.

"Good. You're awake. Can you sit up?" He lifted me to a sitting position and started shining a pen light into my eyes.

I saw the Lieutenant over the EMT's shoulder.

"How is your head feeling, Cara?" he asked.

"Hurts," I mumbled. I was feeling dizzy. I asked the EMT, "Can I lie down now?"

He lowered me back on the couch and I closed my eyes. My head felt like a drum somebody was pounding on.

The EMT said, "We're going to take a trip to the hospital now, Cara. I think you have a concussion and a doctor should take a look at you."

"No! I've had a concussion before. All I need is the ice pack and some aspirin. No hospitals, please."

The EMT frowned. "I can't force you to go, but I think that lump on the side of your head needs to be looked at."

The Lieutenant knelt down next to me. "Cara, would it help if I went with you?"

"Thanks, but no." I looked up at Gavin, who was still crouched at the end of the couch. "What happened? Did you carry me in here?"

"Yes. I was following Ralph, who was going crazy. When I reached the front of the house, I saw that kid hit you with a rock, and you went down." He looked momentarily satisfied as he added, "He's out cold now. I called Lieutenant Fox and he got here in minutes."

The EMT stood up, clearly disapproving. He told the Lieutenant, "Someone should at least keep an eye on her for the next forty-eight hours. I can't do anything more for her here."

He left and I sat up slowly, holding the ice pack against my head. Gavin handed me two aspirin and a glass of water. I swallowed them and attempted to stand. Big mistake.

"I think I'll just stay where I am," I said. I leaned back against the soft couch cushion.

Lieutenant Fox sat down next to me with a pad and pen. "Cara, can you give me a little more information? I wouldn't bother you if it could wait. The man we found in your yard was taken to the hospital in another ambulance. He was still unconscious when they left with him."

He looked over at Gavin. "By the way, what did you hit him with?"

Gavin shrugged. "My fist."

The Lieutenant looked amused for a few seconds. "I suspect he's the stalker we've been looking for, but I'd like to be sure before he wakes up."

Without nodding, I said, "Okay. All I can tell you is that I didn't see him behind me when I left campus. He must have had ninja training because I never heard him behind me. When I heard Ralph barking like mad, I started running. Then it was lights out. I woke up here on the couch."

He said, "Okay, Cara. I think one or more of the other girls he followed may be able to identify him."

He put the pad and pen in his jacket pocket and stood. "Is there anything else I can do for you?" He hesitated. "Cara, I hope you consider me a friend you can call on anytime. I mean it."

"Thanks, Lieutenant. There's really nothing you can do. I'm a disaster magnet. I've accepted it. Maybe you should too." I closed my eyes. The aspirin hadn't touched my headache.

I heard him chuckle. "I seem to remember you mentioning that before. At the time I was sure you were exaggerating. Get some sleep. I'll check in on you tomorrow."

I heard him leave. The next voice I heard was Laurie Williams.

She whispered. "Gavin, is Cara asleep? I can come back later."

I opened my eyes. "No, I'm awake, Laurie. My head is splitting."

"You poor thing. I'm so sorry, Cara. Would you like me to help you into your room? I think you might be more comfortable in bed." My dog sat at my feet looking sad and whimpering a little.

I decided she might be right. I sat up and she helped me off the couch and into my bedroom. Gavin was still sitting on the floor next to the couch. He looked miserable.

"Gavin, not your fault. Really. *Please* stop looking like your life is over. I'll be okay."

Laurie helped me get my jeans and boots off. When one of the knives slid out of its boot sheath, she gasped. "I didn't realize you still carried them, Cara."

As I sank back into my bed, I muttered, "Never leave home without 'em."

I heard her sigh. Then I heard the light switch click and her footsteps leave the room. I felt Ralph jump up on the foot of my bed, and I fell asleep.

I dreamed continuously, always the same dream, the one I'd been trying to erase from my mind. I was at my parents' wedding party in our backyard, in my pink and ivory dress, standing behind a tree with Adam who was kissing me senseless. I felt joyful and bereft at the same time, knowing I'd never have a chance to kiss him again.

When I woke up around dawn, my pillow was soaked. I'd tried so hard to push Adam from my mind, but he was still there, breaking my heart all over again. It had to be the head injury working on my poor brain.

I closed my eyes, flipped my pillow to the dry side, and snuggled my teary face into it. I just wanted to forget.

A few hours later I heard my parents' voices from the living room. Laurie must have called Mom, and, of course, they drove up again. That brought on more tears.

What was wrong with me? I felt like I was dissolving, watering away. I never cried anymore. I hadn't cried in over a year. This had to stop.

I forced myself out of bed and into the bathroom, washed up, realized I was still wearing yesterday's shirt over my underwear, and grabbed my robe hanging on the back of the bathroom door. Unfortunately, it was white terrycloth. I looked in the mirror and saw that I matched it. Except for my eyes, which were ringed in purple.

Being hit on the side of the head had given me two almost-black eyes. Terrific.

Adding to my splendor, my hair was hopelessly snarled. I looked like a wild animal, a wild animal with purple eyes. I groaned and sat down on the toilet seat.

There was a soft knock on the bathroom door. "Cara? It's Mom. Do you need help?"

"Come on in, Mom. But brace yourself."

She opened the door, took one look at me, bent down to kiss my head, and said, "I think this is a job for your father, sweetheart. Can I make you a cup of tea or coffee?"

"Sure. Tea sounds good. Tell Dad I need a little of his magic."

"Okay, why don't you come out to the living room when you're ready. Miss Williams just left. It'll be easier for your father to comb your hair out there. Don't worry. It's just the three of us."

"Okay." I left the bathroom, and for reasons that are unclear, I changed my socks but kept my bathrobe on. I also grabbed my wide-tooth comb.

When I walked into the living room, my father simply said, "Come here, Cara, let me get those tangles out."

I sat down in front of him and handed him the comb. Just as he had once before, he began separating my long hair, one strand at a time, pulling the comb through, again and again. And just as before, he did it painlessly. My father had magic in his hands.

"All done, sweetheart. Now drink your tea and try to relax. I won't ask you what happened. Miss Williams and Lieutenant Fox covered that."

"You spoke to the Lieutenant?" I should have known he'd call my parents.

Mom said, "Yes, he called us last night. He's concerned about the lump on your head. He said you refused to go to the hospital. I think he hoped we'd have some influence on you."

I rolled my eyes. That hurt too.

"Cara, your father and I agree with the Lieutenant. You need some tests that can only be done at a hospital, so here's what we're suggesting. We want to take you to Greenville Hospital where they checked you out the last time you had a head injury. They'll take x-rays and probably a CT-scan. They'll be able to compare the new pictures with your old ones. We have to make sure it's not more than a concussion. Then I'd like to take you home with us for a few days, just to make sure you'll rest."

I didn't say anything right away. Mom was probably waiting for an argument, but I decided to surprise her.

"Okay. I'll bet you also got in touch with Mrs. Barrett to say I'd be out of school for a few days. Right?"

She smiled. "Yes, I did. I'm glad you're not fighting me, Cara. You don't take chances with a head injury. Do you need to pack?"

"I have clothes at home, Mom, so I'll just need a few things from the bathroom."

I went into my room, grabbed a duffle bag, threw a few things into it, and got dressed. Other than my boots, I have no idea what I put on, just that it smelled clean.

When I returned to them, it finally occurred to me that I hadn't seen my roommate.

"Where's Gavin? It's Saturday, so there are no classes."

"Laurie said a few of your friends came by this morning asking about you. She told them you were sleeping, and they took Gavin out with them for breakfast. He hasn't been back."

I groaned, remembering at the last minute not to shake my sore head. "I think Gavin feels responsible for my attack. He'd gone home before I did."

My father said, "I see. If he'd walked home with you, you wouldn't have been attacked. Why did he leave without you?"

"He was upset about something and simply forgot. I'm not blaming him, Dad."

I could see from the expression on my father's face that he did blame Gavin, even if I didn't. He didn't say anything, but I knew he'd be speaking to Gavin first chance he got.

"Okay, I'm ready. I'm not hungry, so I'd just as soon skip breakfast, Mom. Let's go to the hospital and get it over with. I'll just leave Gavin a note."

I jotted a quick note to let him know I'd be gone for a few days, reminded him to feed Ralph, and left him our home phone number so he could call me.

I knew a long car ride wasn't going to do my aching head any good, so I grabbed the pillow off my bed. We got into Mom's car and headed for Greenville.

Mom had given me aspirin before we left, so I got as comfortable as possible in the back seat of her car and fell asleep.

My father had called Dr. Costello, his friend at Greenville Hospital, so I was checked out quickly. The blow to my head had produced nothing more than a concussion and a nasty headache, so we were in and out in two hours. I turned down Dr. Costello's offer of pain pills, and after the necessary paperwork, we headed for Thornewood and home.

When Mom asked me why I'd turned down the pain meds, I said, "Too many dreams." She patted my hand, and I knew she understood.

As she pulled up the driveway next to our house, I was really grateful to be home, safe with my parents. That made me feel about twelve, but I was still a little shaky from being hit over the head again. Being a disaster magnet was wearing me down.

When we got into the house, Mom offered to make me lunch, but I opted to go straight to bed. My head was still pounding, and I was actually nauseated. I just wanted to lie down and, hopefully, sleep.

"Sweetheart, I have to go in to the bookstore for a few hours. Your father will be here if you need anything."

I remembered not to nod my head. "Okay, Mom. I'll be all right." But when I walked into my bedroom and didn't see Ralph on my bed, I felt terrible. He was probably lying on my bed in Syracuse, wondering where I was .

Yeah, I was depressed. And in pain. I pulled my clothes off and sank into my covers as I felt tears in my eyes again. I prayed for no more dreams.

It must have been after dinner before I opened my eyes again. I lay there until I felt capable of lifting my head off the pillow, curious about the voices I heard from below. The pounding in my head was reduced to a dull roar, so I got out of bed carefully.

As soon as I left my bedroom, I could hear Amy downstairs with Mom. The blow to my head was affecting my sense of balance and I took the stairs slowly. When I walked into the kitchen, Amy jumped up to hug me. I was really happy to see her until she exclaimed, "Sweetie, you look like crap!"

I gave her a narrow-eyed look. "Really?"

"I'm so sorry, Cara. I already know what happened. Gavin called me last night. He was so upset, he was practically in tears, swearing he'd failed you *again*."

"I know. I told him he wasn't to blame, that I'd be okay, but he looked miserable the last time I saw him."

"Cara, he didn't tell me why he'd been so upset that he'd forgotten to stay and walk home with you. What's the story?"

I looked across the table to see my father frowning. He apparently wanted an explanation too.

I explained that Gavin had agreed to pose for Lily, the photographer who had taken such great pictures of me the previous year. When I told them that the pictures were nudes and that Gavin hadn't known that crowds of people would see them at our Art Show, Mom's mouth dropped open. However, my father and Amy both looked angry.

Amy said, "So that's why Gavin was upset. Well, I don't blame him, but why did he agree to pose nude in the first place? Lily didn't ask *you* to take your clothes off, did she?"

"No, she didn't. But I should tell you that Lily has been after Gavin ever since he arrived at school." Amy shook her head, still looking highly annoyed.

My father added, "To be fair, you should understand that Elves aren't embarrassed by their physical bodies. We feel that our bodies are beautiful and nudity is perfectly normal. I think that's why Gavin agreed to pose for her. However, he's spent enough time in the human world that he's also aware that nudity is a more sensitive subject for humans. Which is why he was upset when he realized so many people would see those photos."

Frowning, he said, "Nevertheless, running home and leaving you alone was inexcusable. I will be talking to him."

Amy shook her head. "I'll be talking to him too, Mr. Blackthorne, but probably for different reasons." Turning to me, she added, "You're sure you're not mad at him, Cara?"

"Nope. I understand why he was upset and needed to leave campus. Lily's the one I'm mad at, and I'll be speaking to her when I get back."

Mom put some toast in front of me. "Here, dear, you should eat something. You've had nothing at all today."

My appetite had returned and I gobbled down the toast quickly.

"If you're feeling a little better, dear, there's someone in the back yard who'd like to see you." She chuckled. "I've been singing her song at night. I don't have your voice, of course, but she seems to appreciate it anyway."

I wanted to see her too. I walked to the back door and went out on the porch. Amy followed me.

"She won't mind, will she?" Amy asked.

"No, she likes to see my friends."

All I could see in the dark was the dragon's golden eyes.

THE JOINING TREE

I leaned against the railing. "Hi, Rowenna. Mom just told me you wanted to see me. I hope you haven't been waiting too long. I slept all day."

Your mother told me you'd been hit over the head and that she and your father were going to bring you home today. How is your head?

"It'll be fine in a few days. Please don't worry."

I want to know where is the person who hurt you. He should be punished.

"He's in jail. I think he'll be staying there for a long time."

That's too bad. I had my own punishment in mind for him.

I shuddered slightly. Rowenna was a fire-breathing dragon, and I had seen proof of that before.

Cara, I sense that you are in two kinds of pain. You've been dreaming again, I think. It is not just your head that hurts.

I sighed. "You're right, of course. I try very hard not to dream. I try to forget."

No, Cara, you need to be patient. Love can never be forgotten.

I was afraid she was right.

You should talk to your friend with hair of fire. She understands. I think she agrees with me. Please tell her I am glad she is with you. She is good friend.

"Yes, she's my best friend. I forgot that you never met her. Her name is Amy."

Rowenna dipped her head to Amy, who said, "I'm happy to finally meet you. I've heard a lot about you."

Rowenna made that rough coughing noise that I think was laughter.

Cara, please sing for me before I leave.

I sang her song as she closed her eyes and hummed.

Thank you. I am here whenever you need me, my young friend.

The moonlight glittered on her scales as she rose out of our yard and into the sky. Her magic wrapped around us briefly and then was gone.

Amy said softly, "I heard every word she said, Cara. I think she's right. You shouldn't forget the one person you'll probably love forever. I'm sure he'll be back."

I couldn't answer her. But Rowenna's magic had completely taken away my headache. I whispered, "Thank you, Rowenna," and heard her distant chuckle.

CHAPTER 24

I enjoyed Mom's TLC for the next few days, but by the end of the week, I was ready to go back to school. My headache was gone, I looked almost human again, and I wanted to do some drawing for the Albany Art show, but most of my supplies were in Syracuse, along with my car.

While I was thinking about how to get back to school, Amy called to say she didn't have to work that weekend, and she'd be happy to take me back to Syracuse. She wanted to see Gavin, but she also had another purpose for her visit.

"I'd like to have a few words with your friend Lily."

Uh-oh. From experience, I'd learned that Amy's temper was a close match with her red hair. But I needed a ride and didn't want to force Mom to make that drive again.

I spent the next day convincing Mom and Dad that I was well enough to return to school.

"Mom, I haven't had a headache since Tuesday. I've been able to get plenty of sleep while I've been home, and you've probably put five pounds on me. Trust me, I'm fine."

She still looked worried. "All right, but I'll have a little talk with your guardian angel. We don't want you hurt again, Cara."

My father looked resigned. "I wish I could send Rowenna with you, sweetheart. She'd take care of the bad guys in Syracuse very quickly."

That made me smile. "Yeah, she would. Their Fire Department would have their hands full."

Saturday morning Amy came to pick me up after breakfast. Mom had made pancakes, of course. After Mom and Dad had hugged both of us repeatedly, I threw my duffle into the back of Amy's station wagon, and we took off.

Since Amy likes to talk while she drives, I filled her in on everything that had been going on in my life since the Christmas holidays. We hadn't had a long talk since then.

"You said Lily's been after Gavin ever since he's been in school with you. What has she been doing?"

"She asks him out a lot. She likes to party and she invited him to parties off-campus a couple of times. She compliments him constantly." I snorted. "There's nothing subtle about Lily, but she really is a fantastic photographer. I agree she shouldn't have asked him to pose nude, but her photographs of him are beautiful, Amy."

"Well, I want to see them for myself. And she needs to understand that Gavin has a girlfriend and doesn't want to go out with her. Apparently, she can't take a hint. Gavin told me how many times he's turned her down."

"Yeah, he has. He's never encouraged her at all. I was really surprised when he agreed to pose for her. I think he didn't want to insult her work."

"And how about the handsome Lieutenant Fox? Has he called you since you've been home?"

"Yep. I've only been home since Saturday and he's called me twice."

She raised both eyebrows. "He's certainly attentive, Cara. More than any other cop would be, don't you think?"

"I suppose. We've become friends over the past six months. You have to remember: I'm a disaster magnet so I spend a lot of time with the police, wherever I happen to live."

She grinned. "Well, that's one way to meet men, I guess. What does your Lieutenant look like?"

"Amy, he's not *my* Lieutenant."

She laughed. "I still want details."

"Okay. Lieutenant Fox, first name Aidan, is twenty-eight, single, lives with his mom and sister. He's about six feet tall, well built, reddish sandy hair cut short, very light blue eyes that can look right through you, probably a handy feature for a cop. He was suspicious of me at first, mainly because of what he'd been told about my history in Thornewood." I chuckled. "He said he expected someone bigger!

"He's told me to call him anytime I have a problem or need help."

She laughed. "I guess being a 'disaster magnet' has its benefits. Do you think you'll see him while I'm visiting this weekend?"

"I thought you wanted to spend time with Gavin this weekend. Hmm?"

"You know me, Cara. I always have time for handsome guys."

By the time she pulled up in front of the yellow house on Birch Street, we were fully caught up with each other's lives. The catering business at her family's bakery was growing nicely. This was her first weekend off since the bakery opened in September.

As we walked up the steps to the front door, I saw that old green van turn the far corner, heading away from us. I smiled and said to Amy, "Remind me to tell you about my Good Samaritan sometime."

She looked at me with one eyebrow raised.

"Unfortunately, I haven't met him yet."

As we walked through the front door to my apartment, I called out, "Hey Gavin, I'm home and I brought you a present!"

Amy was behind me, laughing.

"Cara!" Gavin rushed in from the kitchen, stopping short when he saw who was with me. "Amy?"

"I needed a ride back and Amy was available for the weekend."

Gavin threw his arms around me first, a concerned look on his face. "I'm happy you're back. You look good. How's your head?"

"I'm fine, my head's fine, now say hello to Amy properly."

He grinned, let go of me, and grabbed Amy for an extremely affectionate hug.

After a sufficient amount of affection had been exchanged, we sat down in the kitchen nook over coffee that Gavin had just made.

He smiled, looking at Amy. "I must have known you were coming.

"Cara, all our friends have been asking for you. Mrs. Barrett even stopped by one night after school. And your Lieutenant was here right after you left last week, sorry he missed you, but glad you were going home with your parents."

He frowned, looking guilty again. "Speaking of your parents, are they very mad at me? I really expected your father would come and take me out of school and return me to my work in the forest. I know he's disappointed in me."

I shook my head. "Gavin, he would never pull you out of school before the term ends. But he does want to talk to you."

He groaned. "I hope you know how sorry I am. I lost my head. That's twice I've put you in danger, Cara. Your father will never forgive me. I hope you can."

"Of course I've forgiven you. The person I haven't forgiven is Lily. She should have warned you that most of upstate New York would be at our art show."

He nodded, regret on his face. "I thought that only her teacher and the other photography students would see her pictures. I never would have agreed otherwise."

"Well, live and learn, Gavin," I said. "But I really thought those photos were beautiful. Lily did a great job."

Smiling, in a dreamy voice, Amy added, "I do want to see those photos, you know."

Gavin's face was bright red. "I was afraid of that," he muttered.

I stood. "I've got some drawings to work on, so the living room is all yours."

I grinned at them. "Have fun!"

Gavin made sandwiches for us when we got hungry. After we ate, I left them to enjoy their time together and went back to my studio.

It must have been after five when Amy knocked on the door of my studio. "We're getting hungry again but I wanted to see what you're working on."

"Come on in." I stepped away from my easel. "What do you think?" I was using watercolors on a drawing I'd been working on before I'd been hit on the head last week. I'd started sketching the two white birch trees in Miss Williams' backyard with the wooded park behind them. I'd also drawn Ralph sitting in front of the tree, looking up into the branches.

"Ooh, I really like this, Cara. The texture of those birches looks so real. You're doing a beautiful job. Will you be selling this one?"

"Probably. I've already done several pen and ink drawings for the Art show in Albany, but I'd like to add a few watercolors if I can."

"Well, put your brush down. It's time to go over to your Café for dinner. I'm looking forward to meeting a few of your friends."

I did an eye roll. I knew exactly who she wanted to meet.

"Amy, promise me. No bloodshed, right?"

She rolled her eyes. "Of course not, Cara. I just want to talk to her."

A few minutes later, we left for the Café, Gavin holding Amy's hand. When we walked in, the usual group was already at our table. Paula and Lily got up and rushed over to me, welcoming me back with hugs. Tim, Joel, and Freddy were smiling as we reached the table.

After assuring everyone that my head was still firmly affixed to my shoulders, we sat down and I introduced Amy to the group.

"I'd like you all to meet my best friend from Thornewood, Amy Strauss. She's spending the weekend with us."

Everyone smiled and greeted her. Except for Lily who just stared at my best friend.

Finally, Lily asked, "You and Gavin are dating?"

Gavin gave Amy an unmistakably affectionate look, and Amy smiled. "Yes."

The look Lily gave Gavin was unmistakably disappointed, even a little hurt.

He noticed and told the group, "Amy and I have been seeing each other since Christmas."

As I looked around the table, I noticed that Paula, Joel, and Tim all looked amused. Everyone knew that Lily had been throwing herself at Gavin. No one said anything for a few minutes.

I broke the silence. "So what's on the menu tonight? We're hungry."

Since it was Saturday night, most of the students were gone for the weekend. One of the third-year students was on duty and kept things simple with homemade pizza, which was really good. Naturally, Paula asked for a salad. He rolled his eyes but quickly tossed lettuce and some veggies into a bowl and brought it over to her.

She grinned at him. "My hero." He winked at her and returned to the kitchen area.

As she poured oil and vinegar on her salad, she asked me, "So how's the handsome Lieutenant, Cara?"

"As far as I know, he's fine. Why?"

Paula smacked her lips. "He is one good-looking man. I might not mind getting hit over the head if he'd pay that much attention to me. Are you sure you haven't been seeing the Lieutenant socially, Cara?"

I snorted. "Quite sure. But I do consider him a friend. He's one of the good guys."

The rest of the table was discussing the reactions to the work they had displayed at Barrett's Art Show. Of course, that brought up the subject of Lily's photography montage.

Lily beamed. "My instructor loved the photos. Of course, they attracted a lot of attention from many of the people who came to our Art Show. Most of the women wanted Gavin's phone number." She looked over at Gavin. "Of course, I didn't give it to them."

Gavin's face was red, but he looked relieved.

Amy's voice was cool as she said, "Lily, I'd love to see those photos while I'm here."

Lily shook her head. "Sorry, the Art Show is over. The photos have been taken down." She sounded equally cool.

Amy wasn't going to let it go. "Lily, everyone says you're a gifted photographer. I saw the photos you took of Cara last year. They were beautiful. I'd really love to see what you accomplished with Gavin's photos."

That put the ball squarely in Lily's court. She couldn't really refuse without looking childish.

She looked straight at Amy. "Okay. They're in my dorm room. If you want to take a walk over there with me, you can see them now." She stood.

Amy got up from our table and Gavin got up with her. She smiled at him. "You should stay here with Cara. I won't be long." She joined Lily and they left the Café.

Gavin put his head down, muttering something I couldn't hear. His face was beet red.

Paula patted his arm. "Gavin, you have nothing to be ashamed about, you know. I think those photos of you are incredible. They make you look like a cross between a Viking god and a movie idol."

Freddy smiled at Gavin. "Definitely a Viking god. Don't ever apologize for posing for Lily. I think it's the best work she's ever done." He glanced at me. "No offense, Cara."

"No offense taken. I agree with you."

Freddy looked slightly worried. "Uh, Cara, your friend Amy is a lot bigger than Lily. You don't suppose she'd . . ."

Gavin's eyebrows shot up as he turned to me.

"No, of course not. I think Amy just wants to talk to her. And see Gavin's photos, of course." I smiled. "You can relax. There will be no bloodshed. I have Amy's word."

Joel poured coffee for all of us while we waited for the girls to return. It seemed we'd all run out of conversation.

It was a half hour before Amy and Lily returned, chatting about models and professional photographers, and had Amy ever considered modeling. They were both smiling, and we all breathed a sigh of relief, especially Gavin.

From that point on, we had a fun weekend. Amy stayed until late Sunday afternoon, promising to drive up the next time she had a free weekend when we had to stay at school. Privately, she told me she thought Lily's photos of

Gavin were gorgeous. Lily had promised to email Amy's favorite photo to her. She'd also promised to stop hitting on Gavin.

I went back to preparing for the Albany Art show and told Gavin it was up to him to deal with all of his new admirers. Since the Barrett Art Show, he'd apparently become very popular on campus. When I mentioned it, Gavin just rolled his eyes, blushed, and left the room.

We drove back to Thornewood the next two weekends, mainly so that I could take the artwork I'd completed to Francis Sullivan for his approval. He would have each piece framed and taken into town to Mr. Callahan who would ship them to the Albany gallery.

As I tried to work on a watercolor in my small bedroom, I realized that what I needed most was a studio, and Mom's house didn't have enough room. A roomy studio with a lot of skylights and a view of the forest I loved. If I continued to make money with my art sales, I might be able to build a studio on the lot that my father had deeded to me two years ago.

The prospect of having my own studio gave me something I could look forward to. And maybe, if I built it big enough, I could live there too. An exciting thought!

Mom decided she couldn't leave her business for two days, so my father and I set out for Albany early on Friday. The gallery's opening of this new show wasn't until seven that night. We'd have time for a leisurely trip and a bit of a rest when we arrived at our hotel, but not the same one Mom and I had stayed at on our first trip to Albany. Mom booked us into the best hotel in that city, after I insisted I could afford it.

Dad looked over Mom's shoulder while she was checking out hotels, and when she chose one she thought would be the safest, my father suggested she book a suite for us. I thought my ever-practical mother was going to argue, but she just shook her head and booked the suite.

My father looked over at me and winked. "Alicia dear, Cara can afford a suite. Her agent keeps raising the prices on her paintings and drawings. I predict she'll be able to support us in another year, and you can retire."

By that time, Mom knew she was being teased. She looked at my father with one eyebrow raised, and said, "Really, Brian."

During the long drive to Albany, I brought up the subject of building a studio on the lot next door.

"Cara, that's an excellent idea. There's plenty of room on that piece of property. Right now it's just a beautiful garden with a practice area for archery and knife-throwing. Since it's yours, you can build anything you want there. Were you thinking of a studio like Francis Sullivan's?"

"Yeah, Dad, exactly. Maybe I could add a living area to it eventually."

"You're not ready to leave us yet, are you? You know, dear, just having you away at school has been hard for us." He smiled a little sadly. "You're missed more than you know."

"Dad, I'll be eighteen in a few weeks. That's considered adult in the human world. I can even vote in the next election. But to be honest, I need a studio a lot more than I need to live away from you and Mom." I smiled at him. "I'm not ready for that much independence just yet."

"Glad to hear it, sweetheart. I know you'll leave us eventually, but we're not ready either."

We talked about the expense of building a studio. "Maybe if I do well at the next few art shows, I'll have enough money to get started."

"Well, you may not have to wait that long. Your college fund is still quite healthy, Cara. Your expenses at Barrett will only make a dent in it. I have no objection if you want to use it to build your studio. It makes more sense to save your art show earnings for that Art Gallery you want to open in Thornewood."

I was thrilled! I'd never even seen the bank balance in my college fund account. I had no idea how big it was. Apparently, my father had been extremely generous.

"I don't know what to say, Dad. That's a really generous offer. Do you think we could get started on the studio this summer?"

"Of course. I'll ask Harry Callahan to recommend a local builder. You'll need things like electricity and plumbing for the studio, so my men won't have all the skills that are needed. I'm sure Harry knows some good people we can hire."

I was so excited, it was hard to concentrate on my driving! Nevertheless, I managed to keep the car on the road, and we arrived in Albany safely.

The hotel Mom booked was a lot nicer than the one where we'd stayed before, and the suite was perfect; two bedrooms separated by a cozy sitting room. Very elegant.

We rested for a few hours, got lunch sent up from Room Service—something else I could easily get used to—and left for the Jourdan Gallery around four. We didn't see Miss Galen when we arrived, but Mr. Jourdan, the owner, greeted us warmly.

"Ah, Miss Blackthorne, so nice to see you again. And this must be your father. Welcome to the Jourdan Gallery, Mr. Blackthorne. Cara, you sent us so many of your pen and ink drawings, my clients will be overjoyed. I can't help wondering how someone so young can create drawings that appear to be from an earlier century. Many of my clients are fans of yours since your first show last year. Please come and see how we have displayed your work."

We followed him to the rear of the gallery where my drawings and the two watercolors had been hung. The lighting was perfect, the placement ideal. My artwork could be seen from anywhere in the gallery. Mr. Jourdan was beaming, clearly pleased. So was I.

He left us to greet some early-arriving clients as Miss Galen emerged from a back room. She was, of course, especially pleased to see my father with me.

We wandered around the gallery, looking at all the beautiful art being displayed at this show. I was delighted to see Win Mason's artwork again.

THE JOINING TREE

His street scenes, full of people and action everywhere, were wonderful. Even my father found Win's work fascinating.

"I'd love to buy one of Win's paintings, Dad. They're so exciting. The people he paints practically jump off the canvas, don't they?"

From behind us, we heard a voice. "Thank you, Cara. Perhaps we can work out a 'friends and family' discount for you!"

I turned to see the short, stocky young man grinning at me.

"It's so nice to see you again, Win. Your work is even more exciting than it was last year."

"Thank you, Cara. Hi, Mr. Blackthorne.

"I've been admiring your pen and ink drawings. I heard that you wouldn't sell any of them last year. I hope you're willing to sell these new drawings. They have a really nostalgic appeal."

We chatted with Win for a few more minutes until Miss Galen waved us over to talk to the same couple I'd met last year, the ones who wanted my 'Elf drawings' so badly. They were delighted that these new drawings were available for sale. I had six displayed, and they were buying four of them—at prices that made *me* gasp.

When I mentioned the very high prices to Miss Galen, she just laughed and said, "It's the law of supply and demand, Cara. Your work is very much in demand."

A few hours passed while we chatted with customers and sipped champagne—I was given the real stuff this time, under my father's watchful eye, of course.

By the time we left around eight, there were "Sold" stickers on all of my artwork.

"Is there a good restaurant nearby, Cara? Your mother told me about a steak house you visited on your last trip."

"Yes! You'll love the steaks." I drove a few blocks to the restaurant where my father and I enjoyed Ribeye steaks, perfectly broiled, along with twice-baked potatoes and Caesar salads.

My father pronounced the meal "perfect." And it was. We returned to our hotel feeling well fed and very tired, and without being mugged. When I showed my father where last year's attempted mugging had taken place, he immediately pulled his knife and hurried me to my car.

On our way back to our hotel, he chuckled and admitted the steak dinner had been almost worth the risk of being mugged. I reminded him that no mugger in his right mind would risk attacking *him*.

We called Mom to let her know the show was a success. I left Dad talking on the phone with Mom while I took a shower and went to bed.

Even though I was well pleased with the way my artwork was selling, I still felt kind of empty, as though something vital was missing. I had hoped my art would fill up my life, soothe that emptiness.

It wasn't enough.

A week later, I turned eighteen. Legally at least, I was now an "adult." Funny, I didn't feel any different.

Mom made Lasagna for my birthday dinner, with Amy, Conor, Arlynn, Kathleen, and Gavin joining us around the kitchen table. Kevin couldn't make it, but he called to wish me a happy birthday and said he'd be home soon, which was good news. I really missed him.

After we had polished off two pans of lasagna, my father took Gavin outside "for a talk", leaving the rest of us around the table.

I had a lot of catching up to do with Conor, Arlynn, and Kathleen since I'd barely seen them for months. But I was worried about Gavin. I was afraid my father had lost confidence in him.

Conor wanted to hear about my plans for building a studio on the lot next door, an idea everyone was in favor of. The prospect of having my own studio was really exciting. Plus, it took my mind off the conversation my dad was probably having with Gavin.

When my father came back into the kitchen alone, I feared the worst. Amy looked worried, and I knew she was aware of Gavin's own fears.

Shortly after my father returned, she said she had to get home. When I walked her to the door, she hugged me and asked me to call her later.

Conor, Arlynn, and Kathleen were the next to leave, all of them again wishing me a happy birthday.

I sat down at the table with Mom and Dad. Mom had made another pot of coffee, obviously aware that a serious discussion was about to ensue.

"Dad, why didn't Gavin come back with you?"

"I think Gavin's ashamed of himself right now, Cara. He'll be at my camp until you drive back to school. He wants to finish the school term. I believe he has several art projects to complete. But he won't be returning to school with you next year."

"Was that your decision or his, Dad?"

"It was his. He thinks, as I do, that you should have some kind of protection while you're at school, but he also knows that he's not really suited for that job. I'm not angry with Gavin, sweetheart. I know how difficult his life has been. For many reasons, Gavin is too emotional and I can see that he lacks self-confidence, which is why I can't rely on him to keep you safe. He still has a lot of maturing to do. He'll have time to do that while he works in the forest with Conor. But I also want him to spend more time in Elvenwood." He smiled. "He has volunteered to give our children art lessons, which I think is an excellent idea."

"Dad, Gavin is so talented, and such a gentle young man, I think he'll make a wonderful teacher. But I want you to know that I'll really miss him." I was already feeling the loss. "He's been more than just a roommate or a bodyguard. He's been a great friend too, something I needed this past year."

"I know you did, and I'm glad Gavin was there to keep you company. But now I have to decide who to send with you next year."

I groaned. "Please don't make that decision now. I'm not sure I want another roommate, not to mention another bodyguard. After all, that missing SUV driver seems to be long gone. I don't think he poses a real threat. I do have friends at school, male and female, and I think I can take care of myself. Lieutenant Fox gave me his home phone number too. He wants me to call him any time I have a problem. Dad, I think I'll be fine without a bodyguard next year."

Mom and Dad looked at each other, clearly unsure what steps they should take next. And we left that subject there for the time being. There were plenty of other things to talk about, like my proposed studio, the most recent Art Show in Albany, and how I planned to spend my summer.

Before I went upstairs, I went out on the back porch to sing Rowenna's song. She didn't stop in the yard that night, but I heard her rusty voice in my head.

Thank you, Cara. I'm wishing you happiness on this day of your birth. I spoke to Alicia a few days ago and she told me there would be a small celebration tonight. Your birth was an auspicious occasion, my young friend.

Her magic felt like a soft hug wrapped around me. That magic was her gift to me. It always made me feel protected.

I sighed and went inside. I still had to call Amy.

"Well, what's the verdict, Cara?"

"You'll probably consider it good news, Amy." I explained my dad's decision, including the fact Gavin would be teaching Art to the kids in Elvenwood.

"Oh! That is good news. He'll also be home more, which will be great for us. As long as Gavin isn't upset about this, I think your father made a good decision."

"Yeah, I think so too. Of course, now he's thinking about sending someone else to school with me as my bodyguard. I'm trying to talk him out of it."

"You don't feel you need a bodyguard at school?"

"Not really. No one's after me, as far as I can tell, and I have friends there. Lieutenant Fox is only a phone call away," I said with a chuckle.

"Hmm. I haven't even met your Lieutenant yet, Cara. Are you sure there's nothing going on there?" That question was part curiosity and part teasing.

"Nothing more than friendship, Amy."

"Well, best friend, don't rule it out if he's as nice and as good looking as he sounds."

"Give it a rest, will you? You know how I feel."

"Okay, okay. Call me next time you're home, okay? And happy birthday again, Cara."

Not tired enough to sleep, I stood at my bedroom window and looked out at the forest in the moonlight. I was suddenly overcome with memories, the kind I'd tried to shut out for almost two years. I could almost hear Adam's voice in my head again, telling me he missed me when we'd been separated for a few weeks. I remembered his laugh when I'd asked him when he'd be going to the Joining Tree. He'd said, "Not until you grow up, love."

Had he meant it? Or was he just teasing me as he often did?

I was eighteen, legally an adult. I finally admitted to myself that I'd held out a tiny hope that he would now consider me "grown up" enough, and come back to me.

But he hadn't.

CHAPTER 25

Gavin and I went back to school on Sunday. School would be out for the summer in less than two weeks, and we both had some work to finish.

The Barrett Art Institute didn't give out grades the way other schools did, although some special projects would be given a grade. Instead, each student had a sit-down meeting with each of our instructors to discuss our work and the progress we'd made in the past year.

The Art History classes weren't graded either, and there were no exams. Mrs. Barrett held the opinion that Art History was simply meant to inspire us, not give us something we had to study and be tested on.

I had really loved my Art History classes. It had been fascinating to learn how artists from hundreds of years ago had worked, especially with the materials they used and the paints they had to make themselves. Modern artists had it easy, by comparison.

I also had to get together with Laurie Williams and arrange for next year's rent. There was always the slight chance that our experience with the police would have convinced her I was not the ideal tenant, but I was pretty sure she wouldn't ask me to move out. She told me once that I had brought some needed excitement into her quiet life. But I knew she'd miss Gavin, who had always been helpful to her around the house.

All of my instructors were pleased with my work, especially in Oil Painting. Miss Alvarez, my instructor, told me I'd made great progress this past year. Of course, I knew my progress was due mainly to Francis Sullivan's help, not my instructor's.

Next year I would have to do some still life painting, not something I was particularly interested in, but it was required. As was the Life Drawing class with Daniel Goldman. That prospect gave me goose bumps. I wasn't sure I would ever enjoy drawing and painting nudes! When I mentioned it to Lily, she laughed and told me I didn't know what I was missing.

Our little dinner group was disappointed to learn Gavin wouldn't be returning in September. Especially Lily and Freddy. He explained it by telling them that his year of art classes had been sufficient training to teach art to the children at home.

"Actually, my main interest is forestry and working outdoors, especially caring for wildlife," he told them at dinner one night. "Art is more of a hobby than a career for me. I love working in Blackthorne Forest. It's a truly beautiful place." He glanced at me and smiled. "Cara can tell you about it. I think she's spent most of her life in the forest."

Joel looked at me somewhat strangely and nodded. "That would explain why she's always seemed different from the rest of us, just as you do, Gavin." I wondered what he meant by "different."

Gavin looked at me, clearly surprised. I don't think either of us realized how we appeared to everyone else. I'd always *felt* "different" until my senior year of high school, but I think my relationship with Sean and getting to know most of his friends had allowed me to feel that maybe I *did* fit in.

Our last night at Barrett, a party was held in the Café, compliments of Mrs. Barrett. We feasted on Fettucine Alfredo, Baked Chicken, several kinds of salads, which pleased Paula, and what was called "Death by Chocolate" cake, seven layers of yummy chocolate goodness. Needless to say, we stuffed ourselves. I'd never seen the Café so packed. We had to eat in shifts.

All the third-year students were getting good-bye hugs, and email addresses and phone numbers were being exchanged. It was a fun night. We'd all be leaving for home in the morning.

After we'd packed up everything we wanted to take home, and cleaned out the refrigerator, we went upstairs to see Laurie Williams and say goodbye. She invited us in for coffee and Danish. I'd already let her know that Gavin wouldn't be back, which saddened her.

"I'm really going to miss you two for the next few months, you know." She leaned down to pet Ralph and told him, "I'll miss you too, Ralph." His little stub of a tail wagged like mad.

"Gavin, it's been a pleasure having you here. I hope you'll be happy back home, and I think you'll be a wonderful art teacher."

We thanked her for putting up with my problems over the past year and for being so understanding.

I knew I'd be back in a little over two months, but I'd miss my cozy apartment as well as the roomy studio—something I didn't have at home.

As we were loading up my car, a police car pulled up behind me with Lieutenant Fox behind the wheel.

He got out and walked over to us. "I hope you weren't planning on leaving Syracuse without saying goodbye," he said with a smile.

"Hi, Lieutenant. I'm glad you stopped by. I wanted to thank you for being a good friend to us this past year."

Gavin took the Lieutenant's arm and led him away from my car. I wasn't sure what he wanted to talk to the Lieutenant about, but I suspected it had something to do with protection for me, which I really didn't think was necessary. The men in my life all seemed to equate my small size with my need for manly protection, which always irked me. And that reminded me I needed to start practicing with my knives again while I was home for the summer.

Finally they walked back to my car, shook hands, and Gavin got into the passenger side after hooking up Ralph's harness in the back seat.

The Lieutenant gave me a warm smile and an unexpected hug.

"Cara, I'm going to miss you, as well as all the excitement that seems to find its way to you." He grinned, which dazzled me, probably because he was usually so serious.

He looked down at me. "I hope you have a good summer. I'll be looking forward to seeing you when you get back. Be sure to give me a call so I can alert the rest of the force." He laughed.

I just shook my head and rolled my eyes.

As we drove away from Birch Street, I saw that green van turn the corner at the end of the block. I couldn't see the driver, of course, so I gave a quick toot of my horn and waved out the window as we headed for the highway. I wasn't sure, but I thought I heard a brief toot in return.

Gavin and I talked about a lot of things on the way home. Every time he began to apologize for letting me down, I reminded him that he was the one who put an arrow in Romanov's back, saving me from having my throat cut!

"Please stop apologizing. And you've been a great roommate—no wet towels on the bathroom floor, clothes always hung up and put away, not to mention you've made more meals for us than I did."

He chuckled, nodding.

"And more importantly, you've been a wonderful friend. I'm really going to miss you, you know."

"Who do you think your father will send with you in September?"

"I don't really want him to send anyone. After all this time, I don't think anyone is after me. Besides, I can take care of myself. I'll be doing more practicing with archery and knives this summer. You should join me when you have time."

"Yes, I will." He grinned. "Of course, you also have Lieutenant Fox at your beck and call. I'm sure he'll come running if you need him."

"Yep. He's asked me to keep his home phone on speed dial, just in case. But I really don't expect any problems next year."

"You know, Cara, I think the good Lieutenant has more than a professional interest in you. I've noticed the way he looks at you."

I rolled my eyes. "Oh, please. I think he sees me as a potential disaster in the making that he needs to keep an eye on. Nothing more!"

He laughed. "Cara, you really don't see yourself the way others see you. For instance, our friend Joel seems to enjoy looking across the table at you. I'm surprised he hasn't asked you out yet.

"I remember you had a boyfriend in Thornewood. Sean, right?"

"Well, yeah. But we're just friends now." I sighed.

"What happened?"

"Sean's a great guy, but he wanted more of a relationship than I could honestly give him."

"Oh. What happened to that guy who was your bodyguard after I got in so much trouble two years ago? I heard you and he were really tight."

I didn't know how to answer. "Well, once I didn't need a bodyguard any longer, he moved away."

"That's too bad. As it turned out, you *did* need a bodyguard."
He frowned. "I wasn't the best choice."
"Gavin, don't start that again. Adam left. End of story."
Out of the corner of my eye, I could tell he was watching me.
His voice was soft. "I don't think it was, Cara."
We stopped talking. I shoved an Oldies CD into the CD player and just drove.

I pulled up in front of Mom's house, glad to be home. Gavin left me at the front door. He was going straight to my father's camp. I hugged him around the waist, surprising him. "I'll miss you. Please stop by my practice area when you have time."

He said he would, kissed me on the cheek and walked through the yard into the woods. It would be strange, not seeing him every day.

Ralph ran around the kitchen, up and down the stairs, finally resting on the foot of my bed, his tongue hanging out. He looked happy.

Mom had left for the bookstore, but she'd left my favorite quiche warming in the oven. My father had waited for us to get home, greeting me with one of his great hugs.

"We've really missed you, sweetheart," he told me with a smile. "It's been too quiet around here."

Over slices of quiche along with coffee, he told me that I had an appointment at Harry Callahan's office the next day. "Harry contacted a builder he's worked with before and he'll be there to go over what you want in a studio. I believe he has plans for a variety of buildings. You just have to look them over and give him your wish list."

I was both surprised and thrilled. "Wow. That's fantastic, Dad. I hope this builder will be able to get started soon. It would be wonderful if we could get the studio completed while I'm home this summer."

He nodded and poured himself more coffee. "It's possible, depending on the builder's schedule. Summer is their busiest season. We'll find out tomorrow."

"I'm glad you're coming with me, Dad. I've never done anything like this before."

"I know, dear. But I have one more reason for going downtown with you tomorrow."

"What's that?"

He grinned. "Don't say anything to your mother, but I'm going to sign up for driving lessons."

I had to laugh. "Yeah, Mom would probably turn green. But I think you'll be a good driver, Dad." I hesitated. "Um, would you like me to go to your driving lessons with you?"

THE JOINING TREE

He shook his head, looking slightly embarrassed. "No, dear. I don't need anyone besides the driving instructor witnessing my mistakes while I'm learning." He looked at me with one eyebrow raised. "I already know enough to avoid mailboxes."

I rolled my eyes. "Well, as Adam said when I was learning, 'If Cara can learn to drive, how hard can it be?'"

My father chuckled. "He went along on your driving lessons, didn't he?"

"Some days it was Adam, other days it was Ryan. Ryan usually turned slightly green during my lessons. Adam just said, 'No one lives forever.'"

My father's smile was sad. "You still miss him, don't you?"

I nodded. Just talking about Adam hurt.

After a few minutes of silence, my father said, "I almost forgot to tell you. Ryan and Lora will say their vows under the Joining Tree in three weeks. They'd like you to be there."

"Of course. I'm happy for them. Ryan was such a good friend through all my troubles." I hadn't seen him during the past year. I'd have to get to Elvenwood as often as possible during the summer. I missed my friends there.

Our meeting with the builder, Jeff Anderson, went very well. He gave me several building plans to look at, and I showed him what I wanted and what I didn't want. I needed water, for a half bath and a second sink in the studio, electricity, a large window facing the forest, and several skylights. He made several good suggestions that I liked, and we drove to the property next to Mom's house so he could look over the site and make some notes.

I told him I wanted to keep my practice area right where it was at the rear of the property, but the lot was so deep, there was plenty of room for my studio plus a flagstone patio behind it. I had thought I might want to add living space on the north side of the studio at a later date, facing the street, so he made some changes to the plans that would make it a simple add-on later.

After I had walked through the property with Jeff and my father, I was beginning to visualize how the new building would look, especially since my father requested that as few trees and plants be removed as possible. It would be beautiful.

Construction would begin in another week. Jeff laughingly suggested we invest in some ear plugs because there would be a lot of noisy power tools being used. He said they usually started work around eight weekdays so sleeping in wouldn't be an option this summer.

My father chuckled. "When it gets too noisy, we can go riding early in the morning." Of course, what he didn't say in front of Jeff was that we'd ride to Elvenwood for breakfast in the dining hall.

And that set the pattern for my summer. Sort of.

Two weeks after I got home, Kevin called to let me know he was finally home.

"Hey short stuff, what's going on next door?"

"Well, it's about time, Kev. How come you didn't call sooner? Have you been home as long as I have?" If I sounded annoyed, it's because I was.

"Sorry, babe. Yeah, I got home a week ago. I'm behind on my game design contract, so I've been working day and night trying to get back on schedule. Today's the first day I've felt like my life is actually mine. But you didn't answer my question. Am I hearing power tools?"

"Yes, you are. Construction has just begun next door on my art studio. I'm hoping it will be finished before I go back to school in September."

"Wow! Your own studio. I'm impressed. I want to hear all about it so how about going to The Grill with me for lunch today?"

"Sounds good. We have a lot of catching up to do, Kev."

"Okay, I'll pick you up in ten."

When he got to my house, we walked through the lot next door so I could show him where my studio would be and fill him in on the details. One of the workers was moving equipment in and tried to stop us, telling us that it was private property and a construction site, and we had to leave.

I didn't like his attitude. "Yeah, I know. I own this property and I'll be over here regularly to see how construction is coming along. My name is Cara Blackthorne. And you are?"

Red-faced, he muttered something unintelligible and walked away.

"Whoa, short stuff. You've become impressively assertive in the past year." Kevin looked surprised.

"Must be the result of being almost killed so many times." My sarcasm was showing.

Kevin shook his head. "We really do have a lot to talk about, babe."

Over burgers and milkshakes at The Grill, we exchanged stories. Kevin had worked his butt off at school, managed to keep up with his studies, but lost twenty pounds doing it. I was afraid those circles under his hazel eyes would be permanent.

He agreed. "I guess that's what it took to teach me not to overestimate what I can handle. My course load for next year will be about half what it was this year. Meanwhile, I lost weight, lost Amy, and I guess I'm down to one best friend now."

"I doubt you've lost Amy completely, Kev. She's dating someone else, but I can't believe she won't want to be your friend anymore."

I told him about my year at Barrett, the campus stalker who'd knocked me out, the three Art Shows where I'd exhibited my work, and my hope I could start my second year at Barrett without a bodyguard.

THE JOINING TREE

He laughed. "Sounds to me like *not* having a bodyguard is asking for trouble. After all, you are the 'disaster magnet.' That's been well established."

Behind us I heard a familiar voice. "Disaster magnet? That sounds like a girl I used to know."

I turned to see Sean McKay grinning at me. Leaping out of my seat, I squealed, "Sean!" and ran into his open arms, both of us laughing. He looked fantastic. He'd filled out, put on weight, and still looked more like a blond Greek god than a college student.

"Hey beautiful, you're a welcome sight," he said as he reluctantly let go of me. "Can I join you guys?"

He sat down with us and told us all about his year at Penn State while he waited for his burger and French fries. He'd played more football than he'd thought he would, and less baseball, which was a disappointment. But, all in all, he'd enjoyed his first year.

"So, Cara, what other disasters occurred since I saw you over the holidays?"

"Just a campus stalker who managed to hit me over the head and knock me out."

Sean shook his head. "They just seem to find you, don't they? Are you okay now?"

"Yeah, another concussion, that's all. I must have an extremely hard head."

Kevin snorted. "I've always known that, short stuff."

Sean tried not to laugh. "But you had a bodyguard, didn't you? Where was he?"

"Uh, somewhere else. He left school early that day."

Looking serious, Sean said, "I'm guessing he won't be your bodyguard next year, right?"

"No, he won't. I'm lobbying for *no* bodyguard next year. Gavin was actually a great roommate and a good friend, but I really dislike feeling that I have to be protected. I think I can take care of myself."

I turned to Kevin. "In fact, after lunch, Kev, you and I are going to do a little practicing. My archery is really rusty, and I'll bet yours is too. I haven't had much knife-throwing practice either. You?"

"Nope. I've had no time for anything extra-curricular. I've got to complete a game design over the summer, but that'll be a lot easier than school was. I'd enjoy getting some weapons practice."

Sean shook his head. "Wish I could join you. I'd love to learn archery, but I've got a summer job doing construction work for a friend of my dad's. I'll be starting on a new site tomorrow building an art studio for some college girl."

Kevin and I looked at each other, trying not to laugh.

Sean looked at each of us. Then his eyebrows hit his hairline. "No. Don't tell me. *Your* art studio, Cara?"

"Yep. You must be working for Jeff Anderson. They did some prep work on the lot next door this morning. I guess the real construction starts tomorrow."

And that was when I realized I'd be seeing a lot of Sean McKay that summer.

The good news: By the end of the summer, I had my own art studio. The bad news: It had been finished the week before I left for Syracuse. I would only get to enjoy using it when I came home on weekends during my second year at Barrett. But I'd know it was there, waiting for me.

Kevin had spent most of his summer designing his video games, only leaving the house to come over for spaghetti night once a week, and, of course, for Mom's Sunday brunch. Other than those two occasions, Kevin was a hermit. I suspected he was afraid of running into Amy, but when I mentioned that, he just glared at me. Which told me I was right.

Amy was still seeing Gavin once a week when he had a day off. He only came over to practice very early in the morning, before the construction workers arrived. I'd barely seen him at all. Which made me sad.

And then there was Sean, working next door all summer. It had been a hot summer. On the hottest days, the younger guys on the construction crew worked with their shirts off, a sight that really cried out for an audience. Especially the sight of Sean, shirtless. Even my mother said, "Wow!" when she saw him carrying some lumber one morning. He grinned and shouted out "Hi" to her whenever he saw her leaving for work. She said it always got her day off to a great start.

We weren't exactly dating. He admitted he'd been dating a girl at school, but said he wouldn't be seeing her until he went back to school in August.

On a couple of weekends, he rode to Elvenwood with me. I even took him to Ryan's wedding. Which might have been a mistake.

It was the first time I'd seen a wedding under the Joining Tree. My parents had been married under the old apple tree in our backyard. But there was something magical about hearing those beautiful words spoken under that majestic tree.

Henry Ferguson, the head Elder, stood under the Joining Tree. Ryan and Lora stood before him, hand in hand. Everyone quieted as Mr. Ferguson began to speak.

"Ryan and Lora, you stand before us today declaring that you are truly Mated and will be bound forever by Elven custom.

"Now you will feel no rain, for each will be shelter for the other.

Now you will feel no cold, for each of you will be warmth to the other.

Now there will be no loneliness, for each of you will be companion to the other.

THE JOINING TREE

Now you are two persons, but there is only one life before you.

May beauty surround you both in the journey ahead and through all the years.

May happiness be your companion and your days together be good and long upon the earth.

And may your years together be fruitful, if it is meant to be."

He looked at Ryan and nodded.

Ryan looked at Lora and said, "Forever, Lora."

The Elder looked at Lora and nodded.

Lora looked at Ryan and said, "Forever, Ryan." I could hear her voice shake.

Looking out at the gathering of Elves, the Elder smiled. "Please offer your warmest wishes to Ryan and Lora, who are now wed."

As the couple turned to us, smiling, I heard a flute playing gaily. Everyone approached Ryan and Lora, delivering hugs, kisses, and good wishes.

Sean and I stood back as the couple made their way through the happy crowd. I'd been so moved by those beautiful words, I was fighting tears. When I looked at Sean, I could see he'd been moved too. He squeezed my hand wordlessly.

When Ryan spotted us, he wore a big smile as he pulled Lora over to us.

"Cara, Sean, what a wonderful surprise to see you here." Ryan let go of Lora's hand just long enough to give me a big hug, dropping a kiss on my cheek, and shaking Sean's hand. "I hope you'll stay for the celebration. There will be plenty of food and drink and music. My father brought his guitar. This probably reminds you of your parents' wedding two years ago, doesn't it?"

"I thought my parents' wedding was lovely, but I have to say that hearing your ceremony under the Joining Tree was even more beautiful. There's something about that tree . . ."

Lora laughed. "Yes, there is. There always has been. The only word for it is *magic!*"

When they left us to receive congratulations from other friends, Sean looked at me as though there was something he wanted to say, but he remained silent. It was all in his warm brown eyes.

I squeezed his hand and we walked toward the grassy area where the younger Elves were gathering as Jason played his flute and the ladies from the kitchen were passing out food and drink. The older people had all headed for the dining hall where there were benches to sit on and tables full of good food.

Sean was wearing a lightweight blazer over his dress shirt. He took off the blazer and spread it on the grass for us to sit on. In honor of the Elven wedding, I'd chosen to wear my green tunic and slacks, made for me by the Elves two years ago. I'd only had to let out the seams a little.

We got comfortable in the grass, with me leaning against Sean. We could smell the grass, the trees, and some roses nearby. It was what I'd always called "the forest's perfume." And there was definitely magic in the air.

"Can you feel it?" I whispered to Sean.

He nodded, smiling down at me. "It's a different kind of magic, isn't it?"

"Yes. I always feel magic in the air when I'm in Elvenwood, but this is something different, stronger."

He chuckled. "I'd call it seductive." He wrapped one arm around my waist and dropped a kiss on my ear.

I closed my eyes for a few seconds and continued to breathe in this very special magic. When I looked around, I could see other couples sitting close together and whispering to each other. Something told me we were all in danger of being bewitched!

Sean whispered in my ear, "I'm guessing this magic we're feeling is always present after a wedding has taken place. Everyone feels more amorous. Including me, Cara."

I sighed. Being in Sean's arms felt awfully good. In this magical environment, it was hard not to get carried away. But I couldn't let that happen.

"It'll be dusk soon, Sean. We'll have to ride back before it's dark."

It was his turn to sigh.

Suddenly I looked up to see my cousin Jason standing near us, smiling. He continued to play his flute, something sweet and romantic. Uh-oh. I knew what he was trying to do.

I spoke to his mind. *Jason, stop it. This isn't fair.*

In my mind, I heard, *Cara, you and Sean make such a beautiful couple.*

I stood up rather abruptly. "Sean, we'd better say our good-byes now. It's getting dark."

He stood reluctantly. "I really hate to go, Cara. This is a magical night."

Jason reached out and hugged me. "See you soon, cousin. Good to see you again, Sean."

My father found us, and I could see the magic reflected in his eyes. "This is a very special day, Cara. I hope you and Sean have enjoyed yourselves."

I assured him we had, but that it was time to leave.

"I'm staying here tonight, dear. I'll be back tomorrow. Hug your mother for me. I wish she could have been here." He hugged me tightly. "Get home safely. The greys know the way. A little darkness doesn't bother them."

We left to find Ryan and Lora, exchanged more hugs and congratulations, and left for the stable.

We didn't talk on the ride home. We were still under that magical spell.

At my back door, he kissed me. I think we were both fighting the magic.

Before he left, he put his hands on my shoulders and whispered in my ear, "I love you, beautiful girl."

He ran down the steps, taking the last strands of tonight's magic with him.

When I was ready for bed, I stood at my bedroom window, enjoying the moonlit forest. I thought I could still hear Jason's flute playing a sweet, romantic tune, but I was probably imagining it.

THE JOINING TREE

Would I ever stand under the Joining Tree with the man I was in love with? That might be too much to hope for.

CHAPTER 26

Sean had to return to Penn State the last week of August for the start of football practice. We went to the Pizza Palace on his last night home. It was a very nostalgic choice.

After he fed all his quarters into the old jukebox, we listened to the oldies as we ate pizza and drank ice-cold root beer.

When he'd managed to consume an entire extra-large pie, he smiled. "This place is full of good memories for me, Cara. How about you?"

"Yeah, of course. Our first dates, dancing to the oldies, my first kiss. They're all great memories."

For just a minute, he looked serious. "It's still him, isn't it?"

I nodded. I couldn't meet his eyes. I still couldn't tell Sean what he wanted to hear.

He gave a decisive nod. "For old times sake, dance with me, Cara."

On the dance floor, with his arms around me, I simply closed my eyes and enjoyed his closeness, his warmth, and that smell of sandalwood and soap I'd always loved. Sean deserved more than being second best.

When the song ended, I pulled away. I said softly, "Thank you for being you, for being wonderful. I'll always care for you, Sean."

He took my hand. "But not enough, I know." The regret showed on his face.

We left and he drove me home. At the front door, he kissed me. It was not a gentle kiss. I sensed his frustration.

I pulled away but ran my hand across his cheek, his lips.

He let me go and said, "If he never comes back, Cara, I'll still be here and I'll still be in love with you."

And I knew he meant it.

I went inside, full of regret that I couldn't love him the way he loved me.

It was time for me to go back to school. After one last satisfied look at my brand new empty art studio, I locked the studio door and got in my car for the drive back to Syracuse. I'd already said my goodbyes to Mom and Dad and to Amy, who promised to call me every week.

Kevin had already left for school.

Over the summer, we'd had fun practicing archery together the way we used to. I had wrung a promise out of him to at least text me if he didn't have time to call. And he knew how much I hated texts!

THE JOINING TREE

Ralph was in his road trip harness, fastened to a seat belt in the back seat of my car. He'd become accustomed to the regular car rides to school last year, so he was curled up with his chin resting on the edge of a window. He'd seemed a little sad to be leaving Mom and Dad and the woods he loved running in.

"It's just you and me this year, Ralph. But if you're not happy being at school with me, I can always bring you home." He yawned and went to sleep, apparently not at all worried.

I put an old Fleetwood Mac CD of Mom's in my CD player and hit the road. Driving out of Thornewood, I began to wish Gavin was still with me. My apartment would seem empty without him.

As I sang along with Stevie Nicks, I told myself I was an independent, self-sufficient young woman who was perfectly capable of living alone. I told Ralph too. He gave a little whine. I didn't think he agreed with me.

When I pulled up to the yellow house on Birch Street, I unloaded the car, unhooked Ralph from his harness, and we ran upstairs to say hello to Laurie. After she made me a cup of tea and treated Ralph with a bacon-flavored dog biscuit, I went out in the backyard with Ralph to look for good scenes I could paint.

Next on the list was food. Groceries were a must, so I left Ralph with Laurie and drove to the nearest market to stock up. When I got home with far too many bags of food, it dawned on me that I only had to shop for one person now, not two. I had definitely bought too much food. Well, that's what freezers were for. I chuckled. Maybe the Lieutenant would stop by for another snack.

I went over to the Café for dinner, but there was a sign on the door. "Closed for Summer. See you in September!" Which was still two days away. I sighed, went back to my apartment and made myself a ham and cheese sandwich.

Ralph was sitting in front of the door, looking over his shoulder at me, wagging his little tail. Ah. He was waiting for his nightly walk, which was up to me now.

I was still in shorts so I quickly changed into jeans and boots, slipped my phone and my keys into my pockets, my knives into my boots, and fastened Ralph's leash to his collar.

"Okay, Ralphie, let's go for a walk."

Since I didn't know the entire neighborhood that well, I decided to stay on Birch Street. We walked six blocks in one direction, then turned around and walked back. I'd have to explore the side streets during the daytime. It was dusk now, but streetlights were going on up and down Birch Street, creating the illusion of safety.

Two blocks from home, I spotted a familiar green van parked at the end of one of the side streets, Oak Street I think. I was tempted to walk down there but there weren't as many streetlights on Oak. Feeling like a big chicken, I decided to wait for daylight to do any exploring. After all, I'd just arrived back in Syracuse. Why go looking for trouble? If past experience was reliable, I was still a disaster magnet.

I sighed. I hated feeling like such a wuss. Ralph whined a little, his head turned toward Oak Street. "We'll explore another day, Ralphie."

When we were back on our own block, I was surprised to see a police car parked in front of our house, Lieutenant Fox casually leaning against the hood, his arms crossed.

As we got closer, I thought he was looking much too serious. I just got here. What could I possibly have done?

"Cara Blackthorne, not even a phone call to warn me. You know it's going to take the rest of the force at least twenty-four hours to get up to speed." Then he smiled at me, laughing softly.

I breathed a sigh of relief. For a few seconds, I thought I was in trouble again.

"Nice greeting, Lieutenant. You had me worried for a minute." I smiled back.

He leaned down to scratch behind Ralph's ears and welcomed him back. When he straightened up, he said, "It's really good to see you, Cara. How was your summer? In fact, before you say anything, can I take you out for a burger? Then you can fill me in on all your summer adventures." I thought I could see a new—and different—look in his eyes, which made me curious.

Standing up straight, he began jingling his car keys. "So, are we on for burgers?"

I'd had a sandwich only an hour ago, but the offer of a burger was tempting.

"Okay, let me take Ralph inside. Maybe Laurie would like his company for a little while."

The Lieutenant drove us to an upscale coffee shop for our burgers. Rudy's was a very classy coffee shop, much fancier than The Grille.

The burgers were to die for, the milkshakes especially creamy.

"Lieutenant, this place is really great. My favorite place in Thornewood is the Village Grille, but this place has it beat."

He smiled. "Glad you approve. I've been eating here for years. By the way, I'm off duty, and you're legal now. I think it would be okay if you called me Aidan."

"Oh." That took me by surprise. He could see it on my face.

"Cara, I'm not being forward, but I'm still in my twenties, not that much older than you. We're friends, right?" Ah, I was beginning to understand that look in his eyes. Gavin might have been right, which made me smile a little.

"Right." So I began calling the Lieutenant by his first name. It felt strange at first, but gradually I got used to it.

Over our burgers, I told him about the art studio I'd had built over the summer.

"My dad gave me that piece of property two years ago. All I was using it for was a practice area for archery and knife throwing. There was plenty of room to build on."

"Were you practicing over the summer?"

"Absolutely. I was rusty. My friend Kevin and I spent one entire summer training, but there wasn't much time this past year. This summer we got together to practice three times a week after the construction workers left. I think I'm now almost as fast as I was two years ago."

When I looked up, he was shaking his head. "Your father told me how skilled you are, but do you really think you need those defense skills now?"

I looked him in the eye. "Aidan, I will never be victimized again if I can help it. Gaining these skills has given me more confidence. I'm not very big and to be honest, being able to throw a knife accurately has saved my life more than once."

He nodded. "Uh-huh. Unless someone comes up behind you, hits you over the head and knocks you out. Or drives his SUV into your car."

I rolled my eyes. "Yes, unless. Maybe, Lieutenant Fox, you and your merry band need to work a bit harder to keep men like that off our campuses and streets." I narrowed my eyes in an accusing look and put down my empty milkshake glass with a bang.

Both eyebrows were raised as he said, "I guess I've been told." He shook his head and chuckled.

As he drove me home, he said, "By the way, I stopped by Barrett's Art Show last Spring. I saw your painting of your father. It was beautiful work, Cara."

"Thank you." I told him about the two Art Galleries that had shown my work in Albany and New York City.

"And they've sold your work?"

"Yes, and at prices I still don't believe." I giggled. "My agent puts the prices on my drawings and paintings. I would never have asked so much!"

"Wow." He chuckled. "At eighteen, you're already a successful artist. That's amazing."

"It's what I've always wanted to do, Aidan. Of course, I expected to be a 'starving artist' for many years. I think I've been very lucky."

"Or exceptionally talented, Cara."

We'd reached my house. He got out of the car with me and walked me to the front door. I thanked him for taking me out to eat. He insisted it was his pleasure.

As he walked back down he stairs, he said, "I'll call you soon!"

When I went upstairs to get Ralph, Laurie said, "So you're dating the handsome Lieutenant now?"

"Not exactly. He wanted to hear about my summer and he was hungry." I shrugged. "I think that's all it was. We're friends."

I wasn't sure she believed me.

Over the next few days, the campus gradually filled up and the Café finally opened. I was grateful for both. The usual group, minus Gavin, met for dinner most nights, talking about our respective summers and comparing notes on this year's classes.

Ralph and I did some exploring during daylight hours, and I learned that the side streets were similar to Birch Street, just rows of older homes, some of which had been turned into student housing. The tree-lined streets were pleasant to walk along due to the very old trees that formed a shady canopy over the streets. Everything was still lush and green, and I enjoyed the smell of just-cut grass. It still felt like summer, which was fine with me. I was in no hurry for winter.

My classes were interesting, to put it mildly. My watercolor class was concentrating on various types of still life displays. It was harder than I expected. I'd always worked on landscapes, flowers, and even the Victorian houses sprinkled throughout Thornewood. Painting a simple bowl of fruit on a tablecloth sounded easy, but it wasn't. Shading, texture, showing the difference between shiny and dull, rough and smooth was challenging.

The Life Drawing class was a different kind of challenge! Seeing naked models at the front of the room always made me want to cover them up with something. Mr. Goldman, our instructor, remembered me.

"Welcome to Life Drawing, Cara Blackthorne." He smiled. "You still look too young to be in my class." He looked at what was on my easel and nodded. "I can see you're having difficulty with this." He walked back to his desk, took something off his bookshelf, and returned to me.

"I don't normally assign homework, Cara, but I think I have to make an exception in your case." He handed me a large, coffee table sized book. "Take this home and study every picture in it. I hope it will accustom you to what we're doing here."

I nodded. "Thank you."

After he walked away, I turned to my drawing again. I'd sketched the model's face in great detail. Nothing more.

When I got home after classes had ended for the day, I took Ralph for a walk first. I knew I was putting off the inevitable.

I kept my eyes open for the green van, but didn't see it parked anywhere in the neighborhood.

After I fed Ralph, I made myself a peanut butter sandwich, just to hold me over until dinner. Aware that I was still procrastinating, I curled up on the couch with Mr. Goldman's book.

The book was full of nudes! Some were drawn, some painted, and some photographed. Men, women, some old, some young, some middle-aged. I leafed through the book until I was accustomed to seeing naked people. But I still wasn't comfortable with the whole subject. I realized that was what Mr. Goldman hoped the book would do for me.

THE JOINING TREE

I went back to the first page and began again. I studied the arms, the hands, the legs, the feet, and yes, everything in between. I concentrated on the lines, the curves, the muscles, the light and the shadows.

Finally, feeling comfortable with all parts of the human body, I closed the book and looked at the clock. Crap. It was nine o'clock and I'd missed dinner. I wasn't sure I could face another peanut butter sandwich.

I had a brilliant solution. Grabbing my phone, I called the Lieutenant.

He answered right away. "Cara, is something wrong? Are you all right?"

I laughed. "I'm fine, Lieutenant. But I was studying and missed dinner. Have you eaten yet?"

I could hear his smile on the other end of the phone. "No, I haven't. How about I bring over a pizza?"

"Sounds great. I'll supply the sodas."

He arrived twenty minutes later, carrying an extra-large pizza covered with all kinds of toppings. I pulled two sodas out of the fridge and we sat down in the kitchen.

"So, tell me. What were you studying so intently that you forgot about dinner?"

I looked at him, slightly embarrassed. "Hard to explain, but after we eat, I'll show you."

He smiled, looking intrigued. "I can hardly wait."

When we'd demolished the pizza, I grabbed two more sodas and we moved to the living room. Aidan saw the huge book on the couch, sat down and picked it up. "This is what you were studying?"

"Yes. It's for my Life Drawing class."

He opened it and his eyebrows went straight up. "Whoa. Your Life Drawing class is drawing nudes, I take it. You're having trouble with this?"

"Yeah. All I've been able to draw is his face. In class, when I look at our model, all I want to do is throw him a towel."

He looked at me and laughed, his eyes crinkling at the corners. "You've never seen a naked man before?"

I shook my head. I felt my face getting hot. I didn't think the photos of Gavin counted.

Chuckling, he muttered, "Well, that answers two questions I was too polite to ask."

I rolled my eyes, still embarrassed. "Two questions?"

"I wondered if you had a boyfriend."

"Uh, no. Just good friends who happen to be boys."

Smiling, he stood up. "I'd better be going so you can get back to your studying."

"Thanks for the pizza, Aidan. By the way, you said *two* questions."

"He walked to the door, winked at me, and said, "I really am too polite to ask, but I think I already know the answer." He was chuckling as he ran down the steps.

"You can call me anytime, Cara."

In my Life Drawing class the next day, I carefully sketched the rest of our model's body, without adding too much detail.

Over my shoulder, Mr. Goldman said, "You're getting there, Cara. But more detail is needed. Keep the book for a few more days, okay?"

I nodded, taking a deep breath. Obviously, another night staring at nudes would be required. But I wouldn't skip dinner this time.

The rest of my classes were going well. I had a different instructor for Oil Painting this year, which made me happy. The subjects he gave us for our class assignments were interesting too. The one I was working on reminded me of Win Mason's street scenes, but I honestly thought Win's paintings were far better.

I continued to go home every weekend. Sure, I missed my parents, but that brand new studio was calling my name. I began bringing a few art supplies home with me on each trip.

One weekend I unlocked my studio to find a large, non-portable easel waiting for me, along with a couple of blank canvases. My father was right behind me. When he heard me gasp, he laughed. "This is a studio-warming gift from Francis Sullivan, Cara. He actually came here to see it. He rarely leaves Elvenwood, but he was delighted to learn you'd used his studio as a model for this one and wanted to see it."

"The easel was his idea. He had Garrett build it for you."

"Dad, I owe Francis so much. I really want to do something for him, just to say 'thank you.'"

"That's really not necessary, dear. But I have one suggestion. As far as I know, no one has ever painted a picture of *him*."

So I did. It would take months to complete because it had to be perfect.

I saw Amy every weekend. She and Gavin were still a steady couple, which I was glad to see. At school, I'd gotten used to living alone, but I still missed Gavin. He'd been a wonderful roommate, but he was happy now, and I felt he deserved to be.

Kevin didn't make it home for Thanksgiving, no surprise, but Sean did. He and his dad had pooled their funds and finally bought Sean a car of his own. He called me as soon as he arrived home to say, "Hey Beautiful, I've got something to show you!" Of course, he came right over.

When I opened the front door, he grabbed my hand with a big smile. "Come on, you've got to see this."

"This" was a vintage Cadillac, much older than we were, so old it actually had fins. It had obviously been someone's pride and joy because it was spotless.

"Sean, it's gorgeous. I'll bet it's been kept in someone's garage for the past forty or more years."

He beamed. "Yeah, it belonged to a client of dad's. The body was perfect, but it needed some engine work. While I was at school, my father turned it over to a mechanic who loves to work on vintage cars."

It was baby blue with a white interior and actually looked like a new car. "How's the gas mileage?"

He made an embarrassed face. "Uh, well, we don't talk about gas mileage, Cara. It takes a full tank to get me to and from school, so I'll have to continue doing construction work during the summers just to cover the gas. But it's okay, I love this car!"

Of course, he had to take me for a ride in it immediately. I ran inside to let my folks know where I was going, and my father came outside with me to see Sean's "new" car.

"This is a very impressive vehicle, Sean. I think I'd like to have one like it when I learn how to drive."

Sean's eyebrows went straight up. "You're going to learn to drive, Mr. Blackthorne?"

My dad grinned. "Yes, and if I succeed, I think I'll need a car this size."

"Have you told Mom yet?" I asked.

"Uh, well, no. I was thinking I'd take lessons like you did, and then surprise her after I get my driver's license." He looked momentarily unsure. "What do you think, Cara?"

I grinned. "She'll definitely be surprised, Dad."

Riding in Sean's Caddy was a real pleasure. It was even roomier than my car, and the genuine leather seats were soft the way only real leather became after years of use.

"Very comfy, Sean. I love it."

He chuckled. "Nice wide bench seat too. All kinds of comfort here." He grinned at me.

I rolled my eyes. "Yep, whatever you say." I hated to rain on his parade, but we wouldn't be getting *that* comfortable.

We had a fun Thanksgiving weekend. Before we left to go back to school on Sunday, Sean was already making plans for our Christmas vacation.

He wanted to spend some of that time riding in the forest, visiting Elvenwood, and maybe attending a few parties. It all sounded good to me as long as I had enough time to prepare artwork for a January Art Show in New York City. This one would be in Greenwich Village.

Miss Galen had called me to ask if I could prepare at least a dozen pieces to show at the gallery. "Cara, your name is becoming more well known, and we never know what will be popular from one year to the next, so I think we should strike while the iron is hot, as they say."

That was fine with me. The more of my artwork that sold, the closer I'd be to that Art Gallery I wanted to open in Thornewood.

Before I left school for our Christmas break, Aidan Fox stopped by to take me out to dinner. He'd been either calling me or stopping by my apartment every week or two. He said he just wanted to see how I was doing. The way a friend would.

But Christmas was only a week away, and he said he wanted to see me before I left for home. I suspected he had a gift for me, but that was okay because I had one for him too.

We enjoyed a good dinner at Rudy's, the stylish coffee shop he'd taken me to before. The restaurant was nicely decorated for Christmas with a live tree in one corner. Twinkle lights were strung up everywhere, reminding me of my parents' wedding in our backyard. That brought back another memory, one I was trying to forget.

Aidan noticed the change in my mood. "What's wrong, Cara? You were smiling a minute ago. Is it the Christmas decorations?"

I shook my head. "No, it's all the twinkle lights. So pretty, but so deceiving." I hadn't meant to say that. I looked up at him. "Can we talk about something else?"

"Sure." He hesitated. "Cara, I don't know how close you are with your friends at school, but if you ever need someone to talk to, I'm here." He smiled. "I may not be able to solve your problems, but I can always listen."

"Thanks, Aidan. But some problems can't be solved, you know?"

He looked at me, his light eyes sympathetic. "I know. Now cheer up. I have a little something for you." He pulled a small box out of his jacket pocket and handed it to me.

"Aidan, you didn't have to do this."

"No, but I saw it in a window and couldn't resist. You'll see why." His light eyes sparkled, crinkling at the corners.

I took the pretty silk bow off the box and opened it. I couldn't help smiling. He was right. It was perfect, a small artist's palette, studded with tiny colored stones to represent the different paint colors daubed on a palette. It was only about an inch and a half wide and had a pin on the back.

"Aidan, this is beautiful, perfect for me." I looked up at him. "This was so thoughtful. Thank you." I immediately pinned it to my sweater.

He was smiling, clearly pleased that I liked it. "It was my pleasure, Cara."

"When you take me home, you'll have to come in. I have something for you too!"

He looked surprised. "That wasn't necessary."

I grinned at him. "I know." His thoughtful gift had put me in a much better mood.

When we got back to the yellow house on Birch Street, he followed me in.

"Have a seat, Aidan. I'll be right back." I went into the bedroom and pulled a paper-wrapped canvas out of my closet."

I returned to the living room and handed it to him. "Merry Christmas, Aidan."

He took the paper off carefully to find a pen and ink drawing of himself. Both eyebrows shot up in surprise. I'd drawn him just the way he'd looked when I got back from summer vacation. He'd been leaning against his car casually with his arms crossed against his chest, looking serious.

To say he looked shocked would be putting it mildly.

"Is this the way you see me?" he asked.

I looked at my drawing again and grinned. "Aidan, I think this is the way everyone sees you."

He looked at me and laughed. "Then why aren't gorgeous women lined up at my door?"

"You mean they *aren't*?" I pretended to look shocked.

He chuckled, looking back at my drawing, shaking his head.

"I now have an original Cara Blackthorne. This is an incredible gift, Cara. Many thanks." He still looked surprised, as though he couldn't believe what he was looking at.

"You're very welcome. I enjoyed working on it."

He stood up and I walked him to the door where he put the drawing down and gave me a gentle hug, dropping a kiss on top of my head.

"You're really one of a kind, Cara," he whispered. "Have a wonderful Christmas. I'll see you when you get back."

He ran down the steps, out to his car, waving as he got into it.

As I watched him drive away, I looked up to see the first snow of the season begin to fall.

Mother Nature wanted to make sure we knew it was really winter. The snow came down for a day and a half.

Yes, it created a pretty landscape, but it was only acceptable to me if the roads cleared before Christmas. Mother Nature must have heard me complaining. I finally made it home on Christmas Eve.

This was my third Christmas with my father, an event that never failed to thrill me. He was the best gift I had ever received. Being greeted with one of his enveloping hugs made my life almost perfect.

But even my father couldn't make me forget what was missing.

I was able to spend some quality time with both Kevin and Amy, but not at the same time, of course. Sean and I double-dated with Amy and Gavin at the Pizza Palace one night. Gavin had never been there before. He loved both the pizza and the oldies music. He and Amy were on the dance floor most of the evening.

Sean was unfailingly polite to Gavin, but not actually friendly. When I asked why, he said, "Because of Gavin, you were physically hurt at least twice, Cara. I understand about his mother, but this last time, there really was no excuse."

"Oh. Well, if I could forgive him, I don't see why you can't."

His expression was totally serious. He put one arm around me and looked me in the eye. "You obviously don't put as high a value on your own life and well being as I do," he said softly.

I had no answer for that, so I kissed him.

It didn't snow again, so a few days after Christmas Sean and I rode to Elvenwood. Storm showed me how happy he was to see me by stamping his hooves on the frozen ground and blowing into my hair until I asked him to let me climb on. Sean was laughing as he sat on Cloud's back, watching Storm's antics.

Riding during the winter months wasn't nearly as much fun as it was during the rest of the year. It was too darn cold. Sean and I both wore layers upon layers of warm clothing, but by the time we reached Elvenwood, we were both shivering. That ended when we passed through Elvenwood's gateway. The air temperature was noticeably warmer, and, as always, there was magic in the air.

We rode the greys directly to the stable and left them with Will, who greeted me by lifting me off the ground as he looked me over, saying, "You still haven't grown, lass. I guess there's no hope, is there?"

I had to laugh. Will's sense of humor was so transparent. "Oh, I don't know, Will. I fully expect to wake up one morning and find I'm as big as my father! It's only a matter of time, you know. Now please put me back on the ground."

Will laughed, finally putting me down.

He greeted Sean by telling him it was getting harder and harder to tell him and Conor apart.

Sean just grinned.

After lunch in the dining hall, we walked to Francis Sullivan's studio. I'd finally finished my pen and ink drawing of him and planned to give it to him that day. Admittedly, I was a little nervous.

Sean asked, "What are you worried about? I saw your drawing, and it's a perfect likeness of Francis. I think he'll love it."

I knocked on Francis' studio door and heard, "Come in, Cara." I had to laugh. He'd recognized my knock, which I had to explain to Sean.

Francis was wiping paint off his hands as he came to the door to greet us.

"It's so good to see you both," he said with a smile. "What have you brought with you today? You know, you don't have to bring your work to me for approval any longer, but I do enjoy seeing it."

I put my leather portfolio on his table and pulled out everything I'd been working on, with my pen and ink drawing of him placed on the bottom.

He looked at each one carefully, nodding and smiling, until he came to the last one.

Looking up at me in shock, he said, "Cara! You drew a picture of me. Why?"

Oh, crap. He's offended. Why did I listen to my father?

Nervously, I answered, "I wanted to do something to thank you for that beautiful easel you had made for me. My dad told me that no one had ever painted a picture of you. I thought you might like to have one." I'd drawn him in profile, at his easel, brush in hand, sunlight shining through the skylight.

THE JOINING TREE

I was relieved when he began smiling. "Cara, dear, it's a wonderful gift, one I'm not sure I deserve. For you to use your gift to draw *me*—it was so unexpected and a complete surprise. Thank you, dear." He leaned down and kissed my cheek.

I took my drawing from him, saying, "I'm taking this to the wood shop to have it framed, Francis. They'll bring it back to you when it's done."

He shook his head, actually looking embarrassed. "This is really too much, Cara, but I do thank you, most sincerely."

We said goodbye to Francis and walked over to the wood shop to see Garrett.

Grinning, Sean whispered in my ear, "I think he liked it!"

I nodded happily. "Yeah, I think he did."

When we walked into the wood shop, the smell of wood shavings filled the air, pine and maple predominantly. I loved the smell.

Garrett looked up from a cabinet he was building, and greeted me with a warm smile. "We haven't seen you in months, Cara. How do you like your new easel?"

"It's wonderful. I use it every weekend I'm home. And the smaller one you made for me gets a lot of use too. You do great work."

"Thank you. And what can I do for you today?"

I opened my portfolio and pulled out my drawing of Francis. Handing it to Garrett, I said, "I made this as a gift for Francis. Would you please make a suitable frame for it? I'll pay for it myself."

He looked at my drawing, his eyes widening. "Cara, this is wonderful! And I know just how I'll frame it. A simple lacquered black frame, I think." He looked up at me, beaming.

"You know, Francis has made so much money for our village. We all owe him a great deal. But he asks for nothing other than art supplies." He smiled. "It's about time someone did something special for him. I'll make sure everyone in the village gets a chance to see this."

"You will let me pay for the frame, won't you?"

He chuckled. "Yes, Cara. I'll send the bill to your father." I wasn't sure he was serious, but before I could ask, the door to the wood shop opened suddenly and I was being hugged so hard, I could barely breathe.

I heard, "Hello, cousin!" He finally let go and I turned to see my cousin Jason's smiling face. "Jason, it's good to see you too. I've missed you. You have to come over to Mom's house while I'm home from school."

He grinned, nodding. "I have the day off tomorrow, and I'd love to spend it with you."

"It's a date. Unfortunately, Sean and I should leave now. I don't want to ride through the forest in the dark, so I'll see you tomorrow."

After I received another bone-crushing hug, and Sean got a "guy-hug," we left for the stable.

As we walked from the wood shop, I said, "I'll have to come back another day. I still haven't seen Kathleen, or Gabe, or Ryan, or Arlynn. I hate these short winter days. It gets dark too early," I grumbled.

"You have time. You're home for another week, aren't you?"

"Yes. But if it snows again, I may not be able to get here." I was still grumbling.

He laughed. "Yeah, I forgot. You hate winter."

I spent most of the rest of my Christmas vacation in my studio, working on some watercolors for the January show in Soho. When Jason stopped by, that's where he found me.

"Cara, can you take a break for a little while so we can catch up?" His smile seemed a bit sad. "I hardly ever see you anymore. We never get a chance to talk."

He was right. "I'm sorry, Jason. Between school and getting artwork prepared for shows, I really don't have much free time. Besides working in the wood shop, what else have you been up to?"

He grinned. "Well, now that Amy's bakery is open again, I'm there a few times a week to buy donuts. Everyone there is so kind."

Of course they were. My cousin Jason was such a sweet young man, as beautiful as he was nice. Everyone who met him was at least a little in love with him.

"I still run errands for your father frequently, and that gives me a chance to come into town. The people I met during your last year in high school always remember me and stop to chat."

I smiled. Of course they'd remember Jason.

He confided, "You know how much I enjoy the human world, cousin. I think if I had a job *here*, rather than in Elvenwood, I would be perfectly happy!"

Jason had once admitted that life in Elvenwood was simply too much of the same old, same old, year after year. He longed for more challenge and more excitement. And that gave me an idea.

"Jason, I have something in mind that might appeal to you. I want to open my own Art Gallery here in town. My father and Mr. Callahan want to be my partners in the Gallery. I think it will probably be a year or more before we're able to open, but when we do, we'll need someone to both work in the Gallery when I'm not there, and to make frames for the work we display. You could handle both."

His eyes were huge. "That would be wonderful! I would love to work in your Gallery, and I've become a fair woodworker too. Making frames would be easy."

He threw his arms around me and squeezed. I gasped. "Jason, can't breathe . . ."

He was grinning. "Sorry, cousin. But what you just described would be a dream come true for me. I can't thank you enough!"

"Well, I'll have to discuss it with my father and Mr. Callahan, but I think they'll agree that you'd be perfect for the job." I was grinning too. I'd never seen Jason so happy.

He grabbed my hand. "Cousin, this calls for a celebration. Do you think you could call for pizza?"

It still amused me how much the Elves loved pizza.

"It's lunchtime. Great idea. Let's go back to the house and I'll order the pizza."

I'm convinced that my father is occasionally psychic. He came in the back door with a big smile. "I had a feeling you'd be getting pizza, Cara. Will there be enough for three?"

Smiling, I called the Pizza shop back and asked them to add another large pizza to my order.

Over our pizza lunch, I told my dad my idea for the Gallery. Much to Gavin's delight, my father agreed wholeheartedly.

"Excellent, Jason. I'm afraid you'll have to be patient, but I'm glad we've finally found work that will make you happy."

He stood, smiling at both of us. "I have to leave for my camp now. Thank you for the pizza, Cara. It was wonderful, as always."

I grinned. "Well, thank *you*, Dad. You're paying for it."

One of his black eyebrows went up. "I am?"

"I put it on Mom's credit card."

He nodded with a rueful smile. "Yes, I guess I am. I'll see you at dinner tonight, dear. Jason, are you staying for a while?"

"Yes, Uncle Brian. Cara and I have a few more things to talk about."

After my father left, I looked at Jason. "What else do you want to talk about?"

He was quiet for a few seconds. "Cousin, it's been over two years. You know what I'm talking about." He wasn't wearing his usual smile.

I looked him in the eye. "Is that why you were trying to get Sean and me closer together at the wedding?" I was seriously annoyed.

He nodded. "Cara, don't you think it's time to move on? I want to see you happy again."

I snorted. "Well, that isn't likely, Jason. And there doesn't seem to be anything you or I can do about it."

"You and Sean used to be close. That could always happen again. He loves you very much, you know."

I shook my head decisively. "Jason, do you really think it's fair of me to encourage Sean when I already know I can't give him what he wants and deserves?"

"Cousin, does he know that?"

"Yes, he does. I've been completely honest with him. He knows about Adam."

"Oh. Adam still has your heart."

I nodded. "You of all people have to understand what that means. I can't love anyone else, even if I wanted to. Although, to be honest, I'm becoming more and more angry with Adam every year that goes by."

Jason shook his head. "I guess I can understand that. When he left, I really didn't think he'd stay away so long. I thought he'd probably come back once you were out of high school."

I looked at him. "Jason, I have to face the fact that he may not plan to come back at all. He may be making his life somewhere else. Maybe he met someone else, someone more his age."

"I suppose that's possible, although I would have bet against it a year ago." He shook his head again, clearly sad for me.

I didn't need any reminders.

CHAPTER 27

My father accompanied me to the show at the Soho Gallery. As usual, he attracted as much attention as the artwork did! The film director from California was there along with a group of other tanned and beautiful people.

He spotted me and approached me with a big smile. "Cara Blackthorne, how nice to see you again. You know, I've spoken to several gallery owners in Los Angeles who would love to show your work. You really must make the trip one day soon."

I thanked him, explaining that I was still in Art school and that I didn't have the time to travel at present.

He handed me his card. "As soon as you can make the time, Cara, just give me a call and I'll see that you receive invitations from the best art galleries in California."

I thanked him again, and he left with a wave and rejoined his friends.

My father whispered in my ear. "How far is California?"

I whispered back, "About three thousand miles, Dad. I'd have to fly there."

"Oh. I've never flown. Have you?"

"Nope. But I think I'll have to eventually. Will you go with me?"

He looked unsure. "In a plane? How long would it take to fly to California?"

"Mmm. I think it takes about five hours, Dad."

"Is that all? To go three thousand miles?"

I grinned. "Jet planes are very fast. You might enjoy it."

He smiled. "I might at that. I do like speed."

The Soho show was successful, Miss Galen was extremely happy, and my bank account was growing nicely. On the train ride home, my father and I talked about the proposed Thornewood Art Gallery until I could actually see it in my mind. I loved the entire concept, although the name I saw over the door was "The Blackthorne Gallery."

I had finally gotten used to living alone at school, although it had taken a few months. The peace and quiet gave me ample time to paint at night. Miss Galen had scheduled me for another gallery showing in April. I got so involved in my painting, I often forgot about dinner. Paula and Lily began calling me the hermit!

One night I heard several forceful knocks on my apartment door, Ralph was barking, and it finally dawned on me there was someone out there. I'd been completely lost in my work.

I opened my door to find Joel standing there with a container that smelled suspiciously like spaghetti.

He smiled a bit uncertainly. "We were really beginning to be afraid you might starve to death, Cara. You've missed dinner three times this week."

Looking me up and down quickly, he added, "You're losing weight, you know."

I looked at the clock in the living room. It was eight o'clock. I'd totally lost track of the time.

I smiled. "Come on in, Joel. I'm afraid I do lose track of time when I'm drawing or painting. It used to happen a lot back home. I'd be in the woods drawing, and my mother would stand on the back porch calling me until she was hoarse."

I shrugged. "I've always missed a lot of meals."

He nodded as though he had already known this. "Well, I come bearing spaghetti, so if you're hungry, I'd suggest we sit down and eat it."

"Okay, Mom. You can bring it into the kitchen. Do you want soda or water?"

He set the bowl of spaghetti down on the table in the nook and sat, grinning at me. "Water please. I don't suppose you have any wine, do you?"

"No, afraid not. I have to be able to function after we've eaten. Wine would just put me to sleep."

He looked curious. "You don't eat much. Do you ever sleep? I can see how productive you are as an artist." He pointed at the far wall, where several paintings were standing up, waiting to be framed.

"Of course I sleep. But my agent has been keeping me busy, booking me into art galleries all over New York State."

I laughed. "What's that saying? You snooze, you lose!"

He shook his head. "Every artist I know would like to be as busy as you are. I don't mean to be crass, but what are you doing with all your money?"

"It's all going into the bank. By next year, my father and I are planning on opening an art gallery right in my hometown. I want to feature local artists as well as my own work."

"Wow. That's quite a goal. But we've all been wondering why you've stayed at Barrett. You're already a successful artist."

I'd finished filling up on spaghetti, so I pushed myself away from the table slightly. "Someone else asked that same question, but I don't feel like there's nothing left to learn. You know?

"I haven't done anything with acrylic paints yet, I haven't attempted any photography so far, and I still have trouble understanding abstract art."

THE JOINING TREE

He laughed. "You must be talking about my abstract paintings. To be honest, I don't always understand it myself. It's like an indescribable energy that just takes over when I'm in a particular mood."

Shrugging, he said, "It's probably not marketable, but it's what I most love to do. Other than staring at beautiful girls, that is." He grinned at me.

"I didn't just come over to feed you, Cara. I wanted to ask if you'd like to visit the Syracuse Art Museum with me some weekend? There's a lot to see there."

"I'd really like to, Joel, but I go home every weekend. I have a studio there and can get a lot of work done over the weekend."

His eyebrows shot up. "Don't you ever take some time off to just, I don't know, have fun?"

I understood what he was asking, but I wanted to be perfectly clear.

"Joel, I don't really date, if that's what you're getting at. I have long-time friends at home that I hang out with occasionally, but that's the extent of my social life. Art is my life. That's all I want to concentrate on right now."

He shook his head as though he understood, but there was curiosity in his eyes. "Lily did say something about a guy in your life, someone you don't see anymore. Is he the reason you don't date?"

I liked Joel. I'd liked him since the day I'd met him at Barrett's Book Store, when I'd been stuck here overnight two years ago. So I would be honest, more honest than usual.

"For the most part, yes. All I have to give anyone is friendship. That's not what most guys are looking for. I've thrown myself into my work because there's nothing else I *can* do."

"And I haven't been that honest with anyone else, Joel. Are we still friends?"

He smiled. "Of course we are. But I'll be honest too. I've been looking at you across the dinner table in the Café for almost two years, and I've wanted to ask you out before, but something always stopped me. I think I knew what you'd say."

Ralph had been circling my feet for a while and finally started whining pitifully.

I slapped myself in the head. "Oh, crap. I completely forgot to take Ralph out for his walk. It's kind of late, but would you be willing to keep us company tonight? I usually walk him before it gets dark."

"Sure, no problem. It'll give us more time to talk." He grinned at me.

I put Ralph's leash on, and we left, walking down Birch Street. Joel was fun to talk with—he was interested in so many things, and he had a good sense of humor. He'd had the same kind of problem with our first year Oil Painting instructor, Miss Alvarez. His solution was to simply ignore her and do his own thing with oils.

I explained where I'd found the best help, and his mouth dropped open.

"Does Mr. Sullivan teach any classes?"

"No, I'm afraid not. He's a bit of a recluse, but he's a good friend of my father's."

"Oh. So that's why he was willing to help you. Cara, you are lucky in more ways than one." He shook his head. "I think I'm jealous."

I agreed with him. "Yes, I am lucky. And I know it. Francis Sullivan has been my mentor for a couple of years. He introduced me to his agent, and the rest is history. Nothing more than dumb luck, Joel."

He looked at me and chuckled. "I wouldn't go that far. I've seen your work. It's top notch. I might even call your pen and ink drawings magical."

I took a quick glance at him, to see if he meant anything by that last statement, but it appeared to be wholly innocent.

On our way back, I saw that green van again as it turned off Birch Street. "I keep seeing that van, but I've never seen the driver. He did me a favor once and I've never had an opportunity to thank him."

Joel said, "Oh, I've seen him. He does gardening over on campus most weekends. But I think he has another job during the week."

"So that's why the landscaping on campus looks so much better this year."

He nodded. "Yeah. And I think he's done some gardening all around this neighborhood." He chuckled. "The guy obviously has a green thumb."

"Have you ever met him?"

"No. He just waves when he sees me. Quiet kind of guy. I've never heard him speak. I guess he might be an illegal, doesn't speak much English. Who knows?"

We'd reached my house, and I turned to thank Joel for keeping me company.

"No problem, Cara. Feel free to call me whenever you need a dog-walking companion." He laughed. "I'm always available."

The look in his eyes told me he was a bit more than just "available."

We said good night and I took Ralph inside. Thanks to the long walk and the spaghetti dinner, I was actually tired enough to go to bed. I took one last look at the canvas on my easel, decided it needed more white paint, brushed my teeth, pulled off my clothes and climbed into my bed.

I guess I'd been too tired to dream these past few weeks, but tonight was a different story. It was more than just his dark blue eyes that haunted my dreams that night. I again saw him leaning against a tree at the edge of the woods, watching me, his face hard to read. When I tried to approach him, he held out one arm, as if warning me not to come too close. I heard his soft voice say, "Not yet, love. Not yet."

In my dream I was frustrated, crying out, "Why?"

There was no answer as he gradually faded away.

I didn't wake up in tears this time. I woke up punching my pillow, angry because I didn't understand why he'd decided we couldn't be together.

I promised myself there would be no more tears. I gave my pillow one more angry punch. I was through crying over Adam Wolfe.

THE JOINING TREE

The rest of my second year at Barrett went smoothly. I enjoyed all of my classes, even learning that a simple bowl of fruit could be beautiful on canvas.

Having dinner in the Café with my small group of friends was a relaxing way to end each day, as long as I remembered *when* it was time for dinner. I always lost track of time when I was painting or drawing. Either Joel or Paula would sometimes bring dinner over to my apartment, or Aidan Fox would surprise me with a pizza. One way or another, I rarely went hungry.

I continued to drive home every weekend, always anxious to get into my roomy studio with its wide windows and bright skylights. I felt I was doing my best work there.

As the weather became warmer, I began spending time on the flagstone patio behind my studio, enjoying a cup of tea as the sun went down. I knew there were Elves in the woods at the rear of my property, and I occasionally had the feeling I was being watched. But it felt "friendly" and no one ever came out of the woods to join me.

Before I knew it, it was time for Barrett's Yearly Art Show, and I had to decide what I wanted to put on display. I already had a few watercolors and some pen and ink drawings set aside for the next art exhibit I'd been invited to, so I wasn't forced to come up with something new.

Paula came over to my apartment after school one afternoon to help me decide what to display. She fell in love with my "Elf drawings," ones that Ian had modeled for months ago. She helped me decide they were the ones I should display at the Art Show.

"Cara, the children hiding in these drawings look like faeries! Don't tell me they're real children."

I laughed. "No, purely imaginary."

She added, "They're like a little secret, carefully hidden in the trees. I love them!"

Looking sideways at me, she asked, "Are you sure they're not real?"

"No, they're not. The woods where I do a lot of my drawing have a rather magical atmosphere, and I think that's what inspired these particular drawings."

I hoped that explanation would satisfy her.

Thanks to warm, sunny weather on the day of Barrett's Art Show, we had a record crowd in attendance. There were even art lovers from neighboring states who had come to enjoy the artwork on display.

My parents drove up for the day, my father, as usual, drawing as much attention as my artwork did! I walked them over to Paula's display so she could meet them. After being introduced to my father, she was definitely starry-eyed for a little while. My friends usually were.

Mom was laughing out loud at Paula's irreverent political cartoons. My father had no interest at all in human politics, so he didn't really understand them, although he told Paula she was very talented. We left her beaming.

We walked around the campus, enjoying the beautiful weather as well as all the beautiful artwork. We stopped at Joel's display, an intensely colorful abstract oil painting. When I introduced my parents to Joel, my father said, "You've used extremely aggressive colors, Joel. May I ask what you were thinking when you painted this?"

I closed my eyes in embarrassment, but Joel grinned. "Actually, Mr. Blackthorne, I was feeling extremely aggressive when I painted it! I'd had a disagreement with one of my instructors. It was either hit him or paint something like this. I guess you can see what I chose."

My father chuckled and patted Joel's shoulder. "Good choice, son."

My mother smiled at my friend. "I understand we have you to thank for not allowing Cara to go hungry too often. We're grateful, Joel."

Joel's face reddened slightly, but he smiled at Mom. "It's been my pleasure."

I took my parents to lunch at the Café where several kinds of salads were on the menu. Mom chose a veggie salad while Dad and I enjoyed a pasta salad listed as "Antipasto Pasta Salad." My father had already discovered pepperoni and was delighted to find it in his salad, along with salami, ham, olives, and provolone.

We had a leisurely lunch before I walked them back to Mom's car. When Dad walked to the driver's side door, I stopped short, suitably wide-eyed. I looked at my mother, who was showing distinct signs of stress.

"Your father has his driver's license, dear." She didn't sound happy about it, but my father was wearing a huge smile.

"I'm trying to convince your mother that we need a larger car. Much larger. Today was the first time I drove on the highway coming up here. We're allowed to drive at a much higher speed on highways," he added happily.

I looked at my mother. Her eyes were closed.

"Well, congratulations on getting your license, Dad. Please take it easy on your way home, okay? You don't want to frazzle Mom's nerves."

Mom looked at me and mouthed, "Thank you."

I hugged them both. I was relieved to see my father pulling away from the curb slowly, his arm waving at me out the window. I sincerely hoped he wouldn't start collecting speeding tickets. That was a legitimate worry because I knew my father loved speed.

THE JOINING TREE

And just like that, my second year at the Barrett Institute of Art was over. It had been a good year, as far as I was concerned. I'd learned a lot, improved all my painting skills, and, best of all, no one had attacked me.

It had been a year *without* disasters. Yay, me!

And I had another birthday, my nineteenth. I was now legal plus one.

My "missing" bodyguard was still missing.

I was now convinced that he had no intention of returning, ever. And I was angry, very angry. If only he hadn't kissed me . . . I might have been able to move on.

Despite those feelings simmering deep inside me, it was a pretty good summer. I spent my days with my parents, and with Kevin and Amy, who were at least willing to be in the same space at the same time now.

Kevin and I continued to practice archery and knife-throwing throughout the summer, getting our speed back to where it had been. Occasionally Gavin joined us, although he and Kevin didn't have much to say to each other.

I wouldn't be seeing Sean at all this summer. He'd gotten a well-paid construction job up in Vermont for the summer and would be staying up there until he returned to Penn State at the end of August. I'd miss him, but I had to admit it would be better for him to be away. He was emailing me every couple of weeks and he sounded good.

I rode Storm a couple times a week and visited my friends in Elvenwood, along with Rowenna who liked to join Jason and me in the old orchard while he played his flute.

One day I wandered out to the old orchard by myself with my drawing pad and a few pens. I was only humming the dragon's song, but she heard me and joined me, landing on the ground close to me.

I'm glad you came alone today, Cara. I have news I want to share with you. Her rough voice sounded both worried and excited at the same time.

"What's wrong?" I asked.

Nothing is wrong. But I'm hoping the village won't see it as a threat.

"Rowenna, the entire village knows you're our friend. You have nothing to worry about."

Cara, if the village sees two dragons in the sky, might they see that as a threat?

"Two dragons? Do you mean that your mate has returned?" She'd waited patiently for him for so very long.

No, my mate has not returned. But I think my egg may be ready to hatch! Although for dragons, the hatching can take many months.

"That's wonderful! This is such exciting news. You must be very happy. I'm happy for you, Rowenna."

Cara, please let your father know what is happening. I don't want any of the Elves frightened when my offspring is big enough to fly.

"Okay, I'll tell him. And I think he'll be happy for you too."

Thank you, my small friend. Will you sing for me before I have to leave?

As I sang the dragon's song, I couldn't help visualizing Rowenna flying in the skies above Blackthorne Forest with a small dragon by her side. The very thought made me smile.

When her song was finished, she took to the sky, wrapping her magic around me like a soft cloak. I watched her until she disappeared behind the purple mountains.

My father was in Elvenwood for the day, so I joined him for tea and told him about Rowenna's hatchling-to-be.

"It was considerate of her to let us know, dear. Of course, I'm happy for her. No one, not even a dragon, should be alone for so long."

When he realized what he'd said, he looked at me, then quickly added, "Rowenna was friendless for many years, dear. That's all I meant."

I snorted. Of course, he was correct. I'd never been "friendless." Rowenna obviously had tons more patience than I had.

"Cara, please let Rowenna know that I will need to speak with her before her hatchling is born. I do have concerns about our village's safety. I'll need to know how long it will take to train a baby dragon to understand that we are friends, and that we're not fireproof."

The sky had turned gray, not a good day for any more drawing outdoors. Instead I walked over to Kathleen's cottage. She had been busy all summer, so my visits with her had been brief.

She was sitting in front of her cottage, making notes in a journal, when I walked up.

She looked up with a big smile. "Cara, dear, it's so nice to see you. It's a slow day for me, so sit down and we can visit. I've had no broken bones or stitches to deal with today." She laughed. "The youngsters must all be too tired to get into trouble!"

I smiled. She was always so cheerful; I really needed cheerful people around me today.

"Cara, I heard about your new studio, but I haven't seen it yet. When are you going to invite me over?" she asked with a smile.

"You're welcome anytime, Kathleen. You don't need an invitation."

"Well, I haven't wanted to interrupt you when you're at work. Francis has told me how well your artwork has been doing at all those shows. Still in school and already a success," she said, shaking her head. "I would really love to go to one of your shows and see what it's like. It must be exciting to see your artwork making so many people happy."

I snorted. "I haven't thought of it that way, Kathleen. But it definitely makes my agent happy."

"Cara, I think you may be missing the most important point."

I must have looked confused because she explained. "If someone loves one of your drawings or paintings so much, they're willing to pay a lot of money for it, don't you think seeing it hanging in their own home will make them happy every time they look at it?"

"Well, yeah, I guess so. That is a nice way to think about the artwork that's been sold. I've been so focused on saving enough money to open an Art Gallery in town, I think I've been pretty mercenary lately."

She nodded. "I understand. But it may bring you even more satisfaction when you think of your artwork hanging in someone's home where it can be enjoyed every day."

"Thank you, Kathleen. You've put things in a much better perspective." I smiled. "I needed that."

She poured a cup of tea for me from the teapot sitting on the bench next to her. "Cara dear, I'm very happy your art is going so well, but I've been wondering how you've been feeling in *other* ways. I couldn't help noticing that you don't smile as often as you used to. Are you still missing Adam?"

That question startled me. Was I that transparent?

"Yes, I still miss him. But I'm angry with him too. It's been almost three years, Kathleen. For a while, I thought there was a chance he'd return when I grew up. But I've been "legal" in the human world since I turned eighteen. I'm nineteen now and there's been no word from him. I don't believe he's coming back, and that still hurts."

"You gave him your heart, didn't you, dear?" There was a slight frown on her normally cheerful face.

I nodded. "It wasn't a choice I made, Kathleen. It just happened, and it can't be undone now."

I felt my nose getting hot, a sure sign I was going to cry. Damn him!

"I'd like to move on. I really would. But I don't think I have enough love left inside me to give to someone else."

I could see the sympathy on her face.

She moved closer and put one arm around me, gently pulling my head to her shoulder.

"Cara dear, I know what you're feeling. There was a time when I thought I'd given my heart to Kelly O'Rourke, but before I could find out if he felt the same, he was banished from Elvenwood. Yes, he's back now, but we're both so much older, I think we've both changed too much. Instead, I dedicated my life to healing those who are hurt."

She sighed. "Like you, I don't know if I have enough love left inside me to give to one man. So much of my love goes into healing others. And you've been putting your love into the beautiful pictures you draw and paint."

Hugging me, she whispered, "The love is still there inside you, Cara. When the time is right, you *will* give it again."

I doubted that but I didn't have the heart to argue.

My last night at home was spaghetti night with my parents and Kevin, who'd been joining us for dinner all summer. He'd be leaving in two days, and I'd miss him.

After we'd cleaned up the kitchen, Kevin and I went out on the back porch. The sun was already behind the trees, even though it hadn't set yet. The peaceful forest was a lovely mixture of gold and green. All we heard were a few birds calling to each other before nesting for the night.

As we relaxed in Mom's deck chairs, Kevin sighed. "I'm gonna miss this, short stuff. Once I'm back in school, I'll have to say goodbye to the whole concept of relaxing. I knew college would be harder than high school, but I honestly had no idea *how hard*!"

I sympathized with him. The dark circles under his hazel eyes were proof how hard he'd been working. Even two months at home hadn't erased them.

"I guess Art school has been a walk in the park by comparison, Kev. Probably because I really love my work. This is exactly what I'd want to be doing even if I wasn't in school. This will be my last year, you know."

He groaned. "Two more years for me. More if I decide to go for my Master's." He shook his head. "I think I may put that off for a year or two. It would be nice to have a life again."

"Are you and Amy at least talking again?"

"Not really. Just 'hello and how are you'. I guess she's still wrapped up in Gavin. He's a lucky guy/Elf/Halfling/whatever." He snorted. "I'm such a shmuck."

He turned and looked at me. "Cara, to be honest, I don't think Amy and I ever had that *'mate'* thing that you had with Adam. But it would be nice if we could be good friends again. I miss that."

"Do you want me to put in a good word for you, Kev?"

"Yeah, why not. It's been long enough, she shouldn't still be mad at me. Should she?"

"I doubt it. She seems to be happy, and there's no reason she wouldn't want you to be happy too. I guess."

He glanced over at me again, half a smile on his face. "Not sure about that, are you? Red does know how to carry a grudge." I heard a deep sigh.

"I'll talk to her, Kev."

"Thanks, short stuff."

The following morning I packed up my car for the return trip to Syracuse. For my birthday, Mom had gifted me with a new down-filled comforter for winter nights. Since she'd bought it in the summer, it had been on sale, half-price, which thrilled her bargain-happy heart. What thrilled me was the extra warmth I could look forward to!

My father had given me the gift I was now wearing. He'd had two small pieces of green jade cut into hearts and crafted into earrings for me.

I'd decided I would never take them off. The first time I put them on, he grinned. "They match your eyes perfectly, Cara."

"I love them, Dad. Thank you."

Amy and Kevin had both given me new art supplies for my birthday, which I really needed. I'd been using up my supplies at a rapid pace.

After exchanging warm hugs from both my loving parents, I fastened Ralph into his harness in the back seat, and we drove out of Thornewood.

Just before we reached the highway, I had an uneasy feeling. I looked around, but there was no car behind me, and I decided I was letting old fears creep into my head again.

I shook my head, slipped an Ed Sheeran CD into my player, sped up and sang along all the way to Syracuse. I replayed my favorite, "Perfect," at least five times. As I turned on Birch Street, "Hearts Don't Break Around Here" began to play. I pulled up in front of the yellow house, glad to turn that one off.

After unleashing Ralph from the back seat, I watched as he made a mad dash for the nearest tree. Once that chore had been taken care of, he ran up to the front door and barked, obviously alerting Laurie that her favorite Boxer was back.

I had to laugh as I unloaded my car, setting everything on the sidewalk and watching my dog at the same time. Ralph sat in front of the door politely, his little tail wagging at top speed. When Laurie opened the door, he dashed in, ran circles around her, and when she bent down to pet him, he immediately licked her face. She was laughing too as she enjoyed all his doggy affection.

She finally was able to get through the door to help me bring all my stuff in. It still took us two trips, but once everything was back in my apartment, we went upstairs for tea and she made lunch for us.

When she sat down, she said, "Hard to believe this is your last year here, Cara. I'll certainly miss you and Ralph."

I grinned. "Well, you still have to put up with us for at least nine more months, Laurie. I'll try to stay out of trouble until then, but there are no guarantees."

She smiled, one eyebrow raised. "Well, you should know that a certain police lieutenant stopped by last week, asking when you'd be back. I know, I know, you're *just friends,*' but I really think the handsome lieutenant has a bit of a crush on you."

My smile disappeared. "Oh, I hope not. All I can give him is my friendship. And I don't want to lose him as a friend."

She looked surprised. "Cara, in the two years you've lived here, I don't think you've had even one date, which I've always found puzzling."

I looked down at my sandwich, shrugging. "Laurie, I'll tell you the truth. My heart already belongs to someone who's not around anymore. It's not fair to anyone else for me to date when all I can offer anyone is friendship."

"Oh no, Cara. I hope you don't mean that he died?"

I shook my head. "No. He simply left town without even a goodbye. That was almost three years ago."

"And you haven't gotten over him yet?"

I snorted. "I guess I'm what they call "a one-man woman.""

Now she was shaking her head. "Cara, you're much too young to give up on serious relationships. Especially when it's already been three years." She chuckled. "You need to get back on the proverbial horse, dear."

I tried to smile. I knew that wasn't going to happen. That proverbial horse had taken my heart with him, wherever he'd gone.

After I thanked Laurie for lunch, Ralph and I went downstairs and I began to put my stuff away and get organized. Once my clothes and art supplies had been put away and I'd made my bed and put fresh towels in the bathroom, the cozy apartment looked like I'd never left. One thing was missing: Food.

I checked the cupboards and made a list. It was late afternoon by then, still partly sunny although some clouds had begun rolling in. I couldn't procrastinate because I wouldn't have any dinner, unless there was some way to turn mustard and crackers into dinner. Even I wasn't that creative.

I stuck my list into my pocket, grabbed my purse and keys, and told Ralph I'd be back in under an hour. I was still in shorts, sandals and a t-shirt but I didn't feel like changing my clothes just to go to the grocery store. Since I was only shopping for one, it wouldn't take long.

By the time I got into my car, the sun was completely covered by clouds. Fortunately, they weren't black, stormy clouds, so I figured I could cope with a few raindrops. I told myself storms didn't scare me anymore.

The parking lot at Family Foods was almost full. I looked at the clock in the car and realized most people were probably on their way home from work at that time.

Oh well. I had to park all the way at the rear of the lot. I didn't have the patience to drive around the lot until something closer opened up. Besides, it wasn't raining yet.

I locked my car and jogged through the parking lot to the main entrance, grabbed a cart and started going up and down the aisles, tossing groceries into the cart. Since I still hadn't learned to cook, my food choices were fairly simple: Cereal, milk, bread, cold cuts, bacon, bagels, tomatoes, microwave dinners, and a few condiments. I included a can of vanilla nut coffee. Couldn't forget the coffee. On my way to the cashier, I grabbed a bag of Oreo's and threw them into the cart too. As far as I was concerned, all the basic food groups had been covered.

I breezed through the cashier's Express line quickly and headed for the door. Of course, it was now raining, and it was more than a drizzle. Everyone was rushing through the parking lot heading for their cars, and most of the cars moving through the lot had their lights on. The parking lot was a madhouse, and I was again getting that uncomfortable being watched feeling.

THE JOINING TREE

As I rushed through the crowded lot to the rear where my car was parked, I thought I saw a green van drive past the store slowly. Without thinking, I stuck one arm up and waved. Then, of course, I realized it could have been anybody. I laughed at myself as I unlocked the trunk of my car and started setting my grocery bags inside.

Thanks to the rain, which was coming down harder now, I hadn't noticed the brown van parked next to me, its motor running.

I jumped into my car, wishing I had a towel, and noticed an envelope tucked under my windshield wiper. Irritated, I got out again and grabbed the envelope as the van next to me backed out of its space. I hoped I hadn't got even more rained on just to learn about a sale on anti-freeze.

Starting my car and turning on my lights, I opened the heavy manila envelope to find a typewritten letter that was actually addressed to me. I suddenly felt cold, goose bumps up and down both arms.

I read: *"Dear Miss Blackthorne, I was driving the car that hit you. Please don't worry. I mean you no harm now. I never wanted to hurt you, and I was relieved when I learned that you weren't seriously injured. I am not a criminal, just a foolish man who got into trouble and was trying to find a way out.*

Even though I relocated and changed my name, I received a message from Nick Romanov recently. Apparently, there's nowhere I can hide. He swears he'll get even with me and with you. I thought you should be warned.

Signed: A Friend

I folded the letter and put it back in its envelope, my heart pounding. I closed my eyes for a few minutes, willing my heart to calm down. When I felt more in control, I grabbed my phone and called Lieutenant Fox.

"Hi, Cara, back from summer vacation, or are you calling from Thornewood?"

He sounded happy to hear from me. I suspected that was about to change.

CHAPTER 28

After I told the Lieutenant about the letter I'd found on my car, he said, "Stay there, lock your doors. I'll be there in ten minutes."

It wasn't even ten minutes when he pulled up next to me. I unlocked my doors and he got in next to me. I handed him the envelope, leaned back against the headrest, and closed my eyes. He read the letter, and I heard him exhale. Then he chuckled.

"You've been back in town for what, half a day?"

"Yeah. Since lunchtime. Twice today I had that uneasy feeling that I was being watched, but I told myself I was imagining things. Guess not."

"Well, Cara," waving the letter at me, "it doesn't sound like this guy is any threat. He actually took the time to warn you, which surprises me."

"Aidan, even though Romanov is in prison, this means he can still hurt me, right?"

"Only if he actually has any influence outside prison. I'll have to contact Chief O'Donnell in Thornewood to see if he's heard anything."

I groaned. "And the Chief will call my parents. Will this *ever* be over?"

He reached over and patted my hand. "Of course it will, Cara. We just have to be patient and make sure you're protected."

I groaned again. "Which means my father will insist I have another bodyguard. Aidan, I don't *want* another bodyguard!" I hadn't meant to yell.

He looked surprised. "Why not? I thought you and Gavin got along well."

I felt suddenly very tired. I brought my voice down to a normal level. "I've had enough bodyguards, Aidan."

He didn't say anything for a few minutes.

"Well, let's get you home now. I'll follow you. Did you buy any bagels today?"

I looked over at him, at his pale blue eyes and a surprisingly affectionate smile.

I nodded. "Okay. You're in luck. All the necessary groceries are in my trunk."

He smiled as he got out of my car. He leaned in to say, "I'll be right behind you."

I waited for him to get into his car, and then I pulled out of the parking lot and drove home.

When we got back to Birch Street, the rain had stopped. We each took a few grocery bags and went inside. I had been in such a good mood when I left the house. It was completely gone.

THE JOINING TREE

Aidan sat down in the kitchen after I'd unloaded my groceries and began making the Sunrise Specials. There was no conversation as I worked although I could feel Aidan's eyes on me.

We ate quietly. When we'd finished, he said, "That was delicious, Cara. Thank you. Getting back to that letter, I think there's one thing you may be overlooking. The man who wrote the letter, the same man who caused your accident, is someone you no longer have to worry about. Of course, the police will still be looking for him, but he's probably no threat to you. You get that, right?"

I looked across the table at him. "I get that it *may* be true. But Romanov used him once. There's really no guarantee he won't use him again, even if this man doesn't *want* to be used."

He nodded. "Yes, there is that possibility. But I doubt it. He must have followed you here from Thornewood just to give you that warning. He'll be in hiding now, probably out of state. I'm not even sure that Romanov has people on the outside who would take on a job like this. We'll be talking to our contacts to determine how much influence he has. He was never a big player in the whole scheme of things. Just a middleman who was trying to impress the people he worked for. Clearly, he didn't."

He looked at his watch. "I need to get back to the office, start making some inquiries. I'll have a patrol car on this block tonight, and I'll be talking to Chief O'Donnell later."

He stood up and I walked him to the door. Before opening the door, he turned and said, "Call me, even if you just hear a strange noise, okay?"

"Okay."

"I'm sorry this happened on your first day back, Cara. But I won't let anything happen to you, trust me." He surprised me with a warm hug and left.

I was restless all night, pacing from the front window to the rear windows, peeking out, seeing nothing, and resuming my pacing. I turned on the TV, immediately turning it off because I was afraid it would cover up any outside noises. I was really missing Gavin.

My second year at Barrett had been so pleasant, so non-threatening, I had convinced myself my third year would be the same. I should have known better. After all, I was a disaster magnet. I snorted, shaking my head. How could I have forgotten that?

I decided to take a long shower. Maybe that would relax me. After some deep breathing exercises in the shower, I was feeling a little better. I dried off and pulled on lightweight p.j.'s, braided my wet hair, and went into the kitchen to make a pot of herbal tea.

I wasn't sure Kathleen's "relaxing" tea would work on this level of tension, but I didn't have anything more potent. I turned the TV on again, without the sound, and watched a movie while I sipped my tea. Naturally, the movie was full of men shooting guns, blowing up cars, and beating the crap out of each other, so I turned it off.

The phone rang and I almost jumped off the couch! Nervous much? Nah.

I was surprised to hear Chief O'Donnell's voice.

"Cara, I thought I should call you right away. I'm sure you'll be hearing from Lieutenant Fox soon, but I wanted to give you a quick heads-up so you can take some necessary precautions. Do you have a bodyguard with you right now?"

"No, Chief. But there's a Syracuse P.D. car parked outside. Did Lieutenant Fox already call you about the letter I got today?"

"Yes, he did, but I have more news, which I'm sure he's received too. Cara, close your curtains and lock all your windows and doors right now. I'll wait."

My heart was in my throat as I flew around the apartment closing curtains and locking everything that had a lock. I picked up the phone again.

"Okay, Chief. Done. And now that you've scared the crap out of me, how about telling me what's happened."

I heard him sigh. "Nick Romanov was being transferred to another prison this afternoon when the van he was being transported in was involved in a serious accident. Romanov and two other prisoners escaped. The other two were picked up within an hour, but Romanov is in the wind. This happened about a hundred and fifty miles from Syracuse, so he might be heading in your direction, although that's just a guess."

"Chief, have you called my parents yet?"

"No, I'll do that now, Cara. I thought you should be warned first. I'm sure your parents will be on the phone to you momentarily. My advice: Stay indoors, stay safe. I'll call you with any developments."

"Thanks, Chief."

I hung up, my heart still pounding. It didn't seem to matter where I was; trouble always found me.

I remembered my knives. They were still in one of my duffle bags along with my boots. I changed into comfy sweats and pulled on my boots, my knives secure in their sheaths. It didn't look like I'd be getting any sleep tonight.

The next phone call was from Lieutenant Fox.

"Cara, I'm sending another patrol car to keep an eye on that park behind your house. We'll have both the front and the rear covered. I'll stop by as often as I can until Romanov is captured. There's an APB out on him too. I don't think he'll get anywhere near you. Try to relax and get some sleep, okay?"

I snorted. "Aidan, you have to be kidding."

"No, Cara, you need your sleep. We've got you covered, trust me."

I thought to myself, *famous last words!*

There was no way I'd be able to sleep.

My parents had called right after I spoke to Lieutenant Fox. He called them to tell them I was being protected by the Syracuse Police twenty-four/seven. Naturally, they wanted to send me a bodyguard immediately.

"Dad, there's only one bodyguard I want, and he's no longer available to us. Please don't send anyone else."

I heard him sigh. "The other alternative is you come home until Romanov is back in jail."

"I'll think about it, Dad. Right now, I'm surrounded by police. I think they can handle it."

Actually, I wasn't sure about that. I wasn't sure about anything anymore.

"Perhaps, Cara, but I refuse to take any chances with your safety. We'll talk again tomorrow. You sound tired."

I was sure sleep would be impossible, but I think I dozed off on the couch around four in the morning.

There was a soft tap on my apartment door around nine. Laurie had just noticed the police cars in front of the house and wanted to know what was going on. I explained they were there to protect me, and that there was a search on for the drug dealer who had escaped from prison.

"Oh my, Cara. You don't exactly lead a charmed life, do you?"

I had to laugh. "You could say that, Laurie. My father is threatening to send another bodyguard too."

I shook my head. "Sometimes I think I wasn't meant to live a normal life. It's kind of depressing, to be honest." That was when I realized that I had gone from feeling happy to seriously depressed in less than a day. A new record.

After we had a cup of tea together, she returned to her apartment, telling me she was right upstairs if I needed her for anything.

I made breakfast along with a pot of coffee to keep myself awake, and curled up on the couch with a sketch pad and a few pencils. Ralph curled up at my feet, looking up at me sympathetically. He knew something wasn't right and had stayed close to me since I returned home from the grocery store the day before.

Lieutenant Fox arrived around lunchtime carrying two brown paper bags.

"What's all this, Aidan?"

He smiled. "I thought you might enjoy a sub sandwich loaded with salami, ham, cheese, onions, lettuce and tomatoes. And I had them add a little oil and vinegar."

It did sound good. He carried the sandwiches into my kitchen, unwrapped everything, and we sat down. Unwrapped, they even smelled delicious.

"Soda or water?" I asked.

He chuckled. "Beer would be perfect, but you're too young to buy any. Which seems strange."

I looked up, confused.

He added, "Well, it just seems someone with your rich, criminal-related history should be a lot older. Know what I mean?" He grinned over his sandwich.

I just rolled my eyes and got sodas out of the fridge. "Very funny, Aidan. But I do know what you mean. I feel at least forty today."

"You didn't sleep, did you?" he asked.

"Not much."

"Is your father sending a bodyguard?" He sounded in favor of it.

"I asked him not to. I think I've had enough bodyguards in the past three years."

"Cara, don't you think you'd feel a lot safer with a bodyguard whose only job would be to protect you?"

The sub sandwich had filled my stomach, but it hadn't lightened my mood.

"No. Been there, done that." I heard how flat my tone of voice was. My total disgust with the recurring problems in my life was showing.

There was silence for a few minutes as we finished our sandwiches and sodas.

His voice was soft as he asked, "You were really attached to one of your first bodyguards, weren't you?"

I frowned and looked up at him. "Who told you that?"

"Not important. I'm right, aren't I?"

"That's none of your business, Aidan. It seems like a long time ago anyway, and it has nothing to do with this present problem."

He shook his head. "I think it has everything to do with your present refusal to have another bodyguard. I think you're afraid to depend on anyone that much. Am I right?"

I shrugged, not looking at him. More silence.

Finally, he stood. "I have to get back to work. Just remember, there are two officers behind this house, and two more in front. Keep your curtains closed, and don't answer your door unless it's one of us. No one can get to you."

I stood. "Thanks for lunch, Aidan. I do appreciate what you and the rest of the Syracuse P.D. are doing for me. I'm not in the best frame of mind, that's all. Not your fault."

After he left I went back to the couch and picked up my sketch pad. When I saw what I'd been drawing, I threw the pad across the room, narrowly missing my TV.

That was the last straw! My subconscious had been doing the drawing, obviously. I'd drawn pictures of Adam all over the page, just quick sketches of him with different expressions on his handsome face.

I put my head down on the arm of the couch and fought the tears that threatened. Sometime later, I fell asleep, feeling totally hopeless.

THE JOINING TREE

The next day was the same, except for a phone call from Amy. She'd spoken to my mother and knew what the situation was. She tried to cheer me up by mentioning all the attention I was probably receiving from the handsome Lieutenant Fox.

He had stopped by for lunch again, looking disappointed when he found me in the same blue funk I'd been in the day before.

Classes would begin in just three days. It didn't look like I'd be allowed to attend, not unless Romanov was captured before then. I was a virtual prisoner in my apartment. So was Ralph, but at least he had a doggy door.

Mom and Dad called several times a day, obviously disturbed to hear me sounding so depressed. Lieutenant Fox brought either lunch or dinner every day, continuing to assure me I was perfectly safe in my apartment.

I gave him a sour look. "You realize I'm a prisoner here, right?"

"It's just temporary, Cara. He'll be picked up soon. He can't survive out there much longer without being seen. And he hasn't been spotted anywhere near here."

He always hugged me before leaving, which was really nice—for a whole five seconds. I could have used a longer hug, or more hugs, or something. Mainly I needed my life back.

The following afternoon I was watching one of my favorite old movies on TV—"You've Got Mail"—I could never watch the ending without crying when "Over The Rainbow" started playing. It had just ended when there was a knock on my door. I went to the door, wiping the tears away, and called, "Who's there?"

I heard a familiar soft voice, "Cara, it's me." I flung open the door and found Gavin on the doorstep, the duffle bag over his shoulder. At the curb I saw Lieutenant Fox leaning against his car, smiling.

I grabbed my former roommate around the waist and pulled him inside, hugging him until he laughed softly and said, "Cara, do you think you can let go of me now?"

Letting go, I looked up at him and felt new tears filling my eyes. I wasn't sure where they'd come from, but I was just so glad to see him. Naturally, that was when they started running down my face.

"Oh, Cara, I'm sorry." Gavin wrapped his arms around me and patted my back until I was able to stop crying.

"Did my father send you?"

He blushed. "No. I sent myself. When Amy told me what was going on here, I packed my bag and started hitchhiking." He took a deep breath. "It took a long time, but then the good Lieutenant found me walking from the highway and picked me up. I couldn't stand knowing you were up here alone. I'll stay until Romanov is back in jail. Okay?"

I was finally able to work up a smile. "Okay. I'm really glad you're here, Gavin."

Over a dinner of Sunrise Specials, Gavin described what had been going on at home and in the forest, and I explained about the letter I'd received and finding out Romanov had escaped shortly afterward.

"The Lieutenant told me there are more police behind this house, in the park back there, as well as those parked on the street out front." He shrugged. "Romanov would have to be invisible to get near you, Cara." Then he smiled. "But at least I can keep you company until the police find him. You can teach me how to play poker!"

So I did. We played poker all night, using pennies for chips. I had a whole jar full of pennies I'd collected from various shopping trips. By five in the morning, he'd wiped me out. Gavin had the perfect poker face.

By five-thirty, we were both asleep, me in my bed, and Gavin in his sleeping bag just outside my bedroom door.

The next day, we both slept late until my phone started ringing. Gavin made coffee while I answered the phone. It was Mom, of course. When I told her that Gavin had hitched rides to Syracuse, she was amazed.

"He really is devoted to you, isn't he?"

"Mom, he's a very good friend who didn't want me going through this alone. Just having his company has made this whole ordeal easier."

She chuckled. "Well, I'm glad he's there. I think your father will be surprised, but grateful at the same time. Please give Gavin our thanks."

I said I would and asked her to give my father a hug for me.

Gavin seemed determined to find things for us to do that would take my mind off being housebound. He made sandwiches for us, kept the coffee pot full, and turned the TV on to every game show being broadcast.

He also picked up my sketchpad from where I'd thrown it the other day, where it was still leaning against the wall behind the TV.

He handed it to me, saying, "I only saw Adam in camp a couple of times after I'd returned, and I never really knew him, except for his reputation as a phenomenal knife thrower. He trained you, didn't he?"

I nodded. I didn't really want to talk about Adam.

"Are you still practicing?"

"Yeah. Several times a week while I was home during the summer."

"Good. I watched you and Kevin practicing a few times. Kevin's a little faster with the bow and arrow, but you're much faster with your knives." He smiled. "Of course, I hope you'll never have to, but you could probably beat anyone besides Adam."

I nodded. "This week, I've been trying to figure out how to take a shower without putting down my knives." I snorted. "Silly, huh?"

He chuckled. "Not really."

Lieutenant Fox brought an extra-large pizza for dinner, which put a big smile on Gavin's face. "Hope you two are hungry," he told us with a grin.

We were. The pizza disappeared quickly.

THE JOINING TREE

The lieutenant had been watching me. "You seem to be in a better mood, Cara. I guess we can thank Gavin for that."

I nodded as I chewed up my last slice of pizza. "Speaking as a prisoner, it's been a lot easier having some company full-time."

The Lieutenant gave me a regretful smile. "Wish I hadn't had to work, Cara."

I looked at him. "I know, Aidan." Out of the corner of my eye, I saw Gavin watching us.

After the Lieutenant left, Gavin asked, "Are you and the Lieutenant more than friends now?"

I thought about it. "Not really. I've thought about it, but my heart belongs to someone else. Unfortunately."

Gavin's voice was soft as he asked, "Would you undo that if you could?"

I looked into his understanding blue eyes and sighed. "Probably not."

I was too tired to stay up for another night of poker, so I went to bed at ten o'clock, leaving Gavin on the couch watching TV.

During the year Gavin lived with me, he had spread his sleeping bag in my studio where the doggy door was located. We were both accustomed to hearing the soft sound of the door flap whenever Ralph went out and came back in. It had become as familiar to me as Gavin's scent of pine and evergreens.

But something was slightly different that night, and I didn't sleep as soundly as usual. I vaguely remember feeling Ralph jump off my bed and hearing the sound of the doggy door flap. A little later I heard the sound of the flap again, which was normal. But I never felt Ralph jump back on my bed, which was odd.

I was more than half asleep, but I thought there was a strange odor in my room, the unpleasant smell of unwashed male. Suddenly alarmed, I opened my eyes and rolled over to see a figure bending over me. I screamed, heard a grunt, and heard the figure—I assumed it was a man—hit the floor with a heavy thud.

The overhead light was suddenly turned on and I saw Gavin standing by the wall switch, staring at something on the floor next to my bed. I looked down and gasped. Nick Romanov lay on his back, a large dagger in his hand and another knife sticking out of his chest. His eyes were wide open in a look of shock, and I knew he was dead.

I leaped out of bed and ran to Gavin, who wrapped both arms around me tightly. "Are you all right?" he asked.

"I'm fine. You?"

"I'm okay. I heard him come in, smelled him too. I'd been resting on top of the sleeping bag tonight, too warm to sleep in it. I waited until I could see him clearly. When he was close to your bed, I threw my knife."

"Gavin, you saved my life."

"It was my privilege, Cara. I couldn't fail you again."

I hugged him until I calmed down, grabbed my phone from my night table and called Lieutenant Fox.

I heard his groggy voice mutter, "What's wrong, Cara?"

"Sorry to wake you, Aidan, but Romanov is on my bedroom floor with a knife in his chest. He's dead." I was rather proud of how calm I sounded.

The Lieutenant woke up in a hurry. "I'll be right there, Cara. Go to the front door and call the officers in. Don't touch anything. You and Gavin should go and sit in the kitchen until I get there."

I took Gavin's hand and led him out of the bedroom. "One of us should make coffee," I said, hoping he'd offer. My hands were shaking.

He started pouring water into the coffeemaker as I went to the front door and yelled. Both officers who'd been sitting out there all night jumped out of their car and ran to me.

"Lieutenant Fox is on his way. There's a dead body in my bedroom," I told them.

They rushed to my bedroom door and stopped. One walked over to Romanov's body and checked for a pulse. He shook his head. "Nada. He's gone." He returned to the doorway and told us, "You'll have to stay out here until the crime techs do their jobs inside. Are you both okay?"

I nodded, wrapping my arms around myself.

Gavin handed me a cup of coffee. "We're fine. Help yourselves to coffee." He led me to the breakfast nook and we sat down to wait for Lieutenant Fox.

In less than five minutes, Birch Street was full of police cars, as well as an ambulance. I didn't think Nick Romanov would need one.

Miss Williams came downstairs in her bathrobe to find out what was going on, and she joined us in the kitchen. Gavin poured her a cup of coffee just as the Lieutenant rushed in, looking relieved when he saw Gavin and me, both of us obviously unharmed.

He looked at me. "We'll talk in just a few minutes, Cara."

I nodded.

He walked a few feet into my bedroom and stopped, taking in the whole scene. "The crime scene techs will be here shortly. I'm afraid you'll have to remain out here until they're done and the body has been removed."

Gavin asked, "Coffee, Lieutenant?"

Several of the officers had taken us up on our offer of coffee, so Aidan got the last cup.

He sat down with us and pulled a notepad out of his jacket and asked, "How'd he get in?"

Gavin said, "The doggy door."

It suddenly hit me. I jumped up. "Ralph went out, but he didn't come back in! We have to find Ralph!"

Laurie said, "There's a door to the backyard at the end of the hallway."

Aidan said, "Stay here, Cara. I'll go look for him."

THE JOINING TREE

"No, Aidan. I'm coming with you." I followed him out of the apartment, through the hallway to the back door. I called out, "Ralph! Time to come in!" There was no answer.

We walked into the yard until we saw a dark lump on the ground at one side of the yard.

"No, oh no, Aidan, not my dog." I was already in tears before we reached Ralph. I put my hand on his side; he was warm. "He's alive, right?"

Aidan was checking my dog's pulse. "His pulse is steady, Cara. I think he's just asleep. Romanov must have given him something to knock him out, probably a piece of meat laced with an anesthetic. We'll probably find it once it's light out here. For now, let's just get him inside where he can sleep it off."

I stroked my dog's smooth head and rubbed his velvety ears. Aidan lifted Ralph in his arms, grunted—Ralph was no lightweight—and carried him inside, putting him down on my soft couch. I didn't want Ralph waking up on the hardwood floor.

Gavin sat down on one side of him with Laurie on the other side. Everyone was fond of Ralph, but no one was as relieved as I was. I knew if Romanov had killed my dog, that would have been it for me. I would have packed up and gone home to Thornewood.

I sat on the floor, right next to Ralph, while Aidan took the blue chair and began asking questions and writing down everything we were able to tell him.

Aidan asked, "Whose knife is that in Romanov's chest?"

Gavin said, "Mine."

The Lieutenant nodded. "Good thing you were here, Gavin. If Cara had been alone, she would have been badly injured, if not killed." He shook his head and looked at me. "Even with this house virtually surrounded, Romanov found a way in. He must have crept through all the adjacent yards; most of them are unfenced."

The E.M.T.'s came through the room with the gurney carrying a body bag. No one said anything until we heard the ambulance doors close and the van pull away. They were followed by the crime scene techs, who had photographed and measured everything, just the way I'd seen it done on TV.

One of them said, "You can use your bedroom now, miss. We're done in there." They left, and we heard another van pull away. Before long, there were only two police vehicles left in front of the yellow house on Birch Street. Just as the sun began to rise, the neighborhood was quiet again.

When the Lieutenant had all the information he thought he'd need, he smiled at me. "On my way over here, I called Chief O'Donnell to update him. I'm guessing your parents will be here very soon."

I had to laugh a little. "Yeah, probably. We'd better make more coffee."

Laurie went back upstairs after telling me she was happy we were all okay, and that the threat I'd lived with was over.

Aidan had to leave too. His shift was about to begin. He looked really tired.

He hugged me longer than usual at the door and said he'd call me later. "I think we finally have something to celebrate," he said with a tired smile.

I agreed.

We were both smiling when he left.

As Aidan pulled away from the curb, we heard the prolonged squeal of brakes as another car pulled up in front of the house, tires bouncing off the curb. I peeked out the window.

My father had arrived.

CHAPTER 29

My father rushed out of his car and ran to the house where I was waiting at the open door. Grabbing me and lifting me off my feet, he held me for a few minutes, then set me on my feet gently. "You weren't hurt?"

"No, Dad. I'm fine. Very thankful Gavin was here. He saved my life."

My father raised his head, clearly surprised. "Gavin's here?"

Gavin was standing in the living room. He raised his hand. "Hi, Mr. Blackthorne." His face was noticeably pink. He probably wasn't sure whether he was in trouble for being in Syracuse when he hadn't been told to come.

One arm still around me, my father went to Gavin and wrapped his other arm around him. "You came on your own? Why?"

Gavin's face was red now. "Well, Amy spoke to your wife. She told me Romanov had escaped from prison and that Cara had received a warning. I left right away."

My father looked at me, then at Gavin, and asked, "Which one of you killed him?"

Gavin took a deep breath. "I did. And I'm not sorry. He was a threat to Cara. It had to end."

My father nodded. "I agree. Thank you, son. We're all in your debt."

We went into the kitchen for more coffee as Gavin told my father everything that had happened that night. I could see my father slowly begin to relax. He'd arrived with a full head of steam. I didn't want to know how fast he'd driven to get here.

"How come Mom's not with you, Dad?"

"Uh, well, I was upset when we got the Lieutenant's call. Your mother thought she should do the driving. I refused because your mother drives too slow; she never goes over the speed limit, Cara."

I was trying to keep a straight face. "I know, Dad. Mom's a very safe driver."

He snorted. "Under the circumstances, I felt getting to you quickly was more important than the speed limit."

I had to hug him, this wonderful, loving father who thought I was more important than speed limits. I leaned my face into his shoulder and muttered, "I love you, Dad."

For the first time that night, he finally smiled.

Ten seconds later, my phone rang. I knew it would be my mother.

"Hi Mom. Yes, he made it here in one piece. I know, Mom. I'm fine, Gavin's fine, Romanov's dead. Everything's fine." I handed the phone to my dad.

My father's side of the conversation was brief: "Yes, dear. Of course. You're right. Yes, dear. She's fine. I will. I love you too."

Gavin and I looked at each other, both of us trying not to laugh. My father was obviously being read the riot act about his driving. He finally hung up, looking satisfied.

He smiled at us. "Alicia worries too much."

"Dad, I've been saying that for years."

The next couple of hours were spent with more pleasant conversation as we enjoyed a breakfast of Sunrise Specials and herbal tea. We'd all had entirely too much coffee.

Gavin was supposed to begin teaching Art in Elvenwood the next day. "I guess I should ride back with you, Mr. Blackthorne. Uh, you'll be driving a bit slower, right?"

My dad chuckled. "Yes. I won't take any chances on the way home. I don't want to give Alicia any more reason to scold me."

He looked over at me. "Cara, would you like us to stay a bit longer?"

"Of course, Dad. I love having you here, both of you. My plans for today include rest and maybe a nap this afternoon. Nothing else. My classes start tomorrow."

We spent the rest of the morning together, talking about all kinds of things. I could tell that Gavin had just become one of my father's favorite people.

After I made sandwiches for lunch, my father and Gavin were ready to leave for Thornewood. I hated to say goodbye to them, but I was half asleep already and desperate for a nap.

In another week, I'd be driving home for the weekend so we'd see each other very soon. Dad invited Gavin to join us for Sunday brunch, which put a big smile on Gavin's face.

After I hugged them both, we said goodbye. I smiled when I heard my father leave rubber in front of the house on Birch Street. I knew it wouldn't be long before my father bought himself a bigger, faster car.

I was still smiling as I stumbled into my bedroom and sacked out, fully dressed. Life was good again.

It was late afternoon when I woke up to Ralph nuzzling my face.

"Hi, Ralph. You feeling all better now?" He licked my nose, giving me his Boxer smile.

He ran to his doggy door and stopped, looking back over his shoulder at me

"You want me to come outside with you?" I asked him. His answer was a soft whine.

I was sure he was remembering the confusing time he'd had the previous night, so I walked through the apartment to the hallway and went out the back door as Ralph popped through the doggy door. I walked along the fence line, all around the backyard, but didn't find anything suspicious. Ralph stayed right behind me.

When I'd completed a thorough examination of the yard, I told Ralph, "I think it's safe out here now. And I hope you now know better than to eat something you find on the ground. Right?"

His big brown eyes looked up at me as if to say, "Yeah, Mom, I'm not that stupid."

I couldn't help laughing. Ralph and I understood each other perfectly.

My phone was ringing as I walked back in the house. Ralph had decided to enjoy the grass and the trees a bit longer, and I left him in the yard, sniffing everything.

I answered the phone. "Hi, Aidan. Did you get any sleep yet?"

He laughed. "Yes, I did. I got home about an hour ago and passed out. But I'm up now and extremely hungry. How about you?"

"I took a nap after my father left with Gavin. I'm hungry too. What did you have in mind?"

"Well, what are you in the mood for? Burgers or something Italian? And I'm not talking about pizza!"

"Mmm. Italian sounds great. I'm already missing Mom's cooking."

"There's a little Italian restaurant near the station that has fantastic food. It's called Bella's and the owners do all their own cooking. Their veal parmesan is out of this world! How about I pick you up in thirty minutes."

"Sounds great. I'll be ready."

I barely had time for a quick shower, so I rushed through one, blew my hair dry as quickly as possible, grabbed a new pair of jeans and my one green silk shirt that matched the jade earrings my father had given me. I had just pulled on my boots when I heard the doorbell.

When I opened the door, Aidan took one look at me and actually whistled.

"Cara, you don't look like the same exhausted girl I left early this morning. Wow! What a transformation." He grinned at me.

Ralph was behind me, whining again.

"Come in for a minute, Aidan. I think Ralph needs a little reassurance that we won't be gone long and that everything is back to normal."

Aidan came in and got down on the floor with Ralph. He'd changed out of his usual suit and tie and was wearing khaki's and a pale blue plaid shirt that matched his eyes. In a word, he was gorgeous. Paula's eyes would bug out if she could see him now.

Aidan played with my delighted dog for a few minutes, then got up off the floor and asked me, "Will he be okay by himself for a few hours? He seems a little unsure."

I thought the same thing. "Maybe Laurie would like some doggy company this evening. Give me a minute to run upstairs."

Laurie was delighted to dog-sit for Ralph. I called him and he practically galloped up the stairs to Laurie's apartment. "He's always welcome, Cara. We'll keep each other company tonight."

I thanked her and ran back downstairs to Aidan.

He drove us to Bella's, which looked like a little hole-in-the-wall, but turned out to be completely charming on the inside. There were the usual red and white checkered tablecloths, candles stuck in wine bottles on each table, murals of Italy on the walls, and soft music that sounded like opera playing in the background. The food smells from the kitchen had my mouth watering immediately.

"Aidan, this place is great. And it smells fantastic!"

He smiled as he pulled out my chair and then sat down across from me. "I'm glad you like it, Cara. You're gonna love the food."

After we placed our orders, I couldn't help noticing that Aidan seemed kind of different than the times he'd taken me out to eat before.

"Aidan, I don't want to assume anything, and I really don't want to offend you, but I have to ask you a question."

He nodded as he munched on a breadstick, looking across the table at me with those pale blue eyes. "Shoot."

I gestured to the restaurant, the candles on each table, the slightly romantic environment. "Something feels different tonight. Is this a *date*?"

He looked amused, obviously stifling a smile. It was a look I was familiar with.

"Well, do you *want* it to be a date?"

I should have known he'd answer my question with another question.

I took a deep breath and looked him in the eye. "No, I don't."

He nodded. No smile this time. "Then it isn't. I just like company when I eat dinner. And I did tell you we were entitled to a little celebration. Okay?"

"Okay." Intuition told me my answer had disappointed him.

Nevertheless, I didn't want our relationship to get complicated. It would be like the situation with Sean, all over again. I really liked Aidan Fox, and I would have had to be made of stone not to be attracted to him, but I already knew that wouldn't be enough.

We had a wonderful dinner. The mood lightened considerably as we enjoyed the best veal parmesan I'd ever had and sipped an Italian wine I wasn't really supposed to have. Aidan winked at me when he ordered it for us.

When he took me home, I thanked him for the fantastic celebration dinner, and he hugged me at my front door, wishing me luck at school the next day.

THE JOINING TREE

Over the next few days, the rest of the student body arrived back on campus. My group had grown smaller. Lily and Freddy had both graduated. I'd already received email from Lily wishing me luck in my last year at Barrett. Joel was back since he had enrolled in a four-year program; this would be his last year too. Paula and Tim were both in their third and last year. Occasionally Ginger would join our table when she wasn't on duty in the kitchen. But without Lily, we were a much quieter group. As annoying as she could be at times, I kind of missed her this year.

Paula had already been on campus for the past few days and, of course, wanted to know why my house had been surrounded by the Syracuse police the previous morning.

Naturally, the whole crew wanted the entire story. They wouldn't accept my "I don't really want to talk about it." They were horrified when they heard how I'd heard a strange man in my bedroom and woke up to find him dead on the floor next to my bed.

"Amazing how Gavin came back at just the right time, Cara. I hope he's not in any trouble." Paula looked worried.

"No, I think my father's ready to pin a medal on him. Lieutenant Fox looked suitably impressed when he walked in after it was all over. No one's filing any charges against Gavin. After all, he saved my life."

Paula asked, "So are you still going to see the handsome Lieutenant?"

"I guess so. He took me out to dinner last night."

She laughed. "I knew it. The way he looks at you, Cara, is a dead giveaway."

"No, no, it's not like that. We're friends, that's all."

She giggled. "Sure you are. It must be a terrible hardship, you poor girl."

Joel rolled his eyes as Tim laughed at Paula's teasing.

I just shook my head and went to the counter to get another helping of spaghetti.

There were a few new classes I was required to take this year: Photography and Graphic Art. I didn't see either one in my professional future, but they were fun. Rather than investing in an expensive camera, as our instructor recommended, I simply updated my smart phone and got one with a better camera. I had fun experimenting with photos of Aidan Fox, who was incredibly photogenic. He continued to bring over pizza for dinner every so often. He seemed to accept the fact that we were just friends.

On the weekends, my parents had to get used to having their pictures taken as well. I thought my photographic skills were improving with practice, but with such good-looking subjects, it would have been difficult to take bad pictures.

I'd also been invited to exhibit my artwork in three different galleries during this school year, so most of my time had to be devoted to drawing and painting. Other than having dinner at the Café, or occasionally with Aidan, my social life was non-existent. During my weekends at home, Amy accused me of being a workaholic but my artwork had become my life. I didn't see anything wrong with that. After all, what were my other choices?

Amy answered that question with "boyfriends, dating, parties! Cara, you're turning into a hermit on the weekends. You know what all work and no play makes you, right?"

I had to laugh. "Yeah, rich! I'll have enough soon to open that art gallery here in Thornewood. Everyone needs a goal, you know."

Amy was still dating Gavin, and occasionally they'd drag me out of my studio to join them at The Grille for cheeseburgers and milkshakes. That was the extent of what passed for my "social life" in Thornewood.

Sean and I still emailed occasionally. He always made sure to let me know he was still waiting for me. I tried to discourage him, but he wasn't ready to give up. Which I knew was a mistake.

In October, I was scheduled to exhibit at a gallery on Long Island. Miss Galen had advised me to bring only four paintings this time. "If there's more demand *and* a smaller supply, I can set the prices higher, Cara." Which she did. I was shocked when I saw the price stickers on each of my watercolors.

My father had accompanied me again. I think he really enjoyed being at these art shows with me, and he seemed to love traveling. Apparently, Harry Callahan had always done the traveling my father's business required. I was fairly sure that was about to change.

My Elven father was becoming more comfortable in our twenty-first century world.

By the end of the show, all four of my watercolors had sold. Even my father was shocked when he saw the prices being paid for my work. He whispered in my ear, "Cara, I think your dream of an art gallery in Thornewood will become a reality very soon!"

Mr. Goldman, who had helped me struggle through my Life Drawing class the previous year, was my Oil Painting instructor this year. I was relieved that I wouldn't be required to paint any nudes this time. I'd always felt that painting a nude model was a terrible invasion of their privacy. When I admitted this to Mr. Goldman, he chuckled and said, "You've obviously led a sheltered life, Cara."

I was happily working on a painting of some maple trees on campus. They were flaunting their glorious fall colors while a student sat on a bench beneath them, wrapped up in a book.

THE JOINING TREE

Mr. Goldman watched over my shoulder for a few minutes, finally commenting, "Your style is evolving beautifully, Cara. You're maturing and that's reflected in your painting. And you're more comfortable with oil paints now, aren't you?"

I nodded. "I'm hoping I'll get as good with oils as I've gotten with watercolors."

He smiled. "I think you already have."

I'd been working hard both at school and at home on the weekends, so when Thanksgiving weekend came around, I decided I was ready for a break. The night before I was planning to drive home, Aidan Fox called and invited me to have dinner with him.

Aidan took me to Bella's again, much to my delight. The smells of Italian cooking hit me as soon as we walked through the door, and I was immediately starving.

Aidan laughed at the hungry look on my face. "I didn't think you'd mind coming back here. At last count, you've made me about twenty Sunrise Specials. Consider this payback."

Over glasses of wine and my favorite veal parmesan, we talked about my classes and art shows, his job with the Syracuse Police, and both of our rather pathetic social lives.

"Aidan, please don't tell me your entire social life consists of an occasional dinner with me. You're much too good looking to have to settle for a teenage disaster magnet."

He laughed. "And you're much too pretty to have to settle for an aging cop."

We were both laughing as we finished our wine. And then I asked a question I had always wondered about.

"Seriously, Aidan, you're such a great guy. Why don't you have a girlfriend?"

He chuckled. "My sister says it's because I'm too picky. But really, who am I going to date? Another cop? No way. The kind of people I meet when I'm working? Absolutely no way!"

He hesitated for a minute. "Seriously, Cara, you're the first girl I've met in the past couple of years that I've really liked. But you don't want to consider me a *date*, or at least you didn't the last time I asked. Why is that?"

His light blue eyes pierced me. He'd been such a good friend to me. I decided that he deserved an answer.

"Okay, true confession time. When I was sixteen I had a bodyguard. We became close friends, and I fell in love with him. Then one day he was gone, just packed up and left. I haven't heard a word from him. Unfortunately, I'm still in love with him. I'm afraid I always will be. I have nothing to offer someone else. And that's why I don't date."

His attention was totally riveted on me, as though he couldn't quite believe what I'd just told him.

"You made a decision that definite at *sixteen*?"

"Yeah, I did. I may be young, Aidan, but I know my own heart."

He nodded, looking serious. "Maybe you do. But do you really plan to spend the rest of your life alone if he never returns?"

"Yes. Would you want to go through life knowing you were second best? I can't do that to someone else."

He shook his head and looked away, motioning to the waiter for our check.

Nothing more was said as we left the restaurant and he drove me home. When he parked in front of the yellow house on Birch Street, he turned off the ignition and sat back, staring through the windshield.

Finally he turned to me. "Don't you think you should at least find out if you can love someone else?"

"Aidan, I have tried. My high school boyfriend is a great guy, like you, and I really care about him, but I'm not in love with him. I've often wished I was."

He shook his head and sighed. "I can't help thinking that you may be wasting the best years of your life, Cara."

"You may be right, but I don't think there's anything I can do about it."

He looked at me sadly. "Come on. I'll walk you to your door."

He held my hand as he walked me in. As soon as I'd unlocked the front door, he put one arm around me, leaned forward and kissed me gently. I wasn't expecting it.

"Have a good Thanksgiving, Cara. Call me whenever you need me."

"I will. Thanks, Aidan."

I went inside and watched him jog to his car and drive away. I was about to close the door when I saw that green van drive by slowly, heading in the same direction. I smiled to myself, strangely glad the green van owner was still around.

It was too early to go to bed, so I curled up on my couch. My date with Aidan tonight had given me a lot to think about. I hadn't even been out with Sean since the holidays last year. Which meant I hadn't been kissed since then either.

Maybe I was wasting the best years of my life.

Any girl would consider Aidan Fox a great catch. He was handsome, intelligent, devoted to his job with the police and devoted to his family. Maybe his sister was right. Maybe he was too picky. We made quite a pair.

Then I thought about his kiss. Being close to Aidan was really nice, but the ground beneath my feet didn't move. It hadn't been like kissing Adam—something I'd tried extremely hard not to think about.

With a deep sigh, I turned on the TV only to see a rerun of "New Moon," the second Twilight movie where Edward had left Bella in an effort to save her human life, resulting in a deep, heartbreaking depression for Bella.

I groaned and went to bed.

CHAPTER 30

Taking a break over the Thanksgiving weekend was just what I needed. I stuck to my guns and didn't touch a pen or a brush for four whole days. I helped Mom in the kitchen, even learning how to make gravy. I did a ton of laundry, only entering my studio to dust and sweep the floor, and went out with friends one night. That was something I hadn't done in a long time. And it was fun.

Amy left Gavin home the first night I was home, and the two of us went to The Grille where we ran into several of our high school classmates, including Sandy, Danny, Matt, and Dion.

It was so great seeing everyone, Dion invited us all to his house for a last-minute party. "When will we all be together again anyway? Let's make the most of this," he said with a big grin.

He glanced at me with a smile and pulled out his cell phone. "I'm just going to leave a message for another member of the group who hasn't made it home yet." I nodded with a smile. Sean was the only one missing.

Dion's parents greeted all of us with smiles and hugs, and we trooped downstairs to their huge family room. That room was so big, Dion threw a bunch of cushions on the floor in a circle and invited us all to sit down.

"I want to hear from all of you, what you've been up to, what your plans are, don't leave anything out!" He looked a little nostalgic. "We haven't done this in years, you guys. I'd hate to lose touch with any of you."

Mrs. Washington brought down sodas and snacks for us, but when she'd gone back upstairs, Dion said softly, "There's beer in the fridge down here for anyone who wants one."

Naturally, Danny and Matt got up and went straight to the beer. The rest of us enjoyed the sodas.

We were all gabbing and laughing when the late arrival came down the stairs. Everyone got up to greet Sean who was all smiles, genuinely delighted to see everyone. Dion got Sean a beer and he sat down on the floor next to me. We grinned at each other as he threw one arm around me, leaning over to give me a kiss. Danny and Matt immediately started hooting and making other rude noises as Sandy and Amy rolled their eyes.

When everyone stopped laughing, Dion said, "It's time to get serious. I want to hear your plans for the future, all of you. Let's start with Amy."

Everyone knew that Amy was running the catering department at her family's bakery. With a smile, she announced that she'd be able to start culinary school the following year, something she'd had to put off when the bakery closed two years ago. I was thrilled for her. She hadn't said a word to me about it.

Matt said he was working at the Post Office while he waited for acceptance to the Police Academy. I think Matt was the last person we thought would ever want to be a cop. He took a lot of good-natured teasing on that subject.

Danny told us, "I'll never be out of a job as long as people's heat and air-conditioning keep breaking down. I'm good for life," he admitted with a grin.

Sandy was in her third year at SUNY, majoring in Science and planning on teaching high school. "Just think, I'll have to deal with characters just like you in a few more years."

We all sympathized along with a lot of laughter.

Then, with a big smile, she added, "Danny and I will be getting married as soon as I graduate." That brought on more hoots and a lot of applause. They'd been a couple since eighth grade. Danny's face was red as he accepted congratulations from all of us.

Amy said, "You really don't deserve her, you know."

Danny grinned. "I know."

Sean was next. "I'm playing a lot of football, which is why I have to get back to school Friday. No long weekend for me, I'm afraid. We have a game on Saturday. I'm majoring in Communications. If I don't play pro ball, and I'm not sure I want to, then maybe I can get a job in the sports department at one of the TV networks."

Sandy said, "You'd be great at that, Sean. Just think! We'll be seeing your face on TV in a few years." I think we all knew that was a distinct possibility. With his looks, intelligence, and personality, Sean McKay was made for TV.

Dion said, "How about our resident artist? Cara, I hear your artwork has been shown at several major galleries already."

I nodded. "Yes, I've been incredibly lucky. A nationally known artist has sponsored me, so I now have an agent, and that's opened a lot of doors. I want to open an Art Gallery here in Thornewood. This could happen as soon as next year."

That got a round of applause and congratulations from everyone.

That left Dion. He'd been our class president as well as a great basketball player.

We all knew he was destined for success.

"You all know I'm studying to be a lawyer. I haven't decided what I want to specialize in, but someday I'd like to go into politics."

There were a few catcalls, and Sandy said, "That's such a corrupt field, Dion."

He smiled. "It doesn't have to be. Maybe I can do some good there."

For the rest of the evening, we sat around talking, munching on snacks, and playing "Remember when . . ." until some of us had to call it a night.

Sean walked outside with Amy and me. I had my car, and he had his. He hugged both of us, and after Amy got into my car, Sean asked if he could come over after Thanksgiving dinner the following night.

THE JOINING TREE

"I have to drive back to school Friday morning, and I'd like to spend a little time with you before then. It's been quite a while, Cara."

It had been. We hadn't spent much time together since last Thanksgiving, and Sean hadn't been home the previous summer.

"Okay. Why don't you come over around six."

He grinned. "It's a date. We should talk."

I got into my car and drove Amy home.

"What's going on, Cara? I didn't think you were still seeing Sean."

I shrugged. "It's just been emails this past year. He says he wants to talk, so he's coming over tomorrow night." I sighed. "Maybe he's finally met someone."

"Would that bother you?"

"Probably, but I think it would be for the best."

Thanksgiving with my folks was great. Kevin hadn't made it home but we invited his dad, Kelly O'Rourke, along with Gavin, Conor and Arlynn, to join us for turkey and everything that traditionally went with it. I did what I could to help Mom put our feast together, slicing and dicing at the breakfast bar, mixing up whatever she needed. She decided to trust me with the gravy this year, and since all I had to do was stir it on the stovetop, even I couldn't mess it up.

Arlynn brought bread she'd just baked that morning, and the smells drifting through the house were heavenly.

Amy stopped by to drop off a pumpkin pie on her way to their neighbor's house. The Strausses and their next-door neighbors had been sharing Thanksgiving dinner for years. Amy collected hugs from all of us as we thanked her for providing our dessert.

We sat down to dinner at three o'clock. By four o'clock the turkey and all the other goodies were just a memory. I think we were all comfortably full as we relaxed over coffee and tea.

I couldn't help noticing the looks Conor and Arlynn kept exchanging. Conor finally told us he had an announcement to make. Arlynn's face was so pink, there was no doubt in my mind what kind of announcement it would be.

"I thought my closest friends should be the first to know," he said, looking just a wee bit nervous. I was smiling already.

"On the first warm day this Spring, Arlynn and I will say our vows under the Joining Tree. We'd like you all to be there." He sat down abruptly, blinking rapidly.

My parents immediately got up to congratulate the red-faced couple, my father slapping Conor on the back and Mom hugging Arlynn. I was next in line to kiss Arlynn on the cheek and congratulate her. I whispered in her ear, "I knew you could do it."

She whispered in my ear, "Cara, this will happen for you too, I know it will." I nodded, even though I had no faith at all in that eventuality.

When I turned to Conor, he wrapped both arms around me, whispering, "You're next, little sister." I think I snorted. *Yeah, in my dreams.*

No one was in a hurry to leave, especially since we now had something else to celebrate. Mom got out a bottle of champagne, my father popped the cork, and we all toasted Arlynn and Conor.

I said, "Sean will be here in a little while. I know he'll want to congratulate you too, so I hope you'll stick around."

They nodded. Conor said, "I've been looking forward to seeing Sean again. I don't think I've seen him since he left for college. By the way, Cara, are you and he seeing each other again?"

"Uh, no, not really. But we'll always be friends. I keep hoping he'll meet someone else while he's away at school. I'd really like to see him happy."

Conor looked sympathetic. "I understand."

Arlynn nodded. Her voice was soft. "We want to see you happy too, you know."

Mom and Dad exchanged glances, Mom wearing a pained expression, Dad simply nodding. "She will be. There's not a doubt in my mind."

I forced a smile. "Hey. This is supposed to be a celebration. I'm as happy as I can be right now. I love my work. I love being home with all of you, and my Art Gallery will become a reality very soon. That's all I need."

There was still some champagne left, so we toasted my Gallery.

At six on the dot, the doorbell rang. I jumped up, smiling. "That's Sean now, right on time."

When he walked into the kitchen, he seemed delighted to see Conor and Arlynn and to hear their big news. "Congratulations to you both." Smiling, he added, "Saying goodbye to your bachelor days finally. It's about time."

He shook Conor's hand and kissed Arlynn on the cheek. "I guess I should welcome you to the McKay family. The news will make my parents happy."

Mom handed Sean a cup of coffee and invited him to sit down with us. Everyone wanted to know how he was doing in college. He talked about football and his future plans in the Communications field.

Finally, he looked at me and said, "Do you feel like taking a ride?"

I said I did, so we said our goodbyes to everyone and left the house.

When we got outside, I asked, "Where do you want to go? If you just want to talk, we can sit in the car and talk, you know."

"Yeah, we could, but I don't really want to sit in front of your house, Cara."

We got in his Caddy and he drove to Thornewood Park, situated a block from the high school. The sun had gone down. It was twilight.

"Okay, Sean, what's on your mind?"

He leaned back against his door and just looked at me. Finally, he asked, "Has anything changed for you in the past year? It's hard for me to realize we haven't really been together in almost a year."

THE JOINING TREE

I smiled. "I know, but we've always kept in touch. I appreciated the emails."

He nodded. "But nothing has changed for you, has it?"

"I'm afraid not. I wish it would, Sean. I feel like I'm in Limbo too." I let out a deep sigh.

"Yeah, Limbo. That's the perfect term. I feel like I've been in a holding pattern for three years, Cara. I'm tired of this." It was obvious that he was no longer going to pretend he was fine.

"Haven't you been dating?"

"Yes, but it never means anything. Because it's not *you*." He sounded angry.

"I'm sorry. But if it's any consolation, I know exactly how you feel."

He didn't say anything for a few minutes.

Finally, he said, "We both want something we can't have. I feel so tied to you and I can't seem to break that tie." I could hear his frustration. "Cara, I *need* to break this tie."

"I know you do. What can I do to make that happen?"

"Maybe you should be brutally honest with me. Tell me the difference between your feelings for me and your feelings for Adam. I need to know!"

I closed my eyes and took a deep breath. This wasn't going to be easy.

"Sean, you gave me my first kiss and it was perfect. You were my first *everything*. I'll never forget you. I always liked being close to you. I was sixteen and it was all wonderful. Until we broke up.

"Then I met Adam and disliked him immediately. But my father thought he was better equipped to protect me from all the mayhem that was going on at the time. I'm sure you remember."

He nodded. "Go on."

"Adam was the one who convinced me to accept your apology when I wasn't speaking to you. He knew I'd feel better if I got all that anger off my chest. He didn't think I was being fair to you. So I accepted your apology and then we both felt a lot better."

He nodded. "I remember."

"As I got to know Adam, we gradually became closer. He understood me and I began to consider him a close friend. I think I had a crush on him too, although I did my best to ignore it, mainly because my mother had made such a big deal about the difference in our ages. She and my dad both had a talk with Adam on that subject. He'd been told to keep his feelings to himself, that he was too old for me. He agreed.

"It was such a gradual thing. I wasn't sure what was happening. I just knew I loved being with him, and I missed him when I wasn't with him. Then my parents got married and Adam was a part of that too. He was always with me around that time.

"After the wedding, he kissed me. Really kissed me. And my entire world came apart. The ground beneath my feet began shaking, and I felt things I'd never felt before. I guess that's what happens in the Elven world when you come together with the person you're meant to be with, your mate. I have no other explanation. From that time on, I knew I'd never want anyone else."

He looked skeptical. "One kiss, Cara? Is that all there was?"

"Yes. One kiss. I haven't been the same since."

"But then he left, right? And that didn't change anything for you?"

"No. He took my heart with him when he left." And I knew how ridiculous that sounded. But it was the truth.

He shrugged, looking kind of beaten. "Sounds like you want the impossible, and I can't provide it. It also sounds like a fantasy, Cara. Has it ever occurred to you that you may be kidding yourself?"

That question annoyed me and I know I sounded annoyed. "Yes, it has. It's also occurred to me that I may spend the rest of my life *alone*. But can you blame me for not wanting to make another man be *second best* in my life? I couldn't do that to you, Sean. You deserve to be first."

"I see. Okay. I am officially giving up. You've been totally honest with me, so I'll be totally honest with you. There was no way I could have loved you *more*, Cara. You've been everything to me, *everything*, for ten years. I'm done. Now and forever. There will be no more emails, no more phone calls. Don't even send me a Christmas card. I want no further contact with you."

His voice softened. "I'm not mad at you. You never promised more than you could give. I know that. But I have to be free of you. I have to give myself the chance to love someone else."

"I know." I could feel tears running down my face.

He pulled a small photo out of his wallet. "Here, I think you should have this."

It was the photo taken at our Senior Prom, me in my black and white gown, and Sean in his white dinner jacket. We really had made a beautiful couple.

"Thanks. I'll treasure this." My voice shook. "I'll miss you, Sean. But you deserve to be happy."

I got out of the car. "Go home. I need to walk."

Maybe a three-mile walk would help me stifle all the regrets and sadness I was feeling.

His big car sat there until I was out of sight. I didn't think I was the only one wiping away tears.

I pretended to be happy for the rest of the Thanksgiving weekend, I talked to Kevin over the phone, and spent most of my time with my parents until I had to drive back to school.

The day before I had to leave, I decided to take a walk into the woods to my favorite spot. The place by the stream held a ton of memories for me, but I felt I had to face them one last time.

THE JOINING TREE

I was halfway through the backyard when I heard my father behind me.

"Want some company, Cara?"

I shrugged. "I'm not in the best place emotionally right now, Dad."

He took my hand as we walked into the trees at the foot of the backyard.

"I know that, dear. You've been upset since you came home from your date with Sean. Can you tell me what happened?"

"We're cutting all ties. We won't be seeing each other again."

We'd reached the stream and sat down on the flat rock, the center of my personal refuge.

"Is this because of Adam?" he asked.

"Essentially. Sean deserves more than I can give him. I want him to be happy. He hasn't been since I told him about Adam. His solution is to cut all ties with me."

"But that's making you unhappy."

"Yeah, but I'll get over it. Sean really needs to get over *me*."

"I see. I'm really sorry you're both unhappy, dear."

I shrugged as the tears began to flow. My tear ducts obviously had a mind of their own, and my father's shoulder was handy.

Mom sent me back to school with a bag full of leftovers from Thanksgiving. I wouldn't need to go grocery shopping for a few days. I hoped I wouldn't have to explain my present state of mind to Aidan Fox. He would have noticed, I was sure.

At dinner in the Café that night, everyone was talking about their holiday weekend, and parties while they were home. I was able to get away with just smiling, laughing at the appropriate times, and not saying much.

There was another Art Show scheduled for the week before Christmas at the Manhattan Gallery. That gave me a good excuse to spend all my evenings drawing and painting.

Per Miss Galen's advice, I would only be exhibiting four pieces of my work, two pen and ink drawings and two watercolors. I dropped them off to be framed on my next weekend at home. From that point until Christmas, I could relax.

Mr. Callahan emailed me a couple of web sites he wanted me to check out. They were for several Art Galleries in the northeast. He thought I should start familiarizing myself with the way they were set up and being run. He also hinted that he thought springtime during the New Year would be an optimal time to open a gallery!

Since he had been keeping track of my art show earnings, I guessed we were ready.

After I had spent time looking at all the web sites he'd sent me, I asked him to start looking around Thornewood for the perfect retail space for our

Gallery. We had already decided we wouldn't need a big space to start with, but the right location was a must. The Gallery was beginning to seem like a reality rather than just a dream, and that lifted my spirits.

Unfortunately, my dreams were doing their best to ruin my mood. One night my dreams would feature Sean and all the "firsts" I'd experienced with him. I'd wake up with an acute case of sadness.

The next night it would be Adam, the way he used to tease me and hold my hand, and that one kiss that rattled my whole world. After those particular dreams, I'd wake up angry, ready to smack someone.

I thought I looked more haggard every day.

Aidan called one night and asked if I was in the mood for pizza. I'd painted right through dinner time at the Café, so I told him he'd be saving me from starvation—or from peanut butter and jelly, take your pick. Half an hour later, he arrived with a large pie, loaded with all my favorite toppings.

"You must have had a good Thanksgiving, Aidan. You're very chipper tonight."

He laughed. "Chipper? Yeah, I guess so. Career-related, though, not personal."

"So what's going on? Are they making you Police Chief? You deserve it, of course."

He shook his head with a smile. "Well, I'm in line to make Captain, although it's not a sure thing. I have a lot of competition for that spot."

He looked down at me and chuckled. "You'd better hope I don't get it. I'll be stuck in the office so much, I won't have time to have dinner with pretty teenagers. But how was your Thanksgiving? You seem a little, I don't know, down, I guess. What happened back in Thornewood while you were home?"

I sighed. "Old friends cutting ties, that sort of thing. Bound to happen, I guess. I don't really want to talk about it."

I saw sympathy on his face, but he nodded. "Okay. But if you ever need a sounding board, or a shoulder to cry on, I'm available." He stood and put his plate in the sink.

"I'd better get home now, Cara. It was good seeing you, as always."

When I walked him to the door, he leaned over and kissed me quickly before he ran out to his car.

"Night, Aidan. Thanks."

He waved as he got into his car and pulled away.

I looked up and down the street, but there was no sign of the green van.

I shut the door and got ready for bed, strangely disappointed.

The following week my father again accompanied me to the Manhattan Gallery. Miss Galen had again raised the prices on my work. My father's eyebrows shot up when he saw the price tags.

THE JOINING TREE

I whispered, "It's getting us closer to our Gallery, Dad. I'm not going to argue with her."

I was glad to see Win Mason again. Two of his extra-large street scenes were displayed. I had been thinking about Win in connection with my own Gallery.

"How are you, Win? These paintings are fantastic. I really love them. My father and I are planning on opening our own Gallery in Thornewood, probably in the spring. Would you be interested in showing your work there?"

He looked delighted. "Of course I'd be interested! I'll take every opportunity I can get to show my work, Cara. Thanks for the invite. Before we leave today, I'll give you my contact information."

He was standing in front of his largest painting, and over his shoulder I saw someone place a "sold" sticker on the frame.

I whispered, "Win, turn around. One of your paintings just sold."

He looked around and broke out in a huge grin. "There *is* a Christmas!"

We each took a glass of champagne off the tray being passed around, and toasted his success along with my proposed gallery.

"I'll see you in the spring, Cara, if not sooner. The holidays will really be happy this year."

A few hours later, both of Win's paintings had sold and all four of mine had also sold.

It had been a pretty good day; I wasn't complaining.

And then it was Christmas, and I was home for two weeks. The smell of pine and bayberry were everywhere. Mom was adding one or two new decorations every year. It occurred to me that maybe I should be adding some decorations to my studio. Right now it was "Bah Humbug" next door.

The next time I went next door to my studio, I took some measurements. I decided the living area in front of my studio was too small. I wondered if I could have the wall dividing the two rooms moved to give the living area more space. I decided to call the contractor, Jeff Anderson, right after Christmas and find out. Maybe it was time for me to begin living like an adult—in my own house.

I didn't have anything special planned during the holidays, but Kevin was home and came over frequently. On days when Kevin *didn't* come over, Amy stopped by. I missed the days when all three of us could be together—at the same time. Amy still didn't think that was such a great idea.

I missed Sean too. I hadn't seen or heard from him since Thanksgiving, which made me sad. But it was what was best for him. Nevertheless, there was an empty space in my life, and I deliberately avoided The Grille and the Pizza Palace while I was home. Which frustrated Amy until I explained why.

"Cara, you never told me that you and Sean had broken things off completely. I thought I was your best friend. Well, your *other* best friend." She snorted.

"I was too depressed, Amy. I just didn't want to talk about it."

"Well, wasn't it your idea?"

"Sort of. Actually, I think it was mutual. I couldn't give Sean what he needed, and he decided he didn't want any further contact with me. I don't blame him. He deserves to be happy, and he can't have that with me. End of story."

"That makes me sad too, sweetie. You two made such a great couple."

I pulled out the photo Sean had given me and handed it to her.

"Oh, the Prom. You two looked so gorgeous together. I remember he didn't take his eyes off you all night. What a shame." She sighed.

Neither of us said anything for a few minutes. Then Amy asked, "It's still Adam?"

I just nodded. There was nothing more to say.

Two days after Christmas I got in touch with Jeff Anderson, the contractor. He promised to review the plans for my studio to see if there would be an easy way to expand my living space. He said he'd call me back before I left for school.

I was spending part of every day in my studio working on more drawings and some watercolors for the next show up in Albany. At the same time, I was mentally designing my redesigned living space, trying to see what I'd need to add to make it more livable. I was hoping there would be enough space for the furniture I'd bought in Syracuse. I had a bed, a couch, an easy chair, and a TV to make room for. I thought it would be cozy rather than roomy, but I could make it work. I would just have to be happy with a smaller studio. Having a home of my own, no matter how small, felt like a step in the right direction.

I was beginning to feel like a grown up. Finally.

Kevin spent New Year's Eve with us. We taught my dad to play poker; he was a natural. We played for pennies, and he cleaned us out.

After we watched the ball come down in Times Square, we drank champagne and apple cider with my parents, exchanged hugs and wished each other Happy New Year. Then they went to bed, leaving Kevin and me at the kitchen table.

He wanted to hear all about our plans for the Blackthorne Art Gallery. Well, that's what I was calling it. Mr. Callahan had cast his vote for the Thornewood Art Gallery.

"It's amazing, short stuff. Your own art gallery! Will you be showing the work of other artists as well?"

"Of course. I'm planning to send out invitations for submissions to several other art schools and colleges. I'll bet I'll find a lot of great new artists, some of them from Barrett."

I smiled. "I'm also going to ask Francis Sullivan for one of his paintings for our gallery. Just one, which may never sell because his work is so expensive. But it will attract art buyers from the city, which will help us become known."

Kevin nodded enthusiastically. "You've really given this a lot of thought."

"Of course. The gallery is my future, Kev."

His eyes narrowed as he looked at me. "Cara, is that because Adam still hasn't come back? I think you're making this gallery your life because you don't think you'll ever love anyone again."

"I know I won't. He's my mate. You know, even if he *did* come back some day, I think I'd be too angry with him to even speak to him!"

Kevin shook his head slowly. "Okay. Anger's good. Nobody would blame you for being angry. But I know you'd forgive him." He shrugged. "You'd have no choice, babe."

I snorted. "We always have a choice, Kev."

It was time to change the subject. We talked about his life at NYU. He had one more year after this one, and had decided to take a break after graduation.

"You know, I haven't really had a life since I started NYU. Granted, that was partly my own fault, overestimating what I could handle without killing myself." He snorted. "Won't make that mistake again. But I think maybe I could take a year off, nothing but R&R for a while. Maybe on a beach somewhere." His hazel eyes had a dreamy look.

He grinned. "With someone to rub oil on my back and mix up pitchers of Margaritas every afternoon. Sounds good, doesn't it?"

I smiled. "For you, yeah, definitely. Send me a postcard, okay?"

"Hey, come with me! By next year, you'll be a huge success and you'll need some R&R. Don't you like beaches?"

"Too much sand."

"I'll find a beach with trees, babe! Just pack your paint brushes and come with me. We'll have fun!"

We were both laughing as Kevin finished off the last of the champagne. He was obviously feeling no pain.

"Kev, maybe I should drive you home. You probably shouldn't drive, not even around the corner."

"Nah, just lead me to my car. It knows the way."

I walked him to his car and watched as he drove around the corner at no more than five miles per hour. I couldn't help laughing. He could have walked faster.

I was still smiling as I walked back in the house, wondering why I'd gone outside without a coat. It was freezing!

The day before I left for Barrett, Jeff Anderson called to tell me what he proposed doing to enlarge the living space in my studio. He thought it made more sense to add on space to the front of the building rather than moving a wall.

"It will be more expensive but more structurally sound. If you want to proceed, we could get started by the beginning of February and finished by the end of that month. How does that sound?"

"Thanks, Jeff. That sounds great. Please put the job on your schedule and email me your cost estimate."

If all went well, I would have my own home when I graduated from Barrett in May. Now I had to break the news to my parents.

Mom made Meat Loaf my last night at home, which put a big smile on my father's face. I hoped they'd both be in a good mood when I told them my plans.

As usual, there were no leftovers, and Dad was definitely in a good mood.

I poured coffee for all of us and began telling them what I wanted to do to my studio.

Mom's first objection, of course, was the expense of the additional construction work.

"My next art show is in Albany in February, Mom. I think I'll sell enough of my work there to pay for the construction."

"But you're only nineteen, Cara. That's so young to be moving out on your own."

I had to smile at that statement. "Mom I'll be twenty in a few months, and it's not as if I was moving out of state. I'll be right next door! Besides, I've been living on my own for the past two and a half years."

My father looked as though he had no problem with my plans. "She's right, Alicia. I'm delighted she'll be next door, rather than farther away. Our daughter has grown up. You knew this day would come."

Mom was actually tearing up, dabbing at her eyes with her napkin.

"But Brian, she's my baby. Having her away at school has been hard enough. At least she's home on the weekends."

I was surprised how emotional Mom had become. This really wasn't like her. She might get mad, but she didn't often cry.

My father whispered something in her ear as he wrapped his arm around her.

She nodded, saying, "I know, I know."

She looked up at me and tried to smile. "Of course you're all grown up, Cara. But try to understand if you can. You've always been my little girl. You always will be. But if living next door in your own studio is what will make you happy, then I guess that's what you should do."

I gave a huge sigh of relief. Arguing with Mom was the last thing I wanted.

My father gave her a look, as if he thought she should say more.

Mom wiped her eyes again and smiled at me. "Sorry, dear. Most women do get over-emotional when they're pregnant."

Dad was grinning.

I leaped out of my chair! "Pregnant? When were you going to tell me? When's the baby due? Holy cow! I'm going to have a little brother or a little sister. This is amazing! I'm so happy for you." Now I was the one in tears.

Mom was beaming. "Honey, I wasn't sure how to break the news to you. But you gave me the perfect opening. I'm so glad you're happy. Your dad and I are beyond happy. The new little Blackthorne is due in July sometime. And since you'll be right next door, maybe I'll be able to talk you into babysitting once in a while." She gave me a hopeful smile.

I had to hug both my parents, a lengthy three-way hug. This was the best news I'd had in years. Finally, something to be truly happy about.

My ever-practical mother had one more announcement to make: "Since you won't be needing your bedroom much longer, dear, I can turn it into a nursery."

They say timing is everything.

I drove back to Syracuse the next day in a much better mood. The kind of good news I'd just received was a great pick-me-up. I sang along with the Beatles for two hours, belting out "I Wanna Hold Your Hand" and "Love, Love Me Do", and carefully avoiding "Yesterday." I didn't want anything raining on my parade today.

It started snowing while I was still on the road, but I kept right on singing.

By the time I pulled up in front of the yellow house on Birch Street, there were at least two inches of snow on the ground. I was glad I wouldn't have to do any more driving this week. But that was before I got inside and checked my kitchen cupboards. I was down to two cans of soup and a box of cereal. No milk, of course.

I had two options. I could slog through the snow to the Café and eat all my meals there. Hmm. I thought about it for all of two minutes and decided to bite the bullet and go shopping. In the snow. At least I had snow tires.

Timing being everything, my phone began to ring. It was Aidan.

"Hi, Cara. How was your Christmas? Just get back today?"

"Yes, just got in. My Christmas was fairly quiet, but it ended really well. I have lots of news to share with you. And I'm afraid my cupboards are bare."

He laughed. "Okay, first things first. I can get off early today, so this is a good day to go shopping. Maybe we could stop at Rudy's for burgers first. You up for both?"

I said I was.

"Good. I'll pick you up at four."

When I opened the door to Aidan at four o'clock, I was struck again by what a good-looking man he was, even covered in snow. His light blue eyes sparkled as he grinned at me. "Happy New Year, Cara!"

"Hi, Aidan, Happy New Year." I couldn't help smiling. With snow in his hair and a smile on his face, he was almost irresistible. Almost.

"Let's get the groceries out of the way first, okay? Then we can relax at Rudy's."

"Sounds good to me."

Once seated at Rudy's, we got our ordering out of the way, and then Aidan asked, "So let me hear your news. It must have been good because you sounded happy over the phone."

I nodded, grinning at him. "Well, I spent most of my two weeks at home with my folks and painting in my studio. For some reason, I began thinking about expanding the studio to make the living space larger. I was thinking maybe it was time for me to move out of my mom's house and live in my own space."

I giggled. "Of course, my studio is next door, so it's not exactly a *big* move."

He smiled. "Sounds more like you'd be making a statement rather than actually moving away."

"Yeah, exactly. So I called the contractor who built it for me and asked him to give me an estimate. We made our plans, and he's going to start construction in February. Of course, I won't actually be living there until I graduate from Barrett because all of my furniture is here."

"How did your parents take it?"

"Well, Mom fussed a bit, but my dad agreed that I'm grown up enough to move out, as long as I'm not going far, and she agreed that I should do what makes me happy.

"Then, she dropped a bombshell, Aidan. Mom's pregnant and she'll need my bedroom for a nursery this summer!"

His eyebrows shot up. "What fantastic news! You're going to be a big sister. I take it you're happy about this."

"Of course! I'll have either a little sister or a little brother." I couldn't get the happy smile off my face. "I'm so happy for my parents. They're totally thrilled, of course. After being separated for sixteen years, they're finally making up for lost time."

Then, of course, I had to explain why they'd been separated for sixteen years. By the time I'd told Aidan as much of the story as I could, we'd finished our burgers and were ready for dessert.

"I recommend the cheesecake if you still have room, Cara."

I had room. Good news definitely deserved dessert, or so I told myself.

Over our dessert, I asked him what he'd done while I was away.

He smiled but hesitated for a few seconds. "Well, you'll probably be surprised, but I've actually been dating."

"Wow! Good for you. Tell me how that came about. You said you never met anyone at work, or through your job, so where did she come from?"

He was still smiling. "She's a girl I went to school with. I haven't seen her in close to ten years. We ran into each other while we were both out Christmas shopping. She's teaching at the junior college here in Syracuse, was married, now divorced, no kids. We went for coffee and we've been dating for the past couple of weeks." He was actually blushing.

I couldn't help laughing. "She must be special, Aidan. You're blushing!"

He looked up at me and smiled. "Well, time will tell, I guess. Now, how about you? Didn't you see any of your old friends while you were home?"

"Oh, sure. Kevin and Amy are my two best friends. We go back to our kindergarten days. I spent time with both of them, but I felt I should avoid all our usual hangouts. I didn't want to run into my ex-boyfriend."

"I see. He's the one you were talking about when you said you were *cutting ties* after Thanksgiving."

"Yeah. He decided it would be better if I were completely out of his life. I couldn't disagree. He deserves to be happy."

"And you didn't want to run into him over the holidays. So you stayed home."

"Yep. If it hadn't been for my parents' great news, it would have been pretty depressing. But I'm feeling lots better now."

He looked more serious and his voice was soft. "And the one who got away? The one you're still in love with?"

I took a deep breath and looked away for a few seconds. Then I focused on Aidan. He sounded concerned.

"I try really hard not to think about him because it always hurts so much. But recently I guess I've changed. Now when I think about him, I feel angry. Still hurt, sure, but mad! He left without even saying goodbye, Aidan. Who does that?"

He nodded with a rueful smile. I could see that he understood my feelings.

"Well, when he does come back, give him hell, Cara."

"What makes you think he'll ever come back?"

He shook his head. I saw the affection in his eyes. "I can't believe that any man would leave you willingly."

"Oh. Thank you."

There was another inch of snow on the ground when we left the restaurant. I was grateful I wasn't the one driving.

Back on Birch Street, we unloaded the groceries from the trunk of his car, and hurried into the house. It was snowing more heavily now. I put on a pot of coffee as I put my groceries away. While it was heating, I slipped into my bedroom to get a small package out of my suitcase.

Aidan was sitting in the breakfast nook trying to brush the snow out of his fair hair.

I handed him the package. "Merry Christmas, Aidan."

He looked startled. "You got me a gift? You shouldn't have done that." Then he grinned and pulled a long, thin package out of his pocket. "Merry Christmas, Cara."

We both laughed. "Great minds and all that," I said.

He unwrapped his package. It was one of the Elf drawings I had kept out of all the galleries. Melissa was featured, half hidden in the landscape, but she was more obvious than most of the Elves I had drawn, so I didn't want to expose her to public view. I thought Aidan would enjoy this particular drawing.

He looked shocked. "Cara, this is too much. This would draw a pretty penny in any good gallery. It's beautiful."

"I want you to have it, Aidan. To be honest, I've never exhibited this drawing because I know the girl in this picture and she's very shy. She wouldn't want hundreds of people seeing it. In most of my pen and ink drawings, I've made the people far more subtle, harder to see. But I couldn't seem to hide her well enough. I thought I could trust you with her."

"I'm honored to have this." He looked into my eyes. "Thank you."

"Okay, now I'll open mine. Hmm. Strange shape . . . unless it's a paint brush!" I ripped the paper off to find a set of three paint brushes, beautiful sable brushes, all different sizes, probably the best brushes made.

"Aidan, you must be psychic. My old brushes are on their way out, and these are perfect. Sable brushes are the finest. Thank you. I really appreciate them."

I got up and hugged him, dropping a kiss on his cheek.

He chuckled. "I don't know the first thing about artist's brushes, but I was told these were the kind most artists want. I'm glad you like them."

We drank our coffee slowly as we digested dinner and the super-rich cheesecake, and then Aidan had to leave. I walked him to the door, gave him another hug, and he kissed me quickly before he ran out to his car. There was another inch of snow on the ground.

"Drive carefully," I called out to him. He waved and got into his car, moving slowly down Birch Street. I thought I saw the tail end of a green van turn the corner. For some reason, that pleased me.

As I got ready for bed, I thought about something Aidan had said. *"I can't believe that any man would leave you willingly."*

It was such a sweet thing to say.

CHAPTER 31

For the Albany Gallery art exhibit, I concentrated on pen and ink "Elf" drawings. Mr. Jourdan, owner of the gallery, had emailed me requesting them on behalf of one of his best customers.

Since I still had my sketches of the younger Elves who had posed for me a few years ago, I simply had to find ways to hide them in the landscapes I was drawing. Everything was covered in snow outside, so I made some of my drawings winter scenes, which I hadn't done before. I hoped Mr. Jourdan's customers would like them as much as the earlier drawings.

When I drove home one weekend to drop off the drawings to be framed, I was happy to see construction on my studio expansion had started.

Mom was excited to show me the baby clothes and paraphernalia she had begun buying. There were now boxes of Pampers and baby clothes stored in my bedroom. I would have to move out soon.

All kinds of wonderful new things were underway.

My father was even washing dishes so Mom could stay off her feet. They seemed closer than ever, which was wonderful to see.

Dad didn't want to leave Mom overnight, so he wouldn't be accompanying me to Albany this trip. Much to my delight, Amy volunteered to take his place. Amy's company would make the Albany trip even more fun. The only thing I was worried about was the chance of more snow.

We got lucky the day we left. The sun was shining and the most recent snow had melted, so it was a pleasant drive. When we reached Albany and checked into the fancy hotel I'd booked, she was beside herself!

"Cara, this hotel is so plush! And there's even room service! Are you sure you can afford this?"

I laughed. "Yes, I can afford this." I knew she'd probably faint when she saw how much my drawings were selling for.

We decided we needed to look our professional best, so we wore tailored dresses, mine borrowed from Mom, and high heels—low heels for me, of course—and drove over to the Gallery around seven. Hank Jourdan, the owner's son, greeted us with a big smile and glasses of champagne.

"You're both old enough for champagne now, right?" He grinned at me and whispered, "I ran out of ginger ale." We weren't complaining.

I hadn't seen Miss Galen yet, so Amy and I walked through the Gallery, stopping to admire all the artwork on display. When we reached my group of pen and ink drawings, Amy gasped.

"Cara, these are incredible. I never saw them framed and hung under gallery lighting before. Wow! They are really—I almost hate to say it—magical!"

Then she saw the tiny price stickers and her mouth dropped open. She whispered, "Cara, am I reading that right? Each of these drawings costs a thousand dollars?"

I was a little embarrassed. "Yeah. Miss Galen has been setting the prices on all of my work, and much to my surprise, they always sell." I shrugged. "In the beginning, I was shocked too."

Amy was speechless. Meanwhile, I continued to walk around the gallery, looking to see if there were any other artists whose work I might like to exhibit in my own gallery. I found two artists working in oils that impressed me. I made a note of the artists' names.

When Miss Galen arrived, I introduced her to Amy.

Miss Galen smiled. "Nice to meet you, Amy." She turned to me, one eyebrow raised. "I've been hearing a rumor that you and your handsome father are planning on opening your own gallery this year. Any truth to it?"

"Yes. Dad's business manager is scouting locations in Thornewood right now. I'm hoping we'll be open by the time I graduate from Barrett."

"Excellent. Just be sure to send me all your gallery's information when you're almost ready to open. I have a few clients that I think you'll be interested in."

She left us to talk to a few people who were clustered around my drawings.

Amy was wide-eyed. "You're that close to opening your own gallery?"

"Yep. Mr. Callahan is handling the business end of it for us. He's looking at all the shops along the nicest part of Main Street. I want our gallery to be in the best possible location."

Amy nodded. "Well, I heard a rumor that York's Jewelry store may be closing soon. The owner is retiring. Mr. Callahan should talk to him." The jewelry store was across the street from City Hall and a block away from Van Horn's Department store.

"Ooh, that would be the perfect location. I'll let Mr. Callahan know as soon as we get home."

Two hours later, all of my drawings had sold, and Amy and I left to celebrate over steak dinners. I drove to the Steak House where I'd eaten before and Amy and I celebrated over mouth-watering Rib Eye Steaks.

Amy chuckled. "I'm not even going to ask if you can afford these steaks, Cara. All six of your drawings sold, so I know you can! It's so nice to have rich friends." She grinned.

I snorted. Despite the prices my paintings and drawings had been selling for, I'd never thought of myself as *rich*. I couldn't help giggling at that thought.

THE JOINING TREE

The weather behaved itself for our drive home, but I was stuck in Syracuse for the next two weekends because of snow and ice. My contractor called to let me know that they had been able to finish the outside work while the weather was dry, so they just had to finish the inside, which would take only a few more days.

The next time I made it home, my studio and larger living area would be finished! I was already visualizing myself living there.

Miss Galen hadn't booked my work in any more galleries until summer. That gave me time to concentrate on some projects I was working on in my classes. And there was also Barrett's Yearly Art Show to think about.

There was one painting I had a sudden urge to do, one that would take courage to paint. It required climbing up into the top of my closet at home and retrieving the box I'd hidden up there three years ago. I wanted to paint Adam's portrait. Maybe that would get him out of my system. Permanently. Hiding those sketches away hadn't helped at all. I hoped painting his portrait might give me some closure.

I had no idea what I'd do with his portrait when it was finished. Maybe burn it.

I spoke to Harry Callahan the next weekend I was able to get home. He'd looked into the location of the jewelry store downtown and learned that the owner was indeed retiring. The store would be available to lease by the end of March. Of course, the interior would have to be completely redone to make it suitable for an art gallery, which meant new wallboard, paint, carpeting, and lighting.

When I thought of all the art galleries I'd visited, the one I'd admired the most was the gallery in Manhattan. One weekend Mr. Callahan and I would take the train into the city to take a closer look at the interior design of the Madison Avenue Art Gallery. As he put it, "Might as well learn from the pro's, Cara."

We were so close to actually opening our own art gallery, I was becoming more excited by the day. This had been my dream years ago. But I never dreamed it would come to pass so soon.

During the next month, I continued to work on Adam's portrait, and Aidan Fox occasionally brought pizza over to share with me. He was still dating the woman he'd told me about and seemed happier than he'd been when I met him. I was happy for him. He deserved good things in his busy life.

As the portrait I was working on began to take shape, Mr. Goldman, my oil painting instructor this year, began to spend more time than usual overseeing my work. He would stand behind me, looking over my shoulder as I painted, occasionally making a comment or two.

"You're taking your time with this one, Cara. But I have one question. I'd really like to know why your brush strokes occasionally seem so angry! I have no criticism of the work you're doing. Your technique is excellent." He shook his head, obviously a little confused. "My first guess would be that this portrait, this man, is someone you're very angry with."

He looked at me, eyebrows raised.

I sighed. He expected an answer.

There was no sense lying about it.

"Yes, you're right. I am angry with this man. He broke my heart when I was sixteen." I frowned. "I think I'll always be angry."

Mr. Goldman still looked confused. "Well, why did you decide to paint his portrait? That would seem counter-productive, Cara."

I shook my head. "I don't know. I guess I was hoping it would help me get over him, give me some kind of closure. Maybe I'll just get sick of his face!"

He nodded with a slight smile. "Well, good luck with that. The painting itself will be memorable."

Yeah, right. I can always shoot arrows at it.

March did its traditional thing, coming in like a lion but going out like a lamb. On April first, my father, Mr. Callahan, and I signed the lease on the space on Main Street, soon to be known as the Thornewood Art Gallery. Mr. Callahan was getting his wish. His rationale was that by naming it after our town, rather than Blackthorne, the gallery would seem to belong to the town itself. I couldn't argue with that.

After signing the lease, we went back to Mr. Callahan's office and made plans for the store's redesign. Mr. Callahan suggested we call Jeff Anderson for an estimate first, before talking to anyone else. Everyone knew that he did beautiful work, so it would only depend on his schedule. Harry would call him right away.

When I asked Harry about our funds, he chuckled. "Cara, your father is putting in funds equal to yours, and I'm adding a smaller amount. Frankly, with this much money, we could probably build two galleries!"

Okay, money wouldn't be a problem. I breathed a sigh of relief. All systems were go!

I was still living in Mom's house on the weekends, although with all the baby paraphernalia being stored in the soon-to-be nursery, there was barely enough room for me to get to my bed now! Even Ralph seemed to be feeling crowded.

Mom had cut back on her hours at the bookstore, only working three days a week. Christina, our favorite Tarot reader, had agreed to work the other three days until Mom was ready to return to work after the baby was born. Baby would be going to work with her, which raised my father's eyebrows, but Mom insisted it would work. Dad was reserving judgment.

Mom's small waistline was already just a memory. I kidded her that she was becoming more well-rounded every day. She had also developed a craving for lemon tarts from the Strauss Bakery, which undoubtedly accounted for some of that roundness.

My father didn't mind. Whenever I teased her, he'd say, "Cara, your mother is beautiful." He was right, of course. Mom was glowing.

Jeff Anderson agreed to take on the job of rehabbing the old jewelry store to turn it into the stylish Art Gallery we envisioned. Work would begin around the middle of April and was to be completed sometime in May.

Mr. Callahan had given me the chore of choosing paint, carpeting and lighting. I'd had no idea there were a gazillion shades of white paint! I realized I was definitely in over my head when it came to the interior of our gallery. It was time to call in a professional designer.

When Mom informed me that Christina, our favorite Tarot reader, was an experienced interior designer, I was amazed. Apparently, there was no limit to the lady's talent. She called Christina who was working at the bookstore that day, and I arranged to meet her on Sunday when the bookstore was closed.

Christina greeted me with a hug and a warm smile. "Cara, it's so good to see you again. Just tell me how I can help."

I unlocked the front door of the gallery and showed her what I thought was needed. The old jewelry store lighting was still in place, but it wasn't suitable for an art gallery. The contractor would install new wallboard throughout the space, and then it would be painted. The old maroon carpet would be pulled up, to make the floors ready for new carpet.

Christina walked through the space, nodding and taking notes as well as measurements. "Okay, this will be fairly simple, Cara. We'll use a bright, pure white for the walls, and I'd suggest a dove gray for the carpet. You'll want flexible lighting in the ceiling that can be adjusted as needed. How does that sound?"

"It sounds perfect. Will it be possible to get the paint, carpeting and lighting quickly? I'm hoping to open the Gallery before the end of May."

"I'll do my best. The paint and carpeting won't be a problem. The lighting might take a little longer. If you want to leave it in my hands, I'll get on the phone in the morning and order everything we'll need. Just let your contractor know he'll have to be available to install the lighting as soon as it comes in. That should be done before the paint and carpet."

I must have been frowning because she laughed. "Don't worry about a thing, Cara. I think May is doable. Would you like me to design a sign for the Thornewood Art Gallery?"

I hadn't even thought about a sign. I was so glad I'd called Christina.

The next chore was lining up the art that would be displayed. That part I was confident I could handle myself. The first person I wanted to see, of course, was Francis Sullivan. One of his oil paintings would be the "jewel" in our gallery.

I rode to Elvenwood the following weekend to speak to him. When I knocked on the door of his studio, he greeted me as he always did: "Come in, Cara."

I told him that the Thornewood Art Gallery would be opening by the end of May and asked if he would allow me to display one of his gorgeous oil paintings.

"I'd be honored, Cara." He walked to one end of his studio where there were three finished paintings and invited me to choose one. "The choice is yours. You'll just have to speak to Miss Galen about the price. That's her specialty, not mine."

His blue eyes twinkled. "I just paint them."

I loved all of Francis' paintings, but there was one I couldn't take my eyes from. He'd painted one of the old, gnarled apple trees with three happy young boys climbing its heavy branches. A much younger child was on the ground looking up at the others, his little hands over his mouth, as though afraid one of them would fall. It was delightful. I could already see it hanging in my gallery.

"Francis, I'm absolutely in love with this one. Are you sure you want to part with it?"

He smiled. "I can always paint another, Cara. You know, I may even pay a visit to your gallery once it opens. But you mustn't tell anyone who I am. All right?"

"Of course." I knew that Francis had always guarded his privacy carefully. I certainly wouldn't give him away.

I had also contacted Win Mason who would be exhibiting two of his charming street scenes. I asked him to ship them to Harry Callahan, but I also invited him to attend our grand opening, the date still to be determined. He lived near Boston and said he'd try to make it.

Miss Galen had proposed two of her other artists. I'd never seen their work, but she assured me I'd love their paintings.

That left my own artwork. I'd already decided to exhibit all of my Elf drawings, although the original drawings from three years ago wouldn't be for sale. They had too much sentimental value for me. I had a couple of watercolors to show, and I'd decided to hang the oil painting I'd done last year of my father. I wouldn't sell that either.

It was time to get my cousin Jason involved. He'd be working full time in the Gallery, and I thought he could help coordinate the decorating jobs still to be done. I'd be at school, and I wasn't sure how much of Christina's time would be available.

THE JOINING TREE

When I drove back to Syracuse that Sunday afternoon in April, my brain was full of everything we'd accomplished as well as everything still to be completed. I had to keep telling myself that everything was under control. I almost believed it.

The Barrett Yearly Art Show was scheduled for mid-May, only one week before I would graduate. When I put the finishing touches on my painting of Adam, I stood back and just stared at it. The sketches I'd done almost four years ago had provided the outline, but I knew that most of my painting had been intuitive. It had come straight from my heart.

Mr. Goldman stopped next to me. "Excellent work, Cara. If I didn't know better, I'd think that you're still in love with this man." He winked at me and walked away.

I gasped from the sudden pain in my chest. I quickly threw a sheet over the painting and hurried out of the room. I needed coffee and people around me right now.

I heard a voice behind me. "Hey, Cara, wait up." It was Joel, who was in the same class. He'd apparently seen my speedy departure.

"You practically ran out of the room, Cara. What's wrong? Can I help?"

I was too embarrassed by my unexpected emotional reaction to look at him.

"Coffee, Joel. I just need coffee. Maybe something stronger, if you've got anything."

He chuckled. "You've come to the right place."

As soon as we sat down at our usual table, Joel poured coffee for both of us and pulled a silver flask out of his jacket pocket. "Irish whiskey, good for anything that ails you." He poured a healthy dose in each cup and grinned at me. "Wait, I think I forgot something." He walked up to the counter, had a quiet conversation with the second year student who was working today, and returned with a can of whipped cream.

I couldn't help smiling as he squirted a healthy dose of whipped cream on top of our coffee. "Joel, you think of everything. Thanks."

We began sipping at our Irish coffee, and I finally started to relax.

"What happened, Cara?"

I took a deep breath. "It's my painting. I finished it today. Now that it's done, I can't look at it."

"I saw your painting. You did an incredible job on it. Judging by your reaction, it must be someone you know."

"Yeah. It was."

"Was? Did he pass away?" He frowned, as though he wished he hadn't asked.

I sighed. "In a manner of speaking. He's just gone, not in my life anymore."

"Ah. I get it. He's the one you've been hung up on for years. He's the reason you don't date. Right?"

I sighed. "Yeah."

He nodded in an understanding way. "You know, I was hoping we might date eventually, but I finally settled for the 'friend' category. And that's fine. I'm glad we've been friends for the past three years."

I smiled. "Me too."

"How's that art gallery coming along?"

"It will be opening around the end of May. And that's something I've been meaning to ask you. I have several other artists lined up for our grand opening, but I don't think any of them are into abstract art. Do you have one painting you'd like to exhibit?"

He grinned. "Of course I do! At least one."

"Well, be sure to give it to me before I leave on Friday. I'll take it home with me. Do you want it framed?"

"No. The canvas is already mounted on stretcher bars. You can hang it that way. And be sure to give me the gallery's address. I'd love to come to your grand opening!"

"You got it. It'll be nice to see you there on our big day."

It would be a few hours until it was time for dinner, so I left Joel and went back to my apartment to take a nap. That Irish whiskey had done a number on me. But at least I was calmer.

As I crossed Birch Street from campus, I spotted the green van approaching. Without thinking, I raised one hand and waved as I dashed into the house. I wasn't sure why, but it made me feel better.

The yearly Barrett Art Show was held a week later. My parents weren't able to make it this year. Mom's pregnancy had made traveling difficult, but she promised they'd be there for my graduation, no matter how many stops they had to make along the way. I didn't really mind that they'd be skipping the Art Show. The only painting I was going to display was my portrait of Adam. It was better they stayed home.

Two short weeks later we had a lot to celebrate! I graduated from the Barrett Art Institute on the twentieth of May, with my parents and Amy in attendance. Amy confided that the drive took three hours because they had to stop at almost every gas station so Mom could use the rest room! She rolled her eyes, saying, "I don't think I'll ever want to be pregnant."

I couldn't help laughing. My Elven intuition told me that Amy would one day have a very large family. I thought it best not to tell her that.

THE JOINING TREE

The work on the Gallery was almost complete. Christina had created a beautiful sign that was now hanging over the door. It was done in an elegant black script, *"The Thornewood Art Gallery."* When I saw it hanging over the gallery's entrance, I was thrilled. We'd done it!

The first time I walked through the thick plate glass entry door, I flipped a switch for the overhead lighting and stopped to admire how the colors of each work of art, some vivid, some soft, glowed against the stark white walls. As I walked across the plush pale gray carpeting, I didn't hear a sound. It was perfect.

There were still a few paintings to be hung, but we were almost ready for our grand opening, scheduled for the Friday before Memorial Day.

Mr. Callahan had placed announcements in a dozen newspapers, including the New York Times. Christina had put him in touch with Winklet Web Design, a popular local web site designer, so that we'd have a presence online too.

Two days after our grand opening was June 1st. I would turn twenty, no longer a teenager. Which felt kind of weird.

Our Grand Opening was a huge success. The gallery was crowded from the time we opened Friday afternoon, until we closed at ten p.m. Mr. Callahan and my parents were there along with my cousin Jason, who was getting a crash course in charming potential art buyers. Needless to say, my handsome cousin was a natural. Everyone loved him, as well as the champagne and appetizers Amy and Gavin passed around. Amy was my caterer, of course!

My friends from Barrett all showed up, including Lily who still had eyes for Gavin, although Jason caught her eye too. She wanted to know if I would consider her photography worthy of displaying in our gallery. I told her I would. I already considered her photographs works of art.

Miss Galen was present, representing Francis Sullivan, myself, and two other artists she had recommended. She'd been right; I loved their work. She was also responsible for the discreet price stickers on each painting. Joel was still reeling from the very high price she'd put on his abstract canvas. I was delighted when she offered to represent him.

Paula and Tim were there too, standing proudly in front of Joel's very large abstract painting, probably the most colorful painting on our walls. It was attracting a lot of attention, I was glad to see.

Thornewood's art lovers mingled with art lovers from Manhattan and even New Jersey. I'd learned that no distance was too far for a true art lover, especially when it had been publicized that one of Francis Sullivan's popular oil paintings would be shown.

Several of those out-of-town art lovers were disappointed to learn that the portrait of my father was not for sale, but happy to meet the live subject of the portrait. My father blushed frequently while my mother beamed at everyone.

At ten o'clock, the last person left, another Thornewood native who told me it was about time our little town had a first-class art gallery. I smiled and thanked her for coming.

Mr. Callahan emerged from the back room, where there was a desk, a sink and a small rest room. He waved a few sales slips at me, smiling widely. "We're a big success, Cara. We sold five paintings tonight, including two of your drawings and that huge abstract piece."

He chuckled. "I won't be surprised if we find we've been cleaned out by the end of the weekend. I hope you can paint fast!"

I felt my eyebrows hit my hairline. Wow. I'd better start lining up more artwork quickly. I only had about four of my own paintings and drawings ready to go. I had to smile. Joel would be over the moon!

We had already decided that the gallery would only be open Friday through Sunday. After all, I needed time to paint, as well as time to collect the work of other artists to show.

As we left for the night, I paused in the doorway to look back at my gallery before I turned off the lights. It was a dream come true. I smiled at Mr. Callahan, turned off all but the security lights, and locked the door.

He walked me to my car and said good night. "Sleep well, Cara. You've already achieved a great deal for one so young. We're all proud of you."

I thanked him and started my car. I had achieved my dreams. All but one.

A surprising number of people drove up from the city Saturday evening, and although the gallery wasn't as crowded as it had been the day before, there was still a respectable amount of traffic until we closed at ten.

My mother stayed home. Mom had been on her feet so much at the grand opening, she complained she couldn't get her shoes on. But other than that, she said she was feeling great. Dad said he'd stop by for a half hour, which attracted a lot of attention as he came through the door. I actually heard a few ooh's and aah's from the ladies present. Not that I blamed them. And once again, there were disappointed sighs when I said that his portrait was not for sale.

I peeked into the back room and found Mr. Callahan at the desk. He smiled but preferred staying in the background. He finally admitted to me that dealing with the public was not his thing. He insisted that my cousin Jason and I should be the public face of the Thornewood Art Gallery and I agreed.

I had achieved my dream. Why did I feel incomplete?

CHAPTER 32

My birthday was on Sunday. Mom insisted on a lavish birthday brunch since I'd be at the gallery at dinnertime.

I'd lost weight during the past six or seven months, and my mother had made it her mission in life to fatten me up. My clothes had gotten kind of loose, so I wasn't arguing with her.

Kevin surprised me by coming home for the day. "I couldn't miss your birthday, short stuff, not this year. Besides, I haven't had your Mom's cooking in much too long!" Mom swatted him with the dishtowel and then hugged him.

I'd already invited Amy to come over for my birthday brunch. When she walked in and saw Kevin already at the kitchen table, she hesitated, then shook her head and grinned.

"Hey, Kev, about time you brought your butt home." He stood up and hugged her, dropping a kiss on her cheek.

"I missed you too, Amy. You look great." He kept his arms around her a lot longer than usual. Judging by the looks they exchanged, they were ready to be friends again.

I breathed a sigh of relief. I'd really missed being with my two best friends, at the same time!

My parents exchanged smiles too. I think they were as pleased as I was.

A few minutes later, there was a knock at the back door and Conor and Arlynn walked in. "Happy Birthday, Cara."

I collected hugs from both of them. Conor leaned down and whispered in my ear, "All grown up now, little sister. Congratulations." I closed my eyes for a few seconds and leaned against his shoulder. He and I both knew what he meant, and I had to fight the tears that threatened.

But this was a birthday celebration. There would be no tears today!

The table was loaded with mouth-watering food. Mom was making very sure I'd start gaining weight immediately. There was my favorite Quiche, a baked ham, home-fried potatoes, pancakes of course, and a bowl of strawberries. It was my kind of feast.

Everyone was talking about the grand opening of our gallery and the artwork that had sold already. My mother wanted to know how quickly we would be able to find new paintings. Kevin asked if we'd be showing the work of local artists. Amy, of course, wanted to know how much money we made at the grand opening. My father chuckled.

I grinned at her. "You're so mercenary. To be honest, I don't even know. I'll have to ask Mr. Callahan. But I think we're doing well."

After we'd all had coffee and tea, Conor and Arlynn left, and Kevin had to drive back to the city. "As soon as I'm finished with school, I'll be home and I expect a personalized tour of the Thornewood Art Gallery, Cara. Seriously, I'm really proud of you."

He gave me a rib-crushing hug and said goodbye to everyone, promising he'd be back soon. Amy got a one-armed hug, and Mom got half a hug, since getting any closer to her was now impossible.

I walked him to the door. "Thanks for making the trip, Kev." He grinned, hugged me again, and ran down the steps to his Jeep. I was really looking forward to spending more time with him while he was home for the summer. He had no idea how often I'd wished I could talk to him to get the more confusing parts of my life straight in my own mind.

After Dad and I had cleaned up the kitchen and run the dishwasher, I went up to my room to take a short nap. I wouldn't be sleeping here much longer. My furniture and other belongings had already been delivered to my next door studio from my apartment on Birch Street. I could start living there as soon as I was ready.

As I snuggled into my pillow, I was wondering if I was really ready. I'd better be. A tiny person would need my room in another month or so. I think I was smiling as I fell asleep.

When I woke up, it was almost three so I leaped out of bed and ran into the bathroom to splash cold water on my face. I brushed my long hair quickly, pulling it up into a high ponytail. Since I knew I looked about sixteen, I coiled the ponytail around itself and pinned it in place, which I thought was a more grown-up look, suitable for a young woman who just turned twenty.

I went to my closet to see what I could find for a "birthday look." I heard my mother's voice at the door.

"Here, dear, try this on. Consider it a birthday present. I saw it at Van Horn's and thought it would be perfect for you since there's no way I'll be getting into it any time soon."

It was a cherry-red sundress with a halter top and a flared skirt. She knew I never wore dresses, but it was really cute. "Thanks, Mom. This is perfect. Definitely a birthday look."

"Well, dear, now that you're a business owner, I think it's time you got some new clothes, and they'd better not be jeans!"

I giggled. "I hear you, Mom."

She went back downstairs and I got dressed. I put on my white sandals and a pair of small gold hoop earrings Amy had given me for my birthday. She'd also given me blusher and rosy-colored lip gloss, so I dutifully put them on after I pulled the sun dress over my head. There.

I looked in the mirror. I didn't look like a teenager anymore. Mission accomplished.

I went downstairs, collected more birthday hugs from my parents and went out to my car.

There were two parking spaces behind our gallery. Mr. Callahan's car was already in one of them when I pulled in. He had undoubtedly already unlocked the front door and turned on all the lights.

I entered through the back door and found Mr. Callahan sitting at the desk, reading the paper.

He looked up and smiled. "Good evening, Cara. Are you manning the gallery alone tonight?"

"I guess so." I rolled my eyes. "I forgot to make arrangements to get Jason over here."

He nodded. "If it gets busy, I'll make the supreme sacrifice and go out there to talk to customers." He rolled his eyes, making me laugh.

I dropped my bag on the desk, walked to the gallery entrance, and froze. Literally.

Standing in front of my father's portrait was a tall, slender man wearing jeans, hiking boots and a blue denim shirt.

I couldn't breathe.

I knew that perfect profile. I knew that shaggy black hair, always a little too long.

He turned and walked to the front door.

I knew his stride, the way he swung his arms at his sides. I knew the way he held his head, moved his shoulders.

Before I knew it, he was outside, heading down Main Street.

I started breathing again and raced to the front door, but by the time I got outside, his long legs had already carried him half a block away.

I stood there staring at his back.

He told me once that Elves have excellent hearing, so I didn't raise my voice.

"Adam."

He stopped abruptly, his head bent down. I saw his shoulders rise and fall, as though he'd just taken a deep breath. He turned and faced me.

Even from this distance, I could see those dark blue eyes pinned on my face.

His voice was as soft as I remembered it.

"Cara. All grown up. More beautiful than ever."

"What are you doing here?"

One corner of his lips turned up slightly. I knew that look.

"I heard there was a new Art Gallery in town. I wanted to visit it, perhaps see more of my favorite artist's work."

He began walking toward me.

I shook my head. "Stay there."

One dark eyebrow lifted. "Do you want to have this conversation here, on Main Street?"

"I'm not sure I want to have a conversation with you at all."

He nodded and took a deep breath. "You're angry."

Didn't he think I would be?

"It's been four years, Adam. You left me without even a goodbye."

"Actually, love, it's been three years, eight months, and twenty days. I've missed you every minute of those three years, eight months, and twenty days."

"Really? Why did you leave? Couldn't you at least have spoken to me first?" *Didn't he understand why I was angry?*

He took another deep breath and looked into my eyes. I'm not sure how he'd done it, but he was now standing only a few feet in front of me. Damn. His dark blue eyes were doing strange things to my heart, which was doing a weird tap dance in my chest.

"Cara, leaving you was the single, hardest thing I've ever done. But I had to."

"Adam, you kissed me, rocked my whole world, and then you left. You broke my heart! Why?" My voice was shaking slightly.

He sighed, not answering for a few long seconds. He looked at me, his dark eyes glittering with emotion, his voice still soft.

"I had given your father my word that I would keep my feelings to myself, that I wouldn't let anyone hurt you." He took a deep breath. "If I'd stayed, I would have broken my word. I would have kissed you again, and again. I wouldn't have been able to keep my hands off you. Cara, you were only sixteen, and I *might* have hurt you. I had to leave. Don't you understand?"

I felt those disloyal tears welling and fought them back.

"You never even said goodbye, Adam."

He shut his eyes, taking another deep breath.

"Cara, if I had seen you again, do you really think I could have said goodbye?"

I didn't know what to say. I was getting lost in his dark blue eyes.

My anger was fading. But there were still things I needed to know.

"Where have you been for three years, eight months, and twenty days, Adam?"

"Never far from you, love."

"But where did you go?"

"I've been living in the human world. I felt I had to."

"Why?"

His smile was tender. "Because that's where you live."

"I thought you would have moved on to another Elven village somewhere."

"No, love. I didn't want to be too far away from you. I hadn't realized that you still needed a bodyguard, but you did. If I'd known, I wouldn't have left when I did. I would never have put your life at risk." Now he sounded angry with himself.

"How did you know I still needed a bodyguard?"

"I learned that a man tried to cut your throat."

"Who told you about that?"

He had the grace to look embarrassed. "I'm a telepath, Cara.

"Gavin has saved your life more than once. He's been doing the one job I should have been doing. I owe him a great deal."

I wanted more answers.

"Adam, how have you been able to live? It costs money to live in the human world."

"I've done all kinds of work. Carpentry, gardening, school crossing guard." He smiled. "That was my favorite job. The children were great."

Gardening?

"Where exactly have you been living?"

He shrugged, looking slightly embarrassed. "Here . . . and there. Never too far."

"How do you get around? Did you learn to drive?"

He wore that familiar amused look. "I sat through your driving lessons, remember?"

"And you have a car?"

"Sort of."

"Sort of?"

He smiled and pointed to the corner at the end of the block. And there it was. An old green van with green curtains at the back windows.

I was barely breathing. "I don't believe it . . . That was you, all those times . . ."

He nodded, his heart in his eyes.

"You got a license? You have I.D.?"

"Yes. Mr. Callahan was very helpful when I went to see him the day I left. I knew I'd need those things to survive in your world."

"He never said anything to me."

"Why would he? He never knew what you meant to me."

He was right.

I looked up at him. "Where do you plan to go now?"

"Nowhere, love. Where you are is where I'll be. Always."

He gave me that swoon-worthy smile I remembered. "You're not a teenager anymore."

I was totally lost in his eyes, in the love shining out of them.

"I have a question to ask you, Cara."

I nodded, still lost in those cobalt eyes.

"Will you marry me? Tonight, tomorrow, as soon as possible. I don't ever want to leave you again. Not even for a day. I love you, Cara. You're my mate."

I had obviously lost what was left of my mind.

"You do? I am?"

He raised one hand to stroke the side of my face. "I've been in love with you ever since you snatched an arrow out of the air and probably saved my life. Ever since that day, you've held my heart in your hands."

"Oh." His soft touch had left me breathless.

He put his other hand on the other side of my face and lowered his lips to mine.

The world started spinning. Then he lifted his lips from mine and said, "Please say yes, love."

I was a little breathless. "Okay. Yes, I'll marry you."

Smiling, he began kissing me again, deeper and deeper, until I totally forgot where we were.

The ground was dropping away from under my feet, the world was spinning again.

I whispered, "Earthquake?"

He whispered back, "Tornado, I think."

I wrapped my arms around his waist and pulled him close.

And he kissed me.

And kissed me.

And kissed me until we were both lost in another world, far, far away.

The End

(Epilogue follows)

EPILOGUE

While Adam and I had our reunion on Main Street on my birthday, we weren't aware we had a fascinated audience.

Customers arriving at the Gallery stopped at the doorway to watch our confrontation with avid attention. Mr. Callahan stood watching too, with a satisfied smile on his face. We were completely unaware of them.

We never heard passing motorists shouting, "Get a room!" as we were wrapped in each other's arms. We heard about all of it later.

Adam came home with me to see my parents. My father greeted him with a huge smile and open arms. "Welcome home, Adam."

Mom didn't even try to get up. She simply smiled and said, "It's about time, Adam."

He smiled and kissed her hand. "You look wonderful, Alicia."

Then he turned to my father and said, "We want to be married, as soon as possible. Do we have your blessing, Brian?"

My father beamed at us. "Of course you do. Cara, Adam, we wish you every happiness. I assume you'd like two weddings, one in Elvenwood and one here."

I looked at Adam. He nodded, smiling.

My father grinned. "Will tomorrow be too soon?"

Adam looked down at me, his eyes dancing. "Do you think we can wait until tomorrow?"

I looked up at him and whispered, "Tonight would be better."

I looked at my father. "Dad, do you think you could talk one of the Elders into marrying us tonight?"

He arched an eyebrow. "We may have to wake up most of Elvenwood, but if you want to be married tonight, we'll wake them up!"

He helped my mother out of her chair. "Come, Alicia, we're riding to Elvenwood tonight."

I suddenly felt terrible. Mom was too pregnant to ride, and the gateway to Elvenwood wouldn't open for her. I really wanted my mother at my wedding.

Mom saw the look on my face and squeezed my hand. "Don't worry, dear. I can ride with your father, and Smoke is very careful to give me a smooth ride."

"But the gateway, Mom. It won't open for you."

She smiled. "It will now." She patted her rounded stomach. "There's a little person with Elven blood in here, and the gateway recognizes him."

She winked at me. "Yes, *him.*"

We walked to my father's camp, collected Conor and the greys, and rode into Elvenwood slowly as the sun was going down.

My father left us at his cottage and went to the dining hall to ring the bell there.

Many of the Elves were still awake and those who weren't got up and came out quickly. My father spoke to Henry Ferguson quietly, and I saw Mr. Ferguson nod and smile.

We gathered under the Joining Tree at sunset on my twentieth birthday. We were married as the sun went down while the ancient tree cast its bewitching magic over us.

There were tears in my eyes as Mr. Ferguson read the beautiful words of the Elven marriage ceremony. Adam held my hand throughout, never taking his eyes off me.

"Adam and Cara, you stand before us today declaring that you are Mated and bound forever, by Elven custom.

"Now you will feel no rain, for each will be shelter for the other.

Now you will feel no cold, for each of you will be warmth to the other.

Now there will be no loneliness, for each of you will be companion to the other.

Now you are two persons, but there is only one life before you.

May beauty surround you both in the journey ahead and through all the years.

May happiness be your companion and your days together be good and long upon the earth."

The Elder looked at Adam and nodded. Adam said, "Forever, Cara."

Then he looked at me. I said, "Forever, Adam."

Mr. Ferguson smiled at us. Looking out at the gathered Elves, he said, "Please offer your warmest wishes to Adam and Cara Wolfe."

An impromptu party followed, and we were mobbed by our friends, all of whom were both surprised and delighted to be attending our unexpected wedding that night.

I was still in my red dress with Adam in his jeans and blue denim shirt. No one minded, least of all us.

I took a few minutes to sing Rowenna's song and we watched her fly over the village, her hatchling at her side, as she mentally sent us her love.

Throughout all of the hugs and good wishes being bestowed on us, Adam never let go of my hand.

Two days later we went to City Hall for our marriage license, and the next day Judge Stone married us in his office. There was just a small group for this second wedding. My parents, of course, Mr. Callahan, Amy, Gavin, Jason, Conor, and Arlynn were with us.

Adam asked me to wear my pink and ivory dress, the one I wore for my parents' wedding. His eyes lit up when I came downstairs in it.

Somewhere my father found a dark blue suit for Adam. He looked incredible.

When Judge Stone said, "I now pronounce you husband and wife," I thought I heard a muttered "Hallelujah" from Amy, which made both of us grin.

Amy reported that Adam and I both had stars in our eyes that day. But she was slightly annoyed that we only gave her two days to cater our second wedding!

Nevertheless, we had a lovely party at my mother's house, spilling out onto the back porch and backyard. Amy had prepared several trays of the little sandwiches everyone loved, there was champagne on ice, and the wedding cake she made for us was, of course, exquisite.

Word had traveled to my father's camp, and we had several unexpected but very welcome guests. Ryan, Gabriel, and Patrick took frequent turns congratulating us and hugging me, much to Adam's amusement.

Adam and I settled happily into my studio's new larger living area, and Adam was building the additional furniture we needed. We were together every day and every night. He vowed that we would never be separated again.

I had never been so happy in my life.

And then, on July sixteenth, my little brother finally joined us. Christopher Blackthorne came into the world, weighing seven and a half pounds. He had Mom's auburn hair, my father's green eyes and a very healthy set of lungs.

We didn't think life could get any better.

But a few years later, it did!

ACKNOWLEDGEMENTS

Where to start? Writing The Blackthorne Forest series has been a labor of love for the past four years. And now that I've typed "The End," I'm sad that it's finished!

There are so many people to thank. I couldn't have done it without any of them.

My first two Editors, Michelle Browne and Laurie A. Will, were my first writing teachers, breaking me of so many bad habits. I learned a great deal from each of them, and I'll always be grateful for everything they taught me.

I turned the editing of this fourth book over to my "Idea Man," Neil Fogel, who made me work harder than I ever had before, as I rewrote whole chapters because he thought it would make the story better. I hope we succeeded.

All of my beautiful covers were designed by Alexandre Rito, who was able to give them the mystical, romantic look I wanted. I still love every single cover he designed for the Blackthorne Forest series.

My main character, Cara Connelly Blackthorne, is a gifted artist. Unfortunately, I can't draw a straight line, so I needed professional advice on the how-to's of watercolor and oil painting so that in writing about art, I wouldn't sound like an idiot. Luckily, I live in a small town that's full of artists. I have to thank Juanita Niemeyer, a talented artist and teacher of watercolor painting, who was my first source for painting insight. She was extremely patient with all my questions and very generous with her time. For additional research I used the excellent Encyclopedia of Oil Painting Techniques, which is full of beautiful oil paintings and clear explanations of how they were created. Any mistakes in this book are mine alone.

Once again, I "borrowed" a portion of a traditional Native American (Apache) wedding vow for my Elven wedding vows because I found it so beautiful.

I have to thank my talented daughter, Paula Hightower, (winkletwebdesign.com) who designed my website, www.clairefogel.com/ where my readers have a place to contact me, and occasionally find out what I'm working on next. I've appreciated – and answered – every message I received from my readers, who have made this journey so rewarding and so much fun!

ABOUT THE AUTHOR

I'm a confirmed bookworm. Have been all my life, beginning with the backs of cereal boxes and graduating to real books. I especially love fiction. Over the years, I've found reading to be the best kind of therapy, taking me away from my problems and into another world because that was all I really needed to cope with life.

I especially love novels in series, which is why I wrote a series. When I find characters I really like and can relate to, I enjoy the opportunity to know them better until they begin to feel like friends. I want to know what happens to them! As I think my readers can tell, I am completely addicted to happy endings, which are the most satisfying parts, both to read and to write!

I grew up in a small town in New Jersey, very much like the fictitious town of Thornewood. Of course, I placed Thornewood in upstate New York, not New Jersey. Although I spent a few years working in New York City, I always returned to the more peaceful suburbs, which is where I've spent most of my life, first on the East Coast and now on the West Coast.

My husband and I live in the central California mountains with our lovable Boxer, Roscoe, who appears in several of my books. When I'm not washing dishes or picking dry dog food out of the carpet, I'm trying to decide which of Thornewood's residents to write about next! I don't think I'm ready to leave the Elves of Blackthorne Forest just yet.

Readers can contact me on my website, www.clairefogel.com. I love hearing from my readers and will always answer questions and respond to comments.

Leaving a review on Amazon always makes my day!

Made in the USA
San Bernardino, CA
18 October 2017